Through My Eyes. Again.

By

Robert Hart
fb: @RobH.Author
IG: @robhartauthor
https://roberthartauthor.com
Twitter: @RobertH62701436
robert@roberthartauthor.com

This is a work of fiction. Whilst some real places are used as settings, similarities to real people are entirely coincidental.

THROUGH MY EYES. AGAIN.
Second edition. April 20, 2021.
Copyright © 2020 Robert Hart.
All rights reserved
ISBN: 978-0-6450169-2-5

Written by Robert Hart
Cover art © Chris Pink, inspired by a Deutsche Demokratische
Republik (East Germany) poster by Klaus Bernsdorf

Saturday, 13th October 1962

He was standing on the far side of the railway line, the untrimmed growth that grazed the fence hiding him from view. The public footpath slanted on up the hill towards the woods at the crest.

Was this the place? he thought. *Or should he go to the greater privacy of the woods? But the climb would be in full view ...*

No, here would have to do.

If he delayed, he feared he would lose his resolve. Shrugging off his coat, he retrieved the drawing compass from his school bag, its newly sharpened point glinting in the thin October sunlight. No knife, so no single smooth slice to a fast fade; it would have to be multiple punctures, the extra pain his reward.

He dropped his satchel, the strap slithering down his arm and sank back into the matted grass edging the scrub. The thick wool of the school jersey moved easily up his arm. The diagrams of the wrist and forearm in his mother's anatomy text were clear in his mind – the arteries boldly drawn in carmine ink. The needle-like point of the compass teased his skin and he wondered how many punctures he would need.

Would he need to pierce both arms? Possibly. He slid his right jersey sleeve up past the elbow as well.

He would probably cry out with each plunge and would need the camouflage of a passing train. A strange sense of detachment enveloped him and his mind drifted until he heard the distant clatter of an approaching train, its low speed and loud clanking marking it as a goods train – perfect.

The point poised over the first chosen spot and the clamour grew. Just a bit closer ... he pressed it down slowly, ready for the first swift puncture.

***

I jerked upright in surprise, pricking my skin with the compass in my hands. A bead of blood formed on my wrist and instinctively I leaned forward to lick it but stopped in shock when I realised my wrist ... was not mine: there was no sign of the greying hair and age-marred skin.

And yet ... it was the wrist of this body: it flexed when I told it to.

I felt my tongue drag across the skin and the sting of saliva in the tiny puncture. The blood left a smear in which a smaller droplet formed. I rotated my hands, revealing fresh, pale skin with none of the blotches and well-known scars that came from seventy years of living.

Above me, I saw the hill crowned with woodland and the footpath that climbed upwards, only to lose itself in the autumnal russets and yellows. From

3

deep in my brain, surging to the surface came the memory: the hill behind my junior school back in England.

I sat there, baffled. My last recollection was relaxing quietly, half a world away with a glass of Australian Shiraz beside me. I must have dozed off. But no previous dream had ever been this sharply drawn; each strand of yellowing grass crushed under my feet was executed in exquisite perfection. *What had stirred this distant memory to surface with such preternatural detail?* And that thought brought me to a halt: *whilst asleep, I was critiquing my dream?*

I glanced around, expecting the images to spiral away, but nothing happened. There was only the sound of the whispering breeze, gradually chilling my bare arms and legs. Minutes passed, as another train slipped into my world, building to a crescendo before rushing away.

I surveyed my body – skinny legs sticking out of grey corduroy shorts, grey knee-length socks, black lace-up shoes, glasses on my face. Such a youthful body, that of my youth – and it had been about to spike its arteries. The dark emotions of my younger self flooded me in a boiling tide. My head jerked up and I felt tears run down my cheeks. The bitter memories of these bleak times flooded through me – the school bullies, my father's beatings, my impotent raging and my loneliness. With my eyes closed, I took a stuttering breath. The rawness of these teenage emotions was agonisingly sharp for a seventy-year-old.

And I knew when I was as well as where: my first contemplation of suicide, aged twelve years.

But I had only thought about it and that contemplation had happened on the other side of these railway tracks. Memory, dream, or nightmare, this was different.

I supposed I could have sat there by the railway line and waited to see what happened, but I was starting to feel cold: time to go. If this were a dream, it could end somewhere else just as well as here.

I was still clutching the compass, so I opened my school satchel and dropped it in, pulled my jumper sleeves down to my wrists, donned the blue school mackintosh and cap and set off, back across the railway line and through the village to the bus stop. I was hoping for a number seven bus, which would take me within a couple of hundred yards of my house, but what came was a number six, which meant a mile walk and a steep climb home. I sighed and went up to the top deck.

The conductor eventually followed me. "Tickets please!" Her lilting West Indian accent was still a novelty in the rural Kent of 1962.

For a moment, I froze and the conductor's sunny smile morphed towards a glower, but my twelve-year-old memories served up the knowledge of my season ticket in its leather case, firmly attached by a cord to a button in my left-hand coat pocket. I dragged it out and the smile returned as she moved on.

Shoving away the season ticket, I wondered what else I had with me. My pockets turned up only fluff and a handkerchief, so I opened my school bag: a French text, a Latin text, Caesar's *De Bello Gallico*, several exercise books. Opening one of these revealed my awful handwriting. I felt my stomach clench – *my father goes wild about this*.

Goes wild?

My twelve-year-old brain was telling me he would be waiting for me at home, ready to thrash me for even an imagined transgression. But twenty-five years ago, I had insisted on viewing my father in his coffin: I had to see his corpse to know it was finished.

Memory was a confusing mélange.

I dived back into the bag finding the *Horse and his Boy*, my favourite from the Narnia series. I escaped into that simpler world for the rest of the journey, trying to shed some of the turmoil I was feeling.

I kept an eye on the passing countryside and my twelve-year-old brain warned me to pack up and head downstairs for my stop at the foot of Mickleburgh Hill. Trudging up the hill, my satchel banged annoyingly against my thigh until my twelve-year-old brain told me to hook the strap over the opposite shoulder. After the climb, the road flattened out before I turned down my street.

About halfway to our house, a boy was sitting on a low wall, idly kicking his heels into the bricks. He glanced up once as I approached and then went on staring at his feet as they banged on the wall.

I stopped – anything to delay the arrival home. "You are new around here," I said, realising I had never seen him before; he wasn't part of my memories at all.

His eyes narrowed quizzically. The feet stopped kicking. He stared up at me with wide, almost black eyes. "*Neu*...new...*Ja!*"

He was speaking ... German. I had learned the language in senior school.

"D...umm." I had nearly replied in German – but my twelve-year-old self wasn't supposed to know his language. "Um...who are you?" I spoke slowly as I suspected he spoke very little English.

He gave me an unblinking stare for a second or so and then jumped off the wall and headed rapidly back down the road in the direction I had come. I almost called after him, but I couldn't think what to say in English that he might understand. I watched him turning the corner at the end of the road without a backward glance. This was becoming quite strange. I had never met – or even known of – a German-speaking boy around here. It seemed like the world of my childhood but at the same time, it wasn't. The weird nature of this dream was rising.

What would I find at home – my mother, father and sister or some complete strangers who would throw me back on the street? Was this reality or a dream?

The kitchen lights were on and I walked warily towards the back door. A head with a long pigtail appeared in the window and turned, glancing at me. It was my bossy older sister as I remembered her as a teenager. I saw her dismissive sniff of recognition as I climbed the two steps to the back door.

My father was seated at the kitchen table, so young and such a malevolent presence as he loomed towards me.

"Why are you so late?" He snapped the question, voice coiled with menace.

Our final physical confrontation, one Christmas day when I was fifteen, crashed into my consciousness. I had silently urged him to just touch me and had gleefully imagined I would hammer him, but after a few nose-to-nose seconds he had turned away for reasons I still could not fathom.

But now? Now, I was too small to do that. All the angst and anguish that drove my afternoon's decision flared through my brain, swamping any control my seventy-year-old self tried to impose. Suddenly I was crying impotently, fleeing through the house pursued by my father's yells up the stairs to my bedroom. Slamming the door behind me I threw myself onto my bed and sobbed.

It was dark when the bedroom door opened and light from the landing crept in, waking me. I lay still. The slight hint of rose scent and swish of a skirt told me it was my mother. I felt her hand lightly touch my shoulder.

I must have flinched, but I remained curled around my satchel.

"Will, do you want to come down for supper?" My mother asked, softly.

I shook my head.

"Shall I bring you something here, then?"

My stomach lurched and, again, I shook my head.

After a few seconds, I felt her hand leaving my shoulder and with the same faint swish, she left. The room descended into darkness as she closed the door and a terrible fear claimed me. I simply could not go through my childhood again. Even with a seventy-year-old perched on my shoulder, I couldn't do it. I would make sure I had a knife next time.

But…was there a way back from here? If this were a dream – what would happen if I went to sleep – would I wake up from my slumber, reach out and find that glass of Shiraz? If I killed myself here, would I wake there? Had I had a heart attack and died back in my old world – and what did that mean if I killed myself here? What was the importance of the differences between what I remembered and what I saw in this world? My brain swirled with questions that had no answer.

Lying there, I became increasingly uncomfortable, so I crept over and cracked open the door. I heard muffled voices from downstairs. I took advantage of the relative quiet and got ready for bed. I pulled the covers over me and finally drifted off to sleep.

When I woke, I glanced round at my childhood bedroom. No glass of Shiraz for me – I hadn't gone back. I lay in bed, immobilised by my crushed hope and this truly strange situation.

I heard my parents heading out for early communion. The front door closed, and the sound of wheels crunching across the gravel drive came to my ears. I decided to make my escape, to find time and space to think. Dressing quickly, I scurried downstairs where my sister was preparing breakfast. I grabbed a couple of slices of bread, slapped on some lime marmalade, slipped an apple into my pocket...

My sister walked back into the kitchen. "Hey! What are you doing?"

"I'm going out. I won't be back until after lunch. Bye!" And I flew out of the door, down the garden, across the back fence and into the field. *Would my childhood sanctuary be here in this world?*

The marmalade sandwich was a bit grubby from its encounter with the fence, but I was starving, so I ate as I walked down the field towards the overgrown garden of the derelict house at its end.

This was my private escape – specifically the massive cedar tree. I could lie back and hide, high in its enfolding arms, invisible from below. With considerable relief, I saw its top branches rising above the other trees in the garden. I clambered over the rickety fence and pushed through the overgrown shrubs to the tree. The cedar was so big and spread so wide that, under its shading arms, nothing could grow through the thick carpet of old needles.

I wiped my slightly sticky fingers in the long, dewy grass at the edge of its shade and walked in beneath it. There was only one way into the tree, and it required some acrobatics. I reached up and grabbed the lowest branch in both hands, swinging my feet up. I scrambled round the cold, dark bark and started the climb.

I was reaching for the last handhold before the fork when a head poked out just above me. This was so startling that I almost fell, waving my wildly grasping hand to regain my balance; another clasped it, placing mine safely on the branch.

"*Vorsicht.*" *(Careful.)* It was the German boy. Those large, dark eyes stared down at me. For a few seconds, our eyes locked together in surprise and then I hauled myself up. We sat in the fork, each leaning back against a spreading branch, staring at one another.

He was the same height as me but slender, wearing long, grey trousers and a baggy blue jumper over a grey shirt. His hair was longer than my short back and sides. Mine, however, was blandly mouse-brown whilst his was black and glossy, matching his eyes. His features were delicate and his skin quite pale.

After long seconds of mutual examination, he flicked the long fringe out of his eyes and tapped his chest. "Col."

Oh, my god, he's completely different – but in this world is this my friend, Colin – Col? My Col was English, well half English, half Canadian. *In this dream, this world, Col was German?* He was not at all like my Colin, who had been (or perhaps is?) blond-haired and blue-eyed.

Bewildered, I tapped my chest. "William…Will."

"Ach so! Willi!" He smiled. *"Wo wohnst du?"* He shook his head when I didn't respond. *"Wo ist dein Haus?"* He wanted to know where I lived. I was trying hard to appear uncomprehending, as my brain was spinning around this huge anomaly.

"House?"

"Ja. Dein…you…Haus?"

"Oh." I waved vaguely through the cedar branches to where part of our roof was visible. "Um ... you?" I was still not thinking very clearly.

He pointed in the opposite direction, across some vacant land to houses along Sea View Road. I remembered where my Col lived, and it wasn't in Sea View Road. Col was eyeing me speculatively as all this bounced around inside my head.

"You are new here!" I eventually said, in a somewhat accusatory tone as if it was his fault that he wasn't my Colin.

"New…here?" he said, pronouncing the words ponderously, testing them for their meaning. "Yes…*zwei Wochen*…two…" he held up two fingers and then shrugged, lost for the right word.

I paused, as my brain started working again. I held up seven fingers. "Week?"

He counted my fingers. *"Ja, Woche…aber zwei…*two." He held up seven fingers, twice.

I nodded, "Week is Woche!" carefully mispronouncing it Wocke.

"Ja – aber Woche, Woche!" He slowly emphasised the German 'ch' sound which didn't exist in English.

"Woche, Woche," I copied and then said "Week."

"Veek." I smiled and corrected him, making much of the shape of the lips for the 'w' sound, which didn't exist in German.

"Veek!" Again, I smiled at him, shaking my head.

We leaned back against the tree branches, appraising one another – and I heard my father's voice in the distance. He knew I used the overgrown garden as a sanctuary.

"William! William! Where are you?"

8

I leaned across and clamped my hand over Col's mouth. "Shh!" I whispered.

Col's eyes stared into mine over my hand. After a moment, he nodded and then, gently but firmly, pulled my hand from his face. He must have felt the tremor in it and our eyes locked as he recognised my fear.

We sat in silence as my father searched the garden below, calling out for me. After a few minutes, he swore loudly and headed back to the house. Moving carefully in the tree, we watched him climb back over the fence and walk quickly across the field.

We sat back down, and Col searched my face.

"That's my father," I admitted, dropping my head in embarrassment.

"You...*Vater*?"

"Father, yes."

Col again searched my face for several seconds. "*Du hast auch Angst vor deinem Vater,*" he murmured.

I frowned, pretending not to understand – but his words made it clear that he also feared his father. Another difference: my Colin's father had died before I met Colin. We sat for a while, each tasting our private fears. After a minute or so, Col reached a decision. He leaned across, grabbing my hand.

"*Komm.*" he said, pointing in the direction of his house and then clambered down the tree.

"*Komm, Willi!*" he said, glancing back up, seeing I had not started down.

My father would be back, searching for me after Matins. It would be safer if I were somewhere else, so I followed Col down.

He led me through the garden, now settling down for winter after its late summer riot of juicy, untamed blackberries and sun-warmed apples. We slipped through a decaying fence into a vacant block which backed on to a row of houses. He showed me how to climb over one of the back fences and led me to the back door.

Col pushed open the door and walked into the kitchen. "Mutti! Mutti!"

I paused on the steps, unsure of what to do.

A woman younger than my mother, with the same dark hair, dark eyes and pale skin as Col appeared. Her eyes travelled past Col and saw me in the doorway.

"*Col, Was machst du?*" *(Col, what are you doing?)* Her voice sounded anxious. I half turned away, ready to make my escape back across the fence. I did not need any more trouble in my life.

"*Mutti, ich habe einen Freund gefunden. Er heißt Willi.*"

Col's mother shifted her attention to me. "Welcome, Willi, come in please." Her English was good, only slightly accented, pronouncing my name the German way.

I stepped hesitantly through the doorway.

"Please shut the door, it is a bit cold today."

I did as she asked, standing with my back to the door, my hand still on the doorknob: I could feel some undercurrent in the room.

Col turned to his mother and started a rapid-fire conversation that my rusty German could only follow in part, but I did pick up "friend", "father" and "fear". During the brief conversation, Col's mother glanced at me several times. Finally, she held up a hand, stopping Col. He tried to carry on. She held up her hand again, *"Genug." (Enough)*.

"Willi, I am Frau Schmidt, Col's mother. Perhaps you would like to join us for some milk and a biscuit?" Col visibly relaxed at Frau Schmidt's welcoming sounding, if incomprehensible, words.

I nodded, slowly realising that my twelve-year-old body had eaten precious little since lunch at school the day before. Frau Schmidt indicated a chair at the kitchen table and Col sat opposite me. Shortly, a plate with half a dozen plain biscuits appeared along with two glasses of milk.

I felt the apple in my pocket and retrieved it. "Would you like half my apple, Col?"

Frau Schmidt's lips curled into a hint of a smile as she repeated my question to Col, *"Er möchte seinen Apfel mit dir teilen, Col." (He is offering to share his apple with you, Col.)*

Col nodded and I saw the smile for me in his eyes. A frisson ran through me and I watched Col's eyes momentarily widen at my reaction. My Col had been my closest, my only friend.

Would that friendship happen again with this very different Col? What if my Col were here as well?

"Eat." Frau Schmidt was smiling as she placed two quarter apples on each of our plates.

I picked up one of my quarters and took a bite.

"Where do you live, Willi?" Frau Schmidt's voice was gentle, encouraging me to answer her.

I finished my mouthful. "About half a mile over that way." I waved my arm towards the back fence.

"And do you have any brothers and sisters?"

I nodded. "A bossy older sister."

"Older siblings can be difficult." Frau Schmidt gave me a wry smile. "And your parents? What do they do?"

"My mother's a doctor."

Frau Schmidt nodded, impressed. "That's unusual for a woman. And your father? Is he a doctor too?" Frau Schmidt asked. Col leaned in. There was something about fathers.

My father...I sat, emotions welling up inside me. I knew I was in trouble and that I had to face it, but I was fast approaching panic at the thought of reliving this life. I struggled to control myself but felt the black tide roaring in. I jumped up, sending my chair crashing to the floor and ran for the door into the garden. In my confusion, I tried to push the door rather than pull it and I stood there pushing futilely at the door, tears streaming down my face.

Arms gently but firmly folded around me and for a moment I struggled against them.

"Shh, shh." was murmured into my ear. "Shh, shh."

Sobbing, I was half carried, half led through into the sitting room, where Frau Schmidt placed me on her lap and cuddled me, rocking me gently. After a while, I managed to calm down a bit. I felt safe, encircled by warm and caring arms. I opened my eyes to see Col sitting half turned towards me, his head leaning on his mother's shoulder, eyes filled with understanding.

Frau Schmidt felt me stir and saw our eyes sharing fear and sympathy.

"We have trouble with Col's father, and he must not know we are here." I heard the tension in her voice, felt it in her cradling arms. The radio was playing a piece for piano and orchestra, so gentle and comforting – the slow movement from the Emperor Concerto, whispered my old brain.

"Perhaps you can tell me about your father another time."

She felt me tensing because she murmured, "Shh…shh…*bleib ruhig*…stay calm, Willi."

We stayed there on the couch for a while, the human contact providing comfort while the music spread its peaceful influence. Finally, Frau Schmidt gave me a gentle squeeze and asked if I was hungry. I nodded and clambered off her lap as she stood up and went into the kitchen. Col and I followed, sitting at the table, picking at the biscuits and milk as she put some soup on to warm and buttered some crusty rolls. At first, I didn't feel very hungry, but the thick chicken soup settled my stomach and I dug into the rolls, following Col's lead in dunking them in the soup, enjoying the delicious combination of soft and crunchy textures. As I finished my bowl, Frau Schmidt smiled and ladled in another serving.

"Thank you."

"*Wachsende Kinder*… Growing children." She said, with a touch of laughter.

When we finally finished, Frau Schmidt sat opposite me. "Do your parents know where you are, Willi?"

My head turned away.

"Willi?"

I turned back and saw only sympathy and kindness in her eyes. I shook my head.

"Well, I think we had better get you home, don't you? Your mother will be worried about you."

I closed my eyes and fought down my young brain's panic.

"Komm, Col, wir werden ihn nach Hause bringen." (Col, we'll take him home).

Col stretched across the table, putting his hand on mine. *"Du wirst es nicht verstehen. Willi, aber du kannst zurückkommen wann immer du willst." (You won't understand, Willi, but you can come back whenever you want to.")*

Oh, Col, I do understand – and thank you, I genuinely wanted to come back to this gentle, welcoming house. I struggled to keep my face emotionless when I felt intense gratitude for the kindness raining softly down on me.

Frau Schmidt smiled. "Col invited you to visit us whenever you can."

I gave Col a heartfelt glance, full of gratitude, noticing that Frau Schmidt had changed 'want' to 'can'.

"Col, benötigst du einen Mantel?" (Col, do you need a coat?)

Col shook his head and Frau Schmidt rose and pulled on her coat and hat. Leading us out of the house, she carefully took a hand from each of us, stopping when we reached the gate.

"Which way, Willi?" I led them along Sea View Road, around the corner to my house. One house short of our destination, I stopped and pointed. Frau Schmidt smiled encouragingly down at me, but kept a firm grasp on my hand, leading us to the front door.

"Col, läute an der Türklingel." (Col, ring the bell.)

Col reached up and pressed the doorbell. After a few seconds, my father opened the door. He was startled to see me in the company of a strange woman but soon resumed his usual glower at me.

"Willi has been with my son and me. He was very upset about something and I thought it best he calmed down before I brought him home."

My father just stared, rudely.

My mother appeared behind him, paused as she surveyed the grouping of her son with strangers, and then pushed past. "I'm sorry, please come in."

My father was not pleased but stood aside and we followed my mother into the sitting room.

My mother and Frau Schmidt touched eyes briefly. "Will, perhaps you can show your friend your room," my mother suggested.

Frau Schmidt turned to Col. *"Bitte, geh mit Willi." (Go with Willi, please).*

I held my hand out to Col.

Frau Schmidt turned to my mother. "Col, my son, does not yet speak English. We have been here only a few weeks."

I led us out, closing the door behind me. Upstairs, Col's gaze travelled round my room. Hanging from the ceiling were my prize *Airfix* models of a Spitfire on the tail of an Me 109. I glanced at Col and blushed at flaunting Germany's defeat at a German boy. Then I realised that on my bookshelves were lined up a dozen or more Biggles books, all featuring images of German defeat at the hands of the RAF and RFC across two wars.

Col did not seem upset. Perhaps he did not understand. He continued his inspection, noting the bed as the only furniture to sit on, and then sat cross-legged on the carpet. Rather than sit on the bed, I sat down opposite him. As far as he knew, we shared no language, but I was aching to find out more about him and his mother. He searched my face and then leaned across and gently took my hands in his.

"Willi und Col...Freunde?"

"Friends?"

"Yes...*Freunde*...friends."

He shook his head in frustration. *"Ich soll schnell Englisch lernen."* (I *must learn English quickly.)*

I squeezed his hand. "You must learn English and I must learn German...*Deutsch*?"

His face showed a mix of surprise and hope. "You spick *Deutsch*?"

"I will learn – and you will learn English!"

He laughed and an idea came to me. I jumped up and grabbed my school atlas off the shelf. Flicking the pages, I came to the map of Europe. I pointed to the two of us and where we were in England and then pointed to Germany.

"Where are you from?"

Col paused. I had the feeling he was assessing me in some way. Then, murmuring, *"Freunde"*, almost as if reassuring himself, he finally pointed at Leipzig. His eyes flicked back to mine, seeking my reaction. For my seventy-year-old self, the Wall had come down and Germany had been unified for thirty years. The old DDR (East Germany) along with the entire Soviet Bloc was now history. But here in 1962, the Cold War was very real...and I started to wonder about Frau Schmidt and her son. Col had expected me to react, perhaps in an unfriendly fashion. *Who were they and what were they doing in England?*

Friendship with this different Colin was far more important to me than some long dead (if strangely still current) global rivalry. I let my face form a smile. "Leipzig," carefully pronouncing it the English way. *"Freunde."* I repeated back to him.

He smiled and I saw his body relax a tension I had not realised was there.

Suddenly, squeezing my hand he pointed at my head. *"Kopf*!" I realised what he was doing.

"Head!" I replied and we started on the process of learning to speak each other's language. I tried hard not to 'learn' too quickly, but I was sure my enthusiasm ran away with me a bit.

After about half an hour, my mother and Frau Schmidt appeared in the doorway. Smiling at me, Col pointed at objects around the room saying the English word and I chimed in with the German. Together, we ran through about thirty words, occasionally helping each other as we stumbled.

"*Ach, Willi,* you speak German well!"

As a novice, had my unusually good accent given me away?

"Will is learning French and Latin at school and he has a good ear for music…so perhaps that helps," said my mother. "Anyhow Will, Col and Frau Schmidt are leaving now."

I felt my buried panic well up at my father's probable reaction to today's absence. Both Col and Frau Schmidt seemed to sense this because Col held my hand tighter, searching my face with concern, while Frau Schmidt knelt beside us, placing her hand on my shoulder.

"Willi, you are welcome at our house. Please come and help Col learn English – and we will help you learn German." She turned towards my mother. "I am certain that will be okay?" Her voice was half question, half statement.

My mother knew that as Col lived close by, her permission or lack of it would not matter much to my twelve-year-old-self. But I knew it would matter to Frau Schmidt – and my father.

"You must let us know where you are." My mother's voice held a touch of that ferocity her recalcitrant patients feared. "You are not to just disappear."

Swallowing, I nodded.

"Right." Her intense gaze rested on my face for a long heartbeat. "Time to see your friend out."

We descended to the hall, where my father was standing, waiting.

"Frau Schmidt and I have agreed that Will and Col can spend time together here and at their house. It will be good for both boys' language skills." I realised my mother had neatly outflanked my father. His face hardened but he was unwilling to make a scene in front of strangers. He managed to shake Frau Schmidt's hand as my mother ushered her and Col to the door.

"Thank you, Frau Doktor Johnstone." Frau Schmidt raised an eyebrow at her son.

"*Vielen Dank, Frau Doktor Johnstone.*" Col's voice was polite but guarded, his eyes flicking anxiously across me and my father before coming to rest on my mother's face.

"*Bitte sehr.*" (You're welcome.)

I turned in surprise. My mother spoke German?

She laughed, as if slightly embarrassed. "I learnt a little German in school before the war…that's all I can remember."

Frau Schmidt smiled and, turning, walked with Col down the drive. As they reached the gate, I rushed after them. "Please, can I come round when I get back from school tomorrow?"

Frau Schmidt's head lifted in question towards my mother, who nodded.

Returning inside, I hurried past my father and up to my room. Nothing was settled with my father, but I felt I had an ally in Frau Schmidt. I also had a friend, but not the one I remembered. A different friend in what was a different world, at least in some small details.

I managed to negotiate the rest of the day without my father exploding at me and that night, safely in bed, I curled myself around this strange, new friendship, revelling in its gentle warmth. At the same time, the discovery of Col had shown me that this world was definitely not the same world I had lived in before.

What did these slowly accruing differences mean?

If this were a dream, I could understand the differences, but this was like no other dream I had ever had.

Sleep came, eventually.

Mid October – Early December 1962

My eyes flicked open and I sighed when I found I was still in my childhood bedroom. My old brain couldn't understand how I had survived the continuous tension of my life here.

At least my father would have left early to catch a train to work in London and so I wouldn't have to face him on weekday mornings. My young brain got me ready for school and after breakfast, I walked up the road to catch a number seven bus. Passing a pair of new houses, I realised that the wall Col had been sitting on was the garden wall of my Colin's home. I stopped across from what had been my Col's house. A young man came out of the front door, accompanied by a woman with a toddler on her hip. The man gave the woman a kiss, patted the toddler on the head, got in the car and drove off – that was not my Col's family.

A great sense of loss descended on me: my Col, my only childhood friend, didn't exist in this world. I saw the woman across the road watching me with curious eyes. I quickly turned and walked on. I would have to make do with the new Col, and though he was not my closest friend from back home, he was kind, and that had to mean something.

At school, the bullies were there as expected, but I reacted differently. I ignored their taunts as we waited for school to start and just got out my book and read. One of the leaders, a tousled, blond boy started shoving me. I pushed back firmly but the bell went just in time. The glare we shared indicated unfinished business.

Schoolwork was trivially easy, given the level of education I carried in my old brain and I tore through what was put in front of me. By the end of the first lesson, Mr. Maple, my Maths teacher, was eyeing me speculatively. He had chided me about showing all the proper working as I skipped over calculation steps but gave each of my solutions a tick as he walked round checking them.

Next period in French as I completed an oral translation with few missteps, Mr. Partington nodded. "Excellent, Will." I could hear he was slightly puzzled at my sudden improvement.

Later in music, Mr. Armitage placed an LP on the turntable and told us to listen and think of the pictures the music created in our heads.

"Tchaikovsky sixth." I muttered to myself, as the music started.

I felt Mr. Armitage's eyes on me and I quickly dropped my head to stare at the floor. At the end of class, I saw the question in his eyes but managed to slip out in the press of students.

I realised I would have to be very careful about showing my knowledge and intellectual skills – assuming I was marooned in this world, which seemed increasingly likely.

On the number seven (hooray) bus trip home, I worried at my situation. If I were stuck here, I needed to find out how different this world was, but there was no Internet, Google or Wikipedia that I could turn to, in 1962. My parents still had a newspaper delivered each day, so I would have to read that. This was a problem as I had never done so in my previous childhood.

But I was still hoping this was some incredibly complicated dream. Then an awful thought occurred to me: *doesn't your life pass in front of you when you die? Was I doing that?* For a minute my mind worried at this possibility – until the differences in this world brought that train of thought to a halt. I surely would not be reliving such a subtly different world whilst I died.

Finally, I realised that as I did seem stuck here, I must act as if this were a permanent arrangement or there could be big problems. Fortunately, I had all the experience of my 'old' brain to make it work. Pondering this nearly caused me to miss my stop and I had to rush to the exit as the doors closed.

"Pay attention, young 'un." The driver's voice was surly as he recycled the doors.

I walked down the road, giving what had been Col's house in my old life an intense scan, but nothing struck me as different, just that there was the wrong family inside. I carried on past my house and turned into Sea View Road, before knocking on Col's door.

"Willi, welcome. Come in." Frau Schmidt smiled warmly.

Col helped me hang up my coat and we went into the kitchen.

"Do you have schoolwork to finish, Willi?"

"Yes, Frau Schmidt."

"Sit down at the table and you can do it there. I will help Col, but he will do the same work and you will learn the German and Col, the English."

I worked on my Maths problems. Frau Schmidt gave Col a pencil and paper and insisted he did the same work. I found to my delight I was able to help Col, once I understood the slightly different way he wrote some numbers. Also, I was learning the German that went with the work as Frau Schmidt explained to Col what he had to do.

Once we had jointly finished, Frau Schmidt provided us both with a slice of cake and a glass of milk – and the double-sided language lesson continued.

That set the course of my days as autumn slid into winter. I continued to avoid my father as much as possible and mostly kept out of trouble, but I knew a major confrontation and beating was inevitable and this reality slunk along beside me, a very dark shadow. I also realised my mother was eyeing me somewhat speculatively. She was a very intelligent woman and she knew there was something different about me but couldn't put her finger on just what it was. I hoped that she would pass it off as part of puberty and growing up.

Each day, I smuggled the previous day's newspaper up to my room. I'd discovered this was pretty easy to do as the old newspapers just went on to a stack beside the kitchen door and I could slip the top one into my school bag as I passed, returning it later. The writing style was very different from that of 2020 and the reporting far more circumspect. Each day I would spend half an hour or so going through the paper, searching my memory for things that jarred. Part of my problem was that I hadn't been into world events and politics until later in my teens and so what was being reported was largely new to my old brain. I didn't even remember the Mariner 2 flyby of Venus, which surprised me when it happened in December. My addiction to space must have developed later than I thought.

But I also worried about what I would do if I did find something different. My main fear was that this world would descend into nuclear madness and there seemed to be precious little I could do about that as a teenager. Life went on, even if my inner life was quite strange by any normal standards.

An explanation of what had happened – was happening – eluded me. I knew this was a different world, but it occurred to me that Col and Frau Schmidt in this world could be significant in geopolitical terms as they had defected to the west. None of this had happened in my world where Col was English.

Most afternoons I went straight to Col's house after school. Col and I would sit at the table and I would do my homework with him. Frau Schmidt would listen to music and act as translator and guide as our knowledge of each other's language deepened. I tried very hard not to 'learn' too quickly, but as we approached Christmas, Frau Schmidt commented to my mother on my 'remarkable language ability' when they happened to meet in the High Street. Col's English was also improving rapidly, although he still spoke it with a noticeable German accent.

We were sitting at the table, homework finished one day, just chatting.

"Willi, how about we meet in town after school tomorrow? There's something I want to show you."

"Okay."

Col smiled, excited at my agreement. "Where shall we meet?"

"How about in the library. That way whoever gets there first can stay warm and dry while they wait."

The next day I caught a number six bus and went on a few stops into the town and then walked to the library. I found Col and greeted him in German. The young librarian at the desk heard me and sniffed, sharply.

"I wonder what her problem is?" I asked Col, still speaking German. As my 'relearned' German was currently better than Col's English, we spoke more German than English.

Col sighed. "Willi, you must understand that many people suffered in the war and blame the Germans for that. Some of them cannot move past that. Mutti and I have talked about it and I can see it happening when some people realise I am German."

"That's not fair."

"No, but I am German, Willi." His shoulders slumped in resignation.

I changed the subject. "Come on, what is it that you want to show me?"

Col's face brightened into a smile. "Oh, wait until you see this. It's the most..." He stopped, realising he was about to give away his surprise. Instead, he grabbed my hand and pulled me out onto the street. At Col's urging, we almost ran a few hundred yards, out of the main shopping area until we came to a car showroom. Col stopped and pointed at the car in the main display area. There, brightly lit, crouched the sleekest sports car I had seen: a Jaguar E-type coupé resplendent in British racing green and glistening chrome.

"Wow." I breathed, softly.

"Isn't it gorgeous?" said Col, sighing. "Do you think we could go in?"

I doubted the salesmen would want a pair of schoolboys putting their fingers all over their gleaming centrepiece, but they could only say no. I grabbed Col's hand and we walked over to the car. Everyone must have been busy as at first we weren't noticed. We walked around this vision of automobile pulchritude, staring at our faces which were reflected and distorted in the chrome and deeply polished paintwork. We peered round the driver's window at the leather upholstery and polished walnut dashboard.

"You like this car, do you?" A deep, rumbling voice practically had us leaping over the car in fright. We both swivelled round to find a huge bear of a man standing there watching us with a crooked smile on his face; a scar ran diagonally from his right eye to pull at the corner of his mouth.

I swallowed a couple of times. "We haven't touched it, sir. We were just admiring it."

"That's all right boys." He looked us over and we must have passed inspection for he leant past us and opened the driver's door. "Would you like to sit in her?"

I pushed Col forward, speaking English. "Go on, Col, it's your car."
Col's gaze was devouring the car.

"Go on, get in, but don't touch anything." I wasn't sure I had ever heard as deep a voice, almost like it rumbled inside me. Col's eyes widened with uncertainty.

"*Mach weiter, Dummie.*" *(Go on, dummy)* I said, with a smile, the German sliding from me without thinking. Col frowned at me but climbed carefully into the car. I caught a sour glance from the salesman.

Col reached out and put his hands on the steering wheel and then grabbed them back into his lap, recalling the salesman's admonition.

"It's alright, son, you can hold the wheel."

Col's face was all question. I nodded, smiling. He put his hands back on the wheel, almost reverently, his gaze roving over the interior.

"Do you want to sit in her?" the deep rumbling voice asked me, and I caught a hint of a foreign accent.

I shook my head. "I'm not very interested in cars. I prefer planes." A strange yearning passed across his face, then he turned back to Col, pointing out some feature or other.

"Brian. Brian. Phone call for you." A voice called out across the showroom.

Our salesman raised an arm to wave his understanding. "All right, out you get and hop it out of here before the boss sees and I get into trouble."

Col climbed out, a huge grin on his face and we scuttled back outside. I saw he was practically walking on air. Col turned, his lingering gaze storing away this view of his dream machine and then we set off for home. I gave him space to savour the experience and walked silently beside him, for several minutes through the town.

"I got to sit in an E-Type." Col almost sighed, still in awe of his experience. He was grinning from ear to ear. I smiled back, knowing I didn't need to say anything. By the time we had walked back to Col's house, he was coming down from his high – but, of course, the whole experience had to be recounted to Frau Schmidt.

At Col's house, our conversations at first were a cocktail mix of English and German, with frequent side trips into grammar and vocabulary with a rich admixture of Latin and French, both of which Col was picking up as we studied together. Col was keeping pace with me except in Maths, despite his learning coming very second hand through me. Eventually, in order to ensure some linguistic discipline, Frau Schmidt decreed we would alternate English one day and German the next. This worked quite well but did not prevent excursions into French and Latin (and to be fair, German on English days and *vice versa*).

At school, I was still having some trouble with the bullies, but my seventy-year-old attitude sapped their energy, and I was increasingly left alone. Even Abbott had not pressed our earlier, unresolved, shoving match. In contrast, my schoolwork improved dramatically, perhaps a bit too dramatically, despite my best efforts to hold back. I saw my teachers scratching their heads at my suddenly sharpened interest and abilities. By the end of the term, I was effortlessly topping the class and constantly reaching for something harder to provide stimulation in otherwise boring classes.

Sitting at Frau Schmidt's kitchen table one afternoon in early December as we worked on translating a section of *De Bello Gallico* into English and German, I realised I had no idea what school Col went to. I had never seen his school uniform or even any schoolbooks. He certainly wasn't at my private school. "Where do you go to school, Col?"

"I don't go to school, not since leaving Germany."

I sat there, surprised. "Why not?"

Col shifted uncomfortably in his chair and didn't reply.

Frau Schmidt, who had been sitting on the sofa, reading, and occasionally joining our conversation when we were stuck for the right word, came to sit at the table with us.

"Willi, I know you and Col are friends and want to share everything. But there are some things we cannot share. I am sorry, but please believe me when I say they are not bad things, just … things we cannot share."

I was perplexed. "Why not?"

Frau Schmidt sighed heavily. "Willi, you know that since the war, Germany is divided?"

"Yes, I've read about Germany since meeting Col."

"Of course, you have." She said, with a smile. "Well, there is bad blood between the two parts of Germany. The DDR, East Germany, is aligned with the Soviets whilst the BRD, West Germany, is aligned with England and the USA. We are caught up in that bad blood … and I cannot say more."

"Col said you come from Leipzig. That's in the DDR, East Germany."

Frau Schmidt's eyes pinned Col to his seat. After a moment, he shrugged shamefacedly. Frau Schmidt leaned across and grasped my hand on the table, her voice low and urgent. "It is very important that you do not tell anyone else that. It must remain a secret."

I stared silently at Frau Schmidt for several seconds as a terrible thought crossed my mind. I saw Frau Schmidt peering into my face, as if trying to work out what I was thinking.

Finally, I blurted out. "*Sind sie eine Spionin*?" The pressure from her hand spiked momentarily.

"Oh Willi, no, no. I am not a spy," she said, with a touch of laughter. "But it is complicated and for Col and me to be safe, you must not tell anyone what you know. No-one else must know."

"But I don't know anything – just that you are from Leipzig, in the DDR."

"And if other people know even that, we could be in danger." She paused for a moment, deep in thought. "It is possible people are trying to find us – or will try to find us – and take us back – or worse." She paused, again. "But you can help us: if anyone asks you about us, please tell me."

I could sense how serious this was to her. I nodded my head in agreement.

After a moment, she patted my hand and stood up. "Once Col's English is good enough, perhaps he can go to the local government school, we cannot afford a private school like yours. Now, how about a piece of cake?"

Frau Schmidt walked into the kitchen and I heard her gasping.

"Col, Willi – come here."

The usual view of Sea View Road illuminated by the streetlights was lost in a softly glowing, thick fog. It was so dense we could not even see the front fence along the road.

"Wow. Let's go outside, Willi."

"Children. Coats, gloves, scarves – and stay in the garden. It will be dangerous on the road."

We surged into our coats and opened the front door. The world sounded quite different blanketed by the fog. The air carried a taint of smoke and tasted slightly bitter from all the coal fires burning against the winter cold. We walked down to the gate and stood there, peering out along the road. We could hear a car approaching and very slowly its lights crawled into view. The driver had his window open, his head half out, following the central white line. Several more cars and a bus crept past.

I heard the front door open and Frau Schmidt came out, carrying my school satchel. "I think we had better walk you home, Willi. I don't want you walking home alone, and I am sure your parents will be happier once you are there."

It only took ten minutes, but we walked through a different world, with the landmarks looming out of a blurred wall of grey as we closed with them.

At my gate, I turned to Frau Schmidt and Col. *"Gute Nacht, Frau Schmidt. Bis später, Col."* (Goodnight, Frau Schmidt. See you tomorrow, Col.)

"Bis später, Willi." Their breath plumed in the cold air as they turned for home.

There were lights on in the kitchen, where my mother was tidying up.

"Hello, Will. I'm glad you're home."

"Frau Schmidt and Col walked with me. I think she was worried I might get lost."

"That was kind of her. The awful weather has upset the trains, so your father is staying in London and your sister is staying with Lucy as the buses are all over the place, too." She finished gathering the breakfast dishes out of the drying rack and put them away. "I'm glad my evening surgery was cancelled or there would have been no one home when you arrived. This is like the pea soup fogs we used to get." She paused, remembering the choking smogs of post-war London. "It's just us tonight. How about sausages and baked beans on toast?" She smiled, knowing this was one of my favourites.

"Lovely."

"Does Frau Schmidt have a telephone?"

"I don't think so. I've not seen one."

"It would be so much easier on days like today if she did. What would have happened if there had been no one here when you got home?"

"I'd have just gone home with her and Col. You know that I'd be there anyway, so you don't have to worry."

"Hmmm…I suppose so. Sit down at the table and finish your homework whilst I cook, please."

"I don't have anything more to do. We finished everything for next week at Col's house."

"What do you mean…we?"

"Col and I do the homework together."

"You mean he helps you with yours? What about his?"

I realised I was on dangerous ground here. I was certain that Frau Schmidt didn't want Col's absence from school spoken of.

"We do our homework together – in several languages. Col is even learning French and Latin a bit from what I have. We do our Maths in English and German and today we translated my Latin homework from *De Bello Gallico* into English and German."

My mother seemed placated. "It's a great advantage to you to have a foreign friend. I know that all Germans were not Nazis, but I was concerned when I first learned Frau Schmidt was German. But she is very nice, and Col is a lovely boy. Do you know where they come from?"

For a moment Frau Schmidt's request ran through my mind, but I knew my mother was merely asking out of curiosity.

"I don't know, just Germany somewhere, I suppose." The half-truth slipped easily off my tongue.

After supper, we listened to "Round the Horn" on the radio and I fell about laughing at Kenneth Williams' "Hand up your Sticks" sketch and then I was sent off to have a bath and to bed. I snuggled in my blankets against the cold night, rediscovering H Rider Haggard's Africa in *King Solomon's Mines*. After a while, my mother came in and kissed me goodnight.

"Lights out."

I lay in the darkness, thinking about my friend's situation. In the world I grew up in, the Cold War had been savage to many people in the Eastern Block, but it had remained a cold war. *Would it do so here? How could I tell?* My need to know if this world was different from the one I remembered was churning inside me.

My friend Col, being German, told me it was a different world, but how different? I knew that in both worlds John Glenn had flown in space earlier in the year – nearly a year after the Soviets put a man in orbit. In my world Valentina Tereshkova would be the first woman in space in the middle of next year, followed by the assassination of JFK in November. But I couldn't think of anything in the immediate future that might show me if this world were deviating in a major way from my world. I would just have to keep reading the papers and watching.

Eventually, I drifted off to sleep.

Mid Dec– 22nd December 1962

December rolled on towards Christmas. Frau Schmidt found a job in a dress shop in the High Street. Final term marks were posted on the classroom noticeboard for every subject and I found I had made top of the class in all but one subject – French. But then, I was competing with a native French speaker in Leurmet, whose father was a French diplomat of some kind. The following day I had confirmation of what I had already guessed: I was top of my class overall, but I supposed I should have been, given what – or rather, who – was in my head.

I usually didn't enjoy Christmas shopping, but this year trying to find something for Frau Schmidt and Col had provided the spice I needed. My small weekly pocket money didn't leave me with much to work with, but after school one day I went a bit further on the number six bus so I could wander along the High Street.

In a toy shop, I saw the perfect gift for Col – a Matchbox car model of an E-type Jaguar coupé – and it was painted British racing green. I had no idea what to give Frau Schmidt, so I meandered along, sampling the various shop windows.

I eventually spied a scarf in swirls of black and crimson that blended into one another. It was tied around a mannequin's neck. When I asked, I was told it wasn't for sale, but a prop used to enhance an outfit. I explained I wanted to buy it as a Christmas present for my friend's mother as it would go with her dark hair and eyes. The owner of the shop must have been a bit surprised at a schoolboy showing such taste. Eventually, she let me buy it for five shillings, a huge sum of money to my young self. On my way back up the High Street, I acquired some blue tissue paper for wrapping and then walked to Col's house. I had to be a bit careful about pulling my homework books out of my satchel when I got there but managed to keep the presents secret. That night in my bedroom I wrapped the scarf and model car ready to put under their Christmas tree a few days before Christmas.

A couple of days later, Col proudly showed me a newly installed phone sitting on the hall table. I wondered how they had managed that so quickly – usually it took weeks if not months for the GPO to install a new phone line. Whatever, I noted down the number to give to my mother.

The winter term ended a week before Christmas and I knew my school report would be arriving by post any day. Because of the bullying at school and beatings at home, schoolwork in my old life had been my lowest priority – so I had continually been close to the bottom of my class. My terrible school term reports had been a cause of some of my father's most explosive ragings – accompanied by thrashings. In my previous life, it had seemed that nothing I did made any difference and I had struggled through school, eventually escaping from home into mindless clerical work before discovering I had a brain. At school, I would try to concentrate and might manage for perhaps a week. Then something would cause my father to explode at me and school passed me in a blur. The only thing that helped was escaping into a book. Books that took me into another world were my favourites – I dreamed of opening a door and finding my way to Narnia or through Alice's looking glass. I knew these worlds were not real, but I needed an escape. Ultimately, they were never enough, and I had found myself beside the railway track baring my forearms as a train approached.

This term, this report, I hoped topping the class and glowing reports from my teachers would make a big difference, so my anxiety when the report arrived was present but muted.

The report arrived the Monday after school broke up for the holidays. Sitting at the kitchen table when he arrived home, my father opened my report and read through it. I was watching his face and it did not soften. He flipped back to the beginning.

"I will be contacting the school to check on these results as I seriously doubt they are correct. You were at the bottom of your class last term. This report must be a mistake – or you have somehow forged it. As a result, you are forbidden to visit your friend Col and you will stay home and study at my direction."

My mother sat there, saying nothing, her faced closed. "No." I heard the anger in my voice and I fought to control it. "You cannot do this to me. I've done really well this term and you dismiss my success as nothing."

My father's eyes narrowed, a storm brewing behind them, but I held my ground. Taking a very deep breath, I stared back at my father. Although I felt the rage blazing through me under the surface, I managed to contain it, enunciating carefully. "You cannot keep me from seeing my friend because you cannot keep me in the house – unless you tie me to my bed."

I sensed my father's temper rising – and I no longer cared. My anger at his injustice had carried me beyond fear.

"You are no better than the bullies at school, but they at least have the excuse of being children."

I took another deep breath as my father towered over me. "William," he growled.

I felt myself lean back in the gusting wind of his menace but somehow held my feet in place. "You no longer control me because I do not fear you." Our eyes were locked together in anger and hatred. "I despise you." Finally, the truth of my feelings about him lay starkly between us.

I knew the slap was coming but held still. He hit me hard and sent me sprawling across the kitchen floor, with a ringing in my head. I ended up beside the sink. Trying not to cry I pulled myself up. I saw the bone-handled carving knife lying on the drying rack.

My eyes moved deliberately from it to my father.

I heard my mother's sharp intake of breath. She understood the threat I was making and there was confusion in her eyes: who was this boy?

Without hurrying, I walked to the back door and out of the house. It was freezing outside and I was in just a thin jumper and pants, but I hardly felt it. I needed to regain control of my temper that was now threatening to surge through me and blank out all rational thought. The siren call of the carving knife disturbed me. I walked along the road and turned on to the cliff-top path away from the town. I knew my father would search for me at Col's house, so I could not go there for a while. Eventually, my fury abated, and I started crying. Not the wracking sobs that marked the end of a melt-down, but steady tears of endless sadness at my strange situation, my terrible father and my loveless home. Starting to feel the cold, I turned back along the clifftop allowing me to approach Col's house from the other direction along Sea View Road. The coast was clear: no sign of my father.

I arrived at Col's door and knocked. The outside light flicked on and Frau Schmidt opened the door to a shivering, weeping boy.

"Willi, what are you doing here at this time of night?" Then she saw the shivers and tears and whisked me inside to sit in the kitchen. Col appeared in the doorway.

"Schnell. Hol eine Decke für deinen Freund." (Quick. Get a blanket for your friend.)

Col reappeared with the blanket that they gently tucked around me.

"What is going on, Willi? Your father was here earlier," Frau Schmidt said softly.

I shook my head…I couldn't speak.

Frau Schmidt picked up a tea towel and started dabbing the tears from my face – and then I watched her caring eyes change as the handprint on my face registered. Slowly, they filled with concern, her brows forming a frown.

"Willi, who hit you?" she asked, softly.

Col pulled up a chair beside me and clasped my hands in his, rubbing warmth into them.

Slowly, Frau Schmidt stemmed my tears. Col went to the sink and filled a glass with water and brought it to me. I took a sip and handed it back, so Col sat and again held my hands in his.

"Can you tell me what happened, Willi?"

I heaved a shivering sigh, finally finding a wavering voice. "My school report arrived, and my father said I had forged it."

"But weren't you top of your class?" Col asked.

I nodded.

"Did your father hit you?" Frau Schmidt asked, softly.

I stared into her eyes for a few seconds. "Yes." My voiced hardened. "I told him I despised him."

I felt Frau Schmidt blanch at my vehemence.

"And then he whacked me across the kitchen."

Col wrapped his arms around me, resting his head on my shoulder. Frau Schmidt's face held something different, something I had never seen there before: something uncompromising.

There was a loud knock at the door.

"I expect that will be my father," I said, retreating into the blanket.

Frau Schmidt peered at us, speaking German. "Willi, does your father speak German?"

I shook my head.

"Well, if I need to say something just to the two of you, I will speak German."

Several hard thumps rattled the door.

"Go into the lounge room but leave the door ajar so you can hear – and unlock the veranda door, so you can escape quickly if you have to. Go."

From the lounge, we heard Frau Schmidt slip on the safety chain and then open the front door. It slammed back against the chain, leaving the door open only a few inches.

"I want my son," my father shouted, angrily.

An arm reached through the gap, trying to snag the chain and release it.

"Why? So you can hit him some more?" Frau Schmidt's voice held an edge I'd not heard before, harsh and almost jeering.

"You Nazi bitch – give me my son."

Frau Schmidt gave a low, contemptuous laugh. *"Ach so.* Because I am German you think I am a Nazi?" Her voice slowed, dripping with derision. "You have no idea how wrong you are." She rolled up her left sleeve, baring her forearm.

"See these numbers? I expect even you know what they signify." She paused. When she continued, her voice was low but intense enough for us to hear. "Amongst other things, it means *you* cannot scare me. I had Elfriede Muller and the rest of the SS scum at Ravensbrück at me for five years and you think you can scare me? You are a mere bag of wind." Her voice was dismissive. "Go home."

"John. John." My mother had arrived behind my father, panting for breath. "Please stop this and come home." Her voice cracked. "Please

John, come home. You're making a spectacle of yourself. We can deal with this in the morning when things will be clearer."

Frau Schmidt stood there. "Yes, go home. I will come tomorrow to your house and we will talk. Tonight, Willi stays here."

"Please John."

My father's arm retreated, and Frau Schmidt stood there staring out into the darkness. I heard some muffled conversation beyond the front door and then footsteps fading down the path. After a minute Frau Schmidt closed the door, walked into the kitchen and sat down, taking a deep breath. Col and I came out and sat down with her at the table. Her eyes were closed, and I saw that her fingers were trembling slightly.

"They have gone," Frau Schmidt said, opening her eyes.

Her left forearm was still bared. In blue dye, six slightly blurred numbers were tattooed there. From my seventy-year-old perspective, I knew what they meant, but not Frau Schmidt's story.

"What does that mean?" I asked, pointing at her forearm.

Frau Schmidt glanced down. In reflex, she brushed her sleeve back to her wrist, covering the tattoo and inhaled deeply. Her eyes closed as she stared through the walls to a different time. Finally, she turned to Col and me.

"Col knows a little of this, but Willi, have you heard about the death camps the Nazis set up?"

I shook my head. Col's right hand snuck into my left and he leaned against my shoulder. He knew I was about to hear something terrible.

Frau Schmidt stared over our heads, pinned by her experience, lost far from the present. "They put people they feared, did not want in their society – people they wished to punish or kill – into camps. My parents were communists. They executed my father, but my mother and I were sent to other camps and finally to Ravensbrück, a camp for women and children. To the guards, we did not have names, just these numbers." She paused, sliding her fingers under her sleeve, tracing the numbers on her forearm.

"The camps were bad from the start with brutal women guards, but as the war turned against the Nazis, the camps got worse." Mutti Frida swallowed and her voice became distant. "So much worse." For a few seconds, she was no longer in the room with us but standing inside the wire with hundreds of emaciated women and children shuffling into rows to be counted as guards shouted and vicious, slavering dogs barked, straining against their leashes.

She rubbed her forehead, her eyes filled with sadness and pity.

"Many prisoners were killed, and many others died from beatings or sickness. Some simply ... gave up on life. Hundreds starved to death." She paused, taking a breath. "My mother was one of them."

Tears formed in the corners of her eyes.

"We had to work, to earn our food, to earn our life each day, one day at a time. I had the job of taking out the slops and carrying such meagre food as they deemed appropriate to some special prisoners kept separately from the rest of us – English girls sent to France as spies and captured by the Nazis. That is where I started to learn English." She took a shuddering breath.

"Those girls were so courageous. They had been beaten and tortured and knew they were going to die, but they befriended me and did not show me their fear. The Nazis did not seem to care if I spent time sitting on the floor outside their cells, talking with them through the meal hatches. The SS kept some of them alive for months, but eventually, the day would come and one or more of the cells was again empty. I would learn from the others that they had been shot or hanged and their bodies burned with all the others. Death was everywhere in the camp, every second of every day – a close companion to us all. As the Russians approached, the remaining English girls were all murdered." Frau Schmidt paused; eyes closed as terrible memories rushed through her. "And then they started on the rest of us."

Frau Schmidt stopped, realising suddenly that this was a very harrowing story to be telling us. Her voice lightened when she carried on. "But then, for some reason, the SS released most of us German prisoners, several thousand women and children, into the spring countryside. Possibly they wanted no witnesses to the final slaughter of the others left in the camp." She paused, perhaps remembering the sudden freedom. "I was picked up by Russian soldiers after a day or so hiding in the woods. I learned from their officer that they had been told to watch for women wearing the red triangle that the Nazis used to label communist prisoners." She turned to Col. "I turned sixteen that May. More than half of my life had been spent in prisons and that camp."

Frau Schmidt stood up and went to the sink, pouring herself a glass of water and then turned, leaning back. She sipped her water, watching us over the rim. "Willi, now you know something of the darkness we all have inside of us. Those SS guards were just people like us: mothers, sisters, daughters but they let the darkness inside them take control." Her eyes came to rest on me. "Perhaps your father is also losing control of his darkness."

Col and I sat, silenced by the brutal intensity of what we had heard.

Frau Schmidt put down her water, walked over and gathered us both to her in a long, fierce hug. "And now, we must eat, for I think Willi will not have eaten tonight? No?"

The evening ended in a strange normality as we sat round the kitchen table, eating, and chatting. After supper, Col and I made up the sofa with sheets and a pile of blankets so I could sleep there. Despite the high emotion of the evening, I slid rapidly into sleep, perhaps because I felt safe in this friendly house.

I was woken by Frau Schmidt clattering quietly in the kitchen. I lay in bed before summoning the courage to throw off the covers and get dressed in the cold room.

"Good morning, Willi. Would you like some hot milk?"

"Yes please." Frau Schmidt opened the small fridge and measured two cups into a saucepan, setting it on the stove to heat.

Col appeared and joined me in sipping hot milk and spreading butter on thick slices of warm rye bread which we topped with slices of cheese. Frau Schmidt had made coffee for herself and that familiar and much-loved aroma teased my nostrils. I wondered if I could one day ask to try coffee – and what my young tastebuds would make of it.

"Now Willi, I am going to phone your mother and see if I can go and talk to her. You will stay here for now as I think it would make it more difficult if you were there."

At that moment, the phone rang, and Frau Schmidt answered it. She turned to me as she said, "Good morning *Frau Doktor*. I was just about to phone you." She paused, listening to my mother.

"Yes. It is I think best if I come to your house without Willi to talk about what is to be done." She paused again.

"That will be fine. I will walk round in about thirty minutes." She ended the call and sat down to finish her coffee. I saw in her face the love she had for both of us as she sat there, thinking about what was to come. At that moment, I realised in wonder just how far she was prepared to go on my behalf, and I understood, half guiltily, that I loved her perhaps more than my own mother.

"Now Willi, you and Col stay here. I will go and speak with your mother."

Col and I cleaned up my bedding and then used the blankets to make a nest for mutual warmth. This being an English day, we continued reading the *Secret Garden*. Col struggled with the Yorkshire vernacular whilst I tried not to find it easy: I had read it to my children and watched a beautiful BBC TV production with them as well.

31

After over an hour, the phone rang. Col answered it and then beckoned to me. It was Frau Schmidt. "Willi, please borrow one of Col's coats and come to your house with him."

We donned coats and walked through some chilling drizzle to my house. At the back door I paused; a bit scared to open it.

My mother opened it from inside. "Will, Col, please come in." She seemed a bit distant, as if still embarrassed at what had happened the evening before. Frau Schmidt was sitting at the kitchen table. She smiled and indicated that we should join her. My father had left for London hours earlier.

Frau Schmidt waited until my mother was seated. "*Frau Doktor*, perhaps you can tell Willi what we think?"

My mother remained silent for an uncomfortable moment, questions writ large across her face. *My implied threat with the knife, perhaps?* After a deep breath, her face hinted at – *embarrassment?* "Will, I am so sorry about last night. I phoned the school this morning and asked them about your report. I know it's real and I am very proud of you, you did very well at school this term." She stared at her hands, resting on the scrubbed wood of the kitchen table. She started to speak, then stopped and cleared her throat. She seemed almost ashamed. Her eyes flicked to Frau Schmidt, who sat impassively.

She started, falteringly, "Your father and I have discussed … what has happened." She stopped and cleared her throat again and started again in a firmer voice.

"There will be no more violence towards you, your father has promised me, but you must promise …" She stuttered to a halt, her eyes narrowing as she searched my face.

Was she worried about the knife? "If he leaves me alone, I will not even speak to him," I spat out.

"Will, he is your father, you must treat him with respect."

"No." I spat it out, my eyes narrowing. "He does not deserve my respect."

Frau Schmidt intervened, "Willi, do not make trouble here." She questioned my mother with her eyes. My mother nodded, so Frau Schmidt continued, "Your mother and father have agreed that your father will no longer be in charge of you as the two of you are so …" She glanced at my mother and then me. "… different. That will be your mother's job. Is that acceptable?"

My father's behaviour last night seemed to have scared at least some of the compliance out of my mother, giving her a forcefulness with my father I was not used to seeing. Perhaps we were both seeing new things in the other.

"Well, Willi?"

I felt Col's hand creeping into mine, giving it a squeeze. I turned towards him and he gave me an encouraging smile and the slightest nod. I wasn't sure I could trust my father not to browbeat my mother into changing her mind, but I had this new refuge with Frau Schmidt and Col. "Okay." But it was dragged from me, unwillingly.

My mother must have guessed I had trust issues about this, but I saw her shoulders dropping slightly as some of the tension left her.

"Okay," she whispered.

Frau Schmidt stood up. "Well now, Col and I will return home. Perhaps you can join us after lunch for tea, Willi?" My mother nodded.

I took off Col's coat and handed it to him. "Thank you. Perhaps we can read more of the *Secret Garden*," I said, meaningfully to Col, but his face remained blank.

We saw them out and I started to go to my bedroom. My mother touched my shoulder and I turned back towards her. "Will, I am so sorry. I know you are hurt by all of this and I know I should have spoken up before and stopped the beatings. But please, help me make this work. This family is close to breaking apart and that will not be good – for any of us."

As I stood there, all the put-downs, all the violence since it started when I was six years old ran through my head. It would be so easy for me to refuse to help – but then I realised that if the family broke apart, we could move away, and I would lose Col. I saw the fear and uncertainty in my mother's eyes…and said, "Okay, I'll try."

"Thank you, Will."

I felt very uncomfortable in my relationship with my mother and needed time to think through this new arrangement. "I'm going for a walk."

My mother cocked her head. "I don't think you should go round to see Col yet. You were invited for tea."

"No – I'm just going for a walk." I rugged up and went out, over the back fence across the field into our secret garden and climbed the cedar tree. I didn't know if Col would turn up as I had hinted he should, but I needed some thinking time, trying to work out how this new agreement might work – and what I would do if it fell apart. After a few minutes of going round in circles, I realised I would just have to wait and see.

After about ten minutes, I heard someone coming through the garden and Col appeared at the foot of the tree. After he clambered up, we sat on the damp boughs.

"I wasn't sure you understood."

Col smiled. "Your mother could see me; I could not show that I understood."

"Oh. I didn't notice that." I paused. "Col, thank you for everything. I know since we met, I have created trouble for you, but your friendship is the most important thing in my life."

There was a strange expression on Col's face – embarrassment at my words, but something else too: shame? *Why would Col be feeling shame?*

Quickly, he changed the subject. "My mother says my English is now good enough for school." He stopped and I read sorrow on his face. "But I can't go to your school – we can't afford it."

I felt a pang of anguish.

"I will start at the local school in January, in a couple of weeks." My stomach clenched – was I going to lose Col? Would he make other friends at the local school that he would spend time with instead of me?

"We will still do our homework together, won't we?"

Col kicked my foot and smiled. In just a couple of months, he knew me well enough to see the faintest flicker of fear on my face. "Of course, Willi. Who else is going to read German novels and poetry with me?"

We sat there, talking about school and the books we were reading, but I could tell there was something on his mind. Eventually, after a pause, Col leant forward, his voice lower.

"At school in Germany, we learned about the camps. We were taken to one and walked around. Everything that happened was explained to us." He paused, eyes downcast for a few seconds. "It is our great shame – and the other people in Europe will not let us forget this for a long time." His eyes rose to meet mine. "But I didn't know my family had been in a camp, that my grandmother died there." I heard his voice catch on this thought. "My mother has held that to herself until now." He took a breath, his eyes wandering through the tree. "Now I can understand why she had to run away from my father for his part in all that."

Col turned back and saw the question on my face. He paused. *What was he going to tell me? What would he trust me with?*

"My mother found out my father was an officer in the *Ordnungspolizei* – the *Orpo*. They were civilian police but under the control of the SS. They were used to round up people for shipping out to the camps – and for execution." His eyes and voice dropped. "My father is a war criminal."

I saw the tears glistening on Col's face and leaned across, taking his hands in mine.

"After hearing...after what we learned last night, I am surprised my mother can bear to have me near her." He gulped back a sob. "I must remind her of everything she despises. It was probably the *Orpo* that arrested her and her parents." Col closed his eyes, as if trying to shut out the shame he felt.

"Oh Col, no. I can see your mother loves you deeply. You know that and I can see it in everything she does for you."

Col raised his tear-stained face to me, shaking his head. "I do not understand how she can."

I wanted to hold Col, to provide the human comfort he had given me, but that was not possible in the tree.

"Come on Col, climb down and we will go and talk with your mother and you will see. She is not ashamed of you, she loves you."

I finally persuaded him to climb down and we walked back to his house. When we entered, Frau Schmidt gathered a still weeping Col into her arms.

"Col, what is wrong? Are you hurt?" Col just shook his head.

Frau Schmidt's frightened eyes found mine. "Willi, tell me what is wrong with Col, please."

I did not know how to say this gently. "He thinks you do not love him as he is the son of a man who put people like you into the death camps." I saw her flinch. "He is ashamed of who he is and thinks you are ashamed of him."

Frau Schmidt squeezed her eyes closed, then with infinite care tipped Col's head up, staring into his eyes. "Col, Col, my sweet child, there is no shame on you for who your father is or what he did. If anyone is to feel shame it is me, for marrying him." I saw the tears on her cheeks. "But I was young, vulnerable and confused. I did not know the world – I had only been out of the camp for a few years and he provided security in a world that had nearly killed me." Tears were running down her face. "It was only later that I began to suspect and finally know what he was."

She hugged Col fiercely. "Col, Col. How can you think I do not love you? You are the reason we ran away – so that you could escape that man. I love you more than my life." She crushed him to her, her arms trying to squeeze all her love into his body.

I pulled a chair up next to them, stroking their hair as they sat entwined, crying softly in one another's arms. After a while, the weeping faded, and they pulled apart.

"Mutti…"

"Col…"

They both spoke at once and laughed, breaking the tension. Frau Schmidt raised her eyebrows in encouragement.

"Oh, Mutti. Thank you. After your story last night, I was feeling so ashamed." He glanced across at me. "You know we went to Buchenwald on a school trip, but it didn't feel real, as I didn't want to believe that we Germans could be like that." He glanced at me. "But hearing your story has

35

made it real. Then I realised that my father had helped put people like you into the camps and … it all got too much."

"My sweet Col, I love you with all my heart. I will always love you." She leant down and kissed him on the forehead, then turned to me. "Willi, thank you for helping Col. You are a good boy." She wiped the tears from her and Col's faces, kissing him again on his forehead.

After a while, she turned to me. "Now – does your mother know you are here?" I shook my head. "Please ring her so she doesn't worry."

I rang and explained I had run into Col whilst I was out, and he was very upset about last night and so I had taken him home. We agreed that I would be home by nine o'clock. Col and I then helped get lunch ready and afterwards, we read the last part of *Secret Garden* and then played games.

As we set the table for tea, Frau Schmidt stopped me "Willi, do you know that in Germany, we celebrate Christmas on *Heiligabend* – Christmas Eve?"

I shook my head.

"Well, would you like to come and celebrate *Heiligabend* with us?"

I gave her a big smile. "I'd love to. I'll ask my mother and let you know tomorrow."

Frau Schmidt nodded.

After tea we sat and read again until it was time for me to leave. I shared huge hugs with Col and Frau Schmidt and then wrapped myself in my coat for the fast walk home. My father glowered at me and I stared back, standing there, my black eye all the reproach I needed. When he turned away, I went on up to my room.

23rd December - 25th December 1962

In the morning I asked about spending Christmas Eve at Col's house. My mother pursed her lips in concern. "I think I'd better ring Frau Schmidt. You are spending so much time over at her house that I am worried you might be a nuisance."

I could hear my mother's side of the conversation and even from that it was clear that Frau Schmidt didn't feel that about me.

I needed to swap my library books over as we had finished *Secret Garden* and I had finished *King Solomon's Mines* at home. I grabbed my books and caught a bus down into the town.

"Excuse me." I asked the young librarian when I reached the desk. "I am learning German and was wondering if you had any books to help me learn the language?"

Her face showed surprise ... and something else. "You want to speak German?" Her voice was tinged with derision at the thought of anyone bothering to learn what she clearly thought was a tainted tongue. Somewhat taken aback, I nodded. She sniffed, her eyes full of ice and fire.

"Well, do you have any?"

The older librarian had been listening. She gave her younger colleague a disapproving glance and moved in front of me. "I think we have a very small selection of books in foreign languages but I'm not sure if they are for children." Her voice echoed her doubt. "Come with me and we'll see." She led me towards the back of the library where there were shelves labelled "French", "Polish", "Russian" – and one labelled "German", with only a handful of books between the bookends.

"There you go – see if you can find anything there."

One title stood out: *"Der schweizerische Robinson"*. On the cover was an illustration of a group of people standing bedraggled on a beach surrounded by wreckage: *Swiss Family Robinson*. I had loved the movie when I saw it in my old life.

It was in the old German Gothic script, which would make reading it a bit difficult, but I decided to take it. One other book that caught my eye – *Die schöne Müllerin und Winterreise* – the poems by Wilhelm Müller that Schubert had used to construct his two great song cycles: beautiful music but both ending in sadness and death. I had heard them many times in my old life and again recently when Frau Schmidt had listened to them on the radio, but I had never read the poems. In the children's library I came across a book with a picture of a dragon sprawled on a hoard of gold: *The Hobbit* – I was sure Col would love this, so I picked that up too, making my three books.

The younger librarian walked away as she watched me approaching. The older librarian pulled my selections towards her. Opening *Der schweizerische Robinson* she was startled by the font. "Can you read this?"

"Well, I can read German and I am sure I'll get used to the old-style writing."

She raised her eyebrows in disbelief and pulled the index cards from the books, smiling at the Tolkien. "I think you'll love this; it's been very popular."

I took my selections home and after lunch picked up the books and carefully wrapped presents and went round to Col's house. Once I had my coat off, I added the presents to the small pile under the little tree in the corner of the lounge room. Col had heard of *Der schweizerische Robinson,* so we started on that, snuggled together under a blanket on the sofa. We both struggled with the font, but it became easier as we persevered.

When Frau Schmidt came home, she picked up the Wilhelm Müller poems. "Why did you bring this book, Willi?" There was a note of disapproval in her voice.

I was a bit surprised at her attitude. "I heard you listening to the songs on the radio and I could see you enjoyed them. But mostly I could not follow the words, so when I saw this, I thought I would give it a try."

Frau Schmidt frowned. "There is some quite grown-up material in the poems, Willi. Let me think about this." She put the book on the table.

"More grown-up than what we saw and heard two nights ago?" Col asked.

Frau Schmidt gazed at him thoughtfully. "Perhaps not, but I will still think about it."

As she turned away, an idea came to me. "Frau Schmidt, would you turn off the radio if the songs came on again?"

Mutti Schmidt' face showed surprise at the question and, giving me a nod of acknowledgement, picked up the book and put it down beside me. "Col, Willi, there are adult ideas here and difficult imagery. Please talk to me about things you are uneasy or unsure about. Okay?"

Her eye caught the front cover of *The Hobbit*, with its red dragon curled over a golden horde. Her face lightened and she smiled. "I have heard about this book and it is very well regarded."

The following day was Christmas Eve and I could hardly wait to go round to Col's house for a German Christmas. My mother and sister were preparing our Christmas lunch, with my sister bustling around, full of self-importance as she prepared the bread and apple sauces under my mother's direction. I was set to cleaning a bag of Brussel sprouts before polishing my mother's small collection of silver.

The day was starting to drag when my mother glanced at the kitchen clock. "Okay Will, you can go and clean up. Put on your long new pants and that white shirt with the lovely red and blue tie. You must be well dressed for a special evening with Col and Frau Schmidt."

Back into the kitchen, my mother and sister were making batches of mince pies. The rich smell of fruit mince filled the kitchen from a tray of cooling pies.

"My, you do look smart, Will," my mother said. My sister just gave me a dismissive glance. I rugged up, ready for the cold outside. "Here, take these to Frau Schmidt." My mother pressed a small cardboard box containing half a dozen freshly made mince pies dusted with icing sugar into my hands. "Now, off you go and wish Frau Schmidt *Frohe Weihnachten* from me."

I smiled at my mother's few words of German.

Frau Schmidt opened the door when I knocked. "Come in, Willi."

I offered her the box of treats. "*Frohe Weihnachten von meiner Mutter, Frau Schmidt.*" She stared questioningly at the mince pies.

"They're fruit mince pies. They're delicious."

Frau Schmidt smiled. "Please thank your mother for me, Willi. Now, come in and take off your coat."

In the lounge, the Christmas tree was sparkling with tinsel and guarding a small pile of presents beneath its green boughs in the corner of the lounge room. Amongst them, I could see the blue tissue paper wrapping I had used.

Col gave me a welcoming hug, pointing to the single candle in front of the tree. "We should have candles on the tree, but we couldn't find any candle clips in the shops. That's why there's only the big one."

Frau Schmidt smiled. "Perhaps it's safer that way. Come and sit down, our Christmas feast is nearly ready."

Frau Schmidt, with Col's help, had prepared a beautiful meal, centred around a roast duck. This was followed by *Dresdner Stollen* – a rich fruit and nut bread that's almost a cake, thickly dusted with icing sugar.

As we sat back from this sumptuous meal, Col smiled at me, "Now, for a mince pie."

"No Col," said his mother, laughing. "Let's keep them for later. But now, it's time for presents."

Col and I ran into the lounge room and sat side by side on the sofa. Frau Schmidt smiled at Col. "You can go first." I was expecting Col to pick up a present to him, but instead, he went to the tree and came back, handing his mother and myself small parcels from him.

I watched as Frau Schmidt opened hers, to reveal a beautiful soap, scented with coconut and frangipani. We all enjoyed this exotic scent – it reminded me of the frangipani trees in my garden so far away in every sense, aromas that were so evocative.

Frau Schmidt kissed Col on the forehead. "Thank you, Col, I will enjoy being clean with this." She went and picked up parcels and handed them to us.

"Go on Willi, open your presents."

I opened Frau Schmidt's present first. It was a German-English pocket dictionary. No longer would Col and I have to wait for Frau Schmidt to come home as we struggled to find the right words. "Thank you, Frau Schmidt." I gave her a hug and then opened Col's present: a small torch – just what I needed.

Col grinned at me. "You are always walking home in the dark and I thought you would like to have something to light your way. It's small enough to fit in your pocket, too."

Col's thoughtfulness was so much a part of him. I threw my arms around him as well.

Frau Schmidt focused on me. "Go on Willi."

I picked up my presents from under the fresh pine-scented tree and gave them to Col and Frau Schmidt, people who had come to be so important in my very strange and difficult life.

Col opened his present – and his eyes lit up when he saw the E-type Jaguar model. He picked it up, admiring its sleek and elegant lines from different angles.

"Perhaps one day I will take you for a drive in my E-type." He smiled and hugged me.

Frau Schmidt carefully pulled the blue tissue wrapping paper from her present.

"Oh. Willi." She picked up the scarf and unfolded it across her lap. "It's beautiful – and it's silk." I smiled at her. "Come here, Willi. You deserve a hug and a kiss for this."

I was again enfolded in her arms as she gave me quite a hug – and a kiss on the forehead. Holding me in her arms, she pulled back. "I think that from now on you should call me Mutti Frida. You are practically family."

I felt tears in my eyes as I clung to her. "Thank you, Mutti Frida." I realised I felt safer and more at home here than in my parent's house.

"But remember," Mutti Frida cautioned, catching my eye. "You do have a real mother and she does love you, even though she is perhaps not very good at showing it."

Mutti Frida's eyes searched my face and I offered her a nod of understanding.

We then played card games and nibbled on chocolate, almonds and muscatels, though we had to keep a watchful eye on Col who seemed to have a chocolate addiction and kept trying to sneak extra bits when he thought we weren't watching.

Eventually, Mutti Frida glanced at the clock on the mantelpiece. "Willi, it is time for you to go home."

Unwillingly I rugged up.

"Thank you so much for sharing your German Christmas with me!"

Col and Mutti Frida smiled.

"Here, Willi, don't forget your torch." Col pushed it into my hand.

"Come and see us on the day after Christmas, Willi."

"Here in England, it's called Boxing Day." I laughed at the stupidity of the name.

Col gave me a bemused stare.

I shrugged. "I don't know why, but it is."

I hugged Mutti Frida and Col and then trudged back to my parents' house. Christmas with my family was going to be different and difficult.

***

Somewhat to my surprise, there was a Christmas stocking on my bed when I woke up. In my previous childhood, I remembered carefully pulling everything out and laying it on my bed in order so I could repack it correctly – we weren't supposed to open our stockings until we were all together. I crept out of my room to the top of the stairs so I could see the cuckoo clock on the wall at the foot of the stairs – half-past seven. As I turned back, my sister stuck her head out of her room and waved me inside, quietly closing the door. We sat on her bed.

"We have to wait until eight o'clock, then we can sing a carol outside our parents' room and go in with our stockings."

I remembered the ritual from my previous life, but I simply couldn't sit on the end of my parents' bed and unpack my stocking in front of my father.

"You go. I'm not going to do that."

My sister jerked away from me. "You have to. You'll ruin everything."

I remained silent.

"Please Will, cooperate. It's Christmas. Mummy and I have worked hard to prepare the food, please don't spoil it all. I know things are difficult between you and Daddy, but…"

"Difficult?" I could hear the anger in my voice. "He beats me. I hate him."

She closed her eyes. I was surprised; usually, she would not talk to me unless pointing out my many failings or giving me orders. The last few days must have shaken her – and perhaps our mother had shared words with her as well.

"Will, I understand. But we all live in this house and you need to compromise a bit." I recalled my mother's warning about the family being on the verge of falling apart.

"Okay, I'll try for you and Mummy." I sat up, firm in my resolve. "But I will not sing carols and go into their bedroom to open our stockings."

I saw that my sister was about to remonstrate with me, but the door opened, and our mother walked in, wearing a dressing gown. "I think we'll get breakfast and do the stockings downstairs. Why don't you get dressed? I'll just go and pop the sausage rolls into the oven to warm and then get dressed myself."

The day unfolded with sharp corners and unexpected edges, even though we were all walking on eggshells. Most of those corners and cutting edges involved my father. I was astonished when he wished me, "Happy Christmas."

For a moment I just stood there, dumbfounded at his hypocrisy. Out of the corner of my eye, I saw my mother stop and turn towards me, her face eloquent in its pleading. I managed to hold back the biting response I had been about to make and walked away saying nothing. From behind my father, my mother gave me the slightest nod of acknowledgement.

By the end of the day, I was exhausted by the effort of restraint – and I think my mother and sister were too. Who knew how my father felt? And I didn't care.

I retired to bed with *Tarka the Otter* and *Ring of Bright Water*, Christmas presents from my mother. I was hoping Col would like these as I had loved them in my old life.

26th December 1962 – early April 1963

The weather after Christmas continued to be wet, cold, and miserable. There wasn't even a decent storm where we could watch from the cliffs as rollers crashed onto the shore or listen to the roar of the shingle as the retreating waves sucked the pebbles back down the beach. It was dark until about eight o'clock in the morning and was dark again by four o'clock in the afternoon.

Col and I spent much time reading to each other from the same book, snuggled under blankets. Mutti Frida had somehow acquired a copy of a slim book of short stories by Heinrich Böll about a soldier's knapsack in the first and second World Wars, but acquiring books in German was difficult, beyond what I had found in the library. Col was loving *The Hobbit* and I had *Narnia* and my otter books to follow.

In my world, the weather had changed on New Year's Eve and we had started the coldest winter for decades. *Would that happen here?*

On New Year's Eve, it was still raining but in the afternoon the temperature had started to drop and as dusk fell, the rain became snow with a driving wind, which was almost a blizzard. I was doubly happy: I loved snow and the weather matching my memories reassured me about this world. Mutti Frida refused to let me go home in such appalling weather, so once again I spent the night on the sofa in the lounge room after phoning my mother.

Come morning, the storm had largely blown itself out, leaving a dramatically changed world. After an early breakfast, Col and I rugged up and walked round to my house. My mother helped us get the toboggan out of the garage from underneath a pile of old potato sacks. We took turns pulling each other along the road to the top of the Downs, where there were already quite a few toboggans racing down the hill. We piled on to ours, with me in front after Col's insistence that it was my toboggan and set off down the slope, feet splayed out either side. By the time we reached the bottom, we were laughing from pure joy. As we came to a stop, Col pulled me so we both fell off into the snow. We lay there, still laughing until we realised there were people hurtling down the hill at us and we needed to get out of the way. We walked back up the hill and started to work out how to get the best speed out of our wooden steed. Half a dozen trips down and back and we'd had enough.

Col pointed to the beach, which was covered with what I first thought was snow, but it turned out to be green-tinged ice crystals, formed when spume was blown off the waves in the storm. The sea surface was also grainy, covered by more ice. On the breakwaters perched a few confused and dejected seagulls, wondering what was happening to their world. I picked up a pebble from the beach and tossed it into the water – its splash was subdued as it splatted through the half-frozen surface. In my world, the sea had quickly frozen, which had been truly amazing. After tossing a few more stones, we headed back to Col's house for some lunch.

We took it in turns to pull the toboggan up the hill and then pulled each other along the snow-covered pavement. The council had gritter trucks out, putting a mix of salt and grit on the roads, but the few cars we saw were still sliding around. We helped push a couple that were spinning their wheels and arrived back at the house quite warm from our exertions.

Mutti Frida had made a beautiful beef and vegetable stew, which we ate with homemade German noodles rather than the usual English mashed potato or dumplings. It was delicious and both Col and I came back for seconds, prompting another *"Wachsende Kinder"* chuckle from Mutti Frida. As we were eating, the day grew steadily greyer and it started snowing again, so we decided to stay inside and play cards. I taught them 'Hearts', which they did not know. We spent a laughter-filled afternoon trying to dodge or offload the Queen of Spades, with Mutti Frida losing very graciously.

It was growing dark early because of the thickly falling snow, so with candles ready in case of power cuts, Col and I snuggled under a blanket to continue reading.

"Do you think the public library can order books in German, Willi?"

I shrugged. "Perhaps. Maybe when Col starts at school in a week, they will have some."

"That's a good idea. Both of you must read in German – Col so he does not forget how to, and you to strengthen your language skills." Mutti Frida seemed to consider this for a moment, then turned to me. "When you go to senior school, will you study German, Willi?"

That seemed a lifetime away for my 'young brain' but also incredibly close for my 'old brain'. I was still somewhat bemused by these two very different perspectives.

"I don't know. I would like to. I don't even know if the school offers German."

"Perhaps you should find out what you can do," Mutti Frida said, with a smile. "You seem very good at most things. Do you know what you want to do after you leave school?"

"I want to fly," I said without having to think – and then squeezed my eyes closed. My old brain knew that was not going to be possible because of my eyesight, but that was all my young brain wanted. There would be tears before bedtime, in this life as in the last, over this problem and I did not want to talk about it.

"What about you Col, when you leave school?" I asked, to deflect the conversation.

"I have no idea. I'll just have to wait and see what I'm good at…and where we are, I suppose."

I hadn't thought about that. My young brain just assumed that the way things were today was the way they would be, yet my old brain knew that change was the only constant in life. The idea that Col might not be here, that I might lose my friend sent a shiver down my spine. He was the best thing that had happened to me, just as his namesake had been in my other life. But that Col had slipped away during our teens as we both moved around the country and I had never been able to find him again later in life. I made a silent promise to myself that was not going to happen with this Col, in this life.

"…Willi? Willi?" Col punched me gently on the bicep.

I turned to face him.

"Oh, so there is someone in there. Where did you go?" he said, smiling.

"Sorry – I was just thinking."

"Right – your turn to read out loud." We settled back into *The Hobbit*, chuckling at Bilbo rushing out of the door without even a pocket-handkerchief. Eventually, Mutti Frida pushed me out of the house to go home. In truth, I felt more like my family was here with Col and Mutti Frida.

The following days before we started at school were very similar. One day, the three of us walked through the snow along the cliff top as a storm built in the Channel. The wind whipped around us, growing stronger after we turned for home. It was clear the ice was forming more thickly as the waves at the foot of the cliffs surged but did not break, due to the layer of ice crystals on top. We also saw great billows of grey-green ice crystals filling the beaches below the sea wall, piled up there by the wind and waves. By the time we arrived back at Col's house, it was snowing increasingly heavily: we were having another blizzard. I hoped Mutti Frida would let me stay the night rather than have me walk home in such bad weather – and that did indeed happen.

Mutti Frida decided it was time we cooked her a meal. She sat on the sofa and gave cooking instructions through the open door. Fortunately, it was a simple meal of toasted ham, cheese and *Gürkchen*, pickled baby cucumbers, on slices of the thick rye bread Mutti Frida loved. She had been delighted to find it a Polish bakery in town that produced something like the *Schwarzbrot* she so loved.

After we finished eating, we again played Hearts, and this time it was me that crashed out. I spent the night sleeping on the sofa as before, swaddled in blankets. That night the sea did freeze – according to the news up to a mile out from the shore – and there were worries that the ice could damage the pier.

A few days later, the holidays ended and it was back to school. After school on the first day, I hurried back to Col's house eager to find out how he was doing.

Col was there in his school uniform, deep gloom apparent in his stance.

"How was school?" I asked, tentatively.

"I hate it." His face screwed up with emotion. "Apparently, I am a Nazi, a hun, a kraut and various other bad names used by you English during the war." He paused, eyes rolling. "Some of them are calling me Adolf. I hate England. I hate you English." I saw the hurt in his eyes and heard the anger in his voice. "There is one Polish girl who insists on calling me *Szkop*, which is probably something rude in Polish."

"Col, I'm so sorry. Have you told them you are not a Nazi – that your mother was in a concentration camp? Surely that would make a difference?"

"I can't tell them. I can't tell them anything because we need to stay hidden!" Col shouted, then turned and ran into his bedroom, slamming the door closed behind him.

I had never seen Col so hurt and angry and I was unsure of what to do. I also realised I had never been inside Col's bedroom and entering now felt strangely like a violation of his space, but I still knocked.

"Col? Col? Can I come in?"

Through the door, I heard faint sobs and stood there trying to decide what to do. Eventually, I decided Col was hurting, and I needed to comfort him. I softly opened the door. Col was lying face down, his head buried under a pillow. I walked rather timorously towards the bed and reached out, touching his shoulder.

"Col?"

There was no reaction. I sat down beside him on his bed. "Col, I'm sorry about what was said to you. Please don't hate the English – at least not all of us."

I felt Col stirring, and he tugged the pillow off his head, before gusting out a stuttering sigh. "*Willi, nein, ich hasse dich nicht.* I could not hate you." He turned to me, eyes a bit red but with a hint of a smile on his face. "Even if you are English."

He got up and we went out into the kitchen. I stood there watching as he filled a glass with water and sipped it.

Could my old brain help Col? "Col, part of my problem is being bullied at school. I've discovered that ignoring it seems to be the best way. It doesn't stop but it does fade over time. I'm hoping this term that it will mostly go away."

46

Col joined me at the table and closed his eyes for a few seconds, gave me a grimace and sighed. "I've always been alone at school. In Leipzig, all the other children knew my father was *Stasi*, so even the children of party members were very careful around me."

"Stasi?"

"*Staatssicherheitsdienst* – the State Security Ministry that has its tentacles everywhere. The rulers of the DDR do not trust the population. After all, the people gave their loyalty to the Nazis – and some of the leaders, like my father, were Nazis too. At least that's what Mutti thinks. No-one trusts anyone very much and no trust at all is given to those with connections to the Stasi."

Even my old brain didn't know much about the DDR – they were hangers-on in the Cold War whilst the Russians, the Soviets, were the real enemy.

"Didn't you have any friends?"

"No. Everyone feared the *Stasi* and I was seen as part of that. I wasn't bullied and called names like I was today, because they feared my father, the Stasi, but I was mostly alone. People were very careful not to offend me, but no-one wanted to be my friend." He sat at the table, toying with his glass of water, so I joined him, waiting for him to find the words he needed. After a lengthy pause, his eyes rose and stared into mine. "You are the closest friend I have ever had…I've never before been able to be this close, to share so much with anyone else." Col flushed slightly, embarrassed at what he was revealing.

I leaned forward. "Col, I've never had such a close friend as you. Thank you for everything you've done for me."

Col flushed red, even more embarrassed. "Do you have any homework?" he asked, changing the subject.

"Not on the first day of term." I said, laughing.

"Neither do I." Col joined me in laughter. "Let's go and read."

Mutti Frida found us in our usual winter cocoon of blankets on the sofa when she arrived home from work. She hung her coat up and came in to sit opposite us. "How was school?" she asked Col.

Col took a deep breath, as if trying to conceal his feelings, but the hurt showed in his trembling voice. "They all hate me because I am German. The English kids call me all sorts of rude names I do understand, and a Polish girl calls me *Szkop* which I don't understand but is probably rude too."

I watched Mutti Frida's face drop, her previous interest morphing into concern and perhaps a little rage – she had heard that slur before. There had been Poles in Ravensbrück, after all. She moved across and sat on the other side of Col, gathering him in her arms. "Oh Col, I'm so sorry. Children can be so cruel."

"Can't he tell them that you weren't a Nazi and that you were in a concentration camp?" I asked.

Mutti Frida shook her head. "No, that would start to identify us, and Col's father might find us." I saw the pain on her face in her frown.

"I'm so sorry Col, but I'm sure it will blow over. Try not to react to the bullies. I wonder," I paused as an idea bubbled up from my old brain. "…perhaps the Polish girl used to be the focus of these attacks because she is different, and she is now trying to fit in by bullying you."

Mutti Frida gave Col another hug and then got up to start cooking tea.

Each day when I arrived at Col's house, I watched the tension rising within him.

"Still happening?" I would ask.

He would nod and I would give him a hug. I was still a target at school because I was a loner – and now my old brain's academic prowess exacerbated the differences between myself and my peers. But some students were starting to seek me out to help them with their work which was, I supposed, progress of a sort.

The weather remained mostly cold, although there were occasional thaws as January slipped into February. One weekend, a Saturday night blizzard was followed by a light, freezing drizzle on Sunday. I made it round to Col's house as the weather turned. Col and I waited outside for a while and watched as everything became coated with ice, as if molten glass had been poured over everything, making every surface treacherous.

Back inside, we warmed up on the sofa with a hot chocolate.

"I talked to that Polish girl earlier in the week," Col said.

"Yes?"

"I found her alone in the Art room."

"And?"

"I asked her if she was bullied by the English kids before I came along. She just stared at me and then ran out."

"Oh."

Col was silent for a moment. "But yesterday, she came and found me and said she was sorry. You were right – she was just trying to fit in with the English kids who had been bullying her."

I smiled at Col, "That's good news." But underneath I felt a frisson of fear. *Would this girl befriend Col and pull him away from me?*

Despite the occasional thaw, there was always some snow on the ground into March, but somehow it was never thick enough to stop my daily bus from running. Col and I had worked our way through *Der schweizerische Robinson*, which we found a bit boring and rather moralistic, although we mastered the old-style Gothic script as a result; but we liked the Heinrich Böll. In contrast, we both loved *The Hobbit*, even though for me it was about the tenth time through. In my head, I heard the fabulous setting by Howard Shore of the dwarves' song from the 2012 movie. I had to concentrate hard to make sure I didn't hum it as we read the song.

At school, my teachers were now giving me individual work from textbooks they acquired from senior school, in Maths most of all, but I was well ahead of the class in everything. I had the feeling that the school was not quite sure what to do with me.

A couple of days before the end of term, Col and I were sitting on the sofa after tea, chatting about what we might do during the Easter holidays.

"I thought I might invite Lili to spend some time with us," Col said, quite suddenly.

"Who?"

"Liliana – that Polish girl. Once she stopped trying to please the English bullies by attacking me, they turned on her again. We have formed a united front against them and are now friends." Col gave me a confident smile.

"Oh." Col heard the lack of enthusiasm in my voice. He stared quizzically at me.

"Are you worried she'll replace you, Willi?"

I turned away, a bit ashamed of the prick of jealousy I was feeling.

"Come now, Willi, I'm allowed to have other friends, aren't I?" he chided.

I knew I was being unreasonable, but Col was my only friend and I didn't want to share him.

"I'm sure you'll like her when you meet her. She is lonely and needs friends, just like the two of us."

My young brain's emotions were getting away from me. I had a sinking feeling in my stomach and the happiness I usually felt in Col's company had soured, replaced by a gnawing fear. I didn't respond and reached for our book. Col raised his eyebrows, but I concentrated on the book, finding the right place on the bookmarked page to start reading. Col sighed and helped balance the book on the blanket we were snuggled under and we began.

I went home that night in an increasingly dark mood. Despite my old brain trying to calm things down, a shadow had settled over me by the time I lay in bed, before sleep arrived.

The following day, the shadow was still on me, deepening through the day, and I went straight home after school, much to my sister's surprise.

"You're gracing us with your presence?" she asked, her voice dripping with sarcasm.

I didn't answer and went up to my bedroom to work on some of the Maths problems I had been set – sine and cosine rule triangle problems – which were still trivially easy for my old brain. I was now well into the 'O' level Maths program, much to my teacher's continuing astonishment.

Later that evening, the phone rang. A few minutes later my mother came into my room.

"That was Frau Schmidt on the phone. Is everything all right between you and Col? You didn't go there as usual today."

"No, I had this Maths to do."

"Don't you usually do this with Col?" I could hear the concern in her voice.

I kept my eyes on my desk. "Col can't do this Maths." This was true – the Maths I was doing was a long way beyond what Col was doing, so now I just helped him with his Maths and did my Maths at school, at home or waiting for the bus.

My mother peered over my shoulder and then picked up the text, flipping it closed over a finger marking my page so she could read the title.

"O Level Maths? Where did you get this book?"

"From school."

"And you can do this Maths?"

I lifted my exercise book and showed her what I had been doing. I could see that this Maths was a long time in her past and she couldn't remember it.

"Let me explain," I said.

I then spent a few minutes going through the two rules and how and when they are used to solve non-right-angle triangles, drawing quick sketches of triangles to illustrate what I was saying. When I finished, my mother inspected the textbook, my examples and stood in thoughtful silence for a moment.

"I can see you know exactly what you are doing." She paused. "I can remember my teachers telling me that you never knew a subject until you taught it – and you've just done that for me." She put down my exercise book. "You don't need this practice, do you?" There was a pause as she gathered her thoughts. "What's going on between you and Col?"

I shifted uneasily in my chair.

"Will, you have so few friends that you need to be careful. I worry about you. Please tell me what's happening. Perhaps I can help."

I felt my fists clenching in my lap. "Col is making friends at his school and I'm being left out."

"What do you mean, being left out?" My mother asked, gently.

I jumped out of my chair and stared out of the window, my young brain's emotions roiling inside me. "I don't want to talk about it. Leave me alone."

My vehemence rocked my mother. After a moment I felt her hand on my shoulder. "Will, I'm sure he's not deliberately leaving you out. He's allowed to have other friends, isn't he?"

I felt the emotions within me surging against my older brain's controls. "He's my friend. My friend." My old brain was struggling to hold things together. I turned and threw myself on to my bed, trying to hold back the angry tears.

My mother sighed. "All right, Will. I'll give you some space." I heard her closing the door behind her.

After a while, I calmed and my old brain started to control things again. It would just have to try to hold things together. I'd had lots of practice with this, after all, but my young brain's emotions were so strong, vivid and all-consuming that calming its turbulent waves was proving difficult.

After a while, I got up, washed my face and went downstairs for tea. My mother watched me, but nothing was said.

Mid-April 1963

In the morning, I went off to school for that last day of the spring term in a dark mood. The bullies must have sensed that I was vulnerable and attacked me mercilessly. I struggled through the day, full of appalling thoughts of what my life would be like without Col's friendship, and without Mutti Frida's deep well of humanity.

Sitting on the bus, I felt my world falling apart. Without Col's friendship, I couldn't face this life. This time, I would get a knife.

There was a calmness within me after that decision, and I sat there, watching the scenery flowing by. Even though it hadn't snowed for nearly a week, there were still white patches clinging to the shade under trees and hedges. I knew they would be talking about this winter for over fifty years.

From the bus, I walked home. My mother was still at work, but my sister might have been home – but not today, it seemed. I scrabbled for the key behind the step of the shed and let myself in. Selecting a sharp knife from the kitchen drawer, I went out, locking the door and putting the key back in its place.

If I wasn't home, I knew my mother would assume I was at Col's house, so I would have plenty of time. I walked down the garden, over the fence and into my secret garden.

Under the cedar, the needles were dry and provided a cushion of sorts. I'd been here before, so I knew the drill. I stripped off my coat and slid up the left sleeve of my school jersey. I would only need to do one arm this time.

I pulled the knife out of my school bag and examined my wrist, reminding myself of the location of the artery. When Seneca suicided after the failed plot against Nero, he had sliced along the artery, not across it, to hasten his end.

So be it.

I poised the knife over my wrist, working out how to best do this in a single slice.

"Willi. Willi, stop."

Col appeared beside me, grabbing my hands.

"No – leave me alone." For a moment we struggled, but my emotions surged up and I collapsed in tears, huddled over the bed of needles. I had no idea how long I lay there as the storm of emotion tore through me and receded. Eventually, I felt a hand softly stroking my hair and stirred, sitting up.

Col saw me glancing at the knife, which was still in his hand. He quickly put it behind him. "What is going on, Willi?"

I closed my eyes, my breath coming in gasps. "I can't go through this again. I can't do it alone."

"Willi, you are not alone." He grasped my hand. "I care for you, Mutti cares for you – your mother cares for you. You are not alone." With each statement, he squeezed my hand in emphasis.

"But you are leaving me for Lili," I said, softly. "And if you go, so will Mutti Frida, and my mother is not enough." Tears started down my cheeks again, loosed by the ineffable sadness suffusing me.

I saw Col stiffen. "You were going to … to kill yourself, weren't you?" I stared at the carpet of needles.

"Because I have another friend?" I heard the anger building in his voice. "A person can have more than one friend. How can you be so stupid, so…so selfish?" His expression changed. "If that's who you are, I'm not sure that I want you as a friend." He stood up, anger suffusing his face. "Here's your knife, then. Get on with it." He tossed the knife on the ground at my feet and stormed off towards his house.

I leaned back against the tree, eyes closed and my old brain started berating me. God, I was being unbelievably selfish – and now I had probably destroyed my friendship with Col. I clasped my arms around my calves and bent forward, resting my head on my knees.

I had no idea what to do. I wanted to go after Col, but I was so ashamed that I couldn't do it. All I could think of was going home and hiding in my room. I opened my eyes – and the knife was lying just in front of me. I reached to put it in my bag.

"Willi. No. No." Col threw himself past me to stop me picking up the knife.

Col just lay there, motionless on the pine needles.

"Col? … Col?" He wasn't moving. I scrambled towards him. "Col!" I screamed.

He levered himself up, rubbing his stomach. "Ouch. That hurt."

"Col. Are you okay?"

He pulled the knife from the ground.

"I'm fine, the handle of the knife just dug into me." He stopped, probing my face, an unspoken question hanging between us.

"No Col, I wasn't going to. I was just going to pick it up and go home."

Col took a deep breath. "But when I first arrived?"

There was a prolonged silence, until I eventually dropped my eyes.

Col touched my arm. "I'm sorry I said … what I said. I was very angry with you. I don't want you to kill yourself. You're my best, my closest friend." Col's voice was cracking, and it nearly broke my old heart. He collapsed forward grabbing me and burst into tears. After a while, he peered up at me with tears running down his face. "Oh Willi, how could you think of doing such a thing?"

"I'm sorry, Col."

He sniffed and sat up. Then he grabbed my wrists, inspecting them intently.

"Have you tried to do it before?" he asked, searching my face.

I closed my eyes and nodded.

"Oh, Willi. When?" I heard the anguish in his voice.

"The day I first met you, I was about to…do it, but something stopped me."

"What do you mean?"

"I don't know – something … happened and I found I couldn't do it. At least not that day."

Col knelt there, holding my hands and staring off into the distance. He squeezed my hands to get my attention and locked eyes with me. "You have to promise me something."

"What?"

"Willi, you have to promise me that you won't do this again."

I took a deep breath. The desert of my remembered life stretched years-long ahead of me. "Col, I don't know that I can promise that."

"You have to. You have to." His face screwed up in heartfelt fear. "I don't want to lose you, but I can't do…" The knife drew his eyes down, holding them for a second before they flicked back up to peer into mine. "…this again. You must promise me."

I swallowed, tears coming to my eyes. I knew I had contemplated this in the future and on occasion gone beyond contemplation to preparation. Yet, somehow, I had survived.

"What if I promise to talk to you…if I ever feel like this again?"

Col scanned my face with his warm, bright eyes. I could almost feel them tracking through my tears.

"You'll talk to me if you ever feel like doing this again?"

"Yes, I promise."

Col pulled me into a crushing hug, only releasing me when I grunted with the strain of it. Then he turned leaning back against the trunk beside me. We sat in shared silence for quite some time as the day faded before he stirred.

"Come on Willi, we need to get to my house. Mutti will wonder what's going on if I'm not there when she gets home." He stood up – and noticed the knife, still in his hand. He paused; lips pursed. "Here. You'd better put this in your bag so you can put it back when you get home."

Wordlessly, I took the knife and stored it at the bottom of my bag. "You've got pine needles all over you." I smiled and started brushing Col down.

"So have you," he said, with a grin.

Once we had removed all the debris, we set off to Col's house.

As we walked in, Col rubbed the dirt on my cheek. "You need to go and wash your face and hands." I could see the tear-moistened dirt smeared across my hands and I saw that on Col's face.

"You, too," I said, smiling.

Shortly we were sitting on the sofa, a blanket tucked around us, about to start reading.

Col stopped suddenly, just as he was about to pick up our current book. "What did you mean, *I can't go through this again?*"

"Pardon?"

When I first arrived, and you were going to ... you said *I can't go through this again*. What did you mean – *again*?"

Had I really said that? I turned to Col, shrugging. "I don't know." I paused for a moment. "I wasn't exactly thinking straight."."

Col sensed the tension in me. "Okay, I just wondered, that's all." He eyed me speculatively, trying to make sense of what he had seen and heard.

Eventually, he said, "Are we going to tell anyone about this?" His voice was soft but laced with concern.

I tensed up, swivelling so I could see right into his eyes. "No." It was almost a shout of fear. I took a breath to calm myself. "Please, please don't tell anyone. I don't know what would happen to me if anyone else found out."

"I'm scared, Willi. What if you try again?"

"I've promised to talk to you if I feel that way again." I was pleading – what would my mother do if she found out I had tried to kill myself? And twice now.

Col's eyes rose to mine. "I know." There was a long pause. "But what if the problem is between us and we aren't talking, like today? What happens then?" I heard the fear in Col's wavering voice.

"If there's a problem between us, we need to talk about it." I saw Col struggling with this. I took his hands in mine. "We must never let it get that far." I felt our friendship was in danger of slipping away and I didn't know what to say to stop it. "I'm so sorry. I know it's very scary and you're right to be worried. Please tell me if this is too much for you ... if it is, I'll go."

Col sat there, his eyes closed. The world seemed to shut down around me. Intent on not showing any emotion, I started untangling myself from the blankets. A hand on my shoulder restrained me.

"Willi, you are one of the most intelligent – no, you are the most intelligent person I know, but you are also the most stupid." The hand shook me, quite hard. "You're my best friend and I don't want you to go." His eyes searched my face. "But you've scared me – and that you have this still in you scares me even more. But you've promised to talk if things are getting too much." He paused, seeking … something. "For us though, perhaps we need a special word we can say to each other if a fight starts going too far, something that will make us both stop and think about what is happening."

I sank back into the sofa, flooded with relief that he didn't want me to go. I turned towards Col. "What do you mean?"

"A word that won't happen in normal conversation. If either of us is starting to feel things are getting out of control between us, we can say it and we both have to stop and find out what's bothering the other person."

"Oh." I thought for a moment. "That's a good idea. What word?"

"Umm ... how about…Gundagai?" I was surprised that Col knew that Australian place name but managed to hide it.

"Gundagai?"

"It's a place in Australia – there's a song about it our geography teacher played us."

I shrugged, to mask my surprise. "Okay, Gundagai it is."

Col took my hand. "Tomorrow Liliana is coming for lunch with Mutti and I. Please, will you come and meet her?"

I sensed this was an important test. "Thank you, Col. I would like to meet your new friend."

Col gave my hand a squeeze and picked up our current book – Müller's poetry – but paused when he sensed me tensing slightly as I recalled its blighted love and dark, suicidal vision which matched my mood but might be too much for Col right now.

"Are you OK, Willi?"

I gave him a smile. "I'm fine." I knew I was going to have a conversation about this with Col.

***

I arrived at Col's house before ten o'clock the following morning, hoping to be there before Liliana arrived.

Mutti Frida answered the door. "Hello, Willi. They are in the lounge room."

I was a bit taken aback that Liliana was here before me, but as I took off my coat, Col burst out of the lounge room.

"Willi. Come and meet Lili." Col dragged me into the lounge room, eager to introduce us.

I hadn't thought much about Lili, except as a rival to Col's affections, so I was surprised when she wasn't at all like I had subconsciously expected. Instead of a slight, dark girl, Lili was a blue-eyed girl, whose fair hair was pulled back into a single long plait. She was taller than me, all in all, more how I expected a Scandinavian to be.

"Lili, this is Willi." Col laughed nervously at the combination of our names.

Lili stood up, very formally. "Hello, Willi." She said in completely unaccented English but used the German pronunciation.

"Oh. Call me Will. Willi sounds strange coming from you."

Lili gave me a shy smile. "But that will confuse everyone here who calls you Willi."

"Oh. All right then." I said, shrugging.

Col picked up a pack of cards from the side table. "I thought we could play Hearts?"

We sat on the floor and explained the rules to Lili.

"I have played something like this game with my parents. They call it *Czarny Piotruś*." She slipped easily into Polish.

"Do you speak Polish at home?" I asked, wondering how much Polish she knew.

"Oh yes. We speak English too, but my parents want to make sure I don't forget my heritage." I realised she knew what she was saying when she called Col *szkop*.

"What does *szkop* mean?" I asked, archly.

Lili sat up, eyes swivelling nervously between Col and me.

"Willi, that's not very nice." Col glared at me.

I glared back. Lili deserved this for what she had done to Col.

Lili swallowed. "During the war, the Germans –," she glanced apologetically at Col. "er, the Nazis – occupied Poland and did terrible things. We Poles had rude names for them and *Szkop* is one." She turned to me. "I have apologised to Col for what I said and he has accepted my apology." She started to stand up. Col leaned across and grabbed her arm, holding her down.

"No, Lili." Col's eyes narrowed. "Willi, I have accepted her apology and I don't want to hear any more about this. I want you two to be friends."

"She hurt you, Col. You came home for days in tears," I said, in German.

"No, Willi. Speaking German to exclude Lili is not right." I saw Col's frustration with me growing. "If you can't be nice to my guest, perhaps you'd better go home."

No. It was happening just as I feared it would. I started to get up.

"Gundagai." Col called out. "Oh, Gundagai, Willi."

I took a deep breath, staring out of the window and sat down.

"Willi, I don't want you to go home but please, don't let jealousy wreck our friendship."

Lili sat there, caught between us, sensing secrets but not understanding.

"I'm sorry, Col. I feel so alone and I'm scared you'll desert me for Lili." I saw Lili's eyes fill with surprise at that.

"Willi, that's not going to happen. This is not about me choosing between you and Lili; it's about the three of us sharing a friendship. Please trust me and let us both be friends with Lili."

With a conscious effort, my old brain clamped down on the fear of abandonment suffusing my young brain. I knew it wasn't real – but at the same time, the emotion was very raw, almost all consuming. Somehow, I needed to stay in control. Now that was interesting – the 'I' was my old brain. It seemed to be the dominant conscious entity in this weird, shared head. But underneath, my young brain was governing my emotions – and they were quite capable of taking over and wreaking havoc. Something to think about…

"Willi? Willi?" Col reached out and touched my arm. I blinked back into the now.

"Um…Okay, Col – and I'm sorry for being rude, Lili."

Lili's face was thoughtful. "I think we three are very much the same. We've been so alone for so long that we're scared of friendship – scared of finding it and very scared of losing it when we do." She turned to me. "Willi, I apologise for hurting your friend and I'm glad you were here to help him when I did." She smiled appealingly at me. "Please, can we be friends?"

Col reached out and took one of our hands in each of his, giving them a squeeze. "Lili, I think you may be right about our fear of friendship." Col questioned me with his eyes.

I nodded my head. "All right."

"Yes." I felt Col squeeze my hand and I saw the smile creasing the corners of his mouth. Lili gave me a tentative smile, which I returned. She reached across, taking my other hand and closing the circle.

The three of us shared a moment's silence before Col picked up the deck of cards and we started playing. I found my fear receding just through spending time with Lili. As she relaxed, her natural cheerfulness started to show. After quite a few hands when Col lost, we stopped for a break.

Mutti Frida popped her head round the door. "Lunchtime in ten minutes." I realised beautiful cheesy aromas had been permeating the house for a while and I was suddenly hungry.

We went and washed our hands and then set the table. As Col and I knew where everything was, we kept bumping into Lili as she tried to help but got in the way. It became a game – side plates in the dresser: hip bump Lili to get past. Cutlery in kitchen drawer: hip bump Col to get past and then hip bump again to set the places round the table. By the time the table was set, Lili had joined in as an active participant and we were all laughing and shrieking, chasing one another and just hip bumping for fun.

"Children, children. Settle down. After lunch, you all need to go out for a walk along the cliffs to burn off some energy." Mutti Frida chided us, smiling.

Her gloved hands carried a still sizzling casserole dish in, placing it carefully on a mat.

"What's that?" Col asked. I saw Lili peering at it, wondering the same thing.

"Willi knows – this is a recipe his mother gave me."

That was news to me. I had no idea that my mother and Mutti Frida had reached the stage of exchanging recipes.

"Cauliflower cheese," I said.

"Absolutely correct, Willi. Oh – I have forgotten the bread and butter. Col, it's on the side in the kitchen."

Col quickly returned with the expected rye bread, already sliced and buttered.

"Careful now, it's still very hot." Mutti Frida cautioned as she handed round plates of steaming cauliflower cheese. "We don't say grace in this house, Lili, so please start."

We helped ourselves to slices of bread. I saw that Lili and Col were a bit apprehensive about this new dish, but I loved it and took a mouthful – wow, hot. I grabbed my water glass and took a cooling drink.

"Willi, I told you it was hot." Mutti Frida smiled at me.

"Sorry, Mutti Frida."

Lili and Col both tried a sensibly small taste – and smiled, sharing a glance. Silence descended on the table.

"More anyone?"

"Yes please, Mutti Frida." I handed my plate across.

"Why does Willi call you Mutti Frida, Mrs. Schmidt?" Lili asked.

Mutti Frida handed me back my plate and I reached for another slice of bread.

"Well, Lili. Col and Willi have become close friends and we have been through some difficult times together." She paused, giving me a gentle smile. "And Willi has become like a son to me."

"Oh." Lili dropped her eyes, a bit embarrassed, sensing there was more to this story.

Mutti Frida seemed to feel Lili's unease and drew her back into the now. "Would you like a bit more, Lili?"

"No, thank you…but it was delicious."

"Col?"

"No, thank you."

"All right children, let's get cleaned up and then you can go and burn off some youthful energy on a walk."

We quickly cleared the table – with an occasional hip bump – and raced through the washing up. Then we rugged up and headed out, leaving Mutti Frida to a concert on the radio.

"Where shall we go?" Lili asked.

"Let's head along the cliffs towards Reculver," I suggested.

Col pursed his lips. "That's a long way."

"We don't have to go all the way. We can turn back when we've had enough."

"Okay."

We set off down Sea View Road to the Downs and along the clifftop path. The day was cold, with quite an easterly breeze in our faces as we walked towards Bishopstone.

Lili pointed at some of the wartime coastal defence works. "What are all these old concrete works?"

"Haven't you been up here before?" I asked.

Lili shook her head.

"These are all part of the coastal defences from the last war." I stopped, a memory washing through me. In my previous life, Col – the other Col – and I had spent hours exploring the slowly rotting concrete bunkers, observation posts and pillboxes. We had even managed to get into some of the dank and dark tunnel network that linked them. It had been a bit scary at times, but we had egged each other on, exploring until we reached a dead-end or our way was blocked by the rusting bars of locked gates. We had been so close, spending all the time together that we could out here on the cliff tops or hidden away in our secret garden.

Col and Lili stopped after a few paces and turned towards me. "Willi?" said Col.

My Col felt so close here, his presence almost tangible. *How could I have let such a close friend drift away? Why did I let it happen?* I turned slowly, seeing ghosts from my past – or was it a different present – flitting in and out of existence amongst the decaying slabs of concrete. I suddenly felt my eyes moistening.

"Willi? Are you all right?" Col walked back to me, staring intently into my face.

I came back to this present with a shiver. "Sorry. I was just…thinking…about what all this meant." I waved my arm over the fortifications that were gradually being reclaimed by nature.

Col cast me a quirky glance and I just shrugged back at him.

We walked on, with Col and Lili chatting and me catching glimpses out of the corner of my eye of those mirages of a different Col. Eventually, I banished the phantasms and concentrated on the Col in front of me: I was not going to let my new friend drift away as I had before.

We came across another cluster of wartime concrete relics as we approached the gully cut by a stream at Bishopstone Glen. I still felt uneasy about Col and Mutti Frida when things linked to the war came up and now there was Lili – I knew nothing of how the war had impacted her family. In fact, I realised I knew almost nothing about her.

We stood surveying the gully and I shivered, only partly from the chilling wind. A buried memory burst over me. My Col and I had been forced to climb the dangerously crumbly sandstone bluffs when we were chased by some older teenagers bullying us for money. The climb was only about five meters, but the frightening memory of foot and handholds starting to disintegrate as we scrambled away from danger was shockingly real. Somehow, today kept tossing memories of my Col at me.

The afternoon was getting on and we turned for home. As we walked back, I kept pace with Col and Lili, unlike the outbound walk when I had the sea anchors of memories dragging on me. Col and Lili chatted about school: students and teachers I didn't know and who had a crush on whom. Even though I could not understand the surface of their chat, I realised I could feel the undercurrents: what and who they both liked and why, what interested them and what bored them. It became clear that Col and Lili were forging a friendship and I would need to have a friendship with Lili. That thought almost brought me to a stop – *would Col and I end up as rivals for Lili's affections?* That was a dangerous possibility in terms of my relationship with Col.

We had the wind at our back and that helped propel us home. As we turned the corner into Sea View Road, we saw a new Ford Prefect parked outside Col's house.

"That's my mother's new car," Lili remarked. "Isn't it lovely?" She was proud of this shiny, pale blue car.

We stopped and inspected the grey leather interior before walking into the front garden and round the back to the kitchen door. I smiled, thinking of *the Hitch-hiker's guide to the Galaxy.*

We tumbled into the kitchen in a blast of cold air to find Mutti Frida and Lili's mother, Mrs. Wiśniewski, sitting at the kitchen table, drinking coffee, and speaking…Polish? Lili stood open mouthed in amazement and then broke into a babble of what had to have been her mother tongue.

Col and I stood and watched.

"Enough," said Mrs. Wiśniewski. "Speak English, Lili, we are excluding your friends."

Lili blushed in embarrassment.

Col stared at his mother. "I did not know you spoke Polish." His voice was almost accusatory.

"Well, a mother needs some mysteries." Mutti Frida smiled, enigmatically. "Did you have a good walk?"

"Oh yes – we got as far as Bishopstone Glen and then the wind blew us home," Col said, with a smile.

"How about a hot chocolate to warm you up and a biscuit?" asked Mutti Frida. "You can stay a bit longer can't you, Daria?"

Mrs. Wiśniewski nodded. Mutti Frida and Mrs. Wiśniewski were forging a friendship of their own, it seemed.

Mutti Frida started some milk to warm and got out the biscuit tin, filling a plate with biscuits and placing it on the table. Shortly, the plate was joined by mugs of hot chocolate and we sat chatting, nibbling biscuits and sipping our hot chocolate.

"What are you children doing for the rest of the holidays?" asked Mrs. Wiśniewski.

The three of us glanced at one another and we all shrugged.

"Spending time together, I hope." I said.

Col smiled at me and then glanced at Lili. "Okay?"

"Of course." I could see the excitement in Lili's face. She turned to her mother. "Can Willi and Col come to lunch tomorrow, Mama?"

Mrs. Wiśniewski glanced at Mutti Frida who nodded. "Willi, do you think that will be okay with your mother?"

"I expect so. I'll ask her when she gets home from her evening surgery."

"Is your mother a nurse then?" Lili asked.

Col jumped in. "No, Willi's mother is Frau Doctor Johnstone."

"Oh," said Lili. "There's not many lady doctors around. That's why I thought she was a nurse. What does your father do?"

I tensed and Col knew I didn't want to talk about my father – and his situation was the same. He cut across the conversation, changing the subject. "What time should we get to your house, Lili?"

"About half-past nine?" Lili asked her mother.

"That will be fine." She stood up from the table." Come along, Liliana. We must be getting back."

After we saw them out, Col and I read more of *Die schöne Müllerin*, getting ever closer to the journeyman miller's fantasy vision of his grave and implied suicide. I was still not sure how I was going to handle this part with Col when the time came as it struck rather too close to recent events.

When I got home, I asked my mother about spending the day at Lili's house and she agreed. I rang Col and told him I would be at his house at about nine o'clock.

Mid - late April 1963

I had breakfast with my mother who sent me off with an admonition not to overstay my welcome at Lili's house. I packed *Ring of Bright Water* and *Tarka the Otter* into my duffel bag, along with *Under Milk Wood*, which I was hoping we could read aloud together. A third voice would make some scenes much easier. It was a typical English spring day with a stiff breeze and showers about. I heard my mother's rhyme in my head: *March winds and April showers bring forth May flowers*. She had lots of these – including the one for all the kings and queens since William the Conqueror. I always thought it unfair that it didn't include the Saxon kings.

I paced along the street, reciting the monarch rhyme to myself, in time with my footfalls, "Willy, Willy, Harry, Steve, Harry, Dick, John, Harry three, one, two, three Neds, Richard two, Henry four, five, six then who?" After a couple of repetitions, I arrived at Col's house, wondering what he was making of English history. I realised I knew very little of German history – apart from the bitter wars we had fought this century – and I always skirted around those if they came up as I didn't want to rub his nose in the defeats Germany had suffered or the horror that was the Nazi regime.

I knocked on the door just as a brisk shower arrived and Col found me sheltering under the eaves when he opened the door.

"Quick, Willi, before you get soaked."

I hung my coat up and we went into the lounge.

"Mutti's already left for work. It will take about twenty minutes to walk to Lili's house I think and Mutti told me to make sure we were not early."

We sat on the lounge at opposite ends.

"What else do you want to do these holidays?" I asked.

"I was wondering about showing Lili our secret garden. What do you think?"

I thought for a moment. Lili lived far enough away so she would only be there when we asked her. "Okay."

"I've seen the apple trees in the garden are blossoming. Do they have apples?"

"Oh yes. And they're delicious when you pick them after the sun has warmed one side, leaving the other cool."

"I've never tried that."

"There are some big cooking apples too. Bramleys, I think they're called. They make a great baked dessert – take out the core, stuff them with raisins and sprinkle with brown sugar."

"That sounds lovely. Do you know who owns the house? Is it alright to take them?"

"Well, I've never seen anyone there and the house seems derelict from the road. I suppose someone must own it, but my mother didn't seem worried last year when I gathered buckets of blackberries there. She used them to make blackberry jam, and blackberry and apple pie."

"Okay." I saw that he was slightly perturbed by taking fruit out of a garden we didn't own. "What books shall we take today?"

"Well, we should take *The Hobbit*. It's not worth taking a German book as Lili doesn't speak the language. I have my otter books and *Under Milk Wood* in my duffel bag. I thought we could read that aloud and having Lili's voice as well as ours would make it easier."

"Good idea. Shall we take a pack of cards?"

"Perhaps we should, just to be safe – though I expect Lili will have a pack."

Col pulled a pack from the sideboard drawer and I added them to my bag.

We chatted a bit longer and then Col peered at the clock on the mantelpiece.

"It's time to go, it'll take about twenty minutes to walk there. Mutti left me an umbrella but we'll need our coats too." Col gave me a serious look. "You'll have to help me remember the umbrella when we leave."

I rolled my eyes – I wasn't the most reliable person even with my own possessions. Col laughed and rolled his eyes back at me.

The weather cooperated for the walk to Lili's house, although from the top of Mickleburgh hill it was clear there were showers further down the coast to the west.

Lili greeted us at the door almost bouncing with excitement. "Willi, Col. Come in. Mama is making hot chocolate for us as she thought you might like a warm drink if you got caught in a shower." Lili's house was on the seafront and quite large with nice furniture and tasteful decorations. It seemed Lili's parents were quite well off – which I had already suspected from Mrs. Wiśniewski's new car.

Lili dragged us into the kitchen and Mrs. Wiśniewski greeted us with steaming mugs of hot chocolate with frothed milk. I pulled our books out of my bag and showed Lili. The otter books attracted her – possibly the simple sketches of otters caught her interest. I also put in a few encouraging words about the Dylan Thomas play. Lili bounced up and went to her bedroom, returning with *The Chrysalids*. That was my favourite of John Wyndham's books and I had to contain my enthusiasm and let Col ask the questions.

After the discussion, we decided to read *The Hobbit* first and then perhaps play cards and try John Wyndham later. We spent a pleasant morning with the Tolkien shared between the three of us on the couch. We started again from the beginning, so Lili had the complete story, and I saw that she was becoming as enthralled as we were. After lunch, Mrs. Wiśniewski pushed us out for a brisk walk onto the pier.

"Off you go, children. You need some fresh air."

I had the impression that she wanted an hour of peace without teens around her feet. We walked all the way to the end of the pier, crossing the bridges that spanned the gaps torn in the pier in 1940 so it couldn't be used to land invasion troops from occupied France.

I had reminded Col about the umbrella and we took it with us, in case. This proved a wise decision as we were caught in a shower on the way home. Three of us didn't fit under one umbrella. Lili insisted Col should be in the middle and stay driest as it was his umbrella, so Lili and I arrived back at her house a bit moist, as the wind made control of the umbrella difficult.

We started on the Wyndham after we hung up our coats, taking it in turns to read a few paragraphs and, after a while, Mrs. Wiśniewski called us into the kitchen to eat some quartered oranges. Col seemed to be enjoying *Chrysalids*. I was having to be careful as I loved it and had read the book several times during my old life.

As we ate, I talked a bit more about *Under Milk Wood* and why I liked it so much, explaining that it was a radio play, not a stage play and so the voices carried far more weight – and it was also very Welsh. Col, understandably, had no idea about Wales and Lili was not much better. It was clear that they saw I liked it, so we would probably give it a try in the future.

We returned to Wyndham's vision of a post-apocalyptic Labrador, reading another chapter before Mrs. Wiśniewski came and asked us how we were getting home. We had been so engrossed in the book that we hadn't noticed that the occasional showers had given way to steady rain.

I shrugged. "We'll be fine. We have Col's umbrella."

Lili turned to her mother. "Mama, why don't you drive them back to Col's house? You could chat with Frau Schmidt for a bit whilst we read some more."

"Well, I suppose I could. After all, what's the point of my own car if I don't use it?" she said, smiling. "Come on, gather your things and let's be off."

We scrambled together our books and stuffed then into my duffel bag, remembering to pick up Col's umbrella which was drying in the porch. Mrs. Wiśniewski reversed her car out of the garage behind the house and

Col and I got into the back with Lili in the front. It took less than ten minutes to get to Col's house where we all piled out and ran through the rain to the front door and into the house as soon as Col unlocked it.

Mutti Frida was not there of course as it was a weekday and she was working. Col and I burst into laughter. We were not used to the holidays yet and had forgotten, thinking it was a weekend because we were not at school. We apologised to Mrs. Wiśniewski and Lili drooped a bit when her mother said they should go home.

"What are you doing tomorrow?" Lili asked, hopefully.

"We haven't decided anything yet," Col said, glancing at me.

I shrugged. "We're probably just going to hang out, read and play games."

Col smiled at Lil. "Do you want to join us?"

Lili's face lit up. "Oh. Yes, please." She turned to her mother. "Is that all right, Mama?"

"That will be fine tomorrow, but don't forget we have to go and see your aunt on Thursday, and you have your drawing class on Friday morning. Tomorrow, though, you'll have to walk up and back as I am volunteering at the Red Cross."

"Okay, Mama. If I leave at nine o'clock, I'll be here by half-past. Is that okay, Col?"

"That's fine, Lili. See you then."

We watched them running back to the car through the rain and then returned to our usual position on the sofa.

"If the weather is fine tomorrow, should we show Lili our secret garden?"

I felt a twinge of something at sharing that place with Lili. What was that – *jealousy, or fear?*

"Willi?"

I took a deep breath and then released it, watching Col's face. "It's our special place, Col."

"I know, Willi, but isn't Lili your friend as well, now? We should trust her enough to let her share that place with us, don't you think?"

I took another deep breath, my old brain pushing down my young brain's irrational fears. "You're right, Col. I should trust her."

Col's eyes showed something that I couldn't identify, nothing bad, unsettling perhaps but … different. "Thank you, Willi." He kept his gaze on me a moment longer and then turned away and picked up *The Hobbit*.

"Perhaps we should keep that for when Lili's here tomorrow, Col. Why don't we read more of Müller's poems as Lili can't read German?"

Col smiled and I saw another flicker of something in his eyes. "That's a good idea, Willi." We were drawing closer to the dark ending of the cycle of poems. I was increasingly uncertain how Col would handle that – and how I would handle his reaction.

After we'd read for a while, I stopped and focused on Col. "Um ... Col. Were you listening to the songs when they were on the radio?"

"Not really. Why?" His expression was quizzical.

"Do you think this is going to end well for the young miller? Do you think he gets the girl?"

Col's expression was pensive. "What are you trying to tell me, Willi?"

"Until we read the last few poems, I'm not certain how it ends. But from what I could make out from the songs when we heard them, I think the beautiful miller's daughter takes up with the hunter, breaking the young miller's heart ..." I stopped, fixing my gaze on Col's face.

His eyes travelled back down to the book for a moment, before returning to mine. "And?" I saw in his eyes that he knew what was going to happen to the miller but needed me to say it.

"He drowns himself in the stream. The last song is sung by the brook – I think it's a lullaby for the dead miller."

Col sat for a moment, his eyes searching my face. "Are you going to be okay if that's what happens?"

"Can you see a different ending? I don't think I can."

I saw the concern mounting in Col's face and he repeated his question. "Are you going to be okay reading this? Do you want to stop?"

"No, it's beautiful poetry, but we can stop if you want to."

Col pulled the bookmark from the back of the book, placed it on our page and closed the book. "Willi, what are you trying to say?"

It was my turn to search his eyes. "We haven't talked about ... what I nearly did that day. And now we are going to read about the young miller drowning himself ..."

Col sat in silence for several seconds, his eyes questing in mine. "Willi, I trust you. You said you would talk to me if things started to get too much for you and I know you would keep that promise." He gave a brief shudder. "I don't like that this is part of you, but I do understand that it is." He paused, deep in thought and then smiled wryly. "That day under the cedar tree we shared something that has brought us much closer. It seems that even awful experiences, when shared, can make a positive difference, in a strange way."

I smiled back at him, admiring his words.

"Willi, I think that literature is full of ... suicides and characters thinking about it. I want us to read and talk about it if it's part of you." He stopped again, trying to crystallise an idea. "Perhaps if we do that, we might end up understanding that part of you ... and perhaps that will be enough to stop you being pushed in that direction."

We sat, staring at one another. I was amazed at the depths of Col's perceptions, but mostly at his care for me, which shone in his eyes.

After a few seconds, Col picked up the book. "I don't want us to be awkward about it when we come across it." His eyes held mine. "Okay?"

I nodded.

Col's gaze lingered for a moment before dropping to the book. "Let's carry on reading."

We read through to the end, the brook's lullaby was gentle and beautifully sensitive to the young miller's anguish. When we closed the book, there were tears in both our eyes.

The following day was fine and quite mild for April and so we made sandwiches from the ham and tomatoes Mutti Frida had left for us and packed a bottle of water and some apples together with *The Hobbit* and introduced Lili to our secret garden. Fortunately, she was wearing jeans as I don't think she would have climbed the tree in a skirt. We spent several hours up there, passing the book between us as we read aloud, sitting on our branches and chatting about books and life as we ate our lunch. I was getting to know Lili and I enjoyed her enthusiasm, which was a contrast to Col, whose situation engendered a more serious outlook and the dark thoughts which swirled inside me. I could almost feel the jig-saw pieces of our friendship drawing together.

As we ate, I had a sudden vision of Bilbo, Gandalf and the dwarves sitting in the pine trees surrounded by goblins and wargs. I had to smother a chuckle as we were mimicking them – without the wargs and goblins, of course, but we hadn't reached that part of the book yet.

After we returned to Col's house, I asked Lili about her drawing classes.

"Well, I enjoy drawing." She smiled at Col. "That was why you found me in the Art room that day, though I haven't worked out why you were there."

"Not because I am any good at art," said Col. "It was just a place I thought I could hide from the bullies for a while."

"Please Lili, could you show us some of your drawings sometime?" I asked.

Lili's eyes dropped, shyly. "Well, alright. I'm just learning but Mama says I have some skills and I should work on improving them."

"Do you enjoy drawing?" Col asked.

"Oh, yes." Her face lit up with enthusiasm but then became suddenly serious. "I get frustrated with myself when I can't get down on paper what I see in my mind's eye. Mrs. Frobisher, my art teacher, says I need to work on seeing more carefully so the picture in my head is clearer and that will come with time." I heard the dedication in Lili's voice.

"I enjoy art, but I don't think I have any skills as an artist."

Col huffed. "When do you look at art?"

"At school, in art class. Our teacher says we should all know a bit about the great painters and their paintings. She has a projector with countless slides. She's been showing us some work by the Impressionists."

"Oh, I love Monet's paintings," Lili said, sighing. "I want to go up to London one day and visit the National Gallery. They have a few of his paintings as well as a sculpture by Rodin."

Col seemed a little lost.

"When we get back to school, Col, I'll show you some of Monet's pictures in the books we have in the art room. I think you'll like them."

Lili couldn't join us again until later in the following week, but she brought a voluminous artist's satchel from which she produced a sketchbook and rather timidly showed us some of her drawings. There were several of a fluffy tabby cat that caught my eye. There was one where it was caught in mid-leap.

"That's excellent, Lili. You captured that in your mind's eye very well."

Lili blushed slightly. "Thank you, Willi. I had to encourage Rupert to jump quite a few times to fix the picture in my head." She paused for a second, glancing down at the drawing. "Mrs. Frobisher says that now I am starting to see more clearly, I need to stop trying to be a camera and show myself in my drawings." She shook her head in frustration. "There's always something more."

"But that's why you like it so much, isn't it?" Col's sensitivity to those around him was showing again.

"Yes, you're right." Lili thought for a moment. "Thank you for asking about my drawings. I'm always a bit scared to show people but showing you two was different. I hate it when Mama makes me get my sketchbook out to show her friends; it feels she's showing me off. I still have so much to learn."

Col spoke softly. "We're your friends, Lili. You weren't showing off but sharing an important part of your life with us. Thank you."

"I think you are talented, Lili." I glanced down at the sketchbook. "There was a drawing of you, wasn't there? How do you do that, in a mirror?

"Yes," said Lili, smiling. "To do it properly, you need two mirrors, to reverse the mirror reversal so you draw what people see rather than what you see in a mirror. I only had one mirror so if you examine the picture," she flipped the pages in her sketchbook and held up her portrait beside her head, "I'm reversed as I see myself in the mirror.

"Of course," said Col, with a smile. "Your mole is on the other side."

"Perhaps I could draw you two one day? I need to practice with lots of different faces and then move on to figures." Her voice was diffident, as if she were unsure of how we'd react.

Col and I nodded our agreement and Lili gave us a brilliant smile.

We spent more time up in the tree that day reading *The Hobbit*. Things were happening in the wildly overgrown garden, with the daffodils and primroses finishing but the fruit trees blossoming. Spring was definitely here, and the bitter winter was receding into history.

When I got home that evening for supper, my mother pointed to an official envelope on the kitchen table that was addressed to me. I had no idea what it was about. I certainly had no memory of ever receiving such a letter in my previous life. My mother offered me a kitchen knife to slit it open – the same one I had taken a couple of weeks earlier. That sent a shiver up my spine and I stood there staring at the envelope and knife for a few seconds.

"Go on then, open it."

I carefully slid the knife under the flap and cut it open. Inside was a letter, with something stapled to it. I read it and then handed it to my mother, rather bewildered.

My mother scanned the document and a smile broke out on her face. "Well, Will, your Premium Bond has just won five thousand pounds."

My mouth dropped open. "My what?"

She laughed, eyes still wide as if she still couldn't quite process what had happened. "When Premium Bonds first came out in 1956, Uncle Joe gave you and your sister one each for Christmas. And yours has just won five thousand pounds."

That was a large sum of money in 1963. I knew my parents had bought our house in 1958 for just three thousand pounds. I sat down at the table, completely dumbfounded.

I had a Post Office savings account that had about thirty shillings in it at present, mostly what was left of my birthday money. I tried to put in a shilling a week from my pocket money, but I missed some weeks. I was thinking about what to do with the money when my father walked in. He saw my mother holding a letter and read it over her shoulder. After a couple of seconds, he snatched it from her hands. "That will go into a special account that your mother and I will set up and require our signatures for withdrawals," he announced.

My mother half rose from her seat. "John, please give that back to me. You know we have an agreement about Will."

"This is completely different." He waved her away, irascibly. "Five thousand pounds is a lot of money and I don't want that stupid boy frittering it away. We need to make sure it's there for his future."

"No!" I stood up, trying to stay calm. "That is my money and you will not have any part of controlling it. I know you; you will simply refuse every request to use it out of spite or hate or whatever it is."

"Will, stop. Please let me handle this. Let me talk to your father." My mother stared pleadingly at me.

I peered up at my father. My thoughts might have been from my old brain, but the frustration and fury were pure teen rebellion from my young brain. "The last time you hit me, I think you realised how this might end up." I watched my mother flinch at the memory. "You made an agreement with my mother. Keep it." I was seething.

My mother used her doctor's commanding voice, "Will. Please go to your room. I will talk to you soon." She frowned at me, afraid I would lose it if I stayed. I turned and walked out, barging past my sister in the doorway.

"Now what have you done?" she hissed. She must have heard the raised voices, but I ignored her and went upstairs.

I sat on my bed trying to read *Allan Quartermain*, but I couldn't concentrate. Eventually, I just lay back on my bed, trying to calm down. Then the implication of what had happened struck me: this was new, this hadn't happened in my previous life. The differences were starting to pile up and I had no idea if they mattered to the rest of the world. I hadn't seen anything in the newspaper that was different from my memories, but I could easily have missed things. The tensions between the east and the west seemed to be the same as I remembered – not getting any worse but not any better either. The next global event I remembered was Valentina Tereshkova's flight into orbit. That happened in the middle of 1963, but I had no recollection of the actual date. Hopefully, it would happen in the next month or two.

I took a deep breath and tried to relax. There was precious little I could do about things, anyway, whether it was world events or my father's virulent antipathy. My mind meandered, finally settling on my current situation. I didn't understand what had happened when I was six years old, when my father turned against me. *Had I done something so terrible that he could never forgive me?* I could remember nothing beyond the sudden and unexpected violence that had crashed down on me. *What could I have done?* I lay on my bed, trying to stop my thoughts spiralling out of control.

After a while, there was a soft knock on my door. This was a first – no-one had ever knocked before. I opened the door to find my mother standing there. "May I come in?"

I blinked and held the door open for her. As she came in, I saw that she had the letter and cheque in her hand.

I sat down on my bed and my mother pulled my desk chair over and sat in front of me.

"Will. Your father has stuck to the agreement and will let me handle this."

"Thank you." If he hadn't done that, I wasn't sure what would have happened.

"There are a few things we need to talk about before we get to the cheque."

I stared at her, wondering what was going on.

"First of all, your father has decided that the travel to London every day is getting too much. He will be staying in London during the week. I hope that will help ease the tension between the two of you."

I simply nodded. I spent as little time as possible at home already so I didn't think it would make much of a difference, but the fact that my mother had thought to help with this warmed my heart.

"Now, we come to your behaviour."

My mother's eyes held a steely determination and a hint of something I could not make out. *Was it concern for me or something else?*

"I should have spoken to you before about the knife the night your father hit you, but I didn't, and you have again implied that threat. You cannot continue making threats like that, for a couple of reasons." She waited until she was sure she had my attention. "First of all because you might find yourself backed into a corner and have to go through with them. Do you understand what I mean?"

I nodded. That was the problem with threats – you could find yourself having to follow through. I wasn't sure I could take a knife to my father, but I was scared I might lose my temper and do it in a cornered rage – controlling my young brain was still problematical. I wasn't sure if capital punishment had stopped in England, but I knew it had sometime in the 1960s. They wouldn't execute a child, but stabbing my father would wreck my life, even if I didn't kill him.

I could see my mother almost reading my thoughts.

"Hmm." She paused. "The second reason not to make threats is that they change things. Your father understands what your threat this evening implies and that changes the relationship between the two of you, for the worse. It also changes how all the relationships in the family work."

I took that in and waited, I could see my mother hadn't finished.

"I told you before that this family was on the brink. I had hoped that things were getting better, but now I'm not so sure. Your father staying in London during the week is not good and things are now…unstable, between us, as well." Her sigh was almost resigned.

I took several deep breaths, trying to control my emotions. I didn't want the family to split up because we could move, and I would lose Col. But I couldn't go on, lurching from crisis to crisis with my father. I sat; my eyes squeezed shut as I tried to contain the turmoil inside. *Why had he turned against me? What had I done?*

"What did I do? Please tell me what I did."

My mother rocked back in the chair, frowning in consternation. "What do you mean?"

"What did I do to my father that turned him against me?"

"Oh Will." She closed her eyes and slumped back in the chair. The seconds dragged out and she said nothing. After a while, I could not stand it any longer – it was so bad she couldn't bring herself to tell me. The emotions from my young brain surged through me, tossing rationality aside.

"Mummy, I can't remember what I did." The emotion knotted round my chest, so I had to gasp for breath. "All I can remember is the beating. Please tell me what I did that was so terrible, so I can try to understand." Tears started down my face and I released an anguished sob.

My mother reached out and drew me into a deep hug, holding my body against hers and I felt her sobs. We stayed that way for some considerable time and then my mother shifted and lifted my chin, catching my eyes with hers. "Will, you did nothing wrong, nothing. What has happened is not your fault at all." Her voice cracked with deep anguish.

I sat there, trying to take that in.

"I must have done something, surely? What else could it be?"

My mother shook her head. "No, Will, no. You didn't do anything wrong." She took a shuddering breath, her eyes wandering. She was struggling. Another shuddering breath and her tortured eyes finally found mine.

"He doesn't think you are his son." The words came softly, as if from a great distance. My old brain grabbed the idea and I pushed away from my mother.

"Whose son am I then?" I felt the bewilderment in my young brain as the foundations of who I was shifted and threatened to crumble.

"No, Will. You are his son. It's just that ... things happened, and he doesn't believe me."

"You had an affair?" The words escaped before I could stop them.

"That's an impertinent question, Will. Please mind your manners." My mother's voice had an edge to it.

"What else am I supposed to think? Why else would my father think I was not his son?"

My mother crumpled slightly, her breath slipping out in a resigned sigh. "There was a man I knew ... a friend from medical school ..." Her eyes became distant, summoning troubling memories, perhaps. "Your father was sent over to America by his job for three months and a couple of days before he got back, George and I happened to meet. Your sister was three and was staying with a friend that night, so George persuaded me to meet for a meal that evening. That's all it was – one meal catching up with a friend I had not seen for a few years. In all the rush of your father returning, I forgot to tell him about the meeting with George." Tears were slipping down her cheeks and she took a deep breath to steady herself. "A few weeks later I realised I was pregnant with you." Her eyes flicked round the room, as if seeking ... something. "But someone had seen me with George at his hotel, although they said nothing for years."

My mother dissolved into sobs and I crouched in front of her and took her hands in mine. She took another deep breath. "More than six years later an anonymous letter arrived that told all sorts of lies about George and me – and gave the date of our meeting, which was near your conception date and said George was your father. Your father completely lost it as he believed the letter. In his hurt and rage, he beat you." My mother retrieved a hanky from her sleeve and dabbed at her eyes. "That's the violence that you remember, Will, that's how it started, and it had nothing to do with anything you had done." She shook her head at the memories. "I am so sorry, Will, that your relationship with your father is so bad and that it's my fault. If I hadn't had that meal with George, none of this would be happening."

My mother's voice became almost fierce and her eyes practically glowed. "I can tell you that you are definitely his son." Then she shrunk before my eyes. "But I cannot prove it, and he does not believe me."

I needed access to twenty-first century DNA testing, I thought, but that was forty years away.

Tears were running down her face again. With all the empathy I could muster, I caught and held my mother's eyes with mine. "I believe you."

My mother pulled me into a hug. "Oh, Will," she said, sighing. "I am so sorry about this, but I can't see a way out. I watch you and recognise lots of your father's characteristics, but he will have none of it." She gave my hands a gentle squeeze and picked up the letter and cheque which had fallen to the floor, sitting with it in her lap for a few seconds. "This is a large sum of money, Will." I could hear the uncertainty in her voice and she peered into my eyes; it was as if she needed me to reassure her about something. "Part of your father's suggestion was to protect you, you know."

She must have seen the scepticism writ large on my face.

"This sum of money could be so useful to you in a few years." She searched my face. "You could buy a house, for example."

I stayed silent.

"I'm not your father, Will. I know you are trying to be a responsible person." She glanced down at the letter again. "Do you feel that you can be responsible with all this money?"

I nodded. "It's so unexpected that I have no idea what I might do with it." I gave her a wry smile. "I'm thirteen. It's not like I'm going to spend it all on fast cars or something."

My mother took a deep breath and I sensed from her face how troubled she was about this. "Well then, here's your cheque. Please put it in your Post Office savings account tomorrow." She passed the cheque and letter to me, her hands trembling slightly.

"I will."

"And please, Will, don't fritter it away. It's a lot of money ... like I said".

"I know. Thank you for standing up to my father and for trusting me with this."

Somehow, sleep found me later that night, despite the turmoil in my head.

Late April – mid November 1963

The following morning, I rang Col and told him I would be a bit late as I had an errand to run. After I packed the necessary books into my duffel bag, I walked into Beltinge and deposited the cheque into my Post Office savings account. The teller gave me a surreptitious smile when she saw it was a Premium Bond winning and advised me that it would take about a week for the cheque to clear before I could access the money. That didn't bother me as I had no desire to spend it any time soon. I was also pondering who I could – or should – tell people about my good fortune. I wanted to tell Col, but it also seemed a bit like boasting, so I decided to leave it for now.

Yesterday's showers and rain had cleared; the day promised to be fine, with fair weather cumulus clouds dotting the sky; it was a pleasant walk back to Col's house. I needed to talk to him about what I had learned about my family from my mother. I pondered this as I walked, and I realised this would be me trusting Col as he (and Mutti Frida) had trusted me with their story. But that brought its own problems: *Mutti Frida and my mother were sharing recipes and so what else were they sharing? Would it be fair to my mother to share what was a family secret with Mutti Frida?* I decided I had to bide my time in talking this over with Col until I had spoken with my mother.

Col greeted me with a smile at the door and we spent a pleasant day together, in part in our cedar tree. A couple of times Col had to call me back to the present as my mind slipped away to think about my family, but as drifting off in thought was not uncommon behaviour from me, he didn't seem to pick up that the undercurrents tugging at my attention were anything out of the ordinary.

I told Col I needed to be home early and arrived home before my mother, so I went up to my room to read. About half an hour later I heard my mother's car and so I went down.

"Oh, hello Will," she said, smiling. "Is everything all right? I didn't expect you to be here."

"Yes, everything's fine, but I need to talk about what you told me last night."

My mother's mood faded. "Okay."

We sat at the kitchen table, a quizzical expression on her face. I took a deep breath, unsure how this would go.

"I want to talk about this with Col, but I know that if I do that, I will have to include Mutti Frida too, as she is so involved."

"And?"

77

"Well, I know you and Mutti Frida exchange recipes, but I suspect there's more to your relationship than that. What I want to talk about is pretty personal and I don't want to embarrass you."

My mother nodded but stayed silent for a few seconds, before finally saying, "Will, thank you for talking to me first. Once again, you are showing maturity beyond your age and I'm proud of you for thinking about this so carefully." She offered me a brief smile. "I suppose this all comes down to how much you trust Col and Frau Schmidt. This is the sort of family secret that could make my professional involvement in this community difficult if it got out. Can you be sure that Col won't talk about this – even inadvertently – at school or with his other friends?"

"If I tell him not to, I know I can trust him."

"What about Frau Schmidt – will she talk about it to her friends?"

"No."

My mother's gaze was piercing. "You seem very sure of yourself about this."

I tried to imbue my voice with certainty. "I am."

My mother sat quietly for a while. "Can I ask why you are so sure they will keep our secrets?"

I wasn't sure how I could answer this. I certainly couldn't tell her they had trusted me with far more important secrets and Col had stayed silent about my suicide attempts. I saw that my mother was trying to divine my thoughts from my face. I remembered reading that the best way to answer a question you weren't sure how to answer was to ask a question back.

"How many people do you think Mutti Frida has trusted with her experiences in Ravensbrück?"

My mother gave a sharp intake of breath. "I didn't know that!"

"You don't remember her showing her forearm with the SS number on it to my father that night at Col's house?"

"No." She shook her head, frowning. "I was concentrating on getting your father home before something terrible happened to either or both of you. That incident with the knife scared me deeply."

"Well, she showed my father the concentration camp tattoo and told him there was no way he could scare her as she'd had the SS at her for years in Ravensbrück and other camps before that."

"I do remember that your father did seem a bit shocked by something Frau Schmidt said, but I didn't know what."

"Well, after you both left Mutti Frida came back into the kitchen with her sleeve still pushed up and I saw the tattoo. I asked her what it meant; she told us about what had happened to her, how her father was taken away and shot, her mother dying of starvation in the camp and, well, lots more."

I managed to stop myself before talking about the red triangle on her

78

overalls saving her when she was found by the Russians, that would have exposed far too much of their secret.

"Dear God, the poor woman." I could see the anguish she felt.

"I think Mutti Frida probably thinks that you at least know that she was in a concentration camp."

My mother nodded, thoughtfully.

"Well, I am also sure that she does not expect you to talk about it with anyone else. She is trusting you on that even though she hasn't asked you to keep it secret."

My mother folded her hands on the table, pondering this. "There's more to that story you are not telling me, isn't there?"

I returned my mother's gaze. Once again, I couldn't answer, so I asked a question in return. "It's not my story to tell, is it?"

My mother nodded, slowly. "No, of course, it's not yours to tell. I'm sorry."

Another first – knocking on my bedroom door before coming in and now apologising. My relationship with my mother was changing quickly and I wasn't sure where it was going.

"Can I talk to Col and Mutti Frida about what you told me last night?"

Across the table from me, I saw my mother's reaction as palpably physical. She was shifting in her chair and glancing round the room. She was deeply uncomfortable with the idea of someone outside the family knowing about this.

"You have nothing to be ashamed off, Mummy."

My mother took a deep breath. "Ah, but you're wrong there."

"But nothing happened between you and your friend, you told me that." *Had she lied to me? Was I not my father's son?*

"Nothing did happen – that's not what I'm ashamed of." I saw tears glistening in her eyes. "I'm ashamed … that for so long I did nothing about your father's violence towards you. I should have stopped it when it started. Before it started." She slowly toppled forward onto her arms, sobbing. This was a totally different mother to the somewhat distant, intensely intellectual person I had known until now.

I reached across and stroked her hair. After a minute or so, she sat up, pulling a hanky from her sleeve to dab her tears and blow her nose. She reached over and took my hand.

"Thank you, Will."

"You've stopped it now, Mummy, that's all that matters."

"That's kind of you to say that, but I failed to protect you. That's what mothers are for and I couldn't even do that."

I saw that she was winding herself in guilt. I stroked her hand. "Please don't, Mummy." I gave her hand a squeeze. "It's over. You stopped it."

79

"Oh, Will."

Our gazes locked. "Thank you, Will." I gave her hand another squeeze. We stayed like that for several long seconds, then my mother leaned back in her chair and gathered herself together. "You need to share this with Col?"

I nodded.

"And Frau Schmidt?"

"Yes. If I tell Col, I will have to tell Mutti Frida."

A long pause, and then she said, "You don't need my permission, Will. This is about you and your life. But thank you again for talking with me first. Once you've spoken to Col and Frau Schmidt, please could you also tell Frau Schmidt that I'd like to talk to her as well? But only after you've told them. Okay?"

I blinked at her, trying to understand why she wanted this.

"It's nothing bad – well nothing bad about you. But I feel I need to speak to her about this, as an adult."

"Okay." I realised I sounded a bit grudging. "If that's what you want me to do."

"She's very important to you, isn't she?"

"Yes, she is." Was she worried Mutti Frida would replace her? "But I know you're my mother."

She was about to say something – and then we heard my sister at the back door and my mother fled upstairs – to wash her face and reapply her minimal makeup, I suspected.

My sister speared me with a vicious glance when she saw me sitting at the kitchen table, went into the hall and hung up her coat and then came back into the kitchen. "I don't know what happened yesterday, Mother wouldn't tell me. But I know you're at the centre of it – again – and now father is staying in London during the week. Are you trying to destroy this family?" Her voice rose until she was practically shouting in my face.

I leaned back in my chair. Damn, I didn't need this.

"This family seems to be doing its best to destroy itself – and you are not helping by yelling at me." My voice and temper were rising.

"Will! Hilary! That's enough!"

My sister had been leaning over me, threateningly. She stood back up. "What's going on? Why is father staying in London during the week.?"

My mother closed her eyes for a moment. "This is between Will, your father and I, so, no, I will not explain that. You know that your father has been…mistreating Will for some years and it has now stopped. As part of reaching that decision, your father decided that perhaps a little space would let things settle down."

I saw that my sister was not satisfied. She wanted the full story, and I was sure it would then be spread far and wide amongst her catty friends.

There was a lengthy silence as my mother and sister stared at one another, then my sister turned away.

"Thank you, Hilary." My mother gave her a nod of acknowledgement which Hilary never saw.

My mother started clattering about in the kitchen, getting supper ready. "Please, Will, set the table."

My sister was silent during supper, sulking I suspected. My mother and I talked about our day. She was interested in the books we were reading, particularly when I mentioned the Muller poetry that lay behind *Winterreise* and *Die schöne Müllerin*.

"They are pretty dark and difficult stories, Will. How did you come across them?"

"I heard the Schubert song cycle on the radio at Col's house. Mutti Frida was listening to them, but I couldn't get the words because the singing got in the way. Then I found them in a book at the library and we've been reading them."

"The library has books in German?"

"Only a couple – the Müller poems and *Der schweizerische Robinson* – Swiss Family Robinson, which was in the old Gothic script which we had to learn to read. They had a few books in French and Polish, too."

"Oh, perhaps they were left over from wartime when there were lots of refugees about."

I shrugged. "I understand what you mean about the poems being dark – but then Shakespeare is pretty dark in places too, isn't he?"

"True."

My sister flounced off at the end of the meal. I stopped my mother from calling her back and we cleaned up together, allowing the emotions of the last couple of evenings to dissipate in shared trivialities.

Later, I lay in bed thinking about these two evenings with my mother. I had wanted to spend some time with her – but I had not imagined that it would be so intense. One good outcome was it seemed that she was starting to see me as something other than a child. The events of the last two evenings had certainly brought us closer together. Tomorrow I would talk with Col and Mutti Frida – and then Mutti Frida and my mother would get together. I was vaguely concerned about this but had nothing concrete on which to base my unease. Sighing, I knew I would have to wait and see what happened.

***

Yesterday's sunshine had departed when I walked round to Col's house in light rain. I was wearing gumboots so we could go for a walk later and had indoor shoes in my bag. Col opened the door when I knocked and I left the gumboots and my coat in the porch.

"Lili's mum is going to drop her round after lunch. We've run out of German books to read and we can't read *The Hobbit* until Lili gets here, so what do you want to do?"

"There is something I need to talk to you about before Lili gets here."

Col smiled knowingly. "I thought something was going through your mind yesterday, you seemed a bit distant."

He had noticed I was more distracted than usual. I went into the lounge room and sat down in our usual place on the couch. Col stood there for a moment before coming to sit down beside me.

"What's on your mind?" he asked in English, with a funny German accent.

"All right, Dr Freud." I smiled and then sighed.

Col's smile faded.

"I know what the problem is between my father and me."

Col half turned towards me.

"He doesn't think I am his son."

"Oh, Willi." I heard the shock in his voice.

"I've always thought I must have done something terribly bad when I was six, but all I can remember is the beating my father gave me. After another row with my father, which my mother sorted out, I finally asked her what I had done that made him hate me so."

I felt Col's hand creeping into mine. "This is a family secret, Col. I'm trusting you not to tell anyone, like how you have trusted me with your secrets."

"You know you can trust me, Willi."

I nodded. I knew that – he had told no-one, not even his mother about my suicide attempts, but of course I hadn't been able to use that as an example with my mother.

"This goes back to before I was born. My father was sent overseas and just before he came back my mother met an old friend from medical school, by chance. She had dinner with this friend – a man – at his hotel. Someone saw them and recognised my mother. A couple of days later my father came back and she completely forgot to tell him about the dinner. I was conceived around that time."

Col gave my hand a gentle squeeze of encouragement.

"Sometime after my sixth birthday, an anonymous letter arrived for my father, telling him about the dinner my mother had and telling him that I wasn't his son. He completely lost his temper and gave me the beating I remember – and plenty more since then."

"Are you his son or is this other man your father?"

"My mother is adamant that all she did with the friend was have dinner. She insists I am my father's son."

I saw the cogs working in his mind, as he pondered what to say next. He picked up both my hands and scanned my face, asking softly, "Do you believe her?"

This was the question that had been slithering around in my brain since the night before last. *Did I?* And by asking myself that question, I had my answer.

"Yes Col, I do. I have no evidence other than her word, but I do. She was completely distraught telling me about it. I don't think she could have been lying."

"I'm sorry to be the devil's advocate here, but are you certain?"

Oh, for a DNA test kit and a laboratory.

"No, I can't be certain. But I do believe her."

Col's gaze held me for a few seconds, as if searching for my certainty and then he nodded. "What now? What about your father?"

"Thinking about him makes me angry." I stopped as I realised there was another emotion hiding beneath my anger. "And sad. He refuses to believe my mother, his wife, rather believing some anonymous gossip. I am angry with him for that and for the way he has mistreated me." I released a sigh of confusion. "But I'm sad because he is throwing away a relationship with the only son he has and he's soured the one with his wife, possibly beyond repair." I turned away, afraid to voice this terrible fear I had. "I think they may be on the verge of separating and if that happens, I don't know where I would be living – I might lose you."

I saw Col's empathy for my situation written on in his face. He gave my hands another comforting squeeze and changed the subject a bit. "I wonder why the gossip waited more than six years to write that poisonous letter."

"I don't know. I have no idea why anyone would write it at all. What had my parents done to them?"

Col heard the anguish in my voice and changed tack slightly again. "What does your father do, Willi? Why was he sent overseas?"

"Oh, he works in some government department about international trade or something like that. I can't see what that has to do with anything."

Col pursed his lips. "Neither can I."

We sat in silence for a few minutes, trying to make sense out of something that happened years ago and about which we knew practically nothing – and for me underneath everything was the gnawing fear that I might lose Col.

After a while, Col stood up, pulling me after him. "Come on Willi, we're not going to resolve that question. Let's go for a walk and clear our heads before Lili gets here."

We walked out on to the Downs and took the long wooden staircase to the beach, where we threw stones at the half-submerged breakwaters. My Col and I had spent so much time along the shore and clifftops, and the memories soothed me. Though he might not exist in this world, somehow his spirit lingered here.

We walked along the sea wall and back up the Downs to have a lunch of tomato soup and rye bread.

"Are you going to tell Lili what you told me, Willi?"

"I don't think so – at least not yet. We're becoming friends but I don't think she needs to know the details – just that I hate my father, with reason." I watched Col wincing slightly when I said that.

"You should not hate, Willi. I hated my father when I learned what he was, but Mutti told me that hatred eats us up from within. I fear him for what he might do to us and I despise him for what he has done, but I no longer let it affect me like that. Mutti helped me, and perhaps she can help you with your feelings about your father."

"Col, your mother is amazing. She has every reason to detest your father."

"But she doesn't." Col locked my eyes in a steady gaze.

I turned away, all the physical hurt and mental anguish my father had heaped upon me seemed in that moment to be a crushing load.

"Willi…"

There was a knock on the door: Lili was here. Col's glance showed his frustration – he wanted to talk more about this, but it would have to wait.

"Willi, get the Risk box out of the cupboard," he called over his shoulder as he went to greet Lili. I pulled it out and started setting up the game. Lili breezed into the room, her smile, bright hair, and face lifting my mood.

We spent the afternoon trying to conquer the world, alliances shifting around the table as first one and then another of us seemed to be gaining the upper hand, but none of us was prepared to form a killer alliance and eliminate a third player, so we declared the game a draw. Lili's mum arrived at about five o'clock to take her home and Col and I worked together in the kitchen, readying tea for Mutti Frida's arrival.

After we had eaten and cleared up, I asked Mutti Frida to sit with us as I needed to share the information about my family with her.

"Are you sure you want to do that, Willi?" Her voice was full of concern.

"It's all right, Mutti Frida, I have spoken about this with my mother." Mutti Frida's face showed her approval. "In fact, she told me to ask you to contact her so that the two of you could talk about this."

"Oh." Mutti Frida's eyes widened with surprise. I went on and told Mutti Frida what I had learned. Col sat close beside me as he knew this was difficult for me. When I finished, Mutti Frida took my hand. "How are you feeling about this, Willi?"

"Like I told Col this morning, I am very angry with my father but I'm also sad about his relationship with me and my mother."

Mutti Frida nodded in understanding. "Anything else?"

"I hate him." My voice was a hard, sharp-edged carving knife.

Mutti Frida took a deep breath and let it out, slowly. "I can understand that."

I waited for her to say more as her eyes travelled across my face, searching for ... something.

"I can understand why you hate him; he has physically and mentally abused you for years." Her eyes were full of sympathy, but then concern washed through them. "But hatred is a dangerous and destructive emotion. If you are not careful, it could destroy you."

It almost felt as if Mutti Frida knew about the knife and my threats towards my father – and my mother's cautioning me about this. *Perhaps this was what my mother wanted to talk with Mutti Frida about?*

"I am not asking you to like your father or even forget his terrible treatment of you, but to move past the hatred his actions have aroused in you." Her eyes were searching mine again. "You don't even have to forgive him, but the anger you have inside you is dangerous." She paused, summoning the right words. "You've heard the story of my childhood in the camps. When I was released, I hated the Nazis and burned for vengeance for myself, my mother, father and the millions who had suffered and died at the hand of the Nazis." Her voice had risen, but now it softened again. "I was lucky; I was helped past this hatred and anger by an older woman in Leipzig. She had survived Auschwitz." Mutti Frida's gaze rested softly on me. "She showed me that my hunger for vengeance could blight my life, allowing its darkness to shut out the love and beauty around me." She cocked her head slightly, a smile of love gracing her face at the memory. "It was her friendship that helped me move past that black, consuming hatred." Mutti Frida gathered Col's hand and reached across the table to hold mine. "I hope the friendship and love you have here in this house and from your mother can help you get past your hatred of your father."

85

I didn't know what to say, so I nodded. "I'll try." But I had no idea how to go about this.

Mutti Frida gave me an encouraging smile. "Thank you, Will. I'll speak to your mother soon."

Col and I sat quietly together on the sofa; he must have sensed my struggle and gifted me his support through his quiet presence.

The Easter holidays drew to a close and we all went back to school for our last term at junior school. Col and I studied together every day, joined sometimes by Lili. Col was able to find some more books in German and we carried on our alternate days of English and German. As the days warmed and lengthened, we were able to spend afternoons sitting in our cedar tree. With the end of term, Lili spent more time with us; she sketched us both, surrounded by the dark boughs with the speckled shade providing interesting contrasts.

Lili seemed to fit into our friendship. I thought it was a bit strange that there seemed to be no sexual tension in our three-way friendship. Although youthful hormones were surging through my body, they were buried under the tensions I felt in my life: I had no desire to complicate things and risk my friendship with Col. It was my rock of stability and Lili's friendship was secondary, even if her generally cheerful attitude to life frequently lightened my day.

Col enjoyed Lili's company and they spent a lot of time together at school. But I detected nothing sexual in their friendship, which I found a bit surprising. On a few occasions, I thought I sensed Lili probing the friendship between Col and me. Our shared language seemed to have deepened our mutual understanding and at times it was almost telepathic. Occasionally, I felt Lili might be jealous of the depth of our relationship, but those flashes from her were infrequent and perhaps I had misinterpreted what I saw and heard.

In June, Valentina Tereshkova orbited the earth forty-eight times: the world seemed to be staying on the tracks it had followed in my previous life, despite the growing number of small discrepancies I had noticed.

The summer holidays felt like a pause – our lives holding their breaths – as we waited to start at our senior schools in the autumn. Col, Lili and I met nearly every day and we shared hopes and fears about the future, although Col usually turned the conversation elsewhere as his future was so unsure. On a few occasions, the weather was warm enough for us to go to the beach. Lili and I swam, but Col always stayed dressed, sitting on a towel. He didn't like swimming and I wondered if he was frightened of the water.

One Saturday afternoon, Mutti Frida sat Col, Lili and I down and insisted we listen to a concert on the radio. It was Jacqueline Du Pré playing the Elgar cello concerto. I remembered my mother had insisted I listen to this same performance all those years ago, in my other life. Then, I hadn't grasped the anguished beauty of the piece and the emotional depth of the performance – and I could see that neither Col nor Lili felt it deeply. Listening to it again almost brought tears to my eyes, knowing the horrible disease that would so shorten Jacqueline's career and life. But the performance was also more reassurance that this world was quite similar to mine.

When the September term started, Col and Lili were able to support one another at their new school and seemed to adjust quite well. But I was alone. Being back at the bottom of the hierarchy – and different in ways the teenagers around me could not quite fathom – made me a natural target for the bullies. This was not helped by being jumped straight into 'O' level classes where I was a couple of years younger than everyone else – and quickly moving to the top of the class. I was studying English (language and literature), History, Maths (ordinary and advanced – which included introductory calculus), French, Latin, Physics and German. None of this was proving hard given my old brain's knowledge and my effortless ease was a source of envy and abuse from a few people.

Once again, I was able to quiet the bullies somewhat by not reacting and again, I was able to help some of my peers with the subjects that were proving difficult to them and this helped defuse the bullying. Slowly, Col, Lili and I settled into the new rhythm of our senior schools as summer drifted into autumn and towards winter.

All the while, though, my father remained a glowering figure on the periphery of my life, my hatred as dark and intense as ever.

Mid November 1963

Large snowflakes were starting to drift down in the still air when I knocked on Col's door. After a minute, the door opened.

"It's snowing," I said, laughing. "Grab your coat and come outside."

I dropped my school satchel in the hall and then we were off outside. Those first few enormous flakes had now been joined by billions of fellows. Already the pavement had a light dusting. We stood watching the thickly falling snow, catching large flakes on our tongues and comparing the beauty of the large flakes we caught on our coat sleeves. Suddenly the streetlights went out and all the windows darkened: a power cut.

The snow-filled darkness had an intense, eerie silence.

Col grabbed my arm. "Let's go back inside."

"Okay."

I pulled out my torch to guide us. Inside, we placed a lit candle in the hall, for Mutti Frida when she returned home from work. We lit a couple in the lounge where we were sitting on the couch. Col grabbed several blankets and we soon made a nest, cuddled together for mutual warmth as we had last winter, relaxing in the dim candlelight.

We chatted about the snowstorm and power cut for a while, before I asked, "Do you wonder where your life is headed?"

"What do you mean?"

"Well, my mother is a doctor and I expect there will be some pressure to follow in her footsteps. But I'm not sure I want that; I don't know what I do want."

"You'll be a pilot, that's what you are most interested in."

I sighed, softly but deeply. "I'd love to, but I don't think so – my eyes are a problem that doesn't seem to be getting any better. I need to think of something else." Again, I was confronting what had seemed to be the great tragedy of my previous youth. I sighed again, staring off into the distance of an impossible future. "Flying is the one thing I want to do and the one thing I'm absolutely stopped from doing."

Col's eyes were full of sympathy and I felt his hand find mine, squeezing gently. "Oh, Willi. I'm sorry, I did not understand that. But there's more to flying than being a pilot."

"I don't know I could be in aviation and not be a pilot. I might not be able to stand it." I felt the moisture in my eyes and was glad of the dim light.

Col snuggled a little closer. "I suppose…it would be like working in a chocolate shop and never being allowed to even nibble some."

"You and your chocolate," I said, chuckling, glad to be moving away from a troubling subject. "What about you?"

"Oh! I don't know – I haven't thought about it."

"You must have some sort of idea?"

Col paused, turning to face me. "What I do doesn't seem to be as important as who I do it with."

"What do you mean?"

He shrugged. "I don't think it's complicated – I want to be with people I like, people I love and doing things with them." Col paused and his eyes drifted uncertainly away from mine. "People like you," he added softly.

What? I wanted to be Col's friend for life, but there was something deeper here. Something scary. "Col, what do you mean?"

He turned back towards me, his face softer and with something in his eyes I had seen hints of before. Then his face hardened again. "I don't know what I meant." He shifted beneath the blankets, trying to hide the emotions that were playing out behind his eyes.

After a second or so, a terrifying thought occurred to me. At school, about the worst insult you could throw at someone was that they were a fag, a poofter. *Was Col saying he had feelings for me like that?*

I grabbed his elbows and for a moment we wrestled under the blankets as I turned him to face me.

"We're boys – you can't…" I struggled to find the right words.

Col sagged back into the cushions, deflated. His eyes were filled with ... desperation? "Yes, I can. I do. But…"

I cut him off, struggling to fight my way out of the cocooning blankets. It was confusing and scary for my young brain as I did feel strongly attracted to him, but not that way – not physically, surely?

"No! We're not like that. I'm not like that!"

Col grabbed my elbows and threw me against the back of the sofa, pinning me. He squeezed his eyes closed for a moment and then held me with his eyes.

"You're right, we're not like that, because ..." he paused, taking a deep breath and squeezing his eyes closed again. After a long pause, his eyes opened, and he practically whispered: "... because I am not a boy."

What? My brain seemed to have taken time out, all thoughts frozen.

Softly, with infinite gentleness, he said, "Willi, I am Colette – a girl."

I had no words. My mouth opened and closed a few times, but I couldn't speak as my entire world shifted around me.

Eventually, "What?"

Col…Colette…leaned closer still, placing a tiny, whisper kiss at the corner of my mouth and then pulling back to engage my eyes, his…no, her hands sliding down my arms raising every hair in a delicious sensuality as they passed on their way to my hands. Reaching there, she turned the palms face up, her thumbs gently exploring and teasing the skin.

"I'm so sorry, Willi. I ...well, Mutti and I – we've been deceiving you, but we didn't have a choice." Tears started down her cheeks. "But I couldn't keep doing it. I know we can trust you – you've shown we can, but we can't grow any closer with this ... this deceit between us." She took a deep breath and batted away the tears. "Anyway, I couldn't keep on pretending to be a boy. Things are happening to my body and it will be difficult to pretend for much longer."

"You're a g...girl?" I stuttered.

"Yes, Willi. You have to believe me, I'm not a boy, I'm a girl."

I sat, completely nonplussed. I tried to speak, but there were no words. She must have seen the doubt on my face. She closed her eyes for several seconds, before coming to a decision. "All right, I'll prove it to you."

She let go of my hands and rearranged herself under the blanket. Then she grabbed my hand and slid it slowly down inside her trousers and knickers. I encountered smooth skin, wisps of soft hair, and a growing warmth. Her eyes flared at my touch and she inhaled, sharply. She held my hand in place. "Does that feel like a boy?"

I shook my head, dumbfounded. She pulled my hand out, slowly, causing her to take another half-gasp. I saw her rearranging her clothing under the blanket.

She shook her head, freeing herself of...embarrassment? "Right – that never happened, okay?" She smiled coyly under eyelashes that must have doubled in length in the last few seconds.

I swallowed convulsively, nodded, and then managed a whisper. "Wow!"

"Wow? Wow, what? Wow, that I'm a girl? Wow at what you just felt?"

I inhaled a breath that was long overdue. "Every one of those!" My brain was still trying to catch up and I leaned back into the sofa. Col straddled my legs and held me by the shoulders, searching my face, aching to understand how I felt.

"Willi, I know this is terribly confusing for you. Please tell me we can still be friends!"

I examined this face I had grown to know so well over the last year, this ... person who had befriended me and helped me cope with the strange circumstances I found myself in.

This person who had saved my life under the cedar tree.

"Oh Col! Of course, we're still friends. You are a huge part of my world. I can't imagine you not being a part of it."

"The same for me!" she said softly and leaned in slowly, placing a soft kiss fully on my lips.

My confusion peaked. I was being kissed by a boy – and then the memory of what I had just discovered asserted itself: the world finished shifting around me. Without conscious thought, my hands slid up her back and pulled her closer to me and our first real kiss was amazing.

Col must have felt the effect she had on me. She swivelled her hips against me and giggled. "Well, the evidence is that you are a boy!"

I felt myself blushing.

"It's all right Willi, we both have bodies, I like your reaction to mine as it tells me you know I'm a girl and one you find attractive." *How could she feel so self-confident and unembarrassed?* Then I noticed a slight, uncertain smile and a faint blush. Perhaps not so self-confident but pushing her boundaries all the same.

Col moved again, to cuddle up beside me, pulling the blankets back into order around us and carefully draping my arm around her shoulders.

"Col, I…"

"Shhh." She placed an index finger on my lips. "Let's just cuddle and allow our minds to catch up, hmm?"

I kissed her finger and squeezed her shoulder. "Okay." And we sat there in the softly flickering candlelight and warmth of the blankets as the geometry of our friendship rearranged itself like the shifting patterns in a kaleidoscope, settling into something new, exciting but also a bit scary.

***

"Hello, sleepy heads. I'm glad you've been keeping warm." Mutti Frida's smiling voice woke us. "I had to walk home as the buses are in chaos because of the snow. The electricity is still out so I'll light the oil heater and we can warm some soup for tea on that."

She busied herself, hanging up her coat and hat. "Have you tried to ring home, Willi?"

"Not yet. We went to sleep!"

Mutti Frida laughed gently.

We stretched and shifted out from under the blankets.

Col took her mother's hand. "Mutti, there's something I have to tell you."

Something in her daughter's voice alerted her because she stopped fiddling with the oil heater and her eyes narrowed, moving between the two of us.

"Willi knows, Mutti."

I saw the tension as it arrived in Mutti Frida's shoulders. "Knows what?" Her voice had an edge, as if she were poised, ready to run.

"He knows that I am Colette, a girl, not Col, a boy." It came out in a rush and then she slowed. "I know we can trust him and I wasn't going to be able to hide it from him much longer."

Mutti Frida pulled a chair out from the table and sat down heavily. "Oh, Col!"

I came up beside Col and took her hand in mine.

Mutti Frida stared at the two of us and sighed. "No, I suppose not." She closed her eyes. "Now, what are we going to do?"

I glanced at Col, then turned to Mutti Frida. "It doesn't change things – at least not yet. Col can still be a boy for the outside world, but she can be who she is here, safe in this house, can't she?"

"For the moment, yes." Mutti Frida's voice was slumped, like her shoulders. "I knew keeping you as a boy was going to cause problems, but it seemed the best way to hide." Mutti Frida closed her eyes in thought. "Well, we don't have to decide anything yet." She got up from the chair.

"Now, Willi, you must phone home and let your family know you're safe here and find out what they want you to do."

I rang home, but there was no reply.

"No one is home." I announced.

"Ah well, I expect they are having problems because of the snow. It was giving everything quite a covering by the time I got here."

She lit the oil stove and opened some tins of beef and vegetable soup.

"This is left over from last winter when I was worried we could be snowed in for days at a time. I hope we are not going to have another winter like that!"

The warmth from the heater spread slowly through the room as it warmed the saucepan of soup sitting on top.

"Willi, set the table, please. Col, what bread do we have in the larder? I think there are still some crusty rolls that will go well with the soup. Perhaps some cheese, as well?" By the time we had eaten, the room was cosy. "Willi, please try ringing your home again."

This time my mother answered, back from her evening surgery. My sister was staying at Lucy's house – again – and my father was staying in London. We agreed the snow and blackout would not be a problem as I was walking. I agreed to be home by eight o'clock as tomorrow was a school day and I hung up.

That gave me nearly another hour with Col. We helped Mutti Frida with the dishes and then sat close together on the sofa and picked up our current English book – Gavin Lyall's *The Wrong Side of the Sky*, which I had picked as it was a thriller with much flying. Tomorrow we would be back to *Das Versprechen* by Friedrich Dürrenmatt, which I was finding quite dark.

We had been reading for about thirty minutes when Mutti Frida stopped pottering in the kitchen and interrupted us. "Col, Willi – we need to have a talk."

We put down the book. I wondered what this was about, but Col, it seemed, knew exactly what was coming. She picked up my hand and gave it a gentle squeeze. "Mutti…"

"No, Col. Please let me speak. I saw how you were cuddled up together when I arrived home and how you are now. I know you are friends, but now that friendship is no longer of two boys, but a young woman and a young man."

She stared at Col. "Col, we have spoken about what is happening to your body and what it means."

Col nodded and gave me a sideways glance. How had I not noticed her long eyelashes before today?

Mutti Frida turned to me. "Willi, has your mother spoken to you about what happens to boys and girls as they grow into men and women?" I was embarrassed at where this conversation was headed but also scared that Mutti Frida might force us apart.

"My mother explained a bit when my sister… got grumpy once a month."

Mutti Frida nodded. "You know that once a girl reaches…" She paused. "*auf Deutsch sagt man erste Regel* … I don't know the English word…when she starts bleeding every month, she can become pregnant?"

I nodded. In a house with a doctor, there was no shortage of medical texts.

"I know you two are close friends and I can see your friendship has now taken a different direction. I need the two of you to promise me that you will not do anything stupid." She stopped, her face almost fierce in its concern. "Col is far too young to have a baby – and I am too young to be a grandmother."

Col gasped. "Mutti." A faint blush limning her face as she gave me a sidelong glance.

Mutti Frida silenced her with a look. "You may be embarrassed, but that's a small price to pay for both of you promising me that you will not be stupid." Her voice softened. "I do not want you to rush into things that have serious consequences."

Her eyes moved between the two of us. "Promise me."

Col laced her fingers into mine, her eyes seeking my agreement. I nodded – I was not going to risk Mutti Frida restricting when we could see one another.

Col gave me a thin smile and turned back to her mother. "We promise."

Mutti Frida sighed, her stance softening as her worry eased. "There will be times when keeping this promise is going to be difficult." She paused, as if interrupted by her own thoughts. "Please, both of you, remember it and help one another to keep it."

Was that coming from her personal history?

Our eyes linked, each of us seeing a glimmer of what she hinted at in the other's eyes.

Mutti Frida took my free hand. "Willi, Col is all I have and I need you to take care of her." She shivered slightly. "At her age, I was in Ravensbrück surrounded by death." She paused again, swallowing. "She is named Collette in memory of one of those brave English girls. I know the dangers here are not as fierce or as obvious as they were for me then, but they are still real."

My eyes searched her face and I nodded, swallowing too. It was so easy, here in quiet Kent, to forget that Col and Mutti Frida were being sought by Col's father, who had the resources of the *Stasi* at his disposal.

"Willi, perhaps it is time for you to go home now?" It was more than a suggestion.

Col pulled a face. I sensed that Mutti Frida needed some time to come to terms with this new dynamic – and I didn't want to cause any friction, so I stood up, with Col's hand still in mine.

"Okay."

Col used my arm to pull herself up and walked with me into the hall to help me dress for the snow outside. As she buttoned up my coat, she leaned in and whispered, "Finish your homework at school or on the bus, okay?"

I just stood there, confused.

Her annoyance came through in the whisper. "Just do it, okay?"

Still not understanding what was going on, I nodded.

Mutti Frida came out into the hall. "Please ring us when you get home so we know you are safe."

"Yes, Mutti Frida."

"Colette, you may see your friend out. Don't get cold out there…" Col glanced at her mother and gave her a slight smile and Mutti Frida walked into the lounge room and quietly, but firmly, shut the door.

Col turned back to me and gently took hold of my coat lapels, pulling me slowly towards her. We managed not to bash our noses together, but I was unprepared for the intensity I felt as our lips came together. My arms went around her slim body of their own accord. The kiss deepened and then I pulled back slightly and brushed my lips against hers. She pulled her face back and took a deep breath, our eyes locked together.

"Mmm!" She smiled softly and leant in to give me a quick, soft kiss. "You had better go now or we might have problems with that promise!"

She pulled herself free from my arms and opened the front door. It had stopped snowing and there was no wind, but the frigid air poured into the room. Col shuddered at the rapid drop in temperature, wrapping her arms around herself.

"Go! Before I freeze to death!"

I gently pulled her to me and brushed a soft kiss on to her lips, then walked out of the door. At the gate, I turned and she was standing there. I gave her a wave and received a blown kiss in return and then she quickly went inside and shut the door.

The snow was about two inches deep, but the sky was now clear, with just the stars providing a surprising amount of light to the landscape, now magically transformed in its coat of snow. My mind was a whirl with what was happening between Col and myself. My old brain had fallen in love several times, but this was the first love for my young brain and it was intoxicated. Somehow it grabbed an image that resonated from its older ... parent? sibling? ... the first time I had swum off the edge of a coral reef. The shock of suddenly hanging above a depth that simply faded into endless blue echoed the feelings surrounding this relationship that was so unexpectedly changed. There was a tinge of fear, for this was unknown territory, but wonder and curiosity at this new place were paramount. As I walked home, the snow scrunching and squeaking around my steps, every soft glint of starlight from the untrammelled surface seemed to have been specially crafted for me.

When I got home, I rang Mutti Frida, while my mum made me a cup of hot chocolate. She gave me several sideways glances, sensing my distraction, perhaps. I finished my chocolate and went off to bed, lying awake, thinking about Col. As a boy, he was my intellectual equal, but not as driven as was I by a desperate need to understand, to know. For Col, knowing and understanding were less ends in themselves but a way of sharing the experience with me, with Mutti Frida and Lili. He had been a friendly, stable rock as life stormed around me. *How would that change now that she was a girl and, at least with me, she was no longer pretending to be a boy?*

And this was yet a further difference from the Col I had known, to add to all the others. Would all these little differences eventually push this world into a different and dangerous direction?

***

The snow had mostly melted by morning – November snow rarely lasted in southern England.

I didn't have much homework and managed to do it all in class, except for English. We were reading "Under Milk Wood" – which I had read in junior school. I had to read a few pages in preparation for taking parts and reading it in class. In my old life, I had a CD of the original BBC radio production with Richard Burton, so I heard his voice lilting in my head as I read it on the number seven bus I had just managed to catch.

"To begin at the beginning …"

When I reached Col's house, the door flew open as I walked up the path and Col stood there, waiting for me inside. When I entered, the door slammed shut and I found myself with an armful of delicious girl giving me a serious kiss.

"I have been waiting all day to do that!" she said, smiling, helping me out of my coat, scarf, and gloves. She dragged me into the kitchen and started unpacking my school bag. "Homework!"

"I've done it all, like you asked," I said.

"Of course you have – but you need to tell me what it is, so I know if Mutti asks me about it – and then I'll tell you about the pages of *Das Versprechen* I have read so you know that. Then you get your reward."

I still didn't understand what she wanted.

"Come on, just tell me."

In spite of my confusion, I lead her through the Maths and French homework and then told her about Under Milk Wood. "You read that before – we read some of it with Lili."

Col shrugged, then told me about Inspector Matthäi's hiring of a housekeeper with a young daughter to use as bait for the serial killer. It sounded even darker than before and distinctly cold-blooded. "Right – now come with me for your reward!"

I gazed at her, questioningly. She smiled and pulled me into the lounge and on to the sofa, wrapping us as usual in a cocoon of blankets.

"Your reward...is me!" and then leaned in for a deep kiss. After a while, she pulled back slightly and nibbled my lips as I had done with her. I wriggled as my trousers were suddenly tight and uncomfortable.

Col smiled. "I'm glad I don't have that problem. Do you want me to help rearrange things?" she teased.

My face must have reflected my embarrassment as I felt it flush. "Perhaps not!" I reached down and untangled myself, with Col watching with interest.

"Now, where were we..." Col's eyes held a smile and ...something else.

Our arms went around one another, and we kissed more deeply. After a while, I tentatively ran my tongue over her lips. Her eyes flew open and she pulled back and searched my face intently, her pale cheeks flushed.

"Interesting!" She breathed and leant in for another kiss, running her tongue across my lips. I slid my tongue against hers and suddenly we were French kissing, pressing our bodies together as if we were trying to climb into one another.

After a minute, I pushed her away and took a deep, shuddering breath. "I think we'd better slow down a bit!"

"Spoilsport!" And she climbed into my lap and started kissing me again, rubbing her body against mine.

After a few minutes, I groaned and pushed her away again. Every iota of restraint from my old brain was needed. "Col, if we don't stop, we'll reach a place soon where neither of us will want to stop."

"But I don't want to!" Her flushed cheeks and rapid breathing showed how aroused she was. She leaned towards me, urging me to continue.

"But we'll end up going too far. We promised to be responsible."

She closed her eyes and took several breaths. "There must be more we can do than kiss? I don't want to get pregnant, but ..."

We kissed deeply. Col's breathing became more rapid and she suddenly pulled back, pushing me away. "Oh, Willi! What's happening to me?"

"Perhaps we'd better read a book," I suggested, trying to control the passion I was feeling inside.

Col nibbled her top lip, taking several deep breaths to regain control of her body and its passion. "You're right, Willi. My body is telling me things I have never heard it say before. I need time to listen to it, to think about all of this."

I gave her a smile and she picked up *Das Versprechen*. We cocooned ourselves in the blankets and lost ourselves in Inspector Matthäi's descent into alcoholic madness. It was such a dark story and quite killed our passion. We were still reading when Mutti Frida arrived home.

In the following days, we slipped into an increasingly easy intimacy, but one defined by unspoken boundaries. We were also conscious of Mutti Frida's watchful but caring eye on us and our relationship.

A few days later, we were sitting on the sofa having finished the *Wrong Side of the Sky*.

Col placed the book on the side table. "Willi, I am worried about Lili and I don't know what to do."

"What do you mean?"

"I think she has a crush on me."

I gave her a sideways, quirky smile.

"Not as a girl, you idiot! She still thinks I am a boy." She shook her head. "What am I going to do? I'm not going to be able to hide this from her for much longer and with this crush, there's a real problem."

I pondered for a moment, remembering my worry that Col and I would end up in a competition for Lili's affections. I had no idea what to say to Col, and I hadn't expected things to turn out this way.

"I want to keep her as a friend – I want her as a girlfriend, so I have someone to talk to about being a girl. We've become close and I'm sure we would be much closer as girls together." She paused, biting her lip. "I'm scared that if I don't tell her the truth soon, she'll feel betrayed when she finds out."

"I didn't feel betrayed – just confused."

"Not confused for long, as I recall!" Col was smiling, impishly, as she leaned in to plant a soft kiss on my cheek.

I returned the smile. "Do you trust Lili?"

"What do you mean?"

"You've trusted me to keep your secrets – that you are refugees from the DDR hiding from your father and that you are a girl, not a boy. Do you trust Lili the same way?"

Col stared off into the distance for several long seconds. "Yes, I think I do. Do you think we should trust her?"

My heart melted at her valuing my opinion on this. "I like her. But Col, it's not me that could get hauled back to Leipzig in a sack if she tells others about your secret – it's you and Mutti Frida. You both have to trust her."

"We should talk to Mutti about this?"

I nodded. Col threw herself back into the cushions, deep in thought.

After a while, a thought occurred to me. "I'm not sure that you are right about Lili. I've not felt that she's crushing on you. I have seen her watching the two of us and I thought maybe it was jealousy at the closeness of our relationship. Now, I'm not so sure either of us is right."

"What do you mean."

"I don't know." I shrugged. "Let me think about it. There's something I can't put my finger on."

We sat back in the sofa, lost in thought. Eventually, Col roused herself and pottered around in the kitchen, starting tea and I got up to help.

When Mutti Frida arrived home, she was met with the aroma of the mutton casserole she had started last night.

"That is a beautiful smell to greet me! Thank you, children." Mutti Frida smiled at us as she hung up her coat. She was an astute woman, and I could tell she sensed something.

"Col, Willi – what is it this time?" she asked, gently.

Col took Mutti Frida's hands in hers. "Mutti, we need to speak to you about Lili."

Mutti Frida sat down at the kitchen table. "Why, what's happened?" I heard the tension back in her voice. It must be so hard to live in hiding, fearing discovery from day-to-day.

Col and I sat down as well, and Col squeezed her eyes shut for a moment.

"I think I need to tell Lili that I'm a girl, Mutti."

"Why?"

"I think she is becoming interested in me as a boy."

Mutti Frida sat back and breathed out, deeply. "Oh. I hadn't thought of that possibility." She paused for a moment, thinking. "Can't you just tell her you only want to be friends? That you're too young for that sort of relationship?"

Col sniffed in frustration. "Yes, I suppose I could. But that might break our friendship and I like her; together we are beating back the bullying." She leaned forward, taking her mother's hand across the table. "But if I don't tell her soon that I'm a girl, I'm worried she'll feel betrayed by the deception."

Mutti Frida sat in silence for a while. Then she patted Col's hand and stood up. "Well, we don't have to decide tonight. Aren't you all going to be here on Saturday afternoon playing Risk?"

"Yes."

"Well then, that gives me time to think about this a bit more."

"You trusted Willi…"

"Col!" Mutti Frida's voice had a sudden edge to it. "I had no choice on that matter right from the beginning, as well you know."

"Yes, and that has turned out okay, hasn't it?" Col didn't sound at all contrite.

"But it could have gone so wrong." Mutti Frida paused, her face reflecting her disappointment in Col. "If it does go wrong, we would need to move away and hide somewhere else and you would lose them both."

Col gasped. "No!"

Mutt Frida put her hands on Col's shoulders, their faces inches apart. "Yes." Her voice became suddenly intense. "If he found us, I don't know what he would do, but he would certainly try to kidnap us back to Leipzig. I don't think he would harm you, but I ran from him and by defecting to the West I must have seriously embarrassed him." She stopped, staring into the night. "I do not expect him to forgive." Her voice was bleak.

Col remained silent as they shared that thought, then she turned away and started setting the table for tea. Mutti Frida saw me about to say something and shook her head.

After tea, as we finished cleaning up, Mutti Frida put her hand on Col's shoulder. "If you can think of a way to show me that Lili can be trusted

99

with our safety, please tell me." She paused, eying her daughter. "My experience is that some people would rather die than break trust and yet others will sell you out for a crust of bread."

I could see the intensity in her gaze, hear it in her voice.

"In Ravensbrück, I saw both of those things."

Col's wide eyes held her mother's for long seconds.

After tea, she pulled me towards the couch where we sat and read until it was time for me to go home.

Lili spent Saturday afternoon with us, but Col remained, for her, a boy.

November 22nd – 24th 1963

We entered the smoky end of November, with the smell of coal fires hanging in the cold air, thickening the fogs and permeating the month's miserable drizzles. I became increasingly concerned about JFK's assassination. I knew it happened towards the end of the month, but I couldn't remember the date even though I remembered it happened in Dallas. *Was it going to happen in this world? What would it mean if it didn't happen?* At home, I scoured the newspapers for information, but I had long realised there was nothing I could do about it. In my searches, I'd found nothing that conflicted with my memories, but Col seemed to sense that something was bothering me. When she tried speaking to me, I passed it off as my usual family angst, but she knew me better than that by now. This created a tension between us and that made us both twitchy as the days passed.

When I arrived at Col's house, it felt as though I had sand scattered under my brain – I had this constant itch I could not scratch, leaving me irritable. Col gave me a welcome kiss, but my response was half-hearted. Col pulled back, eyes narrowing.

"Why are you looking at me like that?" I asked, with a touch of annoyance.

Col dropped her hands from my shoulders "Like what?" Her voice echoed the snippiness in mine.

"Like you're judging me."

Col closed her eyes. She breathed out slowly and I saw the tension flow out of her. She opened her eyes and slid a hand softly across my cheek. "Willi. I'm sorry, I didn't mean to be so unfeeling." She started unbuttoning my coat. "I know something's bothering you and that's making me uneasy and it just got away from me." She pulled my satchel off my arm and hung it on the hall stand as I removed my coat.

I tried to clamp down on my teenage brain. "I'm sorry, Col." I should be better at this by now, but this young body seems to react so strongly to its emotions; they surge and slosh almost uncontrollably.

Col guided me to the table where we usually sat and did our homework. "Can you tell me what the problem is – you've been getting more and more irritable over the last few weeks." She sat me on a chair and swivelled gracefully to sit on my lap. "Is something going on with your father?"

I shook my head. I hadn't been able to tell her the truth about me – that I was a mix of young Will and an old Will from somewhere … different. That truth was so strange that I was scared it might drive her away from me. I still hadn't found the courage do it. "No … but I just feel that something is going to happen…" my voice petered out. I hated this deception.

Col reached her arms around me, hugging me tightly and then leant back, smiling at me. "Well, let's see if I can distract you with our homework." She gave me a playful kiss then retrieved our school bags from the hall. After an hour or so of work on her Maths and our French homework, I did feel more relaxed. Part of that was due to the satisfaction I now felt from concentrated study – but mostly it was due to Col's soothing presence.

After tea, we were just settling down on the sofa to snuggle and read some more *Under Milk Wood* when the music Mutti Frida was listening to was interrupted.

"News has just come in that President Kennedy has been shot. There's no news yet of his condition. It happened as the president was riding with his wife in an open car through the streets of Dallas, Texas. Several shots rang out and the president collapsed into the arms of his wife. One eyewitness said he saw blood on the President's head. The Governor of Texas, Mr John Connally, who was with him, was also shot down. The president was rushed to hospital, where there's still no word of his condition."

Even though I was expecting this, it was still a shock. I heard Mutti Frida gasp and saw tears rolling down her face.

Col threw off the blankets and was at her mother's side in a moment. "*Mutti! Mutti! Was ist los?* What's wrong?"

I disentangled myself from the blankets Col had scattered and stood at Mutti Frida's other side.

After a while Mutti Frida sat up, reaching arms round the two of us. "He was a great man. I had such hopes after his Berlin speech."

She must mean his *Ich bin ein Berliner* speech when he firmly planted himself on the side of the encircled half-city of West Berlin and all western Europe.

"Hopes?" asked Col.

"That one day East Germany would be free, the Party and *Stasi* broken and we could go home."

I ached to comfort her with the knowledge that in twenty-five years that would happen – at least in my world – but all I could do was hug her. I couldn't recall the assassination affecting me much in my previous life, at least until I saw the picture of JFK's small son saluting his father's coffin as he stood with Jackie at the funeral.

We were huddled over Mutti Frida for a minute or so, until she stood up. "I think we all need a cup of hot chocolate." She busied herself in the kitchen whilst we were sitting at the table. In the background, the BBC was playing sombre music.

When the hot chocolate was ready, Mutti Frida sighed and chased us back to the sofa and helped tuck the blankets around us. "Life goes on, children. Read your book."

We sipped our hot chocolate and read more of *Under Milkwood*, but the zest had gone out of our reading and, eventually, we stopped. We remained there, listening to the music and holding hands under the blanket.

After about an hour, another announcement came on the Radio.

"The latest news from America is that President Kennedy
has only been slightly injured and is recovering in
hospital, but the bullets meant for him have seriously
injured the president's wife. She is undergoing surgery
and we wait for further announcements."

A jolt ran through me as if I had been electrified – JFK was alive! My stomach heaved at the shock and I tore myself out of the blankets, reaching the toilet just in time to deposit the hot chocolate and my tea. The solidity of the world I was in had been wrenched from beneath my feet.

I grasped the bowl and vomited again as reality swirled around me. I half-heard Col's anguished cry of, "Willi!" before the world greyed out to darkness.

***

"No!" I tried to sit up but was held down.

A gruff male voice came from above me. "All right, young'un. Settle down."

My eyes tried to understand the strange, swaying environment and the thumping pain in my head.

"You're in an ambulance on the way to the 'ospital, son. Seems like you 'ad a nasty turn and fell down, giving your 'ead a proper crack. 'Spect you'll need stitches." The ambulance attendant glanced down at a clipboard.

"It's Will, innit?"

Nodding seemed to be a bad idea, what with the pain in my head and fluttering in my stomach, so I whispered, "Yes."

"Just lie there, Will. Tell me if you're gonna be sick again." My stomach twinged slightly as I recognised the acrid taste of vomit in my mouth.

"Could I have a drink of water, please?"

"Hmm – just a sip, now and spit it out into this bowl." He held a bottle out, containing a straw, which he brought to my lips. A small suck brought the sweet, cleansing taste of water. I swirled it round my mouth and swallowed. Before I could suck in some more the straw was withdrawn.

"Oi – I said to spit it out! You're not supposed to be drinkin' nuffin 'til the doctor's seen ya!"

I just closed my eyes and let the motion of the ambulance sway me around.

JFK was alive! This was a huge change from my world. Once again, I felt my reality sliding and flowing. The ambulance man must have been watching closely as he had a bowl beside me as I retched several times.

"See, I told ya not to swallow that water!" he said gently, as he wiped around my face with a moist cloth.

I lay there, trying not to think– until I realised that my collapse must have been so scary for Col and Mutti Frida.

"How are the people I was with?" I managed to ask.

"Them Germans?" I heard the distaste in his voice – he was of an age to have experienced the war and all that entailed.

"Yes."

"Dunno," he said, dismissively, "but the woman said she'd tried to phone your mum but there was no one there." His eyes narrowed. "What you doin', 'angin' around with them Jerries?"

The continued swaying of the ambulance was not helping with settling my stomach. I closed my eyes and ignored the question.

"Hey! Don't you go to sleep on me! We're just about there." I felt him picking up my wrist, before taking my pulse.

The ambulance came to a halt and the rear doors were opened. With great efficiency, my stretcher was pulled out of the ambulance and I was wheeled through doors marked "*Emergency*", as the strong aroma of surgical spirit and disinfectant assaulted my nose.

A pair of nurses helped transfer me to a curtained bed and I lay there, eyes closed and glad not to be moving. Outside, I heard the ambulance man speaking to the nurse, "'E was with a pair of damn Jerries an' 'ad a turn, fell over and cracked 'is head on the toilet."

"Germans – is he German, then? Does he speak English?"

"Oh, 'e's English all right, 'is name's Will. 'E was speaking to me just fine in the van. According to that German woman, 'is mum's at work but she wasn't able to get 'old of 'er so she rang the ambulance."

A moment later a nurse bustled through the curtains and placed a bucket by my bed.

"How are we feeling?"

I opened my eyes. "A bit woozy, still."

104

"Well, there's a bucket if you feel sick again. We're going to examine that head of yours in a minute when the doctor gets here. Just you lie still for the moment." After a few minutes, the doctor came and they unwrapped the bandage on my head, mused over the significant bump and gash and decided the latter needed a few stitches, which were duly applied under a local anaesthetic.

I was lying there quietly when I heard Mutti Frida's voice. "But I am his friend's mother – he was at my house when the accident happened. I wish to see him!" A door closed and I couldn't hear any more.

But then the curtain rustled, and Col was standing beside me, holding my hand fiercely in hers. "Oh, Willi. When I saw you lying on the floor in the toilet with blood all over the floor, I thought you were dead! What happened?" She was speaking softly to avoid alerting the staff she was with me, but I heard the fear in her voice.

"I don't know – I must have fainted."

"You hit your head on the base of the toilet – there was blood everywhere. Oh God, Willi, I thought you were dead, but Mutti bandaged it. We tried to call your mother but there was no reply, so we called the ambulance." That all seemed to come out in a single breath and I felt her hand fiercely squeezing mine.

"Please, don't break my hand!"

"Sorry!" She relaxed the squeezing, but still didn't let go. "I've been so scared!" She leaned down to kiss me but pulled back when she caught the whiff of vomit still on my breath.

"Ugh – you need to have a drink and clean your teeth!" she whispered, smiling to take the sting out of her words.

Just then a nurse came in with a clipboard. She gave Col a sideways glance. "Are you supposed to be in here?"

"Sh…Col's my best friend. Please let him stay with me. I feel safer." I gave the nurse my best puppy eyes, hoping she hadn't noticed my near slip.

"Hmmm." She saw Col's hand still holding mine. "I need to take your pulse!" She gave me a pointed stare.

I offered her my other hand.

She flounced around to the other side of the bed, produced a thermometer which she stuck under my tongue and then took my pulse, writing up the results on a clipboard at the end of the bed.

At that moment, my mother arrived.

The nurse raised her head, annoyed at the continued intrusions into her domain. "And who are you?" she asked, irritation flaring in her voice.

My mother was not someone to be trifled with in a medical environment. "I am *Dr* Johnstone," she said, then her voice softened. "This is my son. Please tell me what is happening."

The nurse deflated rapidly. "He had a turn and fell, hitting his head. He has three stitches and the doctor is worried about a concussion."

My mother picked up the chart at the foot of the bed and examined it, then addressed the nurse. "Please let Dr…" She glanced back down at the clipboard. "…Dr Fredericks know I am here so I can talk with him."

The nurse remained there, unsure of what to do.

"Now, please nurse!" My mother's voice was curt, used to lesser medical staff doing her bidding without question.

The nurse left and my mother turned to Col.

"What happened, Col?" she asked, in a much more friendly voice.

I jumped in. "Col had nothing to do with it – it was an accident! I just felt ill and fainted."

My mother sat on the side of the bed, opposite Col. She stared at her hand, which was still holding mine, then picked up my other one. "It's all right, Will, rest easy. I just want to try to work out why you fainted so suddenly."

"Col, can you tell me what you were doing when this happened?"

"We'd had tea and were sitting reading when the news came on that President Kennedy had been shot. We read some more and then the news came that he had only been injured but his wife was in surgery."

"What time did you have tea?"

"About six o'clock, I think. We all had the same – *Gemütlichkeit* – sort of a beef stew with noodles."

I realised my mother was worried about food poisoning.

My mother leaned forward. "You feel fine?"

"Yes, Frau Doctor Johnstone."

"Thank you, Col." My mother patted Col's hand. "Where's your mother?"

"She's here somewhere. They wouldn't let us in the ambulance, so we walked round here straight away. She was trying to get in to see Willi, but they wouldn't let her."

A half-smile played on my mother's lips. "You slipped in here when no-one was watching?"

Col didn't say anything.

"It's all right Col." She leaned across and patted his hand again. "You stay here and I'll go and find Dr Fredericks and your mother."

I was still feeling a bit woozy and had a splitting headache, so I lay with my eyes closed. I felt the bed shift and realised Col was lying down beside me.

Col whispered in my ear, "Well, we're in bed together, but it's not quite what I was expecting."

106

I squeezed her hand. "Wicked girl!" I whispered back, smiling. Then we lay in silence.

After a while, I heard footsteps and the curtain swished back. The doctor and my mother came in, with Mutti Frida and the nurse behind them. My mother frowned slightly at Col lying beside me. Col sat up but kept hold of my hand.

"How are we feeling?" The doctor asked.

"My head hurts."

He gave a wry smile. "I'm sure it does. Seeing as you have a doctor in the house," he said, glancing across at my mother and nodding in acknowledgement, "I think we can let you go home." Having delivered his verdict, he swept out.

"All right, Will, let's get you out of here." She gave Mutti Frida a quick smile. "Can I give you a lift home?"

"Thank you, Frau Doctor, but just to your house. We can walk from there."

Supported between Mutti Frida and my mother, I was walked out to the car. I lay in the back with my head in Col's lap. At home, I was walked up to bed.

Col and Mutti Frida said goodnight and set off for home as soon as I was safely upstairs. My mother fussed around me for a while but eventually left me in peace, leaving the bedroom door open so I could call for help.

I lay there, totally confused by what was happening, the pain in my head thudding with each heartbeat did not help. The world I knew was not this world in a significant way and I had no idea what might happen as a result of this. It would certainly affect politics in the US, but JFK strode the world's stage. *What would this do to the balance of power in the world?* Eventually, the painkillers worked and my head calmed down enough so I could fade into sleep.

I woke to find my mother leaning over me, a hand on my forehead, morning light pushing through the curtains. "How are you feeling, Will?"

"Sore – and thirsty."

She smiled gently. "I'll get you some water."

She was back in a minute with a glass, which she put on my bedside table. "Here, let me help you sit up a bit."

I levered myself up and my mother fluffed up my pillow and put a second one behind me. "How's that?"

I smiled at her and reached for the water.

"Remember, don't drink it all at once!"

I had several sips and put it down.

My mother was studying me, the cogs turning in her mind as she tried to summon the right words. "What's happening with you, Will?" She sat down on the edge of the bed, searching my face. "About a year ago something happened and you...changed." She stared into my eyes silently for several seconds, then her eyes dropped. "I know that things here at home needed to change and I'm so sorry I did nothing until that night with your father. But you aren't that boy anymore – and it feels like you are..." She stopped, searching my face for the right word. "hiding yourself from me."

I held her gaze, saying nothing.

She picked up my hand. "I don't properly know who you are now." Her voice dropped to a murmur. "Sometimes you are so mature that I can scarcely believe it, but mostly..." Her head shook slowly. "mostly, I just don't understand you." She paused, staring off to the side, trying to pull her thoughts together. She gave my hand a gentle squeeze. "Your fainting spell last night doesn't seem to have any physical cause. Talking to Col last night suggested that it was a shock reaction." She paused again, in puzzlement. "But why would you be shocked that President Kennedy ... was alive? I could understand it if you had that reaction to the shooting – but to him being alive? It's almost as if you expected him to be dead."

I stayed silent – I couldn't answer the question. My mother was an intelligent woman and she was picking at the fabric close to a thread that she might untangle and follow. I was pretty sure, though, that what had happened to me was so inexplicable that even if her sharp mind led her to it, she wouldn't be able to accept it.

"I know you've been taking the newspaper to read – and then bringing it back down again," she gave me a knowing smile. "I know you're interested in what's happening in the world. Being shocked at JFK's death I could understand..." She stopped again, frowning in puzzlement. "Was it delayed shock?"

I shrugged, watching her face. "It must have been."

I sensed thoughts and emotions running through her. She squeezed my hand gently as if physical contact would help open a deeper channel of communication between us. "What's happened to you, Will? Who are you?"

"I don't know – I'm just me, growing up I suppose."

My mother sighed. "I've had your school on the phone – they aren't quite sure what to do with you, either. The work you are doing now is well past 'O' level and into the 'A' level curriculum. They want to push you up there. Would you like that?"

This was new to me – and probably dangerous in terms of making me a target.

"If I'm already doing senior work now, what difference will moving up there make?" I was already sufficiently different and jumping me several more grades would make me stick out even more – and could restart the serious bullying.

My mother mused for a few seconds. "Nothing, I suppose – and the maturity of your reaction is one of the things I find so strange. You're only thirteen years old, Will, but I don't understand your thinking most of the time." Just then the phone rang, and my mother went to answer it.

I took a couple more sips of water and then leaned back and closed my eyes. I had been shutting my mother out, replacing her with Mutti Frida and her reaction to this was understandable. We hadn't properly connected since the Premium Bond incident.

"That was Frau Schmidt asking how you were. I told her you were fine, but a bit sore and would be staying home today."

She must have seen my forlorn expression.

"It's all right, Will." My mother smiled. "Col is coming round in about an hour." She paused. "Col is a very close friend, isn't he?" *Was there something in the 'very'?*

"He's my best friend."

"I know he is, Will." She almost murmured and then stopped. "You seemed very close in the hospital yesterday." *There it was again.* My mother paused for a long speculative moment. Homosexuality was not just taboo in 1960's England, it was still a crime. I was now certain she was worried about the relationship between Col and me. A sudden thought struck me: *did Lili think we were gay? Were her subtle attempts to engage Col in a relationship attempts to probe the nature of our friendship?*

"Will, are you okay?"

I realised I had tuned out for a moment, so I smiled at my mother.

"You need to go and have a bath and then come and have some breakfast." She stood up to let me get out of bed. "Don't get your head wet though – if you need a hand in the bath, just call out, okay?"

My mother seeing me in the bath was not what I wanted, so I was careful – something my old brain had been dealing with. *Did you know how many accidents there are in baths with old people?* As I sat there in the bath soaking up the warmth, my mind gnawed at the problem my mother saw with Col's and my relationship. *Did she think Col and I were gay? Did Lili think that too?* I didn't think my mother was homophobic but having that in your family would be challenging in the 1960s. I realised I was making her life problematic, but for the moment I couldn't see a way out. I had no idea how to handle Lili, other than just continuing to be friends. I would need to talk with Col about this, but I needed to think more first.

Col arrived shortly after breakfast. Once we were alone in my room, she hugged me tightly and then kissed me gently. "How are you feeling, Willi?" Her hand strayed up and softly stroked my scalp beside the bandage, where it had been shaved for the stitches.

"I'm mostly okay now, just a bit sore."

"Good!" Col glanced around and sat down on the floor. "Your room hasn't changed much since I was last here when we first met."

"I suppose not – a few more books, perhaps," I said, smiling as I sat down opposite her. "We'd better not tell Mutti Frida that we spent time alone in my room."

Col laughed in nervous agreement.

We spent the morning mostly in my room reading and talking about the attempt on JFKs life. During the day news came through that JFK had been released from hospital and Jackie Kennedy was out of danger.

The secret service and local police had shot the attempted assassin as he tried to escape – and it was being reported that he was from Eastern Europe, a citizen of the Warsaw Pact countries. Yet another difference from my world. *Had Russia just tried to kill JFK? Why would they do that? Were they trying to settle the score from JFK facing them down over the Cuban missile crisis?*

If the Eastern Bloc had been behind the assassination attempt, how would this affect things? Vice President Johnston had put the US (and hence NATO) on to high alert, but JFK had since lowered that. I was in a huge turmoil over the implications of this. I would have to follow the news and analysis closely, which would only give my mother more to worry about.

With all this going on in my head, Col was forced to call me back to the present on several occasions.

During the afternoon, Lili arrived with a bag of grapes, having heard the news of my accident from Mutti Frida. I was having to watch myself closely with her as Col still hadn't been able to persuade Mutti Frida to let her 'come out' to Lili as a girl. It was just one more thing buzzing around in my head.

Col and I were sitting on the floor and Lili joined us after inspecting my room. She noticed the hanging models and perused the bookshelves before sitting down with us.

"You're okay then, Willi?" Concern for me evident in her voice.

Col smiled. "Perhaps it's knocked some sense into him!"

"Don't be so cruel, Col," Lili said, laughing. She glanced back at the hanging models. "You like planes, Willi?"

I smiled. "What makes you think that?"

Lili stuck her tongue out at me and glanced back up at the planes. "You need to get rid of the cobwebs." Then she added, "One of my uncles was a fighter pilot in the war."

"Wow! I'd like to meet him."

"Well, perhaps. But I tried to get him to talk to me about it for a school project and he wouldn't. He said that part of his life was over and we had to concentrate on the future."

She picked up the bag of grapes. "Here, have one."

We shared the fruit between us as we chatted.

"They say the assassin was from the Soviet bloc. Do you think the Russians are behind it?" Lili asked. "I hope he wasn't Polish," she added as an afterthought.

"Or German," Col added.

"I heard he was Hungarian," I said.

"It must be the Russians," Lili said, pensively. "Who else would it be?"

There was an underlying unease in the news brought on by the tone of some of the reporting from the assassination attempt. I thought about the assassinations and attempts I knew had occurred in my world. Whilst many were political, some were carried out by people who were seriously disturbed, usually by schizophrenia. The attempted assassination of the Pope in 1981 had supposed links to the DDR and Bulgaria and, if this was true, back to Russia. But then the attempt on Ronald Reagan and the killing of John Lennon had been at the hands of psychologically disturbed people.

I was drifting again and caught Col's sideways glance. "Crazy people?" I suggested.

"What do you mean?" Lili asked.

"My mother told me about schizophrenia, a brain disease that makes people think they hear voices telling them to do strange things, like to kill important people."

"Brain disease?" Col asked.

"I think it's more like a wiring problem than an actual disease," I said. "You can't catch it, don't worry," I said, smiling.

"That's a relief," Lili said, returning my glance with a laugh. "There are lots of people I know that do strange things!"

Col gave me a quick sideways glance – I saw that we would have to talk about my suicide attempts again.

"How about a game of cards?" I suggested.

And so we spent the rest of the afternoon playing cards. After Col and Lili left, my mother took the bandage off my head and examined the stitches.

"Well, that's not infected and is starting to heal." She stared at me. "You can go back to school, but I'll write a note that you are not to do sport for two weeks."

The following day I still felt a bit shaky, but the news about Jackie Kennedy was good and that buoyed me up somewhat. It had been confirmed that the assassin was a Hungarian who had left during the 1956 uprising. If the US security services knew anything about a recent connection to the Eastern Bloc, they were not letting on. I needed the Internet and the 24-hour news cycle of 2020, but I would have to make do with the BBC news and the papers over the next few days for more information and a deeper analysis. I needed to be careful as I was letting this wind me up – deep breaths and some cuddles with Col were needed.

On the bus home, I found myself wrestling, once again, with the possible fallout from the attempted assassination. Even if the Eastern Bloc were behind it, it would be hard for NATO and the Warsaw Pact to trust one another any less than they already did. I suspected that the CIA would try to stir things up in some of Russia's client states around the world. I doubted there would be any direct confrontation, even if the US were able to prove that the USSR or its client states were involved. It was understood that the west couldn't win a conventional war due to the imbalance of forces in Europe, so a confrontation would rapidly go nuclear. No-one believed a limited nuclear exchange was possible, and it would escalate. We all knew about Mutually Assured Destruction.

I slammed my hand down on the back of the seat in front of me in fear and frustration. I had lived through all this nuclear angst once before and now I was living it again. This truly sucked.

I arrived at Col's house having concluded that nothing much would change, probably, hopefully. Col closed the door and took me by the shoulders, examining at my head from several angles.

"Are you okay, Willi?"

"Yeah – mostly, I think."

Col took my satchel, hung up my coat and led me through to the lounge room sofa. After we sat down, she turned gave me a brief kiss and searched my face.

"What's going on Willi?"

"What do you mean?"

"I feel there are things you are not telling me. I can sense this sort of…vortex churning inside you and I think it's all bound up with your…" She paused, a worried frown on her face. I watched her eyes flicking around the room. "Um…your…um…trying to kill yourself…" She pulled her thoughts together and her eyes fastened on to mine. "But it's also linked to your collapse the other day." She tried to marshal her thoughts.

"Your mother doesn't think you were ill. She gave me the third degree about what happened; I think she senses there's something going on that you are not telling either of us."

I took several breaths. It all came back to trust. This girl had trusted me with her safety when she told me she was from the DDR. But my story was so unbelievable I was worried she would think I was mad. She already had some evidence of my disturbed mental state, after all.

"Willi?"

I would have to tell her my truth as she had told me hers. *How to start?*

I took her hands in mine and breathed deeply – this wouldn't be easy. "You know why I tried to kill myself the second time and, the first time it was basically for the same reason – I couldn't face, alone, the life I had to live."

Col squeezed my hands in hers, nodding sympathetically. She missed what I had been hinting at, that I knew what my life would be like, for years to come. I tried again.

"Do you remember not long after we first met, I said I couldn't go through all this – again?"

I saw from her widening eyes and the way she bit her lip with confusion, that she had no idea where I was going with this.

"I couldn't live this life … again ... because…I have already done it once."

"What?" Col's mouth dropped open, and her eyes widened further. I hadn't thought that was possible.

Trying to explain this was difficult – but I knew that for her, trying to understand would be, too. I started again.

"The first time we met, you remember, you were sitting on the wall in front of a house in my street and I was walking home from the bus?"

"Yes."

"That day I had been on the point of killing myself." I swallowed at how close it had been. "I think I would have killed myself, but something happened." I paused, hoping I would be believed but Col's face was deeply puzzled. I just had to keep going. "What happened was …a future me suddenly found its way into this body."

Col stared at me blankly.

I just needed to keep trying. I took a calming breath. "Col, I grew up here in England but eventually emigrated to Australia, where I married, had children, had a career – or in fact, several – and eventually retired. My last memory from that life is sitting in an armchair with a glass of wine beside me, aged seventy." There was no change in Col's expression. "My old brain arrived in this body just in time to stop my young brain from killing this body we now share."

113

"Young brain, old brain? What do you mean? You've had a brain transplant?" she asked, incredulously.

I half laughed at such a strange thought. "No, Col. Somehow, my consciousness and as far as I can tell all my knowledge just…appeared in that twelve-year-old brain."

Col blinked a few times. I could see from the changing expressions of confusion and disbelief on her face the acrobatics her brain was performing.

Eventually, her eyes locked with mine. "You know what's going to happen in the future!"

I sighed. "That's part of my problem – this world is similar to the one I lived in – but different in several ways that I know about so far." I paused, searching her eyes, trying to work out if she believed me. "I discovered the first way it was different when I met you." *How would she take this next revelation?* "In my world, the Col I knew, my closest friend, was a blond-haired, blue-eyed, English ... boy called Colin. That first time we met you were sitting on the garden wall of what was his house in my world."

"I was a boy?"

"Yes."

Col stared at me.

"The reason I was not shocked when the assassination attempt was announced was… because I expected it would happen sometime in late November, I just couldn't remember the date. That is why I was increasingly tense through November."

I saw things shifting in Col's eyes, but she said nothing, just nodded for me to continue.

"When I heard Kennedy had survived, it was like the foundations of my world had been wrenched away. In my world, Kennedy died. Him living can change so many things."

There was still nothing from Col, which I supposed shouldn't have been surprising. I needed to give her the time to process everything, but I could feel fear of rejection bubbling inside me, so I pressed on.

"One of the things that helped me cope with my strange situation has been knowing that for all the dangerous confrontation between East and West, it never boils over into a war, because in my world it never did. It did come perilously close to disaster several times, but somehow on each occasion, that disaster was averted."

Col was still just sitting there, expressionless, so blindly I continued.

"But now, the future I knew, *know*, is no longer the same. JFK's assassination failing must have a huge impact on the future. It will be different, but I have no idea in what ways and that scared me to the core – it still scares me."

114

Finally, Col's eyes came back into focus. "What else helped?"

I blinked, trying to understand what relevance her question had. "Helped with what?"

"Helped you cope with your 'strange situation', as you described it."

Oh! I took a deep breath. "Knowing you – and Mutti Frida, of course, but mostly being with you."

Col shivered, eyes tightly shut. Her hands flew out of mine and she clasped her arms tightly around herself. "But you're a seventy-year-old man." Her eyes flew open. "You're a pervert." She spat it out, recoiling backwards in the chair.

"No Col, no." I reached for her, but she pulled away. "I'm the same person you've always known – a weird mixture of a boy's body and emotions with a load of knowledge and understanding pasted on top. I'm still thirteen-year-old Willi, with the same mixed-up brain you've always known."

Col stayed silent and we sat, half turned towards one another but not touching for several minutes. Several times, Col almost spoke, but each time, she retreated.

Eventually, she blinked and stared sharply at me. "In your world then, I suppose I don't exist?"

I hadn't thought about that. If my Col didn't exist in this world, this Col probably didn't in mine.

"Well, no, I suppose not." Perhaps Mutti Frida had died at Ravensbrück in my world...

Col sank back into thought for a while and I gave her space, hoping that I hadn't lost my best friend, the girl who had given me so much.

Finally, she stood up. "Willi, I need time to think about this. It's ... we ..." She petered to a stop, took a deep breath and leant down, picking up my hands again.

I felt a seed of hope germinate – she was not rejecting me outright.

"Please Willi, I need some time to think about what you've said, about who you say you are." She paused. "About how I feel about all that you've told me...about who...what you are."

I stood up beside her. She took a step back but kept my hands in hers. "I want you to go home so I have the space to think about all of this."

I felt her hands tightening on mine. "But you must remember your promise to me that you won't...do anything...without talking to me first." She gave my hands a hard squeeze, searching my eyes for reassurance.

I nodded, unable to speak.

"Tomorrow, I'd like you to go to your house. If I'm ready to talk about this, I'll ring you. Okay?"

Again, I nodded, not trusting my voice.

I picked up my school bag, got into my coat and opened the front door. Col was standing in the lounge room doorway, watching me. I paused with my hand on the door. Col's face was closed. I turned and had to pull my feet from a floor that threatened to drag me down with each footstep.

I went through a cocktail of emotions as I walked home – anger at myself for letting out my truth, anger at Col for thinking I was a pervert, hope that she would find a way through this that would leave us as friends and, over all of this, a deep sadness at the possibility that I had lost my best friend and the girl I was starting to love.

Late November 1963

Our house was empty when I arrived, so I went to my room, took out my schoolbooks and tried to study, lost in tortuous, writhing thoughts that reached no conclusion. Col had believed my story – but her reaction had twisted into a completely unexpected and scary direction.

Eventually, I heard someone moving around downstairs and my mother slipped her head around my door. "Will, I saw your coat downstairs! You're back early. Is everything all right?"

It definitely wasn't, but I couldn't talk about it with my mother.

"Yes – Col and Mutti Frida are doing something this evening, so I had to come home early."

"Okay. Supper is leftovers tonight. Come on down in about half an hour – or you could come down and talk to me as I get it ready."

I needed to spend more time with my mother, but I couldn't do it tonight. On my desk, Jean Cocteau's *"Les Enfants Terribles"* lay open in front of me. It's brooding darkness and dysfunctional relationships had seemed to suit my mood when I had picked it up, but I hadn't been reading it.

"I need to get through this chapter of *Les Enfants Terribles*. I'll be down in a bit."

I could see my mother was disappointed. "Okay."

I returned to the deeply disturbed world created by Cocteau, but quickly put it down again. I sensed that it would take me to places I didn't want to visit tonight, so I just sat there.

After about ten minutes I heard the phone ring. My heart leapt. *Could that be Col already?* Then I realised if it was, it might just as easily not be what I wanted to hear. I heard my mother talking on the phone at the foot of the stairs, but not what she was saying.

After a while, she came upstairs.

"Will, that was Frau Schmidt. Something's happened and she asked if Col could stay here tonight as she has to go out and could well be very late – and I said, of course, he could."

"What's happened?"

"She wouldn't say." My mother paused. "It must be something important, though, for her to have to deal with it at this time of night. Anyway, Col is walking here in a few minutes. You might want to go and help him as he will be carrying everything for school tomorrow."

A shudder went through me. It's not something to do with Col's father, is it?

I grabbed my coat and headed towards Col's house. After I turned the corner into Sea View Avenue, I saw her emerge from the house carrying her school bag and a bulging duffel bag. I walked towards her. When we met, I could not see her face in the poor light of the streetlamps, so I was none the wiser about how she felt. I reached out and lifted the duffel bag off her shoulder.

"Willi, I am still thinking, so please don't push me."

I nodded; I saw her tense her shoulders, but I said nothing.

"I don't know what's happening with Mutti, but she's already gone, walking back into town to meet someone who phoned. I'm worried that it's something to do with my father."

I heard the tears hiding behind her voice and desperately wanted to comfort her with a hug, but that could be seen as forcing her, so I just stood there.

She hitched her school bag strap higher on her shoulder, her face closed and set off purposefully towards my house. I had to scurry to catch up.

We walked in silence. Unexpectedly, my father was sitting at the kitchen table as we came in through the back door, glowering silently as my mother welcomed Col.

"We'll set up the camp bed in Will's room after supper, Col," my mother announced.

I watched Col's eyes flare for a second before she sent me a frown.

"Take Col upstairs, Will, so he can leave his bags in your room. Come straight back down as supper's ready."

When we reached the top of the stairs, Col turned towards me and let fly in German, but keeping her voice low.

"I can't sleep in here with you," she spat. "What would Mutti think?"

I knew Mutti Frida wouldn't like this. "I don't know what we can do about it – unless you want to tell everyone that you are a girl?"

"Of course not. Be sensible." The sting went out of her voice and she stared at me with pleading eyes. "What are we going to do?"

I shrugged. "I don't think there's anything we can do."

"Why can't I sleep on the sofa downstairs, like when you stay at my house?"

"My mother will think that's strange. I expect she thinks I sleep in your room when I'm there."

Col closed her eyes and sat heavily on my bed. "We'll have to tell Mutti I slept in your room on a camp bed."

"What? I don't think that's a great idea."

"Willi, think about it. It would be a problem if it came out when our mothers talked. Mutti might be so shocked that she'd let the secret out."

I raised a doubting eyebrow.

118

Col scowled back, then sighed, resignedly. "Don't worry. I'll remind Mutti about our promise and that we are keeping it. I'm sure she will understand, given the circumstances." She didn't sound very convincing.

I gave her a wry half-smile. Given what lay between us, I was certainly not expecting any sort of physical contact and I didn't want Mutti Frida thinking we had broken our promise.

Col sighed. "Come on, we'd better get downstairs. We don't want to annoy your father." We traipsed back downstairs in silence and sat down to tea.

I saw Col suspiciously eyeing her plate of bubble and squeak with beef fritters.

"Es ist gebratene Kartoffelpüree und Gemüse," (It's fried mashed potato and vegetables.), I said.

"Stop that!" My father's voice whipped across the table. "Speak English!"

I watched Col cringe, her face twisted with fear and shock. My mother frowned fiercely at my father. His eyes narrowed, but he remained silent – *not in front of the children*, I suppose.

I turned to my mother, ignoring my father. "I'm sorry. I was just telling Col what we were eating. We don't stop to think what language we are using. I wasn't trying to be rude."

My mother nodded and the incident passed, but I saw Col shifting uncomfortably in her seat and tried to give her an encouraging smile.

The conversation around the supper table was strained and desultory, stretching across long, agonised silences broken mostly by my mother asking about how our days had gone. I felt my father's baleful eye on me throughout the meal and with the question marks hanging over my relationship with Col, I didn't feel hungry – a shame, as I enjoyed the meal, and my mother's cooking.

Somehow, I managed to eat my plateful, as did Col, and then we helped my sister with the clean-up, to her apparent disgust with having to associate with us boys. I wondered if she'd relate differently to Col if she knew Col was a girl.

As we finished, my mother came back into the kitchen.

"Will, you and Col can get the camp bed out of the shed and take it up to your room. Do you remember how to put it together?"

"I think so."

The camp bed was primitive by the modern standards I was used to – basically, canvas stretched tightly across a wooden frame on a set of six legs. There was no mattress, you just put a couple of blankets on top of the canvas to soften it slightly. It took us a while to work out how to put it together, despite my previous experience with it. As we worked together, I could feel Col's mood thawing, to the point of giving me a tentative smile at one point as we struggled with the wretched device.

"Do you think you'll be comfortable on this?" I asked, eyeing off the camp bed suspiciously when we finally had it assembled.

"I expect so." She gave me a full smile. "Even if I'm not, I won't be getting in with you," she laughed softly and then reached across to take my hands. "I'm sorry about earlier – I can see that you are just you, not a pervert. But I do want to try to understand what has happened to you. It must be weird living in your head."

My relief at hearing this was enormous, and I released a heavy sigh. "Thank you for believing me – inside my head is pretty odd at times when my young brain's emotions war with my old brain. But mostly I'm just me – what you see is what you get." I pretty much didn't understand what had happened to me, so I didn't know what else I could tell her. "Ask whatever you want, and I'll try to give you an answer if I have one."

I squeezed her hand – and my mother appeared with blankets, sheets, and a pillow. For a fraction of a second, she froze, assessing the tableau before her, then she shook herself out of it.

"Here you go, Col. Spread a couple of these thick, woollen blankets on the camp bed and then just make up a normal bed on top of that. There's plenty of blankets so you can put more on if you start to feel cold." She dropped the bedding on the camp bed.

We started making up the bed under her watchful eye as she tried to fathom Col's and my relationship. I could almost hear the unasked questions bouncing around in her head.

"Do you want a bath before bed, Col?" she asked.

I watched Col tensing slightly. "No thank you, Frau Doktor Johnstone. Mutti made me have one before I left so I would not be a problem for you."

My mother gave Col a gentle smile. "You are not a problem, Col. It's a pleasure to have you here since Will spends so much time at your house." Again, there was that gazing assessment. I had no idea how to deal with this scrutiny of our relationship.

"Tomorrow is a school day for both of you, so I want you to get ready for bed in half an hour – and when the lights go out, I want you to sleep. No chatting to all hours of the night. Understood?"

"Yes, Mummy!"

"Yes, Frau Doktor!"

Col watched my mother leave and then asked, *"Wenn wir auf Deutsch sprechen, wird deine Mutter es nicht verstehen?" (If we talk in German, your mother will not understand?)*

"I don't think so. I've spoken to her about her German and she told me she only had a smattering and that was from when she was at school before the war." I paused slightly, not sure if I should continue. "Learning German was not popular once the war started."

Col gave me a wry smile and then sat on the camp bed, taking a few tentative bounces to test it. Then she settled, slipped her shoes off, perched her feet on the edge of the camp bed and wrapped her arms around her shins, resting her chin on her knees.

"Willi, I think your mother is worried about how close we are."

I nodded in agreement. "I think you're right. But I don't know what to do about it."

Col paused. "Does she think we are homosexuals?"

I cast her a wry smile. "Possibly. But I don't think she will say anything. That subject is just so taboo, I think we are safe unless she catches us in bed together."

Col chuckled. "If she did, she would know we weren't homosexual." I saw a faint blush creeping into her cheeks at what she had suggested.

I smiled, then raised an eyebrow.

Col shook her head and changed the subject. "Willi, you know the future?"

"I'm not sure."

"What do you mean, you're not sure? You lived through it."

I sighed. "Col, I lived through a future – and mostly this world has been the same as the one I know … knew…?" I shook my head in frustration at a language incapable of expressing my situation without confusion. "…in my other life…but there are differences." I smiled at Col. "You and Mutti Frida are here rather than my Col and his mother. That's a small difference, I suppose, and there have been quite a few other small differences."

I took a deep, calming breath. "But the failed assassination of Kennedy is a huge one. I can see that you being here might just be irrelevant to the future, but I can't see how Kennedy living won't change the future."

"Does it matter, Willi, if the future is not the one you know?"

"Yes, it probably does." I suppressed a shudder. "You see, in my world, in spite of continuous confrontation and sabre-rattling between east and west, the cold war never exploded into a real, all-out nuclear war." I was silent for a moment, recalling that there had been occasions when it had been a perilously close call, even after the Cuban missile crisis. I saw Col wondering where I had gone to this time and smiled an apology. "Then in twenty-five years, the Eastern Bloc collapses, Germany is reunified, and all the Warsaw pact countries gain their independence. Then the Soviet Union collapses, and many of the republics declare their independence from Russia."

Col's eyes flared. "Oh Willi, it sounds wonderful."

"It was a magical time, but Kennedy's assassination must have had a huge impact on what went on behind the scenes with the KGB and CIA – and all that is going to be different now." I squeezed my eyes shut, holding things together. "And I'm back living through an uncertain, dark future – again."

Col leaned across and took my hands. "Oh, Willi. But you managed last time, and you can do it again." She stopped and took a sharp breath in realisation. "Was that…did that…you said before that there were…other times. Was this darkness part of that?"

I tasted my memories from that time. The constant threat of nuclear annihilation was part of the rotten, acrid flavour of my teens and early twenties – but only as a grimy, roiling primer for the canvas on which the rest of my life was chaotically splashed. "It didn't help, but it was so omnipresent that it became part of the background." My voice brightened slightly. "And then I moved to Australia, the other side of the world where the threat was distant."

"Can you tell me why you…tried again?" Her voice soft, enfolding me in care.

My breathing sped up as I trawled through my past which was again my future. After a few seconds, my eyes hooked onto Col's and I grimaced. "I never felt I fitted in anywhere. I knew I couldn't be a pilot, but I tried and, of course, I failed." I took a breath, suppressing the pain caused by pulling at the scab of that memory. "My doubts about my worth in every job I did would be reinforced by something going wrong in my life. I would despair at putting myself in that … place yet again and that would push me … towards that solution."

Col glanced at the closed bedroom door and then leaned forward, taking my hands back in hers. "Willi, you do fit in – with me and Mutti and now Lili. You must learn to trust yourself – if you don't fit in somewhere, it doesn't mean there's something wrong with you."

I sighed. "Col, I'm worried that this time I am even more different because of what has happened to me."

"But you have seventy years of experience to help. Seventy years where you … you didn't do that, however close you came."

I had my head down, so Col leaned forward and peered up at me. "Already that experience has helped you change things with your father and the bullies at school. You even helped me understand what was happening at school, turning Lili into our friend." Her face was lit with encouragement. "And you are so good at everything at school." I saw her eyes gifting me her support and…love?

"Yes – but remember, I've done it all before." I could hear the self-deprecation in my voice.

"Don't put yourself down." There was a fierceness in her words. "Were you ever this good at French and German before?"

I shrugged. "No, but I had only learned things once then – and I wasn't motivated by a German boy…girl …" I smiled at the confusion of Col's disguise, "…I wanted as a friend." I took a breath, suddenly eager to change the subject. "I've just remembered something interesting." Col cocked her head to one side. "When the DDR collapsed and Germany was reunified, all the *Stasi* files were thrown open – and it turned out that almost everyone had been spying on their own family and friends, whilst they, in turn, spied on them."

"That's terrible!" Col cried.

I laughed, ironically. "No, it's not. You see, as almost no one was doing anything bad, most of the reports were completely boring – what people wore, what they ate, where they went, their ordinary everyday conversations. Imagine that - buildings full of filing cabinets of the details of normal people living normal, ordinary lives." I shook my head. "All that work and effort writing reports, cross-referencing them, and filing them was for no benefit at all."

"That doesn't sound like the rumours circulating about the Stasi I've heard – or what Mutti thinks."

"Perhaps not right now, as I suppose people might still be settling scores from the war and its aftermath." I shrugged. "But that's what was in the files when they were opened in the late 1980s: just reams of quotidian detail."

Col laughed in disbelief. For her, the Stasi was a feared organisation. "Anyway, as to the future and you knowing it, we'll just have to see what happens. You need to sit down and write a list of things you do remember; that way we can see what changes are occurring."

I nodded in agreement – I should have thought of doing that, but I would need somewhere secure for that list. *Perhaps giving it to Col was the safest option?*

A moment later. my mother put her head around the door. "Time for bed, boys. Go and clean your teeth, please."

We got back to my bedroom and I could sense tension in Col. "Are you going to change into pyjamas?" she asked.

"Oh, it's all right, I'll go and change in the loo."

"No, Willi. I'll change there, no one will walk in on me there, but they might here." She grabbed her PJs and headed out and I changed and got into bed.

A minute later, Col slipped back in and clambered gingerly into the cot.

"All tucked in?" My mother asked, seeing us both in our beds. "Sleep well, boys." My mother clicked off the light and pulled the door closed.

"Schlaf gut, Col." (Sleep well, Col).
"Du auch." (You too).

***

I woke in the grey, predawn to find Col sitting, fully dressed, on the cot. "Get up and get dressed, Willi, whilst I am in the toilet." She gave me a smile and slipped quietly out of the room. I was dressed for school when she came back.

"Let's get the camp bed pulled apart," she suggested, and we folded up the blankets and battled with the frame, finally getting it into its bag.

"Can I come to your house this afternoon?"

Col smiled. "Yes, Willi. I still don't understand what has happened to you, but I don't think anyone could. We'll just have to explore it together."

A huge knot of tension released inside me.

My mother's head popped round the door. "You're up already, well done Col. Will can be hard to rouse at times." She gave Col an approving smile. "Come on down for breakfast. Leave your overnight at the bottom of the stairs, Col. Will can bring it round this afternoon."

After breakfast, my mother bustled me out of the house to catch my bus. She was going to drop Col at school on her way to morning surgery.

At school, my German teacher, Mr. Sturr, pulled me aside at the end of the lesson.

"Your German is coming along, Johnstone, for someone studying German for less than a term."

I was standing there, not knowing what to say, as I knew my German was pretty good. Mr. Sturr was doing the usual adult thing: trying to motivate by under praising.

"Your mother mentioned that you had a German friend and seemed to have picked up the language quickly." He was gazing off into the distance, almost as if not talking to me. After a few seconds, his eyes returned to my face. "You see, there's an essay competition that might interest you. There's a trip to Germany as a prize. Here."

He thrust a flyer into my hand and walked off, in his usual distant manner.

I stood there, a bit dazed; he was certainly odd.

I read through the flyer: it was from the International Youth Cultural Exchange Program (part of UNESCO) inviting essays in German of not more than two thousand words on the subject *Das Teilen von Musik und Kultur erhöht das internationale Verständnis (Sharing music and culture increases international understanding)*. Winners would spend two weeks as a guest of the program in the DDR.

124

It went on to provide conditions of entry, which I met, a London address for submissions and a closing date of the fifth of December. That was just over a week away and I wondered how long this had been sitting on Mr. Sturr's desk. I stuffed the flyer into my bag and headed off to my next class.

After school, I stopped at my house to pick up Col's overnight bag, locked up again and headed for his house.

She greeted me at the door, nodding when she saw her duffel bag. "Thanks, Willi."

We stood slightly apart, each trying to fathom the other. I was aware of the distance that had separated us when I left yesterday. In spite of what Col had said at my house yesterday evening, I was unsure of where we were and didn't want to make a mistake.

Col reached out, gently pulling me to her by my coat lapels. Our noses were almost touching when she tilted her head to the side, leaned in and softly kissed me. She pulled back and searched my eyes. "I'm sorry about yesterday, Willi. Are we okay?"

I slid my arms around her and pulled her into a kiss that deepened quickly as Col put her arms around my neck, fastening us together.

After a minute or so, Col relaxed her arms and shared a slightly insecure smile. "Are we okay?"

I smiled back in relief. "Yes, Col. We're okay if you are." She leaned back in and I lost another minute of my life to the pleasure of our kisses.

"Come on, get your coat off and let's get the homework done so we can cuddle."

"Is everything okay with Mutti?"

"Oh, yes. She left me a note on the kitchen table, she'll be home from work at the usual time. Come on, let's get the homework done."

We sat down at the table, ready to go through our homework. Amongst my books, I had pulled out the sheet Mr. Sturr had given me.

"What's this?" Col started reading the sheet.

"My German teacher gave me that. It's about an essay competition in German. He thought it might interest me."

"Are you going to enter?"

"I don't know – it would be interesting to visit the DDR and see your home country. What do you think?"

"I'm not sure what to think." She paused. "Part of that is that I'm not sure what my home country is anymore. I'm not sure I want to belong to the DDR." Her eyes lost focus as she gathered her thoughts. "After the school visit to Buchenwald, I was so ashamed to be German. Then Mutti found out my father was involved in putting people in those terrible places." She shuddered at that thought. "I don't feel I belong amongst people like that."

"But Col, remember what Mutti Frida said about all of us having that darkness inside us? I don't know how I would be if I had been caught up in Nazi Germany – neither do you."

Col sniffed. "Anyway, this sounds like party propaganda." Her voice dripped with contempt as she flicked the flyer back towards me. "The whole thing is probably run by the Eastern Bloc communist parties."

I was surprised at her reaction. "What do you mean? It says on the sheet that it's a UN program."

"It's the kind of cynical, hypocritical misdirection that is typical of the Party. They don't mean a word of what they are implying in the essay title. They don't want to increase international understanding. They want to spread their regime across Europe, across the whole world." There was real vehemence in her words, and it startled me.

We hadn't talked about politics and I was surprised she thought so little of the party when her mother had been so close to senior party members – and her maternal grandparents had died because of their politics. "Does the communist party run UNESCO?"

"I'm sure they are heavily involved."

I pulled a doubtful face.

"Mutti and I do talk about this, you know. She has seen it all – as a prisoner in Ravensbrück under the Nazis and then as a party insider in Leipzig. They are the same sort of people – and some of them are the same people, like my father. Ask her about it when she gets home."

Her attitude was puzzling me. "Why are you so against communism?" *Wasn't Mutti Frida a communist?*

Col sighed. "It's not that I'm against communism itself – but the government of the DDR oppresses everyone except the party elite and controls the masses with fear. That's not supposed to happen in a communist state."

I just nodded, still confused, and we turned back to our homework.

Mutti Frida arrived home at the usual time. We already had tea on the go, with Mutti Frida's handwritten cookbook open on the kitchen table. Col and I were gradually being given more control of the cooking as Mutti Frida taught us a variety of dishes.

She had hardly got her coat off when Col pounced. "What was the meeting about yesterday evening, Mutti?"

"Oh, nothing important." She paused, considering what to say. "Well, that's not true. You see it's rather…umm…delicate and you must not say anything to anyone about it." She paused, her gaze flicking between us. "But telling the two of you might serve as a cautionary tale, I suppose."

126

She hung up her coat and went into the kitchen to sit at the table with us in tow. After we were seated. "Remember, this must not go anywhere else."

We nodded our agreement.

Mutti eyed us both seriously. "The daughter of one of the ladies who own the shop has got herself into trouble." Mutti Frida stopped, pointedly watching our reactions. "She's only sixteen and she's ... was pregnant."

Col gave a stifled gasp and Mutti Frida put a hard eye on her and then turned her gaze to me. *She couldn't have heard that Col slept in my room last night.* I felt my stomach tightening.

"I went to look after their younger children for an evening so the parents could help their daughter..." she paused, searching for appropriate words, "help her sort things out."

I did my best to hold a poker face as my old brain realised they must have taken her for an illegal abortion.

"Don't do anything stupid, hmmm?" Mutti Frida gaze pierced us both before she stood up to check the vegetables we had started.

"No Mutti, we won't." Then Col gave me a wink. "But you should know that I slept in Willi's bedroom last night."

It was my turn to gasp.

"What?" Mutti Frida swung around, brandishing a large spoon in her hand.

Col laughed – but I was cringing. "It's all right, Mutti. I was on a camp bed and nothing happened." I could see that Mutti Frida was appalled at this development.

Col frowned at Mutti Frida. "Where did you think I would sleep? Frau Doktor Johnstone thinks I am a boy. She probably thinks Willi sleeps in my room when he's here."

Mutti Frida rolled her eyes and sighed. "Nothing happened between you?"

Col appeared a bit hurt. "Mutti, we promised!"

"Okay." Mutti Frida shook her head in disbelief at how things were turning out. "This subterfuge has more tentacles than an octopus."

I chuckled and in my best mock-Scottish accent intoned. "Oh, what a tangled web we weave, when first we practise to deceive."

Col and Mutti Frida laughed. "Where did you hear that, Willi?"

"It's one of my mother's favourite sayings to encourage my sister and me to be truthful. I think it's from a Scottish poem as my mother always says it with a Scottish accent."

When we sat down after tea, I pulled out the essay flyer and passed it to Mutti Frida. "My German teacher gave me this and encouraged me to enter. What do you think?"

Mutti Frida read through the flyer and then glanced up at me. "Well, your spoken German is excellent now and you have read a lot of written German, so I suspect your written style is reasonable." She paused. "Do you want to visit the DDR?"

I looked at Col and Mutti Frida. "I would like to see the country for myself. All I know is what I have learned from you and Col and what I read in our newspapers. That's not the same as going there and meeting people."

Mutti Frida waved a dismissive hand at me. "But the people you would meet on such a trip will have been carefully selected. All they will give you is the party line. You'll never meet ordinary people, and if you did, they would be too frightened of the *Stasi* and informers to speak to you."

"Surely, it can't be that bad?"

Mutti Frida pursed her lips. "I think Col has told you how lonely she was because of her father climbing the ranks of the *Stasi*." Col nodded in agreement. "You have to realise that, as a foreigner, you would be a real danger to ordinary Germans. If they speak to you, they are certain to be interrogated and quite probably end up in gaol." Mutti Frida leaned back in her chair. "Then there's the danger to us."

"What do you mean?"

"How did you learn the language?"

"You know that – I made friends with a German family…" I suddenly realised where that might lead. "Oh."

Mutti Frida offered me a grim smile. "Oh, indeed."

I sank back into my chair. "I'd better not enter the competition, then, in case I win." I reached for the flyer so I could throw it in the bin.

"No, Willi, I didn't say that. If you want to enter, please do. I am sure the discipline of an essay will be good for your German – and I will certainly read your essay and provide some comment to help you. If you win, there will be time enough for us to make a decision then."

"I'll help too," Col added.

All of a sudden it seemed everything had flipped, and I was now sort of cornered into writing the essay. *This was weird.*

"Okay, I'll think about it."

Later, I lay in bed thinking about it. If I was going to write an essay, I needed a theme. I remembered Mr. Armitage, my junior school music teacher telling us that music bypassed conscious thought and spoke directly to our emotions and my art teacher had said something similar, that art spoke to our emotions and we saw aspects of ourselves in great art. There was a green shoot of a theme there.

I drifted off to sleep, exploring the ideas that flowed from it.

Late November – early December 1963

The essay competition was still on my mind when I woke. On the bus, I started jotting down some ideas and that continued through the school day. If I were to enter the competition, I had to finish the essay in the next couple of days. When I arrived at Col's house, I told her I had some ideas for the essay I wanted to talk through with her after we had finished our homework. We sat at the kitchen table, me with some Physics and Col with her history. Glancing over, I saw an illustration of a Roman soldier.

"What era of Rome are you studying?" I asked.

"We're not studying Rome; we're exploring Empires and my history teacher wants us to think about them from the perspective of the conquered people." Col glanced across at me.

I nodded for her to go on.

"I decided that as we had read *De Bello Gallico,* I would study the Roman Empire here in Britain and its effect on the native peoples of Britain."

"That should be interesting. Will you be able to find enough material in the school library?"

Col gave me a slightly wry smile. "I went there at lunchtime, but I couldn't find anything useful. I'm going to the town library tomorrow afternoon."

"I could meet you there if you like. I could do my homework and work on the essay whilst you did your research."

Col smiled. "That would be nice. I think Lili will come with me as she wants to study the Russian empire, in particular its colonisation of Poland."

"Oh." I paused for a moment. "But that's still going on, isn't it?"

Col's face stilled as she thought about that. "I suppose so, but Lili wants to cover several centuries as far as I understood from what she was saying."

"I don't know much about the history of central Europe," I mused.

"Well, it's important to Lili so I expect we'll learn a bit more from her." Col gave me a knowing smile. Lili had proved to be quite a talker with people she trusted.

We settled back into our work. Thermal Physics only required a quick read to refresh my knowledge, despite the appalling Imperial units and conversion factors, so I pulled out my notes for the essay. I realised that hiding underneath my current ideas was the assumption that there was a shared cultural language across Europe – for without that there was unlikely to be any sort of understanding. It was a truism that we are alike beneath the skin, but within Europe, for all the different languages and subtleties of *Weltanschauung* between countries, our similarities greatly exceeded our differences. Perhaps that explained why European wars had always been so bitter – they were almost civil wars.

We worked quietly together for an hour before Col pushed back her chair and stretched. "That's enough for today. Let's get supper cooking."

I chopped carrots, swedes and turnips and Col cubed some skirt beef and quickly browned it. Then it got dusted in seasoned flour and into the pressure cooker with beef stock. We'd add the vegetables later. Col pulled three decent-sized potatoes out of the sack in the larder and carefully washed them.

"Aren't you going to peel them?" I asked.

"What can you do with unpeeled potatoes?" She arched her eyebrows.

I thought for a moment. "Baked potatoes. Yum."

"Yes indeed, but with a German twist, as you'll see," Col said enigmatically as she set a clockwork timer for forty minutes, turning the oven on to warm up for the potatoes. She took my hand and led me into the lounge room to the sofa. "Can you think of something we can do to keep us occupied for forty minutes?"

Did they run secret classes for girls where they teach them how to gaze at you from under their eyelashes? I gave her a half-smile and picked up our book from the side table. That earned me a frown and a slap on the arm.

"You had something else in mind, my essay perhaps?" I asked, innocently, returning the book to the table.

"Stop teasing and come here." Col's frown disappeared as she grabbed my arm and pulled us closer together.

After quite some time spent sharing kisses, Col turned round, sitting in my lap, and leaning back, her head on my shoulder, relaxing back into me with a sigh.

We sat there like that, in intimate and gentle silence for a few minutes.

"You know, we are going to break our promise to Mutti sometime in the future," Col murmured.

Oh, my. I thought for a moment, shifting Col to so she did not crush suddenly uncomfortable parts of my anatomy. "I don't think we should do that."

Col stirred and twisted round. "You don't want to have sex with me?" Astonishment and a touch of anger vied with an embarrassed blush.

"Shh." I placed a finger against her lips. "That's not what I said – and no, I don't want to have sex with you."

Col frowned, tensing slightly and I sighed. Even though we now spoke each other's languages well, communication between the sexes still had its problems. "I want to make love with you, not have sex with you."

Col relaxed and I gave her a slightly wry smile.

"But I don't think we should break our promise to Mutti Frida. When the time comes, we should tell her we are moving in that direction."

"What? You want to tell my mother that we're going to have sex…er…make love?" Col scrambled to the other end of the sofa, a mixture of fear, anger, and accusation on her face. "She'd lock me in my room and never let you in the house – or me out of it."

I leaned towards her and took her hand. "If we spoke to her, I don't think she would do that."

Col's face reflected her disbelief.

I tried a different tack. "What would happen if we just went ahead and broke our promise?" I asked. "What would that do to your relationship with your mother?" Col became pensive. "What would it do to my relationship with her?" By now, Col was frowning. "And what would all of that do to us?"

Col's eyes held real pain. She was about to speak and then closed her mouth and thought some more. She was about to say something when the kitchen timer pinged.

"Rats."

She got up and went into the kitchen and I followed her. She carefully reduced the pressure in the pressure cooker and opened it. Rich, beefy smells wafted through the kitchen.

"All right then, put in the vegetables." I did that and she returned the pressure cooker to the stove. Col, cut a deep cross into each of the potatoes, arranged them on an oven tray and slid them into the hot oven, setting the timer for another forty minutes. She turned to me. "You think my mother would be less disturbed by us telling her we were going to be…" she paused for a moment and I could see a faint blush. "Um…intimate than by finding out later?"

"It's also about how we feel about her. I do not wish to lie to your mother, even by omission."

Col sighed. "This is going to be more difficult than I thought."

"Big decisions are always difficult." I took her hand, and we went back and sat side by side on the sofa.

"Our promise to Mutti Frida was not to do something stupid – which I think meant something that could end up with you pregnant."

Col thought about that for a minute. "Yes, I suppose so." Col's voice had an edge of frustration to it.

"Well, there are things we can do that can't end up with you getting pregnant." Col stayed silent, her dark eyes wide pools, filled with unspoken questions. "When you're ready to try something more, you can ask me."

Col pondered what that meant, holding me at arm's length. After a moment, she snuggled up to me and gave me a gentle kiss and then leaned back, releasing an explosive breath. "It's so difficult for me. I can see the other girls get together and talk about boys…and things. But I'm not part of that. And the boys seem mostly to just boast about what they say they've done." Her hand smacked down on to the chair in frustration. "I don't even know what I don't know."

"You can ask me," I said gently. Her head turned and our eyes locked onto each other for several long seconds.

Col paused, contemplating our present and future – and my past, with all that implied. "I need to think about that." Her voice was laced with uncertainty.

I gently squeezed her shoulder. "When you're ready. I'm in no hurry, nor should you be."

Col sighed and snuggled into me and we sat that way until we heard Mutti Frida arrive home. She greeted us, putting a full shopping bag down beside the kitchen table. Smiling at us, she sniffed the aromas permeating the kitchen. "Something smells good."

"Well, you know what it is as you gave us the recipe and pointed out the ingredients yesterday."

Mutti Frida smiled and we started setting the table. It turned out the German twist to baked potatoes was yoghurt with a mixture of herbs, rather than butter, which gave the potatoes a refreshingly sharp flavour.

"Of course, it should be *Sauerrahm* – sour cream, not yoghurt," Mutti Frida said, sighing.

How difficult must it be to hide away from all the normal things in your life? I suspected it was small things like having to substitute yoghurt for sour cream that highlighted this.

After tea, I went over some of the ideas I had for the essay as we sat around the table. We also talked about the communist party in DDR and other Eastern Bloc countries. Mutti Frida was more nuanced than Col, suggesting that picking up the pieces of a shattered society after the war was difficult and some central control of the populace was necessary.

"Do you think your position is influenced by your being part of the ruling elite?" I asked, playing the devil's advocate.

Mutti Frida's head swivelled towards me. She was about to speak when she stopped herself and thought for a couple of seconds, then nodded, ruefully. "I suppose I was part of the ruling elite…in a way." Shaking her head, she went on. "Of course, I had no power, but at first because of what had happened to me, who my parents were, and then because of my husband, I was around the leaders of the Party in Leipzig." She gave me a nod of acknowledgement. "My ideas are probably influenced by that." She

132

paused again, while sadness seeped into her face and her voice grew softer. "But the camps influenced me more. There we had no control and only one decision to make: to work together trying to survive or to die alone."

I watched the deep sorrow filling her eyes.

"And even when we worked together, many of us still died."

Col's hand crept across the table to hold her mother's.

"I understand what you are saying," Col said, gently. "But that central control hasn't been needed in West Germany, has it? And they seem more successful than the East, from what I have seen and read."

"Perhaps…" Mutti Frida nodded, deep in thought. "Perhaps, though, it depends on how you measure success."

That night I lay in bed thinking about our discussion and what it could have meant. There were clear, some might say irreconcilable, differences between east and west, but could I justify the central argument of my essay? It was to be centred around the shared cultural language of Europe and the power of the various arts in that shared culture to speak to our emotions and so increase international understanding. I would focus on music as that seemed to speak directly to our emotions. With no Google to quickly find quotations to support my thesis, I would have to see if the library had a copy of the Oxford Dictionary of Quotations – a once well-used book, known in my family as the ODQ, that had sat on a shelf in my old life, although unopened for quite some years, thanks to Google.

I hurried to the bus stop after school and caught a number six that would take me into the Herne Bay town centre. When I arrived at the library, I joined Col and Lili at their table.

"Hello, Lili." She gave me a brief smile before returning to her notes.

"How is the Roman research going, Col?"

She leaned back, stretching in her chair. "There's not much information about the society that existed before the Romans arrived." She gazed, contemplatively, into the distance. "Perhaps it's because none of the Celts' few writings survived. There's more information about them in *De Bello Gallico* than any books here." Col gestured at a couple of books on the table. "Anyway, it seems from what I've read so far that in some ways, the Celtic people may have conquered themselves."

"What?" That was completely paradoxical, but I saw Lili smiling: it seemed they had already talked about this.

Col smiled, pleased to have surprised me. "What I've read suggests that the Celts adopted the new Roman ways without much pressure from the Romans."

"What about Boudicca and the other revolts?"

"Well, the entire military campaign in England only lasted about the first forty years out of the four hundred the Romans were here. And even during the military campaign, the rulers of the Celtic tribes seemed to adopt the Roman way and that set the tone for everyone else."

I considered this for a moment. "Hmm, I think I see what you mean." I turned to Lili. "How are you doing?"

She shook her head in frustration. "There's almost nothing here about central European history. I've found a little bit in the encyclopaedia but that's all, so I'll have to ask my parents if they can help me find some books."

I left them to it and went over to the library desk. Unfortunately, the younger librarian was on duty – and she recognised me as the boy wanting books in German. "Yes?" I heard the disdain in her voice.

I pushed down on the annoyance surging up from my young brain. "Do you have an Oxford Dictionary of Quotations here?"

"What?" She hadn't even raised her head.

I stopped my eye-roll before it started and repeated my question. I heard a bit of an edge in my voice none-the-less, but I couldn't help it.

"Oh, yes," she said, indifferently. "In the reference collection." She waved her hand vaguely towards the library stacks.

I could stand here and argue with her for more detailed directions, which would gain me nothing, or I could explore the reference collection. I walked towards the end of the stacks, watching as the Dewy Decimal labels counted down towards zero and the reference section.

"Can I help you?" The older librarian appeared from within the stacks, leaving a trolley piled high with books.

"Thank you, I'm trying to find the Oxford Dictionary of Quotations."

"That's just down here. Follow me." She started off and then stopped, turning back towards me. "You're the boy that wanted books in German, aren't you?"

"Yes."

She glanced towards the main desk. "I'm sorry that Mrs. Price was so unhelpful. She has never recovered from losing her husband to the Nazis in 1945. They'd only been married a few months..." Her voice trailed off.

I didn't know what to say, so I said nothing. After a moment, the librarian turned and walked between two stacks. She ran her finger along a shelf, stopping to pull out a familiar, fat volume.

"Here you go," she said, smiling. "Do you know how to use it?"

"Yes, thank you."

She handed me the book, a raised eyebrow signalling some scepticism, and walked back to her trolley.

I took the ODQ back to the table where Col and Lili were working.

I plonked the book on the table, making Lili start. "What's the book, Willi?"

"It's a book of quotations. I'm trying to find material for an essay on art and culture's benefit to society."

Lili raised her eyebrows. "That sounds a bit deep."

Col glanced up from a map she was poring over. "It's for an essay competition – in German."

"Oh." Lili glanced at me and went back to her homework.

I started searching for quotable quotes, noting down ones I thought useful. After a while, I had a dozen or so, including one by Goethe that I thought might be useful to place beneath the essay title. *Nichts kann mit dem neuen Leben verglichen werden, das die Entdeckung eines anderen Landes für einen nachdenklichen Menschen bietet. (Nothing can be compared to the new life that the discovery of another country provides for a thoughtful person).*

I would be suggesting that art and music, through our shared European culture, was able to help take us to another country – to Europe, a country we shared. It occurred to my old brain that this was a bit paradoxical, given Britain's exit from the European community in 2020.

Eventually, Col roused me. "Come on Willi, we must head home to get tea ready. I'll see you in school tomorrow, Lili."

"Okay, I'm not finding much here for my project." I heard Lili's frustration in her voice. "Mama is asking around her friends to see if they have any Polish history books." Her disappointment at the library was palpable. "I might need to change the topic of my project."

I shared a sympathetic smile. "I hope your parents can turn up some books to help, Lili."

On the way out I returned the ODQ to the loans desk. The older librarian was there.

"I hope that was useful." She sounded a bit sceptical.

I smiled. "Thank you, yes. I have a dozen or so quotations for my essay on European art and culture." From her expression, it was clear that she wasn't quite sure what to make of me.

Outside, we split up, Lili heading for her home, Col and I for hers. It was about a twenty-minute walk through the town and up the Downs. We chatted about Col's project and my essay. We started getting tea ready as soon as we arrived home and Mutti Frida arrived not long afterwards.

When we had cleared the table after tea, I pulled out my essay notes.

"If I'm going to get this essay written in time, I will need to work on it tonight." I hoped she would understand.

"That's okay, Willi. I can work on my project." She retrieved her school bag from her room, and we worked opposite one another, with Mutti Frida's radio playing a concert in the background.

After about an hour Col stretched. "You'll have to go soon." Her eyes dropped back down to a map she must have traced in the library.

"What's that?" I asked.

"It's the Roman road network across England and Wales. There's a road called Watling Street that linked *Londinium* to the ports of *Dubris* and *Rutupiae*." Col smiled at her own ability to flaunt these Roman names at me.

I raised a questioning eyebrow in return.

"All right – London, Dover and Richborough. Watling Street also went here to Reculver…umm," her finger traced the road on the map, "*Regulbium*, that is."

I could see she was deeply involved in this investigation of Roman Britain. "It's terribly interesting though, because the Roman road was constructed on top of an ancient track that had been used for thousands of years. Most of the other Roman roads were also built on ancient tracks. It's just one example of the way the Romans absorbed a country into their culture." She moved the map and flipped a couple of pages in a book. "Did you know the Romans adopted many of the Celtic gods into their pantheon? The Romans called Bath *Aquae Sulis* – the springs of Sulis – after the Celtic god of the hot springs. I'm starting to feel that the cultural adoption was not just the Celts adopting Roman ways."

Now that was an interesting idea.

"It seems that empires are not just the oppression of the conquered, but also the adoption of some of the oppressed culture by the conqueror." I smiled, recalling how worked up Lili was about the Russians in Poland.

Col paused for thought, then continued, "I think it probably works more or less like that in all empires."

"I think you're probably right, but that doesn't make it any easier for the conquered." Col gave a slightly distracted nod; her attention was back down at her papers.

I started packing up my stuff. Col's head was still down in her project. "I'd better get going, Col."

She smiled and helped me into my coat. "Where's your torch, Willi?"

I pulled the torch Col had given me for Christmas out of my school bag with a flourish and turned it on. "Ta da."

"I think you need a new battery – it's quite dim."

She was right, I'd have to pick up a new one from the shops, but even with a new battery, the torch was like a glow-worm compared to the LED torches from my old life: just one more thing I missed.

Mutti Frida came out of the lounge room. "We'll see you tomorrow, Willi. Take care on the way home." She kissed me on the forehead and returned to her concert on the radio, giving Col and me some privacy to say goodbye a bit more intimately, which we did.

***

I worked on my essay at school the following day and had a rough version finished by the time I caught the bus home. As I was well ahead of my homework, I got stuck into writing the first draft whilst Col did her homework, and I was able to give it to Col and Mutti Frida to read after tea.

"It's very good, Willi." Col smiled and passed it to Mutti Frida.

I sat there, waiting for Mutti Frida's comments.

"Hmm...yes, the logic and flow are excellent. I like the quotations you have used and that you've sourced them from across Europe." She smiled. "But I think it needs a bit of polish and some tweaks in a couple of places." Mutti Frida pointed out several places she felt the wording was a bit clumsy or the meaning less than crystal clear. I took it to school the following day and did some polishing. Then I wrote out a fair copy for Mutti Frida and Col to read that evening. After some discussion with them, I decided I had my essay. *But should I send it in, wouldn't that risk the exposure of Col and Mutti Frida?*

I leaned back in my chair. "So ... Col, Mutti Frida – should I send this into the competition?"

Col gave me a puzzled look. "Why not?"

Mutti Frida huffed. "You're worried about exposing us if you win, Willi?"

"Of course. I don't think there's much chance of that as there will be much more experienced essay writers than me."

Mutti Frida nodded. "It's a good essay, Willi. If you do win, you can always turn down the prize."

"You think I should send it in, then?"

Col reached across and squeezed my hand encouragingly. "Go on, Willi. I know you like testing yourself academically against other people."

"If you're sure ...?" I gave them both a querying stare.

They both nodded.

"Okay. I'll post it in the morning on the way to school."

At home that evening, I asked my mother for an envelope and stamp.

"What are you posting?"

"I'm entering an essay competition and I need to send off my entry."

"Oh. Will you let me read your essay?" she asked, tentatively, not wanting to intrude into my life where I didn't want her.

I smiled. "Of course you can." And handed over the pages.

She flipped the pages and peered up at me, smiling.

"Well, you got me there, Will." She handed the pages back to me. "What is it about?"

"My essay is about our shared cultural language." I dug out the original flyer and handed it to her.

"You could win a trip to East Germany?"

"Well, I suppose so, but that's not likely. I did it mostly as an exercise – I like writing essays."

"Did you write this in English and then translate it?"

"No – I think that if I did that it would show in the language construction."

My mother nodded. "That's probably true, but I've never been so fluent in another language to have a sense of that. I still find it hard to believe the speed with which you learned German." Her eyes lingered on me and I felt her speculation about the changes I had undergone. "I'll get you that envelope and stamp."

She turned away, then back. "You should write a covering letter for your essay, giving a bit of information about yourself, how long you've been studying German and that you have a German friend."

"You think so?"

"Yes, I do. I'll get you some sheets of letter writing paper."

This presented a bit of a problem. There was no way I could talk about having a German friend as this could endanger Col and Mutti Frida, so I would restrict the letter to information about me and my school.

My mother brought me an envelope and stamp, so I addressed it and licked the stamp, sticking it on. I folded my essay and was about to put it in the envelope, when I realised I should write out a copy to keep – no photocopiers here, yet another technology I missed. Once that was done, I started writing the letter.

My mother wandered off and I was able to write the letter, giving information about my school and German teacher but no mention of Col and Mutti Frida or how long I had been learning German. I had just finished sealing the envelope with the essay and letter in it when my mother came back into the kitchen. "Would you like a hot chocolate?"

"Yes, please."

My mother put some milk on to warm. "Oh – you've sealed up the envelope. I wanted to read your letter."

"It's just a letter about me – you already know everything I could put in there." I smiled.

My mother raised an eyebrow at me. "Well, I may know most things about you, Will, but that's not the same as understanding you, is it?"

I applied my policy of answering this sort of question with a question. "Do you think we ever understand anybody – even ourselves?"

My mother was silent for a while, searching my face. "I think the answer to that is probably not. I don't think we are ever sufficiently honest even with ourselves to permit true self-understanding, so how can we truly understand someone else?" Her eyes lingered on my face until a loud hissing from the stove announced that the milk was boiling over. My mother rushed to retrieve it and mop the stovetop. I put the envelope in my school bag.

"Here you go, Will."

"Thank you. I think I'll take it up to my room as I'm a bit behind on my homework due to the essay."

"Okay, Will. Lights out by 9:30, please. Sleep well."

"Night, night."

Up in my room, I revised standard integrals and differentials for about half an hour, resurfacing and polishing old knowledge from deep in my brain, and then went to bed.

***

Christmas was on the horizon and that meant spending several days around my father, a thought which made me increasingly anxious. But I was also starting to feel a real anxiety about my school results. I had started the term in the 'O' level group but had been bumped up into the A level classes in Maths and Physics, despite not wanting to move. I should probably have been in the A level English, German and French classes as well, but that hadn't happened – yet. As the term drew to a close, I had no idea what my results would be on my report and the events of the previous year came back to haunt me. Whilst my old brain knew my father was, hopefully, not going to be involved, my young brain was becoming increasingly anxious and that afternoon Col sensed there was a problem.

We were working on our homework when Col slapped a book on to the table. "Willi, where are you?"

I jerked in my seat, startled out of my fugue of angst. "What?"

"You were staring off into space – I spoke to you, twice, and you didn't hear!"

"Sorry."

Col's face showed her concern. "What's bothering you?" she asked, softly.

I leaned back, eyes closed, and flexed my neck and shoulders which were painfully tense. Talking about my anxieties with Col was difficult. I knew she would be concerned that I might be heading into another suicidal episode – but not talking about what was making me anxious would convince her that I was. I opened my eyes and sighed, before recalling my worries.

I saw a flicker of fear in Col's eyes.

"You remember the explosion my report caused a year ago?"

Col nodded. "But you must be doing well, Willi. You've been bumped up to O level in everything except the subjects you're in the A level classes for. If you weren't doing well, they would surely have moved you back down, wouldn't they?"

I breathed out, heavily. "Yes, I suppose so. But in senior school, there is no form order posted so I don't know where I am against the other people in the class." I almost heard the whine in my voice, which disgusted me.

Col leaned across the table, gently taking my hand. "Does that matter, Willi? I'm sure your report will be exceptional." She stroked the back of my hand, her face full of concern. "In any case, your father won't be involved in talking about it, will he?"

"No, I suppose not – at least I hope not." Col's hand continued gently stroking mine.

"Thank you, Col. I'm sorry I'm so insecure about this sort of thing." I gave a self-deprecating laugh. "You'd have thought with all my experience I would be over such things by now, but my teenage brain has such strong emotions I find it difficult to manage them."

"I wouldn't know about that. I don't have your unique perspective." Col smiled at me and then tapped the back of my hand. "Come on, let's get tea underway and then have a cuddle."

Tonight, we were having another of my mother's recipes – Toad-in-the-Hole with peas and broad beans. Once that was underway, we cuddled together on the sofa, waiting for Mutti Frida to arrive home.

"If you win the competition, will you go to East Germany?"

"No, Col, you know I can't do anything that might risk exposing you. Anyway, it's most unlikely that I am going to win. There will be students who have been studying German for years longer than I have."

We sat and chatted for a while until the timer pinged to get the Toad-in-the-Hole out of the oven. Mutti Frida was always home about this time, so we turned the oven down to keep it hot and started the water heating for the peas and broad beans. We sat down again and cuddled together with our current book, waiting for her to arrive.

After about half an hour, Col glanced at the clock. "I wonder what's keeping her? She's usually home well before now."

"Perhaps something is keeping her at the shop," I suggested.

"Perhaps. I wonder why she hasn't phoned?"

We carried on reading and Mutti Frida finally arrived after another half an hour. "I'm sorry about this, children." I could see she was quite flustered – more than you'd expect because she was delayed at work. We hurried to get tea together and sat down.

Col voiced our concerns, "Is everything all right, Mutti?"

"Yes, everything's fine," Mutti Frida snapped back, her voice sharp-edged with tension.

I had never seen Mutti Frida be short with Col before and her attitude was upsetting Col, who fidgeted and frowned opposite me. I gave Col a supportive smile and the meal descended into silence.

Mutti Frida kept her head down, avoiding eye contact with either of us. Eventually, the tension became too much for Col and she put down her knife and fork, got up and went and knelt beside her mother's chair.

Still, Mutti Frida ignored her, so Col gently took her mother's hands, making her release her cutlery. "Mutti, what is wrong?" Col asked, softly. "You are frightening me."

Mutti Frida took a deep breath. "I'm sorry. It has nothing to do with anything you have done, my dearest Col." She paused, glancing at me over the table and I saw fear in her eyes. Our eyes locked for a second, questions of loyalty passing between us. Then she turned back at her daughter. "You remember when we first arrived, we were asked a lot of questions by British security?"

I hadn't known that, but it made sense.

Col nodded.

"When I left work today, they met me in the street and bustled me into a big car. They wanted to know more about why we fled your father and what evidence I had that he was a Nazi war criminal." The experience had shaken her, and her voice was tight, her words clipped. "I could tell them nothing new, but they kept asking." She stopped, trying to calm herself. "I'd told them before that I had hidden all the evidence in Leipzig before we fled. It was too dangerous to carry that with us in case we were caught – it was our insurance." She paused, thinking, her eyes moving around the room, searching for understanding. "I can't work out what they want. Why do they keep asking me the same questions and why this sudden renewed interest in me?" I heard the frustration and fear in her voice.

I stared across the table at her. "Perhaps it has something to do with the attempt on JFK's life?" I suggested.

"I don't see how it can be…" Her voice trailed off as she pondered what was happening. "It was a Hungarian that shot JFK, not a German." Her voice echoed her puzzlement. She lifted Col's chin. "They did tell me that your father is searching for us, using his position in the *Stasi* to gather information from outside the DDR."

Col's eyes tightened at that news.

Mutti Frida shook her head. "Anyhow, finish your dinner, you two. Don't let my worries destroy your appetite."

Col went and sat down, and we resumed eating, but the undercurrent of fear remained.

Col steered the conversation towards mundane matters, trying to ease the tension. "When does your term end, Willi? Mine ends in two weeks."

"Mine, too."

"Would you like to join us on Christmas Eve again, Willi?" Mutti Frida asked.

"Oh, yes please." Sharing their Christmas Eve celebration last year had been the brightest moment in a dark and troubled time.

"Well, please ask your mother to ring me about it, Willi."

I smiled gratefully. "I certainly will."

The following day, Col was bouncing with excitement when I arrived, waving a stiff card at me. "We've been invited to a Christmas party at Lili's house, Willi, on the Saturday after school breaks up. It's a proper grown-up party in the evening. Mutti is going as well."

"Oh yes?"

She handed me the card – a beautifully scripted formal invitation on stiff card. Col's mood switched suddenly. "But I will have to go as a boy – I want to be able to dress up as a girl and show you how pretty I am." I heard the sulk in her voice.

I gathered her into my arms. "I know how beautiful you are, Col. You don't need to dress up for me to see that."

"But I want to dress up. Boys' clothes are so boring." Frustration with her situation coloured her voice and her hands tightened as she leaned forward on the back of a chair.

I turned her towards me and lifted her chin, brushing her lips with a kiss. "Come on, let's get our homework done."

She gusted out a sigh. "I don't have much to do – we've had our end of term tests in everything except Maths." Col's face showed her insecurity about this subject. "Could you help me with quadratic equations, please?"

"Of course." And we lost ourselves in the three solution methods and three types of equations, keeping us both busy until we stopped to get the evening meal ready.

Early to mid-December 1963

Gradually, December accelerated towards Christmas and school was finished for the year. Col brought her school report home on the last day and gave it to Mutti Frida that evening. When her mother opened it, there was an accompanying sheet of paper. After reading the report and smiling at Col, she unfolded the letter. After a while, she glanced up.

"You are doing so well that they want you to move to the grammar school in Canterbury."

Col gasped in surprise.

I smiled. "Well done, Col." I knew from working with her that she was bright.

Col gave me a worried glance, then turned to her mother. "Can we afford it, Mutti?"

Mutti Frida searched through the letter again. "It doesn't say what the fees are."

I leaned across the table. "I think it's free – apart from books and uniform, which you pay for at the secondary modern school here."

Mutti Frida glanced over at me. "Are you sure?"

I shook my head. "No, but I'm sure they want to speak to you about this."

Mutti Frida read the letter again. "Yes, you're right. They want me to phone on Monday."

"Col, we could travel to Canterbury on the same bus." I said, excitedly.

Col smiled at me.

Then another even more exciting idea occurred to me. "Mutti Frida, perhaps Col could become a girl at her new school?"

Two heads snapped round, Col's eyes flaring with hope and Mutti Frida's with fear. Neither said a word.

"It's worth thinking about as a possibility, isn't it?" I stared between Col and her mother.

Mutti Frida found her voice. "No, it is too dangerous."

"But Mutti…" Col's voice ached with hope.

"No, Col. It's too dangerous."

Col opened her mouth, as if to say something.

Mutti Frida's voice brooked no discussion. "Enough."

She then turned to me, a deep frown creasing her forehead.

The glance that Col and I shared was forlorn at this denial. The conversation at tea was a bit subdued. I silently chided myself for spouting the idea without first talking it over with Col. Together, we might have come up with a way to lead Mutti Frida gently to support Col in becoming a girl again.

Now that school was over, I had time for Christmas shopping. This was a bit easier as I had my Premium Bond winnings to fall back on and I ended up using a small amount to buy Col a delicate gold chain necklace and Mutti Frida a new folding, umbrella as hers was falling apart.

Lili's party would run late, so I was to sleep at Col's house that night. We wore coats, hats and gloves over our smart clothes and walked through the chilled, blustery darkness down to Lili's house. It felt like a storm was developing.

The party started out as great fun. Lili's much younger brother was in bed and so mostly Lili, Col and I spent time together drinking lemonade and snacking from the delicious mix of English and Polish food in the buffet. Neither Col nor I knew anything about Polish food and so Lili educated us.

"These sausages are called *kabanos* – they've got a smoky flavour and go well with that *oscypek* – which is a smoked cheese."

Col smiled at the selection of sausages. "They're almost German," she said, picking one up.

"What are those?" I asked pointing at rings of bread.

"They're *bagels,* sort of like bread rolls – and you have to try some of my aunt's *pierogi. "* She pointed at a plate of things that looked like a small pasty.

Col eyed them a bit suspiciously "What's in them, Lili?"

"These ones are savoury minced pork and those ones down there," Lili pointed to the far end of the table where there were recognisable mince pies and even a trifle. "are cherry ones."

Lili continued loading our plates before we retreated to our corner to eat, plates perched awkwardly on our knees. The eating stifled the conversation until Mrs. Wiśniewski and Mutti Frida came over to where we were sitting.

Mrs. Wiśniewski checked out our plates and smiled at Lili. "I see my daughter's been educating you about the food of our country."

I swallowed my mouthful of *pirogi.* "Yes, thank you, it's all delicious."

"Excellent." She turned to Mutti Frida. "Come with me Frida, I'd like you to meet one of my friends who has connections to the fashion world in Paris."

Mutti Frida, smiled and allowed herself to be led away.

Once we finished eating, Lili gathered up our plates, depositing them on the buffet table. "Come with me, there's someone I want Willi to meet." She pulled Col and me through the crowd until we stood close to a group of people in the far corner of the lounge room.

"Wujek Brajan?"

A large bear of a man turned round when Lili spoke to him. He had a scar across his face: it was the car salesman.

"To mój przyjaciel Willi, który chciałby być pilotem myśliwca." (This is my friend Will who wants to be a fighter pilot.")

"Thank you, Lili. Please speak English in front of your English friends." He turned towards us. "Please call me Uncle Brian – which is what Liliana just called me, in Polish." He examined us more closely. "Ah." A smile of recognition lit up his face. "One likes fast cars but the other prefers fast planes. Eh?" His smile was slightly distorted with the scar that crept to the corner of his mouth.

I nodded, slightly embarrassed that Lili was pushing the fighter pilot thing when she had told us her relative wanted to put that behind him. Given the scar on his face, I could understand why that might be so.

Uncle Brian smiled at Col. "Perhaps I can arrange for you to go for a drive in an E-type sometime?"

Col's eyes widened with excitement and she nodded. "Yes, please."

The smile faded as he turned to me and his voice darkened. "Being a fighter pilot is not so glorious as you might think. Perhaps one day you and I will sit down and talk about that." His face was sombre, then he inhaled deeply. "But not today." His voice lightened and he smiled at the three of us, lifting Lili by the waist and twirling her round. "Today is for smiling and dancing with pretty girls, enjoying friendship and *wódka*." He placed Lili daintily back on her feet, her face flushed. "Off you go, enjoy yourselves. I need to refill my glass." As he turned away, his smile evaporated and his shoulders tensed. I had the feeling he was escaping from us because we had stirred up memories that he wished to stay buried.

We went back to our corner and replenished our glasses with lemonade. Mutti Frida emerged smiling and slightly flushed from the throng. "Are you enjoying yourselves?"

We nodded and she slipped back into the crowd.

Lili smiled. "I'm sure your mother is speaking Polish to my family and friends and that would delight them." Her smile broadened. "Perhaps also she is enjoying the vodka."

I excused myself and headed off to the toilet. When I came out into the shadowy corridor, I saw Lili and Col standing in the hallway, where a bunch of mistletoe was hanging. It is an English tradition that you may kiss anyone under a bunch of mistletoe at Christmas. It seemed that Lili's family had adopted this decoration and knew of its significance.

Lili put her hands on Col's shoulders and leaned forward only to have Col gently push her away. I walked out of the shadows and when Lili saw me, she turned and disappeared back into the party, obviously flustered and hurt by Col's rejection.

"What was that about?" Col frowned in confusion. There was a window seat in the half-lit hallway, and I pulled Col across to sit there and explained about mistletoe.

Col's concern showed in her eyes. "Lili was caught up in that and decided to push along the relationship with me as a boy?"

I nodded and sighed – life was complicated. "We need to find a way to let her know you are still friends – just not that sort of friend."

Col was distraught. "I want Lili as a friend, but I don't know what to do now." Her voice acquired an edge of frustration. "I told Mutti that this was a problem, but she wouldn't listen." Col dissolved into tears and without thinking I drew her into a hug, holding her while her tears soaked my neck. After a minute or so, Col's tears slowly faded. "What are we going to do, Willi?"

I shook my head. "I don't know, Col, but we'll need to talk to her." I leaned in and gave her a gentle kiss, trying to lend her some emotional strength.

"Oh, God!"

The voice startled us, and I glanced up to see Lili standing in the hallway, her mouth gaping in shock.

"Now I know why you pushed me away, Col." A shudder passed through her. "I knew the two of you were close, but I didn't realise just how close or in what way." And she rushed away, leaving Col and me sitting there, minds in turmoil: we had just made a difficult situation so much worse.

We sat there for a minute or so, silenced by the enormity of the problem we had just created.

Col started talking but had to clear her throat and start again. "Please Willi, find Mutti and ask her to come out here. We need her help."

As I had no idea what to do, asking Mutti Frida seemed like a good idea. I went back into the party throng trying to find her. Before that, I caught sight of Lili, who scowled balefully and turned away. Mutti Frida was deep in conversation with some of Lili's parents' Polish friends. I was able to catch her eye and told her, in German, that Col needed her urgently.

Mutti Frida's eyes widened, and she quickly excused herself, grabbing my hand. "Where is Col? What's wrong?"

I didn't answer but guided her out into the dimly lit hallway.

She saw Col and rushed to her side. "What's wrong, Col?"

Col's eyes pleaded with me and I grasped her hand. "Lili tried to kiss Col under the mistletoe and she pushed her away, which upset Lili. Col told you that Lili had a crush on her ... er ... him."

146

Col's hand squeezed mine, urging me continue.

Mutti Frida must have sensed our silent communication. "There's more?"

I took a deep breath. "Col was upset too, and was crying, so I gave her a hug and then ... well, Lili saw us kissing." It came out in a guilty and embarrassed rush.

Mutti Frida closed her eyes and remained still for a few seconds.

"Well, I don't think we can talk to Lili during this party. Stay here for a minute or two, children and then I'll come and find you so we can thank our hosts for their hospitality before we leave." She stood up, caressing Col's cheek and squeezing my shoulder. "I'm sure we can find a way out of this, but it won't be today."

After Mutti Frida disappeared back into the party, Col and I sat dejectedly in silence. My old brain was insisting homosexuality wasn't a big deal, but my memories of the 60's told me this was a different time, with starkly different attitudes. We – and our families – could get into all sorts of trouble if it were suggested Col and I were homosexual. After a minute or so, Mutti Frida appeared in the doorway, with Mrs. Wiśniewski beside her. "I told Mrs. Wiśniewski that you were feeling unwell, Col, and that we have to leave the party a bit early."

"Col's certainly a bit flushed. I hope he's feeling better in the morning."

Mutti Frida nodded. "I'm sure he'll be fine. Come along." She glanced at us both, pointedly. "I said your goodbyes and thanks to Lili, so we can leave straight away."

"Will you be all right to walk home? I could drive you." Mrs. Wiśniewski offered, kindly.

"Thank you, Daria. I'm sure the walk and some fresh sea air will help Col. Come along children. Put on your coats, hats and gloves."

Mutti Frida bustled us out of the house. Col started to say something as the door closed but Mutti Frida hushed her with a squeeze of the hand, so we walked in silence for a few minutes through the cold and windy streets. Eventually, Mutti Frida gusted out a sigh of frustration that was whisked away in the blustery air. "I found Lili and told her that what she thought she saw was not what really happened." Mutti Frida drew us along for a dozen more silent steps, allowing that to sink in. "She likes you both a great deal and is prepared to come tomorrow and listen to what we have to say. Until then, she told me she won't talk about this to anyone."

Mutti Frida took a few more steps before glancing down at the two of us. "We just need to decide what it is we will tell her."

We walked on in silence, thinking about that.

When we arrived back at Col's house, Mutti Frida warmed some milk and made us all a hot chocolate. We sat at the kitchen table, gazing at one another.

Col took a deep breath. "We have to tell her I'm a girl." She stared pleadingly at Mutti Frida.

Mutti Frida closed her eyes. "Col, we can't. What if she tells someone? Remember what MI6 told me: your father is searching for us and I am sure there are Eastern Bloc agents here in England." She jerked to a stop with a worried frown. "An *émigré* Polish community would be a good place to hide such an agent."

Col was aghast. "Lili's family hate the Russians."

Mutti Frida nodded. "I know, Col. But what about their friends?"

Col stared at her mother for a few seconds and then collapsed back into her chair. "But we have to tell Lili. What she thinks is terrible."

I turned to Mutti Frida. "But you've half told Lili already."

Mutti Frida frowned. "What do you mean?"

"Well, you said you told her that what she thought she saw wasn't the reality, or something like that. What is she going to think now?"

Mutti Frida's face paled slightly as she realised what I was getting at.

I took her hand from where it was resting beside her mug. "Lili's an intelligent girl and I am sure she's pondering what you said to her."

Col leaned into the conversation again, as I continued arguing her case.

"She probably won't guess that Col's a girl, but she might." I gave Mutti Frida's hand a gentle squeeze of encouragement. "But I'm certain she will expect an explanation in the morning."

Mutti Frida closed her eyes and shook her head. "But it's too dangerous to tell her the truth."

Col picked up Mutti Frida's other hand. "I don't think it is." Col peered at me. "We've already told you Lili and her family hate the Russians and all the puppet Eastern Bloc governments. If we told her the truth I think – no, I'm certain – she would understand the need for absolute secrecy."

I gave Mutti Frida's hand another encouraging squeeze. "Col's right, you know. Lili and her family hate the Russians. She would not betray you."

Mutti Frida nodded in silent agreement: she had been speaking to Lili's family and Polish friends. Perhaps she picked up on their hatred of Russia.

"But she's so young." I heard the fear and tension in Mutti Frida's voice.

I put a light pressure on her hand until she turned towards me. "But so am I – and so is Col."

Mutti Frida pulled her hands from us and picked up her mug. Taking a sip, her eyes moved between us and then shook her head. "Yes, you are both young and you have kept our secret – up until today when you did something that may have exposed us."

I gave Col a chagrined frown. She frowned back and turned to Mutti Frida. "Yes – and we've learned a lesson through that mistake. We'll be more guarded in future." Her eyes flicked across me in irritation. "But what Willi said is true. Lili will not rest until she gets to the truth behind your words."

Mutti Frida sighed. "I should not have said what I did, that is clear, but I felt I needed to say something to stop Lili from explaining to her parents why she was upset." She picked up her mug and took another sip of chocolate. "What this needs," she said, pausing to savour the chocolate, "is some Schnapps." She rose and went to the dresser, retrieving a bottle from one of its cupboards. Returning to the table, she lifted the bottle to gauge its content and then poured a generous tot into her chocolate. She recorked the bottle, swirled the mug and took a sip, letting out a sigh of contentment. "That's better."

Col leaned forward and sniffed Mutti Frida's mug. "Oof. That's quite strong."

Mutti Frida chuckled. "Perhaps, but what's the English?" She stopped, thinking. "Ah yes. It warms the cockles of my heart."

Col's face showed her frustration at this language without logic. "That's a very odd saying; we dug up cockles on the beach and pickled them in vinegar. How can a heart have cockles – shellfish?"

I shrugged. "I don't know. English is a strange language."

Col gave me a friendly frown and then turned to Mutti Frida. "Anyway, back to Lili. When she comes tomorrow, we have to swear her to secrecy and then tell her I'm a girl."

Mutti Frida shook her head.

I took Mutti Frida's hand. "I think we have to. I can't see what else we can do without it causing more problems." I stopped, thinking. "It won't matter to me if Lili thinks Col and I are homosexual as I don't mix with the local kids apart from Col and Lili."

I stared at Mutti Frida. "But think about how it would affect Col if Lili told her friends at school what she saw tonight. The bullying would start up again only much worse."

Mutti Frida's eyes practically bored into me.

"I don't think you want that happening to Col."

Seconds of silence followed. Eventually, Mutti Frida almost muttered. "Would that be better or worse than being thrown into gaol in East Germany?"

I peered over at Col, hoping for some inspiration that was not forthcoming. "I don't know about that. But I know that if you stay here and

149

don't explain things to Lili, life will be awful for Col. And what about the future? Are you going to make her hide herself forever?" I realised that I was pushing Mutti Frida hard, perhaps too hard and tried to soften my words with a smile.

Mutti Frida was silent again before standing up. "Well, I need to sleep on this and so do both of you. Come on, we need to make up the sofa for Willi."

Col and I shared our frustration in a shrug and a sigh. Then we went through the now-familiar ritual of setting up my bed on the lounge room sofa. Later, I lay huddled under the blankets in the dark. I was certain we could trust Lili as she would understand Col's situation.

As I drifted into sleep, I half decided to tell Lili myself if Mutti Frida wouldn't. Whilst that would make life difficult between Mutti Frida and me, it seemed the best option for Col.

***

I woke early, stomach churning as rain slashed against the house: the storm had arrived. My old brain must have been gnawing away at the problem during the night and now my young brain was reacting to the stress. *Could I go against Mutti Frida on this?* It had seemed so possible last night, but now, in the cold light of day, I was far less certain.

Eventually, Mutti Frida stirred and I helped with breakfast. The three of us were all feeling tense and we sat silently around the breakfast table. After a while, Mutti Frida put down her coffee cup. "You are prepared to trust Lili with our safety?"

Col swallowed and glanced across the table to me. I nodded my support. Col cleared her throat. "Yes."

"What do you think, Willi?"

"I don't think we have any other options."

"Hmph. It's not 'we' in this situation, Willi. It's just Col and I who are at risk." There was a sharpness to Mutti Frida's voice, the tension creating an edge. I stared down at my half-eaten toast, shamefaced after including myself in their danger.

Col pounced on her mother. "Mutti, that's not fair," she said, her voice showing the hurt she felt on my account. "You know Willi would do anything for us."

Mutti Frida's eyes held Col's until Mutti Frida let out an explosive breath. "You're right, Col." She smiled, wryly. "I'm sorry, Willi, that was uncalled for."

Just then the phone rang. Mutti Frida got up and answered it. The conversation was short and mostly one-sided. Mutti Frida put down the

150

phone. "Lili will be here in an hour. Her mother is dropping her off because of the storm."

We sat, silent, at the table, our faces filled with indecision, fear – but also, at least for Col and me, perhaps a touch of hope.

After about a minute, Mutti Frida stood, clapping her hands. "Don't just sit there, we have the breakfast things to clean up and your bed to unmake, Willi." She opened the pantry door. "Oh, and I'd like you to pop up to the corner shop and buy one of those nice fruit cakes, so we have something to offer Lili. Eating together helps strengthen bonds of friendship."

We got busy cleaning up the house and then Col and I donned hats and coats and grabbed a shopping bag. We would share Mutti Frida's rather tatty umbrella to walk up to Mr. Searle's corner shop. Once out of the house, Col turned to me, wrestling with the umbrella in the wind.

"Do you think Mutti is going to tell Lili the truth.?"

"I'm not sure, Col. But I do think she is leaning that way." I took a deep breath. "If she doesn't, I've been thinking that we – that is – I should tell her."

Suddenly Col was no longer beside me and I was getting wet. I turned and she was standing a couple of paces behind me, consternation on her face. I quickly walked back to her and ducked under the umbrella. I wanted to take her hand, but we were in public.

Col's mouth worked a couple of times before she almost stuttered out, "You'd go against Mutti?"

I nodded. "I couldn't bear to see you being bullied again, if Lili told everyone what she saw." I tried to send her waves of love and confidence through my eyes. "Besides, you think we can trust Lili to keep your secret, don't you?"

We started walking again. "Yes, yes I do. But…" I saw that Col was struggling. "But we've seen how easy it is to make a mistake. Do you think Lili can manage not to do that?"

I thought about this for a moment. "You know her much more deeply than I do, so what do you think?"

We walked on for a bit in silence and, just before we got to the corner shop, Col turned to me. "I think Lili is no more likely to make a mistake than we are. We will need to talk with her about our mistakes so she can see just how careful she will need to be."

"Our mistakes?"

Col dropped her head, sheepishly. "Well, we've made one together, yesterday and I made one right at the beginning, telling you we came from Leipzig."

I had forgotten about that.

Mr. Searle was his usual bright self. "Good morning, boys – quite a storm, isn't it? What can I get you?"

Col pointed to the square fruit cakes in the display cabinet. "A fruit cake please, Mr. Searle."

"Right ho." He carefully put a cake into a paper bag and passed it to Col. "That'll be three and sixpence, please."

Col counted out the money and put the cake into the shopping bag. "Anything else?"

We shook our heads.

"Right ho. Have a good day then. Don't let the wind under that brolly or you'll get airborne, like Mary Poppins," he said, chuckling.

We walked in silence back to the house. About half-way there, Col stopped and turned to me. I saw her throat working, she was trying to decide something and find the right words. "I … I can't let you tell Lili." Her eyes were almost pleading.

"What?"

Her voice firmed. "I can't let *you* tell Lili. *I* must tell her. It's not right that you should be the one to tell Lili if Mutti won't. It might wreck your relationship with Mutti."

I was stunned into silence.

"I'm her daughter and if I tell Lili, Mutti will be angry but she won't stop being my mother, nor will I stop being her daughter."

Once again, we were standing on the street and I couldn't even hug her. I had thought for a moment she was about to risk serious bullying, but she wanted to protect my relationship with Mutti Frida.

I smiled at Col, shaking my head. "You have hidden strengths"

She smiled back as we started walking, with a glimmer of coyness in her eyes. "I hope so. After this, we have to tell Mutti we are going to break our promise to not do something stupid."

It was my turn to stop walking, allowing the rain to smack me in the neck. Col turned and walked backwards a couple of steps, smiling broadly. "Come on, slowcoach, or Lili will be there before we are – and you will be drenched."

As I caught up to her, she swung around and we walked silently, side by side beneath the umbrella, knowing what we would do, if we had to.

We arrived in plenty of time as Lili didn't appear for another ten minutes or so. Mutti Frida watched the car as it pulled up. "She's here, children. I'll let her in. You stay here, please." She shut the kitchen door behind her.

We heard Mutti Frida open the front door and then muffled conversation.

Col and I shared a glance, brimming with tension and fear.

The kitchen door opened, and Lili waited in the doorway, her emotions visible in her rigid stance.

"Have a seat at the table, children. I'll get the cake."

The three of us eyed each other silently, whilst Mutti Frida put the cake and a knife on the table and placed four plates at her seat.

"Would you like a glass of milk, Lili?"

Lili's head turned towards Mutti Frida in surprise and nodded. I didn't think the banally domestic atmosphere was quite what she expected.

"Col, reach three glasses from the shelf there, please."

Mutti Frida poured milk into our glasses and put the bottle back in the fridge. She returned with her coffee cup, sat down and cut the cake, passing over a slice for each of us. Then she sat back. "Try the cake, Lili," Mutti Frida suggested.

Lili frowned but picked up her slice and tried a nibble.

Mutti Frida watched her. "I like Mr. Searle's fruit cake – it's so moist. Don't you think so, Lili?"

Lili appeared slightly bewildered. She had probably arrived expecting a fight and the end of a friendship and here she was being asked to critique cake.

Mutti Frida took a sip of her coffee and carefully placed her cup down on the saucer. "Thank you for coming Lili. I know what you saw at the party upset you."

Lili glowered across the table at us.

Mutti Frida to paused for a moment, before continuing in a very gentle voice, "Lili, perhaps you could tell us what you saw last night."

Lili paused, examining her hands in her lap and then stared between the three of us. "I saw…" Her voice was so faint we could hardly hear her. She cleared her throat and started in a stronger voice. "Col and Willi kissed." Her eyes flashed at Col. "That was…after Col refused to kiss me." A blush crept into her cheeks and her eyes filled with anger. "And when you kissed Willi, I knew why." She sat, breathing hard for a few moments and then started to push her chair back. "I hate this. I shouldn't have come." I saw the great hurt glistening in Lili's eyes.

Mutti Frida leaned across and took Lili's hand. "Please wait. Do you remember what I said to you last night, Lili?" Mutti Frida's voice was sympathetic and encouraging

Lili half-tried to shake off Mutti Frida's hand and then collapsed back into her chair. "I don't remember, and I don't care." Tears were running down her cheeks and her chest heaved with emotion. *This was not going well …*

I squeezed my eyes shut in trepidation. *Where was Mutti going with this?*

Col leaned forward. "Lili…"

Mutti Frida hushed Col with a glance.

"Look at me, please, Lili," Mutti Frida's voice was gentle but firm and Lili eyes rose slowly to Mutti Frida's face.

"Last night I told you that what you thought you saw was not real."

I watched confusion fill Lili's eyes, but I felt a surge of relief wash through me: *Mutti Frida was going to tell Lili the truth.*

"But I saw Col and Willi kissing – I did," Lili hissed. Her head dropped to examine her hands once more.

"Yes, Lili, you did." Mutti Frida inhaled, glancing across at Col and me. "I still need you to look at me please, Lili." Mutti Frida paused and Lili raised her head, tears visible on her cheeks. "What I am about to tell you is a dangerous secret – and if it is revealed it could lead to terrible things happening to Col and me."

Lili's eyes swivelled between Col and Mutti.

"Can you promise me that you will keep this secret?" Mutti Frida's voice lightened slightly. "You can talk about it with us but no one else – not with your other friends, with no one in your family – with no one outside this room at all." Mutti Frida paused. "Ever."

Lili's face showed her growing confusion. Mutti Frida reached across and brushed the tears from Lili's cheeks. "Can you promise me…" she glanced at Col and me, "…us, that you will keep our secret?"

Lili sat still for a few seconds, her eyes flicking questioningly between the three of us.

Mutti Frida sent Lili a reassuring smile. "I want you to know that Col and Willi both told me we could trust you to keep this secret."

Lili's eyes darted to each of us again before returning to Mutti Frida's face. She paused and then nodded.

Mutti Frida nodded in acknowledgement. "Last night, you thought you saw the boy you wanted to kiss you, kissing another boy." I saw a small shudder pass through Lili. "But that's not what happened."

Lili's eyes narrowed and her voice was vehement. "But that's what I saw."

Mutti Frida's voice remained gentle. "No." She took Lili's hand again. "You saw my daughter, Colette, kissing her boyfriend, Willi."

Lili sat there, immobilised in consternation. Eventually, she stuttered, "Wh…what?"

Mutti Frida's voice was almost a caress. "Col is a girl, Lili, not a boy."

I could see the moisture in Col's eyes as she leaned towards Lili. "I'm so sorry I have deceived you on this, but you will understand why when Mutti explains." Col's hand slid halfway across the table towards Lili's, but Lili pulled her hand from Mutti Frida's and placed her hands into her lap.

Lili stared at Mutti Frida. "Well?" Her voice was tinged with accusation.

Col and I sat there in silence as Mutti Frida explained that she and Col had defected from East Germany and were in hiding from her husband, an ex-Nazi, now an officer climbing the senior ranks of the *Stasi*, the secret police. Partway through Mutti Frida's explanation, I felt Col's fingers interlacing with mine. I gave her hand a gentle squeeze, but we kept our eyes on Lili and Mutti Frida. I saw the disbelief slowly ebbing in Lili's eyes.

Once Mutti Frida had finished, Lili turned to Col, searching her face. "You're a girl?"

"Yes."

I saw doubt lingering on Lili's face.

Col glanced sideways at me. "Come with me, Lili, and I'll prove it." Col stood up and walked around to Lili's chair. "Well?" Col was almost pleading as she took Lili's hand and gently urged her to stand up.

Lili looked at Mutti Frida in confusion.

Mutti Frida smiled softly at them both. "It's alright, Lili. Go with Col if you need proof that she's a girl."

In silence, the girls disappeared into Col's bedroom. As the door closed, Mutti Frida turned to me. "And did you believe Col when she told you, or did she have to prove it?"

I felt a blush rising across my face.

Mutti Frida held my eyes for a few seconds then half-smiled, raising an eyebrow.

The heat in my face intensified. "We've kept our promise." My voice sounded strained, doubtless because my throat felt tight. I didn't want Mutti Frida to think I had betrayed her trust.

"Relax, Willi." Mutti Frida leaned across and patted my hand. "I know you always try to do the right thing." She sighed slightly. "I'm not so sure about Col, though."

I wondered if she'd say that if she knew about the conversation Col and I had about our promise to her. After all, I had suggested that 'something stupid' meant getting Col pregnant and that left a gap wide enough to drive several fleets of trucks through, line abreast. We sat in silence as I pondered this, and we waited for the girls to reappear as I nibbled on my slice of cake.

Col's bedroom door opened, and the girls came and sat back down at the table. I saw that Lili was still tense – something, perhaps several somethings, were still bothering her. Her eyes travelled round the table and her gaze settled on me. "How long have you known Col was a girl?" The question arrived with a hint of venom.

I glanced at Col, who just shrugged infinitesimally.

"I've known for a couple of months."

Lili pursed her lips and glared at me, then turned to Col. "And you kept me in the dark? And led me on until I made a fool of myself under the mistletoe?" Lili's face darkened in anger.

Mutti Frida leaned across, keeping her voice calm. "Lili, you have to remember Col's situation. Imagine yourself in her position – likely to be dragged back to Poland and probably imprisoned if someone there found out who you were."

Lili remained with her arms crossed, staring down at the table. We all stayed in silence for a while.

"You didn't make a fool of yourself under the mistletoe, Lili." Col's voice was soft, caressing. "Even if you didn't know quite who I was, you showed me how much you cared for me. You showed me that you wanted to be my close friend."

Lili's face was losing some of its pique.

Col's voice remained low, but now with an added intensity. "You have no idea how much I wanted to hug you under the mistletoe, Lili, to show you how much you mean to me." Her lips pursed in frustration. "But I couldn't do it – not as a boy – and that was the only reason I pushed you away. Mutti knows I have been wanting to tell you the truth about me since early this year."

Lili glanced at Mutti Frida, who nodded in confirmation.

"Please Lili, can we still be friends? There's so much we could share as girls together?" Col reached a hand across the table, pleading with her eyes.

Slowly, Lili's hand slid across and the two hands met. I realised I'd been holding my breath and slowly released it. Col's other hand found mine and lifted it onto the table, bringing it across to rest on hers and Lili's. Finally, Lili brought her other hand to rest on top of the stack.

We sat that way for a few seconds and then Lili spoke softly. "Okay, friends." Then her eyes twinkled. "But it's not fair that you have already taken the next-best boyfriend around." She paused, enjoying our confusion and then grinned at Col. "After you, that is."

We laughed, releasing the tension and I felt Col's hand squeezing Lili's. "I'm sorry about that, but finders-keepers."

"What am I, just an ornament for someone's arm?" I teased.

Their, "Yes!" was exclaimed in unison.

Mutti Frida gave me a reassuring smile. "Eat your cake, children."

"There's something else I need to tell you." Col leaned across towards Lili. "I may not be coming back to our school in January. I may be going to the grammar school in Canterbury instead."

"Oh." Lili flushed slightly. "I was going to tell you at the party last night, but then…" Lili's voice faded.

"You were going to tell me what?" Col sounded anxious.

"That I was going to the grammar school in January," Lili said, a smile bursting over her face.

Col jumped from her seat and rushed round to Lili, clasping her in a fierce hug. "That's wonderful, Lili."

And so as had happened several times before, our tension drained away as we sat round the table, sharing food.

Col licked a milk moustache from her upper lip and put her glass down. "You'll need to be careful about our secret, Lili. It's so easy to say or do something that arouses suspicion or lets the cat out of the bag."

Lili glanced up. "What do you mean?"

"Well, you saw Willi and I sharing a kiss last night – that was because we didn't think and made a mistake. Fortunately, it was you that saw us and not someone else. When I first met Willi, I told him we were from Leipzig. And then I…err…told Willi I was a girl without talking it over first with Mutti."

Lili arched an eyebrow at Col's hesitation, and she smiled slightly in return. I started to get the feeling that there could be a downside for me to this new style of friendship between Col and Lili.

"Would you like to stay for lunch, Lili?" Mutti Frida asked.

"Yes please, but I'll have to phone home first."

She agreed with her mother to be picked up at five o'clock, and we spent the rest of the day in a cut-throat game of Risk that eventually saw the girls forming an alliance to destroy me. Lili had manipulated things so that she came out on top of that exchange and rapidly eliminated Col. *Or had Col set things up that way?*

As we were packing up the game in the fading daylight, Mutti Frida came in, turning on the lights. "I was wondering, Lili, do Poles have their main celebration on Christmas Eve or have they adopted the English Christmas day?"

"We've gone English in that, but we have been to one of my parents' friends' houses on Christmas Eve."

Mutti Frida smiled. "Would you like to join Col, Willi and me for a European Christmas celebration on Christmas Eve, then?"

"That would be fun." Lili focused on Col and me, smiling. "I'll ask my mother when she picks me up."

Mrs. Wiśniewski arrived a bit early and enjoyed a cup of coffee with Mutti Frida, chatting away in Polish. Lili waited for a gap in the conversation and spoke to her mother in Polish.

Mrs. Wiśniewski's voice showed her displeasure at what she saw as Lili's bad manners. "Liliana, you've been told before not to speak in Polish in front of your friends. It's not polite to exclude them from the conversation."

Mutti Frida switched to English. "Oh, Daria. I'm sorry, but that was my fault. I have so little opportunity to speak Polish now that I always try to do so with you and your friends. Lili was just following my lead."

I stared at Col, smiling. "Perhaps we need to stretch ourselves and add Polish to English French, German and Latin, Col."

"Oh, yes," Lili exclaimed, delight shining on her face. "I'll help you and I'm sure we can find some textbooks, too."

Col gave me a slight frown. "Okay." She turned to Lili. "But only if you agree to learn German at the same time."

Daria laughed. "Well, Lili?"

There was a silence of a few seconds before Lili gave her mother a slightly sheepish nod. "All right, I'll learn German while Col and Willi learn Polish."

"We could work in the public library after school," I suggested.

Mutti Frida smiled at me. "Do you want to annoy all the library staff with your foreign chatter, not just the one that doesn't like Germans?" Mrs. Wiśniewski's face showed confusion, so Mutti Frida explained what had happened with the younger librarian.

"Oh." Daria thought for a moment. "It would probably be best to meet at a house, then. I'm happy for them to come to my house."

We were all going to be travelling from Canterbury, so we could meet up on the bus.

"You'll need to speak to your mother about this, first Willi."

I nodded. "I'll speak to her – and I expect she'll want to speak with you, Mrs. Wiśniewski."

"Possibly, but I know Dr Johnstone as she is my doctor – and Lili's too."

I didn't know what to say to that – in my old life, I'd not been deeply involved in the community where my parents lived and so hadn't previously experienced people I knew having a professional relationship with my mother. I just nodded. I wondered how Lili felt about this – she hadn't mentioned it before so perhaps she didn't mind.

Daria and Lili left soon after and I helped bring in the small Christmas tree that was sitting upright in a bucket of beach pebbles. Col and I had gathered these a week earlier, struggling back to the house with the pebbles divided between a bucket each. It was good that we were wearing gloves as the galvanised iron handles cut into our fingers and we'd had to take a few rests coming up the Downs from the beach. It took the three of us to manoeuvre the tree into position, but I loved the pine aroma it gave off, filling the lounge room with its fresh smell.

Once we had it in position, Mutti Frida carefully poured in several pints of water to help the tree stay fresh.

I was a bit perplexed. "Won't the salt from the pebbles kill the tree?"

Mutti Frida smiled. "It's all right, Willi. We washed the pebbles yesterday morning. Now Col, get the decorations and Willi can help us dress the tree."

Col retrieved a box from the hall cupboard – and squeaked with delight when she saw the set of Christmas tree lights on top. "O, Mutti. These will be amazing on the tree. Thank you."

We spent a happy hour or so turning the tree into a glittering green cone before Col ceremonially turned on the lights. Their soft glow made that corner of the room almost magical.

Mutti smiled at her daughter's delight.

"Now we can start putting presents under the tree," Col said, clapping her hands with glee.

I realised we would need to find a present for Lili. "What do you think Lili would like for Christmas, Col?"

Col turned from her infatuation with the tree. "Hm, I think we should get her some art supplies. She always has a sketchbook in her school bag, and she's started using some sort of special crayon as well as pencil and charcoal. I wonder how we can find out what she likes?"

"How many art supplies shops are there in the town?" Mutti Frida raised her eyebrows.

"Um – just the one, I think," replied Col.

"Well then, I suspect that if you went there and asked what Lili likes they would know her and could help."

Mid-December 1963 – late February 1964

My mother did indeed want to speak with Mrs. Wiśniewski about Col and I spending time with Lili in her house, possibly alone and unsupervised. There was an unspoken undercurrent of whether it was appropriate for two boys to be alone in a house with a girl. I suppressed a smile: my mother didn't know Col was a girl, and I was spending hours each week alone with her. But then she didn't know about the promise Mutti Frida had extracted from us or about my re-interpretation of that promise.

"Are you sure you can cope with adding another language on top of everything else you are doing?" I heard the concern in my mother's voice.

"I'm not going to let it interfere with my other studies. After all, it will be just like what Col and I did when he was learning English and I, German. That didn't seem to cause a problem." I thought back to how we'd worked together. "In fact, because we had to explain things several times in both languages it deepened our understanding."

"Well, we'll see. I still have to sort things out with Mrs. Wiśniewski."

"OK." I passed my mother a smile. "May I take some mince pies to Col's house on Christmas Eve? Lili will be there too, so I think we might need a dozen this time…"

My mother laughed. "I'll see what I can do."

I picked up yesterday's newspaper and sat at the kitchen table, leafing through it. The attempted assassination of JFK didn't seem to have stirred things up – at least not on the surface, and there were no indications of increased tensions between the east and west. In fact, the opening of the Berlin Wall for the first time, allowing westerners to visit the east, suggested that tensions might be easing. International politics was strange.

An item well back in the newspaper discussed the recently started trial of twenty-one Auschwitz guards in Frankfurt. It seemed the prosecutor was unhappy with the charges brought against the defendants. Under German law, even for the guard responsible for operating the gas chambers, charges of accomplice to murder could only be brought as he was *'following orders'*. I wondered what Mutti Frida thought of this. I knew she had stopped hating them but had never forgiven those responsible for what had happened to her and her parents – along with millions of others.

Despite the surface seeming calm between east and west, MI6 had been pushing Mutti Frida about her husband. *Did they want to use his Nazi past against him, blackmailing him to pass information to them?* I wondered if there had been any pressure brought to bear on West Germany to conduct these trials. *If so, would it remind those involved in the Nazi regime of what they had done? Would that make Herr Schmidt more biddable?*

I pondered this as I lay in bed, before drifting off to sleep.

***

Col and I walked into town the next day and visited the art supplies shop which was just off the High Street. They knew Lili well and pointed out the sketchbook she liked, so we picked one up. Col asked about the special crayons Lili had been talking about and we were shown the huge colour-sorted array, picking out a dozen with the help of the shop owner.

"We could wrap each crayon separately, you know," Col said, smiling with a wicked glint in her eye. "That would make it all look much more impressive."

"But that would take lots of paper too," I countered.

"True." Col gave me a sideways smile, with a tinge of devilry. "But it would be fun to see her realise what we'd done." Smiling, I shook my head, as we wandered along the High Street, browsing the shop windows.

"Will your father be there for Christmas?" Col asked.

He had been increasingly absent during the year, staying in London almost every week and some weekends. Memories of last year flared, raising spectres my young brain quailed before. "I suppose so." Even I knew my voice sounded monotonal and dead.

Col sensed my sudden tension. "I'm sorry, Willi, I didn't mean to worry you. I was just thinking of the Christmases we had when I was little, before Mutti learned of my father's past. It all seemed so magical: Mutti, father and I singing carols in front of the Christmas tree with the glow of the candles flickering gently about us."

We walked on in silence for a few paces.

"I don't think either of us will have a family Christmas again." Col's voice was also flat now.

I glanced at her and I could see my pain echoed in her eyes, and then something occurred to me. "No, I think you're wrong there."

"What?"

"Think about it." I smiled at her. "We will have our own families one day."

"Or our own family." And she gave me a slightly coquettish smile.

I raised an eyebrow. "Is Mutti Frida ready to be a grandmother, then?"

Col blushed faintly, stuck her tongue out at me and we both laughed, lifting our mood.

Once back at Col's house we wrapped up Lili's present, with the crayons in one parcel and the sketchbook in another and added them to the pile under the tree. I had my presents for Col and Mutti Frida in my bag and added them. I was pleased with finding a collapsing umbrella that Mutti Frida could put in her bag. It was quite expensive but worth it for her.

At home that evening, my school report had arrived. My mother had left it on the kitchen table, unopened.

I stared at her, confused. *Why hadn't she read it?*

"I left it for you to open and read it, Will," my mother said, softly, as if reading my thoughts in my silence, or in my blank expression.

I sat down at the table, turning the envelope with the school crest on it over in my hands.

My mother sat down opposite me.

"You're not worried about what it says, are you Will?"

I glanced at her. "No." I knew my voice sounded unconvincing. What had happened the previous Christmas hung silently between us.

I slid a finger under the flap and folded open the report. I read through it in silence.

"Well?"

I slid the report across the table and my mother picked it up. After a minute or so, she folded it carefully and smiled at me. "Excellent, Will. All your teachers speak highly of you." She picked up the report again, re-reading some of the entries. Then she peered up at me. "You've come such a long way in the last twelve months, Will. It's almost unbelievable, seeing it laid out here in your report."

I shifted uncomfortably in my chair, slightly embarrassed. My old brain found the schoolwork ridiculously easy, but I couldn't tell my mother that, so I changed the subject, "Col and Lili may be going to school in Canterbury next term."

My mother raised an eyebrow. "How so?"

"Their school has recommended they transfer to the grammar school there."

"Good for them." My mother stood up, smiling. "Well, I can't just sit here. There are mince pies and everything else to make, after all." As my sister was not around to chase me out of the kitchen, I spent a cosy hour with my mother, helping with making the stuffing and forcemeat balls for the goose.

Both Col and Lili received confirmation of their transfer to the Grammar School in Canterbury before Christmas. When Col got her letter, I had assumed we would travel together on the number seven bus I had been taking, but with Lili going as well, that wouldn't work so well. It was easiest for her to take a number six. We talked about this the next time we met, with Lili pointing out that we would all be travelling back together if

162

we were going to work our language program at her house, but that was not certain yet, as my mother and Mrs. Wiśniewski hadn't spoken.

"I'll chase her up about this tonight when I get home and let you know tomorrow."

Col smiled. "Okay, I hope she lets us do it. It will be so much fun working together."

Lili gave Col a tentative smile.

"Come on, Lili. It will be fun – don't worry. The three of us will work on our homework together in German and Polish." Col glanced over at me. "Do you think we should do the alternate day thing again?"

I nodded. "Good idea."

Lil seemed a bit lost, her eyes widening. "What do you mean?"

"Sorry, Lili. When Willi and I started learning each other's languages at my house after school, Mutti made us speak only English or German on alternate days."

Col stared at Lili, smiling. "It will be a bit easier for the three of us as we share English. With Willi at first, there was a lot of fumbling around trying to explain things when we had almost no language in common."

Col stopped, delight brightening her face. "Oh, I can't wait to see your uncle Brian's face when I turn up at the garage and ask, in Polish, for a drive in an E-type."

Lili chuckled at that.

As I was leaving, Col told me that she was busy in the morning. "Mutti and I have to go into the school to sign some papers and pick up an information pack."

"I've already got mine," Lili interjected.

I gathered Col in my arms. "That's okay. My mother wants me to help her with some stuff anyway. I'll see you later?"

"Yes, of course. Why don't you come over about three o'clock?"

We shared a kiss, interrupted by a cough from Lili.

I was a bit embarrassed. "Sorry, Lili."

We broke apart and now Lili seemed embarrassed. "No, I'm sorry. I was just joking. It's fine by me for you to kiss."

Was Lili feeling left out?

Rather than cause further problems, I just gave Col a peck on the cheek and turned to the door, but Lili grabbed my shoulder and spun me gently round. "No, give her a proper kiss." Her eyes apologised, so Col and I kissed and then Lili and I both left, heading home along Seaview Avenue in opposite directions.

In the morning, I helped my mother with cleaning around the house, hoovering through the downstairs and then polishing the parquet floor in the hall. As I worked, I could smell baking aromas wafting in from the kitchen. When I finished and put the hoover and polisher back in the cupboard under the stairs, I wandered into the kitchen. Several racks of mince pies were cooling, and my mother was finishing off a couple of trays of sausage rolls, brushing them with milk, ready to slide them into the oven.

I leant over a rack of mince pies, savouring their rich, fruity aroma. "Mmm."

"Don't you touch them, Will," my mother scolded. "They're for Christmas."

I was already imagining their rich taste on my tongue as I glanced questioningly at her.

My mother smiled. "Yes, there's a dozen for you to take tomorrow."

"Thank you." I gave my mother a smile and then pottered around helping her and my sister with the preparations for Christmas day, peeling potatoes to sit in salted water so they did not brown, preparing a pile of Brussel sprouts and breaking up bread for the bread sauce. When we were finished, I went to spend the afternoon with Col.

Christmas Eve dawned cloudy, cold and wet – a typical English winter's day. After breakfast, I was set to polishing the dining room table and sideboard, ready for Christmas dinner. I was to be at Col's house at four o'clock and the day dragged slowly onwards. I went and got myself ready an hour early and had to wait around trying to read before finally heading to Col's house as dusk settled the clouds lower over the bare-armed trees.

Mutti Frida answered the door. "The girls are in the loungeroom, waiting for you." She smiled and cocked an eyebrow. *Hmm...*

I took off my coat and gloves and opened the door. The Christmas tree lights gave the room a soft glow, but I was stopped in my tracks by two beautiful girls standing beside the tree. Lili's golden hair caught the lights as it cascaded over her shoulders, setting off her pink floral chiffon dress. Beside her was a dark-haired beauty with shining eyes wearing a dark blue dress, her hair unfashionably short but tastefully arranged to accent her face.

"Oh, wow. You are both so pretty." But my eyes were mostly on Col.

They both smiled and then Lili nudged Col towards me, and we embraced.

"You're beautiful, Col," I whispered, and Col leant up and we kissed.

I held her at arms' length. "I love your dress. Where did you get it?"

Lili came over and fiddled with the material on Col's right shoulder, readjusting its already perfect fit. "Well, we couldn't take Col out and buy her a new dress," Lili smiled at me. "It's a dress that no longer fits me – I only wore it a couple of times before a growth spurt made me too big for it. We – well, mostly Frau Schmidt – adjusted it for Col. What do you think?"

"It's beautiful." I gazed at Col again, unable to focus on anything else. "You are beautiful." I leant in and planted another gentle kiss on Col's lips, and she snuggled up to my side. Col usually wore somewhat baggy clothes to help disguise her shape, but this dress showed off her figure. She was more svelte than Lili, but had gentle curves in all the right places, which I could see for the first time.

I cast Lili a stare that was filled with gratitude. "Lili, thank you for helping Col with this." I noticed Mutti Frida standing in the doorway, smiling at us. I caught her eye and smiled back. "You have a beautiful daughter, Mutti Frida."

"Ah, yes. But she's not my little girl anymore," she sighed, wistfully, her love shining through. Then she clapped her hands. "Come along, dinner is ready."

The traditional meal I had first enjoyed a year before was repeated, but the Dresdner Stollen was accompanied by my mother's mince pies, served warm with clotted cream. After the meal, we exchanged presents. Lili was delighted with the sketchbook and crayons. Apparently, the lady in the art supplies shop remembered exactly which crayons Lili had purchased and had told us to buy the ones that would complement those.

When it came to my present to Col, her face lit up when she opened the box.

"Oh, Willi. It's beautiful." I smiled and she lifted it so Lili and her mother could see it.

"Go on, Willi, fasten it around her neck," Mutti Frida said, smiling softly.

Col's short hair made it easy. As I fastened it, a shiver of delight passed through Col. When I stepped back, I saw Lili watching, a smile on her face but her eyes betraying her sadness. I realised that just a week ago, she had hoped Col, as a boy, would have these feelings for her. On an impulse, I gently pulled Col to her feet and beckoned Lili to join us. As she approached, I took her hand and placed it on Col's far shoulder and then softly gathered both girls into a three-way hug. For a moment, Lili resisted, but then she reached round, pulling us more tightly together. We held the hug for a few seconds and then almost telepathically pulled apart until we stood there, holding hands and smiling at one another in our deepening friendship.

As we finally separated to sit down, I saw Mutti Frida watching, a sad smile on her face. I couldn't tell her that I knew her juxtaposed joy and sadness: I had watched my son and daughter growing into their teens, then becoming adults and all too soon forging their own paths in life. I went over to where she was sitting and gave her a soft kiss on the cheek.

"Thank you, Mutti Frida."

She held my eyes for a moment and then nodded, almost imperceptibly.

***

Christmas day at my house passed in subtle tensions but last year's sharp edges and gouging points were more rounded – or perhaps just buried beneath our father's growing disinterest. It had none of the love and joy of the previous night. I tried to help my mother as much as I could, but I found my sister glaring at me – she must have felt I was trying to usurp her position. As soon as I could, I retreated to my bedroom with my mother's Christmas present – a beautiful, boxed set of *The Lord of the Rings*. She had noted my delight in *The Hobbit*.

After another discussion with Mrs. Wiśniewski, my mother agreed that Lili, Col and I could gather at Lili's house after school to start our Polish language program. Mutti Frida would meet us there when she finished work at the shop so Col and I could walk home with her. After consulting the bus timetables, Lili found that the number seven bus left from the Herne Bay bus station not far from her house, so she could catch it there. Col and I would join her at our bus stop at the end of my road.

As the holidays ended, Mutti Frida finally decided that Col would have to continue as a boy in public, as there were too many problems with becoming a girl again. Col wasn't happy about this, but at least she had Lili as a friend at school who knew she was a girl. They were in all the same classes, so they would be able to support one another if there was any bullying. Lili had no discernible foreign accent and Col's German accent was almost imperceptible – but their last names were still foreign and that might be a problem.

On the first day of school, Col arrived at my front gate and we walked to the bus stop together. As the bus pulled up, I saw Lili waving at us. After showing our season tickets to the bus driver, we walked down to join her. The single-decker bus was four seats across, with two on each side of the aisle. The only wider seat was right at the back – and that was occupied by some other teens, so Col joined Lili and I sat across the aisle, which made conversation difficult.

Col turned towards the back of the bus. "We need the back seat so we can talk together."

Lili turned around as well. "Oh, right. I didn't think of that. Those kids got on after me, so I should be able to get the back seat from now on as I get on at the bus station."

"We'll need to do the same on the number six on the way home," Col reminded her.

I gave her a frown. "But there's no wide back seat on a double-decker."

"Of course not, silly me."

Lili leaned across. "Oh well, we'll just have to sit like this, then."

That afternoon, as I hauled myself aboard the bus the girls had found a solution. Lili was sitting at one end of the sideways bench seat with Col in the two-seater in front of it. I sat down next to Col and with Lili leaning between us we could converse over the noise of the bus. The following morning when we boarded, Lili was in the back seat, smiling broadly. Col and I received a few glares from the kids who had been there the day before as we walked past and sat with Lili.

"Well done, Lili," I remarked. "Possession is nine-tenths of the law."

Our after-school homework and language program began that afternoon. Of the three of us, Lili was the least confident. I thought she found the fierce rate at which Col and I worked a little off-putting. At first, Lili would fall back to English far too readily on German days and it took some gentle pushing from Col to change that. Both girls had a bit of catching up to do on academic subjects at their new school, but I was able to help them in almost everything, to Col's delight and Lili's surprise. German wasn't offered at their school, but French was compulsory. Col had a reasonable start on that from studying it with me for a year, but Lili was starting from scratch. Once she applied herself to both languages, she progressed rapidly – her bilingual background probably providing favourable brain wiring. For our walks back from Lili's house, Mutti Frida insisted on all conversation being carried out in Polish, so Col and I were progressing fairly quickly.

We also realised that there was one language we shared that neither Mutti Frida nor Mrs. Wiśniewski spoke – French, so that became our 'private' language, which helped us all in that language and annoyed the mothers somewhat, although they took it, mostly, in good spirits.

One evening in early February, I scrambled into my house with a gale and sheets of rain at my back. I'd had tea with Col and Mutti Frida, but within a hundred yards of their house, it started pouring down. My legs were soaked beneath the reach of my raincoat, as were my shoes and socks. Water was dripping down my neck underneath my shirt and I was starting to shiver.

"Goodness gracious." My mother sprang to her feet. "Why didn't you stay at Col's house?"

Another convulsive shiver ran through me. "It was only blowing with a bit of rain when I left."

"Never mind. Take your shoes and socks off here – there's no point treading water through the house – and get yourself upstairs and have a hot bath."

"Okay." I struggled out of my shoes and socks, the latter hitting the kitchen floor tiles with a distinct splat.

"I'll have a hot chocolate waiting for you when you come down."

I grabbed pyjamas and dressing gown from my bedroom and stripped off in the bathroom as the bath filled. The water felt almost scalding on my shivering skin at first, but it soon warmed me. I relaxed for a while but far too soon the water started to cool and so I got out and went downstairs in my PJs and dressing gown. I saw my shoes, stuffed with newspaper to help dry the insides, sitting on the hall radiator shelf.

My mother had milk simmering on the stove and quickly placed a mug of hot chocolate in front of me. I cupped my hands round it and carefully sipped the froth off the top.

"Oh, I nearly forgot; there's a letter for you." My mother went out into the hall, coming back with an envelope, which she placed in front of me.

I slipped a finger under the flap and opened it.

It was from the International Youth Cultural Exchange Program thanking me for my entry but telling me I had not won the competition. I hadn't expected to and at least that solved the problem of having to refuse the prize. I handed the letter to my mother.

"I'm sorry about that, Will." My mother put her hand on my shoulder. "I'm sure your essay was excellent."

"As I said, there would be lots of people older than me who had learned German for much longer."

"What did you do with your wet clothes?"

"I hung my trousers over the towel rail in the bathroom to dry for tomorrow and put the rest in the laundry hamper." I sipped my hot chocolate. "I think I'll head to bed now."

"Okay, Sleep well."

***

In the morning, my shoes and trousers were dry. I watched as usual for Col to arrive at the front gate and we walked to the bus stop together. Every morning I had to remind myself not to take her hand or kiss her. It was difficult, but we needed to be careful.

"I didn't win the competition."

Strangely, Col smiled at me. "I'm glad."

I couldn't help but feel a little hurt and was certain it showed in my eyes. "Why?"

"Oh, I'm sorry Willi, I didn't mean to sound like I didn't care. But it would have been awkward for you to turn down the prize. How would you have explained that to your mother?"

I shrugged as she was right. "I have no idea, but it doesn't matter now."

February progressed in its usual miserable weather and so the weekends were spent indoors, reading and playing games. Lili always had her sketchbook with her and frequently sketched, listening to Col and me as we read out loud. We managed occasional walks out on the cliffs, frequently getting blown about and occasionally wet.

Late in February, Mr. Sturr asked me to stay after class. "How did the competition go?"

I was a little surprised, as I hadn't told him I had entered.

"I didn't win."

"Hm." He picked his glasses off his nose and started polishing them with a handkerchief. "The competition people rang me yesterday. You told them I was your teacher."

It was a statement, not a question, so I just sat there, rather surprised none-the-less.

"It appears they were impressed with such a thoughtful entry from so young a person." His lessons were like this – statements and questions punctuated by pauses which students rapidly learned to use as thinking time. He didn't want quick comments and shallow answers and could be brutal in his destruction of loose thinking.

I waited for him to reach his point as he polished his spectacles.

"Yes, very impressed." His manner was almost proprietorial. "It transpires that one winner has had to withdraw and they are offering you his place." He replaced his glasses and gave me a lengthy stare. "That is quite an honour."

My stomach lurched slightly.

"An honour, indeed, for you – and also for this school."

How was I going to get out of this? With pressure from the school, I could see my mother would push me hard to go and, of course, I couldn't do that.

"Well done, boy." Mr. Sturr leaned forward and clapped me on the shoulder. "They told me you should be getting a letter in a day or two."

I sat there, trying to think of a way around this problem.

"Well, off you go or you'll be late for your next class." I scrabbled my books together and scurried out.

The rest of the day passed in a bit of a daze as I worried at this problem. By the time I reached the bus stop, I realised Mutti Frida and Col would have to help me. After all, it was them I would be putting in danger.

The girls' bus arrived, and I swung up and took my usual seat beside Col with Lili behind us. I knew Col would sense something was wrong so, in my still rather broken Polish, I told the girls I had something important to say to Col and it would need to be in German as our Polish wasn't good enough yet. Our excursions into Polish and German were now accepted as normal on the bus, so no heads turned.

Col nodded and turned to Lili. "Don't worry, we'll tell you soon."

Lili nodded at us both and I told Col what had happened and how I expected the school to pressure my mother and me to accept the award. By the end of my explanation, Col's lips were pursed, and she leaned back against the window.

Lili leaned forward between us, a question on her face. She had probably followed some of what we had discussed, but her German was not as good as our mediocre Polish.

Col took her hand. *"Nie martw się."* (*Don't worry.*), and then finished in English, "We'll explain when we get home."

For the rest of the bus journey, conversation was limited, and it wasn't until we reached Lili's house that Col and I felt safe to talk about what was going on. Col asked Lili to check to see there was no one else home – there wasn't – and then we took a seat in the kitchen.

"What's going on?" Lili's impatience was obvious.

"We should get our homework out first," Col commented, calmly. "That way if someone comes home early, they will see what they are expecting, and we can start talking about that."

I nodded. "Good idea, Col." And the three of us got out our books and spread them in front of us.

Col then quickly told Lili what was happening and the problem as we saw it.

"But how will the competition people know about Col?" Lili was clearly perplexed.

"My mother told my teacher, Mr. Sturr, that I had a German friend and that he had helped me pick up German faster than usual."

"But your teacher's not going to tell them that, is he?"

Col peered at me and then sighed. "We don't know. He might have already told them."

"But he might never tell them, either. And even if he does, that doesn't mean Willi's friend is Col. There must be other Germans with children living in England," Lili countered.

I stared at her. "True. But how will we know one way or the other? I can't ask my teacher as he would want to know why I was asking. As for there being other German children in England, you're probably right. But I would expect Col's father would be investigating any and all that come to his attention."

"We have to assume the worst – and that means that Willi can't go." Col leaned across, taking my hand.

Lili paused for a moment, deep in thought. "But…this teacher might already have told them – and Willi going to East Germany or not won't change that. The people you are afraid of may already know."

That hadn't occurred to me – and, from the fear on Col's face, it hadn't occurred to her either. Needless to say, little homework was done that afternoon, even after Mrs. Wiśniewski came home from her volunteering. Col and I desperately needed to speak to Mutti Frida and when she arrived from the shop, we hustled her back out of the house as quickly as possible.

Once we were on the street, Mutti Frida pulled us to a stop. "What's going on, children?"

I gave Col a nod of encouragement. In German, Col explained that would have to wait until we got home and we continued our usual Polish lesson, telling Mutti Frida about our day, interrupted by occasional tense silences.

Once the door was closed and we had removed our winter attire, we sat round the table and brought Mutti Frida up to date. As she realised that word of her and Col's whereabouts might already be back in East Germany, Mutti Frida sat back in her chair, her face drawn.

"I need to go out again and make a telephone call."

"We have a telephone here." Col responded in a confused tone.

I put my hand on hers. "But someone might be listening to that line."

Mutti Frida was surprised. "What makes you say that?"

I shrugged. "I've read some James Bond books."

Mutti Frida raised an eyebrow; she must have heard about the raunchy nature of parts of those books.

Col clapped her hands in delight. "Oooh, Sean Connery is so sexy."

"Col. That's enough." I saw that Mutti Frida was a bit shocked by her daughter's admission. "Please get tea ready." Her voice softened. "There are lamb chops in the larder, and we'll have beans and mashed potatoes with them. I won't be long."

Mutti Frida donned her hat and coat and slipped out. We topped and tailed the beans, peeled the potatoes and put them on to cook.

Mutti Frida was only gone for about thirty minutes. Col quirked an eyebrow at her when she walked back in.

I saw that Mutti Frida was distracted, thinking about what was said on the phone call and its implications. *"Bis später*, Col." (*Later, Col.*")

I knew Col wasn't happy at this; as we set the table, I gave her a couple of hip bumps, trying to cheer her up, but she almost snarled at me after the second one, so I left her alone.

Once we sat down to eat, Col leaned towards her mother and rather grumpily said, "Well?"

I tried to take her hand, but she shook me off. "Mutti, I'm involved too. You have to tell me what's going on."

Mutti Frida took Col's hands in hers, holding them fast when Col tried to jerk them free. "Col, if I knew what was going on, I would tell you. Please believe me." Mutti Frida's face begged me to support her.

"Col, you know Mutti Frida would tell you if she had anything to tell." I gave Mutti Frida a shrug. "Why don't you just tell us what happened on the phone call?"

Mutti Frida sighed. "Yes – you are both involved in all of this, so telling you is the right thing to do. But first, eat your tea whilst it's hot."

I glanced at Col and she offered me a slight nod. My stomach was quite uneasy as the fear I might be about to lose Col mounted, but my young body was still hungry enough to put away everything, as did Col.

Mutti Frida mostly just moved her food around her plate. When she saw Col and I had finished, she pushed her plate away.

"I spoke to Herr Watling, he is my contact." She paused for a moment. Col leant across impatiently. "And?"

I took Col's hand. "Just let her tell it in her own time, Col."

"Thank you, Willi." She smiled wryly at Col. "It will be much easier if you don't interrupt."

I saw that Col was about to speak and gave her hand a squeeze, shaking my head slightly.

"I told him about you, Willi, the competition and your German teacher's discussion with the competition organisers." She sighed. "He asked lots of questions about you and your family, Willi. I hope we haven't brought you any problems with the authorities."

I hadn't thought about that possibility. "What do you mean?"

Mutti Frida cast her eyes up, searching around the room, as if there might bugs. "Oh, Willi. Back in the DDR, no-one wants any attention from the authorities, particularly the security services. Such attention only ever brings trouble."

I reached across and found her hand. "Mutti Frida, this is England. The authorities are bound by law and can't just cause trouble for someone without a reason." Rumbling in the back of my head was that I hoped this was true in 1960's England because it certainly wasn't in the twenty-first century, where all sorts of skullduggery went on in the name of national security.

"I hope you're right, Willi. I do so hope you are right. I do not wish our troubles on you," and she gave my hand a squeeze.

"I am part of your family now. If there is trouble, it is my trouble also."

Mutti Frida closed her eyes for a few seconds. "Thank you, Willi. But you don't know what people like my husband can do."

A shiver ran down my spine. I had, after all, read about the Gestapo and their interrogation techniques.

I needed to stop thinking about that. "What does your contact, er ... Mr. Watling, want you – us – to do?"

"For the moment, nothing. He wants us to keep living our lives as normal." Mutti Frida gave a slightly bitter laugh. "As if living in hiding in another country is in any way normal."

"What does he want Willi to do about the competition? He'll be getting that letter any day."

Mutti Frida shook her head. "I don't know, he didn't say. All he said was that he would be back in contact with me soon."

I shrugged. "We'll just have to wait, I suppose."

Mutti Frida stood up and started gathering in the plates. "You're right, Willi. We'll just have to wait." Then she stopped. "But I suggest you keep a good lookout for any strange people following you or people asking questions about you."

We cleaned up our meal and then Col and I sat together on the sofa, trying to provide some comfort by being physically close in what was suddenly a much more threatening world. Eventually, I walked home, ears pricked for footsteps following me or anyone strange on the streets.

Unsurprisingly for Beltinge at nearly nine o'clock on a February night, I was alone on the streets. Despite this, I slept uneasily.

Late February 1964

In the morning, when we joined Lili on the bus, she was practically jumping out of her skin with the need to know what was going on. Col and I had talked about this as we walked to the bus and decided that Col would tell her in the playground at their school where there was little chance of them being overheard in the general hubbub. Lili frowned when Col told her she had to wait, but I hope she understood why we felt it necessary.

I was a bit distracted at school and received a few frowns from teachers as a result, something they were not used to giving me.

At the end of my Maths class, Mr. Pollock walked over to my desk as I gathered up my gear. "You seem unusually distracted today, Johnstone."

I was surprised by this intervention as, whilst he was an excellent teacher, he had always seemed a bit aloof. His expression showed his interest and concern. "Sorry sir, I've got a lot on my mind at the moment." I hope I didn't sound rude; I was just unused to this from a person who had always seemed so removed from everyday vicissitudes.

Mr. Pollock's lips curved up hinting at a kindly smile. "I see." He pondered for a moment. "If you think I can be of assistance, please come and see me."

I was quite off balance and just nodded. Mr. Pollock's concerned eyes held mine for a moment longer and then he turned away, his academic gown swirling around him. This was a side of him I hadn't seen before as he'd always come across as the distant professor, content in his ivory tower surrounded by the Maths he so loved.

Fortunately, I didn't have a German class, so I didn't have to talk to Mr. Sturr about the competition.

I wanted to reach my house as soon as possible to see if the letter from the competition had arrived. Perhaps the wording would offer me a way to turn it down – but I couldn't think what that might be. Boarding the bus, I sat down in my usual place.

Lili leant in from behind,

"Col told me…" Col frowned at her and Lili stopped. "Of course, sorry."

And we spent the bus trip and the walk to Lili's house avoiding the giant elephant in the room.

Once we reached Lili's house, she checked the house was empty and, after we spread out our homework, we started rehashing what was happening.

"Like I told you, Lili, Mutti told us to watch out for anything odd or people asking questions about us." Col gave Lili a grim smile. "But as you're our friend, they might want to get to us through you, so you need to watch out for your family as well and tell us if anything strikes you as odd, no matter how small."

Lili nodded, her face taking on a serious mien as she realised that her closeness to us might put her and her family at some risk.

Col, as ever, sensed Lili's concern. She leant across the table. "I know it sounds all a bit farfetched, but I'm afraid it is real." She sighed, shaking her head. "I'm sorry we got you into this, Lili."

Lili's bright blue eyes found ours across the table. She shivered slightly and then shook out her hair, as if scattering her fears. "It's not your fault – and I'll help any way I can." Her soft voice strengthened as she spoke.

Col smiled at Lili, her voice gentle and filled with gratitude. "Thank you, Lili. I…" she glanced across at me. "We knew we could count on you."

Lili blushed slightly. "I'll keep my eyes open and certainly let you know if I see or hear anything unusual."

I saw the redness in her cheeks and knew she was embarrassed at Col's praise, and she quickly changed the subject, "I need some help with conditionals in German, Col." She picked up her exercise book and flicked it open.

We settled down with our homework. Col and Lili had been a term behind the rest of their class in everything as they had only started at Grammar School in early January. Despite this, they seemed to be caught up. They were both bright and I was sure that our homework club was helping, particularly with Lili's focus and motivation. It also distracted our minds from the worries we faced, about our families.

Mutti Frida arrived at the same time as Mrs. Wiśniewski, with Lili's young brother, and the two mothers shared a cup of coffee before the walk back to Col's house. In spite of what was going on – or perhaps in an effort to retain normality because of that – Mutti Frida insisted we talk to her, in Polish as usual, about our day as we walked home. I struggled to explain in Polish about Mr. Pollock and the 'ivory tower' metaphor – to Mutti Frida's amusement.

When I finally returned home later that night, there was no letter waiting for me. But the following morning the postman was a bit early, arriving as I was walking out of the door – and there was one for me. I put it into my pocket and left the others for my mother.

Once we were on the bus and safely ensconced on the back seat, I took it out. As expected, it was from the International Youth Cultural Exchange Program offering me the place turned down by one of the winners on a two-week visit to the DDR during the upcoming Easter school holidays. Col and Lil read it over my shoulders.

"Well, now what am I going to do?" I peered at both Col and Lili, but neither had anything to offer.

We stayed like that, in silence and after a minute or so, Lili stared at me and said, rather tentatively, "Couldn't you just lose the letter? That way your mother wouldn't know you'd been offered the trip."

Col huffed. "That's not going to work – Willi's school knows he's being offered the trip and they want the glory of one of their students winning the prize. If Willi says nothing, I expect they would contact his mother."

"You think they'd do that?" Lili asked.

I nodded, thinking of Mr. Sturr's interest. "I'm afraid so."

Silence descended upon the three of us again. I wondered what Mutti Frida's contact was going to do about all of this.

Lili's mind must have been wandering down the same track because she asked, "What do you think *they* will tell Mutti Frida?"

I shook my head, partly in amazement that she had put my thoughts into words. "I've got no idea, but I think I'm going to be forced to go to the DDR by the school and my mother."

"Perhaps if you could convince her that travelling behind the Iron Curtain was dangerous, you could get her on your side?" Lili suggested.

"Now, there's a thought." My tone was grateful. "Do you think your family would be able to talk to her about this? I don't expect she'd need much convincing. The DDR and other eastern bloc countries don't have a good reputation in the west after the way the Russians put down the Hungarians in 1956."

Col perked up at this. "Oh, please, Lili. Could you get them to help?"

"Well, we can talk to my mother later today and see what she says."

"Okay." I paused for a moment. "It'll probably be best if I raise the subject with your mother, Lili. That way she will know I am worried about travelling behind the Iron Curtain."

"Are you saying you are not worried about it?" Col's voice was dismayed.

"Yes...er...no. Of course I am worried." I managed not to grab Col's hand. "I'm just thinking that if Lili's mum knows how worried I am she might push a bit harder with my mother."

Col subsided back into her seat. "Oh, yes, of course."

That afternoon, we gathered around the table at Lili's house, working on our homework until Mrs. Wiśniewski arrived home. It was Wednesday, early closing day, so Mutti Frida would have gone home at lunchtime and we'd be walking home alone.

After a while, Mrs. Wiśniewski came into the kitchen where we were working. "Would you like a glass of milk and perhaps a biscuit?"

A chorus of *"Tak proszę," (Yes, please)* ran round the table.

Mrs. Wiśniewski smiled. *"Twoje lekcje języka idą dobrze. " (Your language lessons are going well.)*

Col thought for a moment and then replied, *"Tak dziękuję. Twoja córka dobrze nas uczy." (Yes, thank you. Your daughter is a great teacher.)*

Mrs. Wiśniewski smiled broadly at Lili and then gazed at Col and me. "And she tells me you are helping her in every other class. Thank you." She whisked about the kitchen, getting glasses of milk and a plate of biscuits.

I glanced at Col and then at Lili's mother as she put the plate of biscuits on the table. "Mrs. Wiśniewski, can I ask you something, please?"

Lili's mother was a bit surprised by this. Our interactions had always been superficial up until now. "Yes, of course, Willi."

"I've won a trip to East Germany, the DDR, at Easter and I'm worried about going behind the Iron Curtain." I paused for a moment, staring into her eyes. "Is it ... safe?"

Out of the corner of my eye, I caught Col suppressing a slight smile. *Had I laid it on a bit too thick?*

Mrs. Wiśniewski pondered my words for a moment, so I pulled the letter from my satchel and gave it to her. She read through it and then pulled up a chair and sat down.

"First of all, Willi, congratulations on doing so well. You have been learning German for only a year and you win an essay competition."

"Well, I didn't win it, as the letter says."

Mrs. Wiśniewski waved my objection aside. "Rubbish, don't be so modest. Your essay was so good they offered you the prize." She reached across and helped herself to a biscuit, nibbling it as she thought. "You are right to be worried about visiting the Eastern Block as they are not trustworthy and twist the words and actions of others to fit their purposes." She finished her biscuit, leaning back in her chair. "It would be dangerous for Col or Lili to visit behind the Iron Curtain as they are European, and the Russians see them as their slaves – even a West German." She nodded at Col, thinking that Col and Mutti Frida were from West Germany, the BRD. "But you are English, and that's different."

"How is it different for me?" I asked, confused.

Mrs. Wiśniewski's face was stern. "Willi, you are English, part of the free west. You are their declared enemy in everything, so they have to treat you carefully." She paused. "You are not in the military, invading their airspace like Gary Powers or that unfortunate pilot shot down and killed over Cuba during the crisis. You are a child and someone they can, perhaps…influence. Someone who might help them in their war of ideas with the West."

I saw Col's gaze flickering towards me when Mrs. Wiśniewski called me a child, but I managed not to react.

Col covered her reaction. "Yes, Willi, they would take anything you say and twist it so that it seemed you support their world view."

Mrs. Wiśniewski gave Col an approving glance. "Indeed, but I think it is most unlikely that they would arrest you or prevent you from returning home on time. There is too much for them to lose in the propaganda war by throwing a child of the West into gaol."

This was not headed in the direction I had hoped or expected.

"You think there is no problem with me going to East Germany?"

Mrs. Wiśniewski pursed her lips. "I did not say that. Of course there is some danger. But that danger is more the propaganda value of having an intelligent young Englishman visit their country and say nice things about it." She leaned across the table and patted my hand. "But there is a great propaganda risk for them, too."

She must have seen the confusion on my face. *How could I be a propaganda risk?*

"They will show you the very best of their country and carefully pick the places you go and the people you will meet, hoping you will sing their praise when you return home. But they risk you seeing past all of that to the reality they are trying to hide."

Mrs. Wiśniewski leaned back in her chair, marshalling her thoughts for a few seconds. "I think you have a responsibility to go. You are an intelligent young man and will see beneath the propaganda veil that they draw across their society. You can tell young people here in the west the reality of life behind the Iron Curtain, why we must resist them and strive to bring freedom to the oppressed people of the eastern Europe."

This was totally unexpected. Mrs. Wiśniewski wanted me to become a propaganda tool in her fight with the oppressors of her country. It sounded like she would be pushing Mutti Frida and my mother to not just let me go but to send me. "Um, thank you. You've given me a few things to think about."

Mrs. Wiśniewski stood up, giving me an encouraging smile and left us to our homework. Lili's eyes were wide, almost shocked at her mother's vehemence.

The three of us sat in silence for about a minute before Col leant forward and took my hand. "I hope she doesn't call our mothers. We don't need that."

I nodded. Slowly, we returned to the books in front of us.

On the walk up to Col's house, I turned to Col, "You need to be careful."

She stared at me, wide-eyed. "About what?"

"I saw the expression on your face when Mrs. Wiśniewski called me a child."

Col tossed her head. "It's difficult for me, Will. Most of the time you are a teenager. It's only occasionally that you say something unexpected or react slightly differently that I remember what you are." She shrugged. "When Mrs. Wiśniewski described you as just a child, it struck me as funny."

"We both have things we don't want everyone knowing – although I don't think most people would believe me like you have. They'd probably just lock me away." I pulled a wry face at her.

Col nodded. "We both have to be careful not to give our secrets away."

We walked the rest of the way in silence, pondering the strange realities and dangers we both lived with.

When we arrived at Col's house, Mutti Frida sensed our mood and asked what was wrong. I took the letter out of my bag and handed it to her.

Mutti Frida's face was sympathetic. "Willi, we knew this was coming. It's not the end of the world."

I sighed. "I know, but…" My voice petered out in uncertainty.

"Well," Mutti Frida smiled encouragingly. "We will just have to convince your mother that it is not safe for you to travel to East Germany."

Neither Col nor I wanted to tell Mutti Frida what Mrs. Wiśniewski thought about this, so I nodded, and we worked on setting the table for tea.

What to say to my mother occupied my thoughts on the walk back to my house that evening. If I could convince her that it wasn't safe, that would stymie the school's efforts to use me for their propaganda – and Mrs. Wiśniewski 's efforts too. I was slightly distracted when I pushed open the back door.

"Hello Will." My mother glanced up from the kitchen table where she was sewing replacement buttons onto a couple of my father's shirts. "I hear you got the letter confirming your place on the trip to East Germany."

I was shocked to silence for a moment. "What?"

"Manners, Will." She chided me softly.

"Sorry. I beg your pardon."

My mother gave me a nod of acknowledgement. "Mrs. Wiśniewski rang earlier. She told me you showed her the letter."

Good grief. That was fast work; Mrs. Wiśniewski must be fired up about this.

"Yes. It arrived this morning just as I was leaving, so I took it with me."

"May I see it, please?"

I retrieved the letter in its envelope from my satchel.

She carefully lodged her threaded needle in the shirt collar. "Hm – the trip is during the Easter holidays, so it won't interfere with your school." She paused. "Do you want to go, Will?"

Finally, an adult was asking what I wanted. "No." I was emphatic.

My mother was surprised. "I would have thought you'd jump at the chance to go somewhere different – in particular, Germany." She stopped. "Why don't you want to go, Will?"

I couldn't tell her my real reason. "I'm scared of going behind the Iron Curtain. They are not like us and I'm frightened they might not let me come back."

I was slightly worried that my mother might not take me seriously, but she did. Her face hardened. "You're right, Will. The governments of those countries are not like us and they will use people to suit their own ends. But I think the people in those countries are just like us in the West." She paused thoughtfully. "Frau Schmidt showed me that not all Germans were Nazis and I'm sure that the ordinary people in East Germany have concerns about their government, even if they cannot speak about them. I think it would be good for you to visit and learn this for yourself."

This was terrible: even my mother wanted me to go.

I knew she saw that I was unconvinced. "Anyhow Will, we don't have to decide yet." She focused on the letter again. "You don't have to let them know for a week, so have a good think about it and come and talk to me some more about your concerns if you need to."

My sleep that night was a bit disturbed as all this rolled around in my head.

I updated Col and Lili on the bus to school in the morning.

"Willi, I'm so sorry." I saw that Lili was deeply embarrassed at what her mother had done. "I heard her on the phone to your mother, but I couldn't stop her."

"It's not your fault, Lili." I shrugged. "Your mother must feel strongly about this."

"Oh, she does, she certainly does," Lili said, sighing. "After she phoned your mother, I heard her talking to some of her friends that came over to play Bridge last night and they all agreed it was important for the English to learn what Russia was like." She paused, reaching back to what she had overheard the previous evening. "They said they are worried that the alliance with Russia during the war still colours British thinking about the Soviets and their global intentions. Educating young English people about the reality of the Soviet Empire is important to them."

I knew Col saw that I was becoming increasingly worried because she said softly, "Come on Willi, don't let this bother you." She winked at me and chuckled. "After all, what can a bunch of Polish ladies do about it?"

I smiled, as a measure of relief washed through me. "Thank you, Col, I don't suppose they can do very much."

The rest of the trip to Canterbury passed with Lili and Col discussing various boys and their suitability as boyfriends for Lili. It seemed that none of them passed muster for a variety of different reasons – and the discussion continued on the bus trip home. By the time we got off the bus at the Herne Bay bus station, I was forming the impression that there was a standard against which boys were being judged and that perhaps that standard related to Col-as-a-boy and perhaps me in some way, which was an uncomfortable thought as I was far from being a 'normal' boy, nor was Col.

As we turned into Lili's street, we passed a man leaning against the wall. We had gone a few steps further on when he called out. "William Johnstone?"

Reflexively, I turned around and was almost blinded by a flashbulb going off in my face. He had taken my photograph.

"What?" I was rooted to the spot in confusion.

The man just turned and walked swiftly away into town. This was so strange that we just stood there for a short while, gazing at one another.

"What was that about?" Lili asked as we finally walked the few yards to her front gate.

I could see the fear on Col's face. Was this part of her father searching for her? But if so, why take a photo of me?

When Mutti Frida arrived from the shop, Mrs. Wiśniewski buttonholed her, pushing her view that I should go on the trip. Mutti Frida was surprised at her vehemence and quietly suggested that it was up to me – and my mother.

"Yes, of course," Mrs. Wiśniewski agreed. "But it's such an opportunity for Willi and through him for his friends to discover the truth about the Russians and their lackeys. We should be encouraging him to go and his mother to let him."

The incongruity of Mrs. Wiśniewski talking to an East German about 'Russian lackeys' struck me, and I had to suppress a grim smile.

I saw Lili fidgeting in her chair: her mother's attitude was making her uncomfortable, so I leant close to her and whispered, "Remember, this is not your fault – but you can't let on the real reason I cannot go."

Lili gave me a small but grateful smile.

On the walk home, we started telling Mutti Frida about the photographer, but she stopped us. "When we get home, children."

Instead, Col started telling her about the boys at school showing interest in Lili.

181

Once the door was closed behind us, Mutti Frida sat us down and asked us to go through the incident in detail.

"It happened so fast." I thought about it for a moment. "We passed this man leaning against the fence a few doors away from Lili's house and then he called out my name. I turned round and he took my photo – dazzling me with the flash – then he took off up the street back into town."

Mutti Frida gazed at us both. "Did you see his camera as you went past him?"

We glanced at one another and then shook our heads.

"Hmm, he was hiding it." She thought for a moment. "It sounds like he was waiting for you, that he knew you would be there at about that time," Mutti Frida mused.

That was quite a frightening thought.

"But he called out your name, Willi, not Col's." Mutti Frida paused for a moment. "Col, had you turned round when the flash went off?"

"No, I don't think so." She closed her eyes, casting her mind back. "No, I'm sure about it. I wasn't dazzled like Willi."

"Hmm...I don't think they were trying to photograph you, Col. I don't think this man was working for your father. But why would he want a picture of Willi?"

I shrugged...and then a terrible thought occurred to me. "It couldn't be about that anonymous letter, could it? Someone's not going to drag that up, are they?"

Col grabbed my hand. "Oh, Willi. I hope not."

Mutti Frida smiled kindly. "I think perhaps you should tell your mother about this incident and your fears about it." She moved to her feet. "And I must go and make a phone call, even though I think this has nothing to do with us. Please get tea started – I won't be long."

In fact, she was away nearly forty minutes, so we had tea nearly ready to put on the table when she returned.

"Well?" Col asked, bearding Mutti Frida at the front door.

Mutti Frida shook her head. "They don't think it has anything to do with us." She hung her coat up and turned back. "It now seems from their contacts that your father, Col, believes we are in America as we disappeared into the American zone. He doesn't know that we simply went through the American zone and contacted the British." Mutti Frida chuckled. "I was commended on my subterfuge, even though it was entirely accidental."

I saw that the worry lines around Mutti Frida's eyes had lessened. Then she turned to me with sympathetic eyes. "But I think, Willi, that you may be right in your fears. Please know we will support you and your mother if things become...difficult."

"Thank you, Mutti Frida. I know you will."

Mutti Frida smiled sympathetically and then busied herself in the kitchen, dishing up the tea.

Col pushed me across my chair to sit beside me, wrapping her arms around me and whispering in my ear. "Remember your promise to speak to me, Willi, if things get too much."

I turned and fixed my attention on this beautiful young lady, ready to give me her total support, in spite of her own troubles. Her eyes were full of care and she slowly leaned forward to share a whisper of a kiss. Our eyes locked and I lost several seconds. I reached up and caressed her cheek in thanks for her deep well of compassion. Her eyes smiled into mine in understanding.

A cough from Mutti Frida roused us and we both blushed. Mutti Frida's smile was both a blessing and gentle reminder of our promise. Col and I shared a glance full of love tinged with embarrassment and we set about setting the table for tea.

***

My mother was sitting in the kitchen, reading the paper when I got home. I hung up my coat and sat down opposite her. She glanced at me over the top of *The Times* and then lowered it.

"Yes, Will?" She had seen the worry in my eyes.

The incident with the photographer poured out of me, propelled by my fears.

My mother waited for me to finish and then sat in silence, eyes closed, for a minute or so. Then she stirred, took a deep, strengthening breath and stiffened. "If that is what this is about, I am not going to let it rule my – our – life." Her voice was firm. "There's nothing we can do about it now and I'm not going to let it worry me." She took another deep breath and slowly released it. "If someone stirs this baseless allegation against me, I will fight them this time. I'm not going to let them control our lives any longer."

My mother had grown within the last year. Standing up to my father had, it seems, given her much more self-confidence outside her medical domain.

I nodded and shared a grim smile with her.

"Will, please let me know if anything else strange happens. I want to get to the bottom of this and put a stop to it." She slapped her hand on the table in emphasis, making me jump. "Once and for all."

Despite the looming problems, I went to bed heartened by my mother's increasing confidence.

***

Even though Col, Lili and I were alert to our surroundings, nothing odd happened, at least to our eyes and I was nowhere closer in convincing my mother that I shouldn't go on the trip at Easter. Mr. Sturr was pressing me for a positive response to the letter, but I told him that at home we were still discussing the dangers.

He gave a dismissive snort and walked away.

On Saturday afternoon, Col and I were sitting on the couch reading when a breathless Lili arrived, having run most of the way from her home. As she took off her coat, she produced a newspaper. "This is yesterday's *Dziennik Polski*, the Polish language newspaper here in England." She opened it to an internal page – and there was a photo of me with the blurry back view of Col and Lili, accompanied by a short column of text.

"What's my photo doing in a Polish-language newspaper?" I gazed at Lili in complete astonishment.

"I think this is my mother's influence at work." Lili's tone was apologetic. "She has many contacts in the Polish community. She has worked for many years helping Poles to settle in England, find a job and somewhere to live."

My Polish was improving but still not great and I was struggling to understand the article.

But Mutti Frida had scanned it over our shoulders. "Yes, Lili, I think you are right. This article is pushing your mother's view that the young people of this country should learn just how dangerous and devious the Soviet bloc is. And it's commending you for going to the DDR to learn that."

I glanced again at the photo. I was half-turned towards the camera, but full face. The girls were behind me and hadn't turned round, so Col was safe. I breathed a sigh of relief.

"You were right Col, neither of you girls had turned around when the photograph was taken."

Mutti Frida inspected the photo again. "He only took the one?" I nodded, and Mutti Frida sighed with relief.

"Lili, please can I take this copy home to show my mother? She will … want to see it."

I just managed to stop myself in time before I revealed to Lili a tendril of our family secret. I saw Col's eyes flaring with alarm and then relax as I wormed my way out of the near mistake.

Col quickly jumped in. "I expect that's the only copy your family has, Lili."

Lili nodded.

Col stared at me. "Is your mother home this afternoon?"

"Probably. She's on call; unless she's been called out to see a sick patient, she'll be there."

Col jumped to her feet. "Good. Let's walk round and show her the paper and then you can take it back home, Lili."

Mutti Frida stood up. "All right children, I think I'll come with you."

I saw that Lili was a bit cautious when we arrived. She had mostly met my mother professionally. My mother soon put her at ease by offering us homemade cake and milk, with a pot of tea for her and Mutti Frida. As we took our seats in the lounge room, Lili translated the article for her, with Col and I jumping in occasionally to substitute words, showing off our Polish to my mother.

I saw my mother's relief in her heavy sigh as she understood the recent photograph had nothing to do with our family secret, and she caught my eye and gave me a gentle nod of acknowledgement. I smiled back at her.

We sat and chatted for a while until the phone rang. My mother went out into the hall and answered it. She came back after a couple of minutes with a slip of paper in her hands. "I'm afraid I have to go and see a patient."

Mutti Frida stood up. "We will clean up the tea things, Frau Doktor. Willi can show us where things go and lock up when we leave."

"That's most kind of you. There's no need to wash up, just leave things on the sink. The cake goes back in the tin, Will." My mother gave us all a smile and whisked out, cloaked in her doctor's demeanour.

"Finish your cake and milk, children." Mutt Frida picked up the teapot, gave it a gentle shake and poured herself another cup of tea. "I don't drink much tea, but this is quite different. Do you know what it is, Willi?"

"It's black Chinese tea, I think. My mother always serves this at teatime. Some people put milk in it, but my mother says it should only be drunk black, with a slice of lemon as you are having it."

We munched on our slices of cake.

"Why did you not offer to translate the newspaper, Mutti?" Col asked.

Mutti Frida carefully returned her teacup to the saucer. "Well, we have a native Polish speaker with us and that gives Lili precedence, don't you think?"

I saw Lili preening slightly at that comment.

"In any case," Mutti Frida continued, "I do not want to have to explain to your mother how I came to speak Polish."

I tried to remember if I'd told my mother that Mutti Frida spoke Polish and was involved in our Polish lessons – I couldn't remember if I had, so concluded that I probably hadn't. I made a mental note not to do so in the future as Mutti Frida wanted to keep that to herself.

Shortly after, we were in the kitchen washing up and putting away the tea things, chatting in our usual mixture of English, German and Polish when I heard the front door open and shortly after my father walked into the kitchen. "What is going on?" His voice was hard and flat, eyes glaring at me. "Who are all these foreigners?"

Mutti Frida stepped between my father and me, her right hand fingering her left forearm. "You remember me, I think, Herr Johnstone." Her voice was cold and suddenly a slight German accent could be heard. I saw my father glance at her arm and shift back slightly. "We were having tea with Frau Doktor Johnstone when she was called out. We are cleaning up and will shortly be leaving." She glanced at the teapot. "I think the tea is still hot enough. Can I pour you a cup?"

My father tried to see me round Mutti Frida.

She shifted slightly, blocking my father. "Tea?" she queried again, now brandishing the teapot almost aggressively. There was a definite edge to her voice.

"Hmmph." My father grunted, turned and walked out of the kitchen.

We were subdued as we quickly finished washing up and drying the tea things, dressed and slipped out of the back door.

"Your father is very different from your mother, Willi," Lili remarked. "He is a bit scary."

I just nodded. His behaviour in front of my friends embarrassed me and that made me angry with him. The short walk back to Col's house helped settle me and by the time we arrived back there, my mood had lifted somewhat.

"Lili, does your mother know you are here?" Mutti Frida asked.

Lili finished hanging up her coat. "She was out when I found the newspaper. I left her a note on the kitchen table."

"She would be expecting you to be home for supper. Would you like to phone her to make sure she knows you are here?"

"Yes, thank you."

Once Lili had phoned, we played cards for a while before Lili had to leave.

"Don't forget the newspaper, Lili," Mutti Frida reminded her.

Lili grabbed it off the side table and waved it at Mutti Frida. "Thanks, Frau Schmidt."

I was wary when I got home in the evening. The afternoon's confrontation with my father was on my mind. My young brain was ashamed of his behaviour towards my friends and my old brain was fed up with having to pussyfoot around him. There was a light on in the kitchen, but no-one was there. As I hung my coat up in the hall, I heard music playing on the radio in the lounge room.

I stood there for a minute, listening for voices – I truly did not want to be in the same room as my father.

"Will, is that you?" My mother called.

I opened the door ... only my mother was in the room. "Your father left for London early this evening. It seems he has an early meeting tomorrow."

I felt myself relax. "On a Sunday?"

"Apparently." I heard the disbelief in my mother's voice. "Come and sit down and we can talk about the trip to Germany."

"I still don't want to go," I bridled.

My mother raised her eyebrows. "I don't understand why not, Will."

I shrugged. "I just don't feel I would be safe."

My mother nodded. "I understand your feeling that way." She looked at me slightly sideways. "But lots of people do go ... and return without any trouble."

I shrugged again as I didn't know what to say.

My mother was silent for a moment. "I think it would be good for you. It would give you new perspectives on the world." Her eyes searched my face. "You live a fairly constrained life, you know – just school, Col and Lili. I think you need to widen your horizons and meet more people."

Unbeknownst to her, I had a lifetime of perspectives stored away in my head. "I read a lot, including the newspaper every day ... and I'm learning French, German, Latin and Polish and reading their literature. I think my view's wide enough, don't you?"

My mother frowned slightly. "Will, you are an intelligent person. You need to get out and see the world and this Germany trip is a great opportunity. How many people your age get a chance like this?"

I stared at my mother for a second or two: it was clear she thought I should go. "Okay, I'll think about it."

The rest of the weekend passed quietly, and Monday seemed normal until Col and I joined Lili on the bus to Canterbury.

March 1964

On Monday morning as we walked down the aisle of the bus towards Lili, she stood up and waved a newspaper. Before we even sat down, she blurted out, "Willi, you're in the local paper."

What now?

Lili handed me the paper, folded to an inside page. There was that photo of me again and a short article that basically repeated what the Polish newspaper had said, except it added that I was the son of Dr Johnstone, a local doctor in Herne Bay. It felt like everyone was conspiring to force me to take the trip.

I shook my head and sighed. "I have to reply to the letter tomorrow, telling them whether I will accept the award or not."

Neither Col nor Lili said a word, but Col surreptitiously squeezed my hand sympathetically.

At school, Mr. Sturr was on my case about it, too. The feeling that I was being hemmed in grew ever stronger.

On the bus home, my impending decision stifled most normal conversation and it got worse at Lili's house as Mrs. Wiśniewski was home early and pushed her view strongly until I insisted we needed to get on with our homework. She gave me a hard stare before turning away.

Mutti Frida was later than usual in meeting us at Lili's house.

She apologised to Mrs. Wiśniewski, "I'm sorry I'm late, Daria. I was delayed at the shop for a while."

"Nothing serious, I hope?"

I noticed that Col was searching her mother's face intently.

"No, just a mix up in the stock list that took a while to sort out." She turned to Col and me, keeping her face blank. "Come on children, we need to let these good people have their supper."

We bustled out of the house and once we were a few yards along the road, Col grabbed her mother's hand. "What's going on, Mutti?"

Mutti Frida shook her head. "When we get home, Col."

Col frowned, but we walked home mostly in silence, my sword of Damocles suspended above us all.

Col pounced as the front door closed behind us. "What's going on?"

Mutti Frida hung up her coat. "Come and sit down, you two."

Col grabbed my hand and pulled me into a seat.

"Well?"

Mutti Frida pulled out a chair and sat down. "Herr Watling was waiting for me when we closed up the shop." She paused, glancing sideways at me, before continuing. "It seems that the Polish community has tentacles that reach even into MI6 – and then there's the article in the local newspaper today." Another pause ... and Mutti Frida' s face was apologetic when she turned to me. "Willi, they now think it would be suspicious if you did not go."

Col sat bolt upright in her chair. "What?"

I stared at her, equally stunned.

"It seems that you have become a bit of a *cause celebre* for the awarding committee. Your tardiness in replying is seen as a reluctance to go, yet there is a cheer squad pushing for you to 'see through' the front the DDR will put up for you." She sighed, apologetically. "All of this has made you rather...visible."

"If it was just you ... I mean if it were not for your fears about our safety, would you go?" Col asked.

"Um ... I don't know, that's something I haven't considered. Your safety is the most important thing to me."

Col gave my hand a gentle squeeze.

"Herr Watling doesn't think there is any risk to us if you go. In fact, they think that you must go now. That if you don't, the *Stasi*, my husband, will wonder why and they may send someone to investigate you, which would be dangerous for us."

Good grief. Now even Mutti Frida was pushing for me to go. All of this ran through my head as we ate supper and sat there reading afterwards – rather distractedly on my part.

My mother and sister were in the lounge room when I arrived home. My sister briefly raised her head and then returned to her book, but my mother put down her newspaper and patted the settee, inviting me to sit beside her. "Hello, Will. You're becoming a bit of a local star." She smiled as I sat down beside her. "Are you any closer to deciding what to do?"

My sister frowned. "I don't see what all the fuss is about. Surely it can't matter what some random boy does?"

My mother ignored the remark. "Well?"

"I don't have to make up my mind until tomorrow."

"That's true. So...?"

"So, I want to sleep on it tonight."

"Okay, Will." My mother paused. "I want you to know that it is your decision. You've heard my views ..." she paused and gave a humourless laugh. "... and those of lots of other people, too. But it's your life and you should decide for yourself."

I nodded. If only it was that easy. My problem was that it wasn't just my life that would be affected, whichever way I decided. "I'm going to bed. Perhaps it will be clearer for me in the morning."

My mother smiled gently. "Goodnight, Will. Sleep well."

Surprisingly, sleep came quickly, but when I woke in the morning, confusing shards of dreams afflicted me. I lay there, pushing them aside for a while, but I now realised that I had to take up the offer. It seemed too problematic for Col and Mutti Frida if I did not go. That everyone else and their dogs wanted me to go for their own reason did not carry any weight.

I dressed and headed down to breakfast, where I told my mother of my decision.

"Okay, Will. I'll pick up a passport application for you and make an appointment for you to get a photo taken late one afternoon this week."

Of course – no photobooths or even Polaroid cameras. "Thank you."

I wandered down to our front gate. Col arrived shortly after and we set off for the bus and joined Lili on the back seat.

I gazed at the two girls. "I've decided I have to go."

Col nodded. "But you don't want to?"

I sighed in frustration. "It's almost like I've been pushed into deciding this way." I saw that Col was frowning.

"Not by you and Mutti Frida, Col, but by everyone else. All this stuff in the newspapers has made it difficult and it now seems that you will be safer if I do go." I released a frustrated breath. "Even though I find that hard to believe."

"Oh, Willi. I'm sorry things have turned out this way."

I snorted. "It's not your fault, Col. I should never have entered this wretched competition." As I spoke, I felt shame flood me: *I had been showing off and entered without thinking through the implications.*

Col's sensitivity showed again as she gently squeezed my hand. Lili had been silent through this and I could see she was upset about her mother's part in this.

"It's all right, Lili. What's happened is not your fault. Please don't let it worry you."

"But I do, Willi. If Mama had not interfered and got that article published, none of this pressure on you would have happened." Lili was almost in tears.

I reached across and clasped her hand until she glanced up. "It's not your fault, Lili." I held her gaze for a few seconds until she gave me a tentative smile.

I shrugged. "It's all water under the bridge now, anyway. My mother is arranging my passport application and a photo, and I'll tell my German teacher, Mr. Sturr, today that I'm going. Things are moving along and now I have to make the best of them."

"Do you know where you are going?" Col asked.

"Not yet. I suppose they'll tell me that once I accept the prize."

As usual, I got off the bus a couple of stops before the girls and walked into school. I had time before morning assembly to write my letter of acceptance. I could pick up an envelope and stamp in Herne Bay as the post office was almost on our route to Lili's house.

After my German class, I told Mr. Sturr that I was accepting the prize and he was delighted.

"Excellent, excellent. It's a great honour for the school and I'm sure your parents are proud of you." He tipped his glasses forward and peered at me over them. "Hmm...I expect you to write a report of your visit to East Germany for the school magazine."

"Yes, sir." I escaped quickly to avoid him from loading me with anything else. He was a pretty good teacher but could be quite pompous at times.

As planned, on the way to Lili's house we diverted via the post office and I posted my acceptance letter. I was now committed, like Julius Caesar crossing the Rubicon: *Alea iacta est.*

The next few days felt strange: there had been so much tension building up to the decision and so many threads had seemed to be weaving into a knot of truly Gordian proportions, that I felt almost lost and, well, empty now the decision was made. This put a strain on things with Col and Lili, who tried, without success, to lift me out of my grey mood. I knew this depression worried Col and several times over the following days I noticed her thoughtful assessment of me. Despite her care for me and Lili's cheerful outlook, I found the emptiness hard to shake.

I duly had my passport photo taken and my mother and I completed the passport application and took it to the post office.

On Friday evening, my mother and I checked on the old suitcases stored in the loft. They were all rather tatty. We went shopping on Saturday afternoon, acquiring a new suitcase. It was eye-opening to see how primitive suitcases were compared to the strong, light, wheeled ones from my old life. I would have to carry the one we selected: none of the suitcases we saw had wheels. We also bought a couple of shirts and pairs of slacks. My school uniform was essentially a black suit and my mother decided that, dry cleaned and pressed, would do for formal occasions in the DDR.

A few days later, a thick envelope from the International Youth Cultural Exchange Program arrived in the mail. I went through it that evening with my mother and took it with me the following day on the bus, but I did not bring it out until we arrived at Lili's house in the afternoon.

Col and Lili pored over it, asking questions which I could not answer: the documents were the sum total of the information I had. All the winners (*how many?* I wondered) were to meet at the Victoria Station Hotel in

London on the Tuesday after Easter, the 31st March, by noon. There we would get to meet everyone else, staying for the night. On Wednesday morning, we would go by bus to Heathrow airport to catch a BEA flight to West Berlin. We would spend one night in West Berlin before going by bus to East Berlin. We would stay there for four days, visiting the *Staatsoper* for a performance and several museums and art galleries. We were going to visit a school – a *Polytechnische Oberschule*, a combined primary and grammar school Col explained, and we'd spend time with members of the *Freie Deutsche Jugend*.

"What's that? Were you a member?" Lili asked, sharply

"No, Lili. You have to be fourteen before you can join." She paused, raising an eyebrow at Lili. "I know what you're thinking and its nothing like the *Hitler Jugend*." Then her voice softened. "I was a member of *Pionierorganisation Ernst Thälmann*, but then all young children were. They're like the Cubs and Brownies here in England."

We would then travel to Dresden for more of the same and then on to Leipzig before returning to Berlin, where we would visit the *Volkskammer*, the East German Parliament before returning via West Berlin to England.

On several occasions when Lili was asking questions, I sensed that Col was holding back. We both knew she was from the DDR and specifically Leipzig, so I didn't understand her reticence.

Mutti Frida duly arrived and we walked back to their house. After tea, I gave Mutti Frida the documents. She slid the papers out of what was becoming a well-worn envelope. After a while, she glanced up from the papers. "You will have a busy time on this trip, Willi."

"It certainly doesn't seem we'll have much time to ourselves."

Mutti Frida carefully folded the papers and slid them back into the envelope.

"Can you tell me more about what to expect?" I asked.

Out of the corner of my eye, I saw Col shaking her head. "I don't think we should do that Willi."

"Why not – you know all about Leipzig and you must have visited East Berlin and Dresden."

"Col's right, Willi. We can't tell you much – they would be suspicious. After all, how would an English boy know much about East Germany?"

"Oh, I see what you mean." I thought for a moment. "Perhaps the library has some information, we can stop there on the way home tomorrow. Oh – and I'll ask my German teacher, too."

At the end of my German class, I told Mr. Sturr I was trying to find information about East Germany and the cities we were visiting.

"Hm…I was in East Berlin a few years ago." He paused, casting his mind back to his visit. "It's not as well developed as West Berlin – but then

192

it's not seeking to develop a capitalist society, but one of cooperation." His eyes drifted away from mine as he thought. "Hmm…perhaps I can find you some information." His gaze returned to my face. "When are you leaving, boy?" He knew my name well enough, his refusal to use it was an unconscious indicator of his old-fashioned attitudes. I didn't like it but showing that would not get me what I wanted.

"Immediately after Easter, sir."

He nodded. "Excellent, excellent. That gives us a couple of weeks. Leave it with me and I'll see what I can do."

That afternoon, Mrs. Price was at the library desk when we arrived and gave me the evil eye as usual. I found the older librarian and asked for help, but unfortunately, there was precious little information in the library about post-war East Germany, just a few slightly disapproving paragraphs in the Encyclopedia Britannica covering some basic information.

Col continued in her refusal to answer any questions, insisting that I could only use the information that I found out myself. But then help arrived from an unexpected source: Mrs. Wiśniewski. Lili must have told her about my search for information and through her contacts turned up some copies of *Neues Deutschland* – the newspaper of the government of the DDR.

She sat down at the table where the three of us were doing our homework. "Now Willi, I have managed to get some information for you." She laid the four newspapers on the table but kept her hand firmly on them. "You need to understand that this newspaper is run by and for the government of the DDR – it is propaganda aimed in part at the people of East Germany but also at the west – particularly West Germany."

I started to reach for the papers, eager for any insight into the society I was to visit, but Mrs. Wiśniewski was not finished with her admonitions.

"Willi, read them carefully – read between the lines and behind the words, knowing that many of them are lies." Her voice was emphatic. "Do not be taken in by their lies, Willi." She then pushed them across the table towards me.

"Thank you, Mrs. Wiśniewski."

The papers were from the last week in February, about a week old, but I was not seeking current news from them but a feeling for the society and its culture. As today was a Polish day, I reluctantly folded the papers and slid them into my satchel for later.

Once we arrived back at Col's house, I pulled them out.

Mutti Frida's eyes widened in surprise. "Where did you get those, Willi?"

"Mrs. Wiśniewski got them for me. I don't know how."

Mutti Frida picked up the one on top and started skimming over it. I grabbed the next one and, after watching her mother and me disappear into their pages, Col picked one up and flicked through it in a desultory fashion, turning pages.

I was deep in an article lauding the education system when I heard Col gasp. "*Mutti, Mutti. Er ist es*." She pushed the paper across the table to her mother.

Mutti Frida's eyes dropped to the page Col had pushed across and closed her eyes, opening them after a few seconds. "Yes, Col, that's him." She picked up the paper and started reading the article.

"Who is it, Col?" I asked, although I had a pretty good idea.

Col slumped back in her chair. "My father." Her voice held a quaver; seeing him had shaken her, so I leaned across and took her into my arms.

Mutti Frida scanned through the article. "It seems he has had a promotion to *Oberstleutnant*, making him the second in command of the Leipzig office."

I didn't understand. "Why would a secret policeman have his photo in the paper?"

Mutti Frida glanced up. "The *Stasi* is not a secret police force. They are responsible for internal security. Whilst they have undercover police, spying on dissidents and such, their senior officers are known." She reached across and took Col's hand. "That's why Col was lonely – everyone knew her father was a *Stasi* officer and kept their distance."

I nodded; Col had explained this before. I pulled the paper across and read the caption under the photo. It was taken on the steps of the Leipzig Opera house – several senior party officials had attended a gala performance. Herr Schmidt was in the front row, a tall, somewhat gaunt-faced man with receding, grey hair.

Mutti Frida tugged the newspaper back towards her. "He's starting to show his age," she mused. "But he's still climbing the ladder inside the *Stasi*. My defection does not seem to have harmed his career."

"Don't the authorities care that he was a Nazi?" I asked.

Mutti Frida shook her head. "After the war, most bureaucrats that survived had been involved with the Nazis. But the Russians soon realised that someone had to run the country and only those people had the skills." She peered at me. "It was the same in West Germany too, I expect."

"But what about the trials of war criminals?"

Mutti Frida shrugged. "Being a member of the Nazi party didn't make you a war criminal. Only the worst of the worst went on trial – and not all of them. Everyone else just faded into the background and got on with rebuilding the country and their lives."

I was confused. "Why did you have to flee if Col's father was just a Nazi policeman?"

Mutti Frida leaned back in her chair. "I knew when I first met Axel that he had been an officer in the *Orpo* – and that meant he almost certainly was a Nazi Party member, but he assured me his duties were just policing inside Germany and he had left leaning sympathies. It was what I discovered later that showed he was a liar and a war criminal."

I could see her pondering what to tell us. "And?"

Mutti Frida gazed at each of us and came to a decision. "I met an Auschwitz survivor ... I told you she helped me get past my hate. Dora recognised Axel as the commander of the *Orpo* group that rounded up her family in June 1941 when the Nazis broke the treaty with Stalin and attacked what had been eastern Poland on the way to Russia." She paused, sadness suffusing her face. "Dora was in the fields when they arrived at her village and hid in the woods, escaping the initial round-up." Mutti Frida paused, fiddling with the newspaper. I saw that this was making her uncomfortable, but she took a breath and carried on. "Axel's *Orpo* group was working with an *SS Einsatzgruppen* – the death squads that followed behind the army and did the killing of Jews and other undesirables. Dora saw some of the executions from her hiding place and Axel was there ... watching. That was when my suspicions about him started." Mutti Frida pursed her lips as if tasting something bitter. "Dora was rounded up a few weeks later and eventually ended up at Auschwitz. It was through her that I met others that gave me more information about Axel's wartime activities. I collected names, places and have statements from six people about them." She stopped, staring at Col before reaching across and taking her hand. "Two of those people saw him shooting an old Jewish couple that didn't move fast enough for him."

I focused on Col, who was quite pale. This was her father ... *what must she be feeling?* I pulled her onto my lap. She leaned her head against me, and I felt a tremor running through her.

"Did you give this evidence to British security?"

Mutti Frida shook her head. "I was scared it would be destroyed if I were caught. When I realised Axel suspected I had information about his wartime activities, Col and I fled, leaving the evidence in a safe place. I explained what I had found out to British security, but they didn't seem interested." Mutti Frida sat down in silence for a few seconds and then shrugged. "Come on, let's get supper started."

After supper, Col and I read the newspapers. I saw some of what Mrs. Wiśniewski was talking about. Unlike in our newspapers, it seemed there was little wrong within the society of the DDR and there were many examples of how life was improving for everyone. In the few places where

195

the West was mentioned, it was mainly to draw unfavourable comparisons with the 'more advanced society' in the DDR.

Eventually, I folded up the newspapers and put them in my bag.

Col hugged me tightly after I put on my coat. "You should be looking forward to your trip, Willi. After all, you're going to be flying to and from Berlin."

I gave her a wan smile. "I know, but I'm finding it hard to muster any enthusiasm."

Col gave me another hug. "It'll all be fine – and I will be here when you come back."

I found Col's confidence difficult to emulate. As I walked home, I realised that underneath all the feelings that I had been manipulated into going to the DDR, was a gnawing fear. I was scared that because of me Herr Schmidt would somehow discover Col and Mutti Frida and they would be forced to move away.

I went to bed troubled: would Col be there when I got back?

***

In the morning, when Col and I walked to the back of the bus to join Lili in our usual back seat, she leapt up as we approached. "Willi, Col. Have you heard that the Russians have shot down an American plane over East Germany?"

Good grief! Did this happen in my world? I couldn't recall such an incident but that did not mean it didn't happen. We sat down.

"What happened?" Col asked.

"The BBC said that an American plane had radio trouble and flew into East German airspace by mistake. Russian fighters intercepted it, shot it down and everyone on board was killed. The Russians are claiming the plane was on a spying mission and they are not letting the Americans into the DDR to recover the bodies."

"Do you think this will affect your trip, Willi?" Col asked.

"I have no idea." I shrugged, but inside, I was hoping the trip would be cancelled. "We'll have to wait and see I suppose." I wanted to grab my mobile phone and check the news…*in my dreams*. But the school library had a copy of the newspapers. I could at least read what had happened thus far. I headed straight to the library when I arrived at school only to discover that the newspapers were still in the librarian's office and he was out somewhere.

I groaned with frustration and turned away, only to bump into Mr. Pollock.

196

Once we disentangled ourselves, he blinked in recognition. "Hmm, you seem a bit down. Can I help?" I was surprised – he had meant it when he offered me help.

"I wanted to read the newspapers about the American aircraft shot down in East Germany. It might affect my upcoming visit there."

"Oh yes. You're that boy, aren't you." He gave me an encouraging smile and glanced over at the empty newspaper racks. "The papers must still be in the librarian's office." He walked over and tried the door: unlocked. Mr. Palmerston, the librarian, was still nowhere to be seen.

"I'm sure he won't mind me bringing the papers out for you." And he did just that.

"Thank you, sir." I was truly grateful for his help and sat down with *The Times,* opening it as it stubbornly still refused to print headlines on the front page, covering it with classified advertisements. It seemed the Russians were not denying having shot down the plane near Vogelsberg. They were, however, insisting that the plane was on a spying mission and had refused to allow US inspection of the wreckage or released the bodies of those on board. The article hinted that the US might take the issue to the UN security council.

Throughout the day, my desire to check the news kept bringing me to a standstill. My old brain expected to be able to satisfy its desire for news at a moment's notice. At school, I didn't even have access to the BBC radio news bulletins. By the time I met the girls on the bus I was almost screaming with frustration.

Col sensed my tension was running high. "Take a few deep breaths, Willi."

"I can't believe I have to wait until six o'clock to get the BBC news."

Lili leaned forward from her seat behind us. "There will be a newspaper at home unless Mama has taken it with her."

"But that will be talking about the situation as it was last night. I've already read *The Times* at school. Things will have changed by now." I heard the frustration in my voice and closed my eyes, taking a couple of deep breaths. "I'm sorry Col, Lili. It's not your fault, I'm just used to getting news regularly."

I felt Col tensing beside me – *had I really said that*? Fortunately, Lili did not seem to pick up on my mistake. I had tried to explain to Col about smartphones and the Internet, but to the technology of the 60s, the concepts were completely alien and I'm not sure she understood much at all.

"Well, if you have the money, we could pick up the evening newspaper on the way home," Lili suggested.

"Good thinking." I smiled at her.

We diverted slightly and picked up the early edition of the *Evening News*. Things seemed to have reached a stalemate. The US maintained that the plane, with an instructor and two students on board, was on a navigation training exercise when it experienced radio problems, no longer responding to radio calls on any frequency. The US was demanding access to the crash site to examine the wreckage and recover the bodies of the airmen. For their part, the Russians were insisting that they shot down a US plane on a spying mission. The *News* also reported that there had been some Warsaw Pact troop movements in the area where the US plane crashed. *What did they think the US would do?*

After we had all read the article, we were none the wiser as to what the future might hold, so we just worked on our homework and practised our Polish. When Mrs. Wiśniewski arrived home, she saw the newspaper I had bought. She leaned across towards me from behind Lili's chair. "You can see the sort of monsters the Russians are, Willi, shooting down an unarmed plane."

I saw Lili roll her eyes at me as she realised her mother was on her hobby horse again.

Mrs. Wiśniewski grasped her daughter's shoulder, squeezing hard enough to make Lili wince as she warmed to her tirade. "You, Willi, have to help the young people of this country see through the Russian lies."

"Mama, you're hurting me." Lili almost squawked.

Mrs. Wiśniewski snatched her hand off Lili's shoulder. "Oh, Lili. I'm sorry. I got carried away." She leaned down and kissed her daughter on the cheek.

Lili frowned and rubbed her shoulder. "Don't get so wound up, Mama." Still rubbing her shoulder, pulling a sour face.

Mrs. Wiśniewski was flustered and changed the conversation. "How about some cake and milk?"

"That would be lovely, Mrs. Wiśniewski. Thank you." Col smiled, helping Mrs. Wiśniewski past her embarrassment. Mutti Frida arrived as we were picking up the cake crumbs and the odd currant with our fingertips.

"Come on, Col." I stood up, chivvying Col towards the door. "If we leave now, we'll be back at your house in time to hear the six o'clock news."

"All right, Willi," Mutti Frida laughed. "I know you want to hear the news."

As we walked to Col's home, I felt a bit like a sheepdog, always nudging Col and her mother to move a bit faster. As it was, we arrived in plenty of time to listen to the BBC news. The Vogelsberg incident led the bulletin.

Following the refusal by the Russians to permit a US team to visit the crash site and recover the bodies of those on board, Russia has moved military units closer to the East German border. The US has responded by raising the alert level for its European units and has asked that NATO respond in a similar fashion. As yet, NATO alert levels remain unaltered.

With neither the US nor the Soviets backing down and indeed both making moves with their military, the UN Secretary-General U Thant has called for calm. President De Gaulle has offered his services as a negotiator to bring this matter to a satisfactory conclusion, but neither side has responded to the offer.

I certainly didn't remember anything like this from my previous life. Both the US and Soviets were rattling their sabres and neither side seemed to be listening to the other. I just hoped that JFK would pick up the red phone and sort things out directly with Khrushchev before a military commander did something stupid.

I went to bed that night worried about the rising East-West tension but hopeful that this situation would cancel my trip, which was a truly weird mix of emotions.

At breakfast, the BBC news again led with the Vogelsberg incident. It sounded as if neither side was backing down and both were accusing the other of moving military units in such a way as to exacerbate tension.

My mother saw that I was getting increasingly worried because she asked, "Is there a phone number you can ring to find out about what's happening to your trip, Will?"

There probably was if I looked. I retrieved the envelope from my bedroom: there was a London phone number.

"I don't expect anyone will be there before nine o'clock, Will. I will phone them during the day if you like?"

"Thank you." I copied the number and gave the slip of paper to my mother, then returned the envelope to my bedroom. I was unsure of my sister and didn't want to tempt fate.

The girls sensed my mood because they left me alone on the bus, chatting amongst themselves.

Once again, I headed for the library to read *The Times,* but there wasn't any new information. That afternoon I again purchased an *Evening News* on the way to Lili's house. It seemed that things were much the same, both sides claiming the movement of the other side's military units was provocative, but nothing of import had happened. We set to work on our homework – in German today.

We had been working for about forty minutes when the phone rang, and Lili got up to answer it. A moment later she called out. "Willi, it's your mother." She must have news about the trip. Lili handed me the phone.

"Hello?"

"Will, it's Mummy. I must be quick as I'm between patients. I spoke with the Youth Exchange people and they told me the trip is still going ahead. They expect this trouble will blow over in a couple of days."

"Okay, thank you, Mummy."

"I'll see you at home, later. Bye."

"Bye."

Col and Lili sat there, expectantly.

I sighed. "The trip's going ahead. The organisers expect this to blow over in a couple of days."

Which was what happened, eventually. Ten days after shooting down the plane, the Russians returned the bodies of the 'three spies' to the Americans and the incident slipped quietly out of the news as the winter term came to an end, just before Easter.

Easter – early April 1964

School ended for the three of us on the Wednesday before Easter and we made plans to spend time together over the Easter period. I had to travel up to London on the Tuesday after Easter and my mother insisted that I came home on the Monday evening. I eventually negotiated that I would be home by eight o'clock that evening: Col and Mutti Frida wanted to give me a farewell dinner.

When I arrived, I found the girls dressed up in the finery they had worn at Christmas, which made me feel a bit underdressed, in slacks and a pullover. As we finished the delicious *Strudel mit Schlagsahne* Col and Lili had prepared under Mutti Frida's supervision, Col slid her hand into mine. "What time's your train?"

"I'm catching the twenty-five to ten train which gets me to Victoria before eleven o'clock. That gives me plenty of time to get to the Victoria Hotel where I'm meeting the rest of the group at noon."

Col gave me a strained smile. I knew she was going to miss me, but I also knew that lurking underneath was the fear that, despite all the advice, my trip would reveal her location to her father.

I slipped my hand into hers and gave it a gentle squeeze. "Please don't come to the station to see me off. You never know who may be watching."

Col frowned at me and I saw that she was about to argue.

Mutti Frida leaned across. "Col, Willi is right," she said, sadly. "We shouldn't go."

"I'll come and see you off, Willi." Lili said.

I watched Col stiffen. *Was she jealous?* Since the near disaster at Mrs. Wiśniewski's Christmas party, our three-way friendship had experienced few problems, something which only now I realised was unusual. I saw Mutti Frida glance between Col and Lili.

"If that's all right, Col?"

Lili's gentle question drew a small, self-deprecating sigh from Col. "I'm sorry, Lili. Yes, of course that's all right." Her eyes were full of sadness. "I just wish I could be there too."

After we cleared the supper table and washed up, Mutti Frida retrieved her bottle of Schnapps and filled a tiny glass.

"Willi. Wir wünschen du eine sichere und glückliche Reise in den Osten." (Willi. We wish you a safe and happy journey to the east). She raised the glass to me and tasted it.

Then she passed the drink to our friend. "Just a sip, Lili."

"Yes, Will, have a safe trip to East Germany." Lili touched the glass to her lips and made a bit of a face. She shuddered slightly at the taste, quickly passing the glass across to Col.

Col picked up the glass, holding my eyes over the rim. *"Zwei Wochen sind so lange. Komm sicher zu mir zurück, Liebling."* (Two weeks is such a long time. Come back to me safely, darling.) She sipped but mostly suppressed the shudder, wanting to put up a brave face. Slowly, she reached across the table to hand me the glass.

I took the glass glancing at Mutti Frida and Lili but returning to hold Col's gaze. I thought for a moment. *"Tu es toute ma vie. Reste en sécurité ici en sachant que je penserai à toi tout le temps."* (You are my entire life. Stay here in safety, knowing that I will think of you all the time).

Col's eyes closed for a moment and I heard Lili's soft intake of breath. French was our secret language and Lili's weakest, but she too had understood what I had said. When Col's eyes opened, I saw the moisture gathering at the corners.

I took a sip, the alcohol exploding the taste of Schnapps across my tongue and I nearly coughed, even though I had expected it – my young body was not used to spirits. I placed the glass down in front of Mutti Frida, whose eyes lingered on me. She may not have understood the French, but she understood the emotional content of what had passed between her daughter and me. She gave me an understanding smile, picked up the glass and drained the remaining mouthful.

Col jumped up and retrieved a package wrapped in blue tissue paper, tied with a delicate bow of thin white ribbon, from the dresser drawer. She sat down and slid it across to me.

I smiled at Col, recognising the carefully preserved paper, and opened the package: a leather wallet.

"Something to take with you to remind you of all of us during your travels."

"Thank you," I said, smiling at all three of them.

"And now, Willi, you must leave to be home on time."

We all rose from the table. Col hung back whilst Lili and Mutti Frida gave me intense hugs.

Mutti Frida's sensitivity showed again. "Col will say goodbye to you in the hall, Willi."

I put the wallet in my trouser pocket and went out into the hall with Col, who firmly shut the door behind us. We shared several lingering kisses before Col gently pushed me away. "You must go, Willi." I heard the trembling in her voice before it became firmer again, more in control. "And when you return, we will have that talk about our promise with Mutti." Her eyes held mine.

I saw that there was trust, fear and desire in them, and a frisson ran through me, lifting the hairs down my back and arms. I leaned in and planted a gentle kiss on the tip of her nose and caressed her cheek.

"Take care of you." I turned and walked out of the door. I paused at the gate, turning to receive and return a blown kiss before the door closed.

As I walked home, the moisture on my cheeks was cold in the night air.

My mother sensed my mood when I walked into the kitchen, even though she did not know the actual reason for it. She gathered me into her arms, staying silent for a while. Eventually, she relaxed the hug.

"I know you're worried about this trip. I'm sure everything will be fine, but be careful over there, Will." Her voice firmed. "Don't make life difficult for yourself, or anyone else."

I nodded.

"Hot chocolate?"

"Thank you."

I hung about in the kitchen and then took the mug up to my room and checked my suitcase again. I transferred the money I had taken out of my Post Office account into my new wallet, putting it on my desk with my passport and the information about the trip. That would go in my duffel bag, along with a jumper and a few other things I might want with me all the time. I had pondered what books to take and had settled on Thomas Mann's *Der Tod in Venedig* and Shakespeare's *Sonnets*, both of which were set texts. After a moment, I added my pure Maths textbook to leaven the mixture and slipped the picture of Herr Schmidt I had cut from the newspaper into it. I wanted to make sure I recognised him in the unlikely event that I saw him. After a moment's thought, I also slipped in the copy of my essay that I had laboriously written out: photocopying was another technology I missed.

Despite my worries over the trip's possible consequences for Col and Mutti Frida the emotions of the last few days had drained me. I slept so soundly that my mother had to wake me when she checked on me at half-past seven. I hustled through my morning ablutions, packed my wash bag and did one final check on the suitcase before closing it up.

I was treated to a lovely breakfast of scrambled eggs, bacon and toast, causing me to raise my eyebrows.

"You need to start with a full stomach, Will. Today's going to be all over the place and heaven knows when you'll eat – or tomorrow, travelling to Berlin."

As I tucked away my breakfast, my mother sat opposite me, sipping her coffee and glancing at the paper.

"Try to send us a postcard from West Berlin when you get there before you go into East Germany, Will."

I smiled at her.

"Allow me to have a mother's concerns over her chicks, Will." There was a self-deprecating smile on her lips.

I smiled. "Okay – I'll try to send a postcard from West Berlin. I'm not sure about from inside East Germany through."

My mother nodded in understanding.

I sat and read the newspaper for a while before my mother said it was time to go. I took my bags out to the car and my mother drove us to the station. She insisted she pay for the return ticket to London and as we turned away from the ticket office, Lili walked into the station.

"Have a safe journey, Willi," Lili said, in Polish, shyly leaning forward to give me a brief kiss on the cheek.

Mustering my Polish, I took her hand. "Thank you for coming to see me off. Please take care of Col."

Lili gave me another shy smile and nodded.

"Your Polish is coming along then, Will?"

"Yes, he and Col are learning quite quickly," Lili explained.

"Col's not coming to see you off?" My mother asked.

Before Lili could answer, I turned to my mother, "I asked him not to come. He told me he's not good at goodbyes."

My mother was a bit surprised and then gave a small shrug.

"Dr Johnstone?" We turned around to find a photographer. "I'm from the newspaper. I'd like to take a photograph of you and your son as he heads off on his prize trip. Perhaps the three of you could stand together." He shepherded us against a British Rail cream wall. "Young Mr. Johnstone in the middle, please." Lili moved from beside my mother to beside me. "Excellent." The camera flashed. "Just one more."

He quickly changed the flashbulb and the camera flashed again. As it did, I saw a man in a trilby hat staring at us from across the station foyer. He was probably wondering what made us special.

"I'm sorry, but we must be going. My son has a train to catch." My mother used her doctor voice and moved us towards the platform ticket machine.

The photographer doffed his hat. "Thank you for your time, Dr Johnstone."

My mother inserted two thruppenny bits into the platform ticket machine, handing one of the tickets to Lili. We moved out on to the platform as my train was announced. It rolled in with an electric hum: none of the hissing clouds of steam and smoke I had enjoyed as a boy.

My mother watched the coaches slow to a halt and made sure I was entering one with open seating, not compartments. The train was fairly empty, and I had no trouble finding a seat on the platform side. I stowed my case, plonking my duffel bag on the seat and waved to Lili and my mother.

The train started moving so smoothly that it was almost like the station was bearing Lili and my mother away as they waved farewell; then the carriage jerked and reality reasserted itself: I was leaving them, my stomach fluttering queasily at what the next two weeks would hold. The train moved inexorably down the platform, past a few people including the trilby hat man. Disinterestedly, they watched our accelerating departure, waiting for a different train.

As we picked up speed, I sat down and pulled the Thomas Mann novella from my duffel bag to distract myself from my worries. I'd been finding Gustav's obsession with Tadzio a bit uncomfortable. This was probably coloured by Col's initial reaction to the revelation of my strange circumstances and the confusion of her gender for Lili and myself. It is fascinating how we read ourselves into other's art – or perhaps it is because great writers leave room for the reader to see themselves in their work.

We clattered through the Kentish countryside, which drew my attention from Gustav's obsessions. The blossom in the orchards was being replaced by exuberant green leaves. I was still coming to terms with the startling greenness of the countryside after decades of the much sparser, greyish Australian greens. I sighed; there was so much of my previous life that must remain hidden except with Col and for the next two weeks I would need to be extremely careful. Eventually, the Kentish fields and orchards gave way to London's expanding suburban sprawl and we rolled into Victoria Station.

I carefully checked my wallet and repacked my duffel bag, making sure for the umpteenth time that my paperwork and passport were safe in the internal pocket. My first time through as a teen I had been somewhat absentminded, prone to leaving a trail of unintentionally abandoned possessions, but decades of life had trained me to be more careful. Nevertheless, I was concerned that my young brain might betray me – so I checked.

With my duffel bag over my shoulder and my suitcase bumping awkwardly against my legs, I set off to find the Station Hotel. A porter gave me directions and pausing occasionally to swap my case between hands, I found the hotel and went into reception.

"Yes?" The bored man behind the desk asked, staring down his nose rather like Mr. Sturr.

"I'm part of the UNESCO group, the International Youth Cultural Exchange program travelling to Germany."

He waved at a sign pointing down a corridor. "In the Mallard Room." He dismissed me by dropping his eyes back to the work on his desk. I walked past a couple of rooms, also named after famous locomotives of the steam age.

There was no-one in the small Mallard room. I put my case on the floor beside a sofa, sat down, retrieved *Der Tod in Venedig* and, with nothing to distract me but my still fluttering stomach, started reading. As it was only just gone eleven o'clock, I wasn't surprised I was the first to arrive.

The clock was showing nearly half past eleven when a harried man poked his head in and then stood out of the way for a young man. "Well, that's two, anyway," he muttered and disappeared.

The young man glanced at me, noting my young age. "You must be the runner up," he said rather dismissively. "Do you actually speak German?" I heard the sneer in his voice.

I realised he was trying to establish some sort of pecking order; I smiled and returned to my book, making sure the cover was visible to him. After a moment, he dropped his case loudly beside an armchair and sat down, drumming his fingers on the armrests.

Almost immediately, a girl in her late teens stepped rather tentatively into the room. "Is this the UNESCO trip to Germany?" she asked in a soft voice, her eyes on the floor rather than us.

The young man leapt to his feet. "Indeed it is. I am Peter Farquar." His hand came out ready to shake the girl's, but she shuffled back and did not put out her hand.

"Oh, I am Virginia Dawson." Her voice held a trace of west country in it.

"Come and sit over here with me." Peter grabbed for her suitcase, but Virginia pulled it away searching for a safe refuge in the room. There was an armchair beside my sofa and she quickly retreated, her pale, freckled skin blushing slightly beneath her red hair.

Peter gave her a frown and went back to his seat, trying to hide his embarrassment at the failure of his advances. The three of us sat silently for a few minutes. I thought about returning to my book but decided I should introduce myself to Miss Virginia Dawson.

I turned towards her. "Hello, Miss Dawson. I'm Will Johnstone."

The freckled face turned towards me and there was a pause. "Hello, Will." She glanced furtively across the room at our companion and turned back to me. "I'm pleased to meet you. Please call me Ginnie. Are you going to East Germany too?"

Peter Farquar's voice cut across the room. "Little William is our runner up."

I heard the sneer in his voice again. It seemed we had someone in our midst who needed to shore up his self-image by putting other people down.

I watched Ginnie stiffen slightly and make as if to respond. Instead, she held my gaze. "Is that Thomas Mann you are reading?" She nodded towards my book.

"Yes, it's one of my set books."

She was slightly startled. "You're reading that for O Level?"

I gave her a slightly embarrassed smile. "No, for A level."

"Goodness." She gave me a closer inspection, blushing faintly when she realised this was a bit rude. "How old are you, Will?" she asked, curiosity sounding in her voice.

"Umm…" I was worried that this would just intensify Peter's unwanted attention. "I'm fourteen."

"Goodness," she repeated.

Just then the rather harried man came in, followed by two other boys, both in their late teens.

"Right ho," the man said, putting a bunch of room keys on the coffee table. "I'm Mr. Stock and we'll be joined shortly by Miss Turner. We are your guides and chaperones for this visit to East Germany." He paused, identifying us. "We'll get you settled into your rooms and conduct introductions over lunch."

He pulled a sheet of paper out of the clipboard he was carrying. "Here are your room assignments. Peter Farquar and William Johnstone." He picked up one of the keys and tossed it to Peter. "Henry Ruthven and Timothy Charles." Another key was tossed. "Virginia Dawson, you are with Miss Turner." He picked up the remaining key and handed it to her.

"Okay, off you go." He waved at the door. "Be back down in the dining room by one o'clock." He glanced at his watch. "That's about fifteen minutes. Don't be late." He bustled out without waiting for us to start moving, quickly followed by Henry and Timothy.

I packed my book into my duffel bag and stood up, but there was no movement from Peter. As he had the key and knew our room number, perforce I had to wait. As the Ginnie gathered her gear, Peter stood up. "I'm stuck with the baby of the group," he said disgustedly, half to himself. "Listen, you little oik. Stay out of my way or there will be dire consequences for you. I don't want to see or hear you." He leaned down and picked up his case. "The room is mine and it's bad enough that you have to sleep there. Just stay away, apart from that. D'you understand?"

His attitude was not unexpected given his initial reaction to me, but I had not been expecting to share a room with him. I was unsure what to do, so I just stood there.

He dropped his case, took several steps and towered over me. "Did you hear what I said, oik?"

I was now quite scared. He was built like a rugby scrum player and would have no trouble flattening me. Before I could summon up a safe reply, he grabbed my shirtfront and pulled me up onto my toes. "Cause me any trouble on this trip, oik, and…"

"What," asked a commanding female voice, "is going on here?" I presumed it was Miss Turner standing in the doorway, bristling.

Peter dropped me back on to my feet and pretended to be brushing down my chest. "We were just discussing arrangements about our shared room." It slipped glibly from him: he was well-practised in this sort of ploy.

"No, you weren't," Ginnie's enraged voice appeared angrily from the corner where she had been fiddling, unnoticed, with her case. "You were bullying William."

Peter's eyes narrowed.

"Miss Dawson, is it?" Miss Turner asked.

Ginnie nodded, visibly controlling her fury. "Peter Farquar was…intimidating William."

Miss Turner saw the room key in Ginnie's hand. "I see you have our room key. I suggest you take your bags there. I'll join you shortly."

Ginnie made me a sympathetic face and sidled past Miss Turner.

Peter turned and picked up his case.

"Where do you think you are going, Mr. Farquar?"

It was a rhetorical question, but Peter answered in a tone that assumed unassailable superiority. "To my room," and he attempted to push past Miss Turner, who had moved back into the doorway after Ginnie left.

"I think not, Mr. Farquar." Her tone was icy. "Please give me the room key."

Peter stayed there, unused to being commanded by a woman and yet concerned that a confrontation could see him in trouble. After a few long seconds, he tossed the key at Miss Turner, who caught it deftly.

"Go and wait at reception for Mr. Stock and we'll decide what to do with you."

Trying not to seem like he was following her instructions, he sauntered out past Miss Turner.

She tapped the key on her palm several times. "I thought putting the two of you together might cause problems, William, but ..." She paused, surveying me. "From what I hear, you are probably used to being a bit out of place. Hm?"

Just what had Mr. Sturr told them? I wondered, staying silent. I was grateful for Miss Turner's intervention, but I did not want her mothering me for the next two weeks.

She tapped the key against her palm a couple more times and sniffed. "Very well, here's your key. Take your bags up and hurry down for lunch."

Room 104: I shouldered my duffel bag, picked up my case and headed off to my room. It had two single beds and I pondered which one I should take to avoid more confrontation with Peter: *close to the window or close to the door?* I had noticed the bathroom was down the corridor; I tossed my bags on the bed nearest the window, wondering what to do as I suspected he would complain whichever bed I chose. Shrugging, I locked the room behind me and went back downstairs to lunch.

When I walked into the dining room, I found Miss Turner sitting at one end of a table with Henry, Timothy and Ginnie. I walked over and joined them, wondering where Mr. Stock and Peter were. Miss Turner had kept an empty seat next to her and she waved me over to sit there. It seemed that she had appointed herself my guardian.

I hesitated for a moment.

"Come and sit here, William." She patted the chair.

There was no point in fighting it, so I sat down. Ginnie was opposite me and flashed me a quick smile. I suspected that Miss Turner was keeping a close, chaperoning eye on her too.

"Mr. Stock is having words with Peter Farquar about his unacceptable behaviour." Miss Turner's eyes travelled round the table, pausing at Henry and Timothy, who both shifted in their chairs despite having done nothing wrong. "Peter Farquar will be sharing a room with Mr. Stock for the rest of the trip," she said, before turning to me. "You have the luxury of a room to yourself, William."

Given Peter Farquar's odious attitude, I felt that Mr. Stock was coming out on the short end of this stick.

"I would ask you all to remember that on this trip you are representing our country. People will be making judgements not just about you, but about this country and our society." Her piercing gaze traversed the table again, checking to see that her message had been understood. "Good. Now, let's have lunch."

About five minutes later, Mr. Stock arrived with Peter Farquar and lunch passed at our end of the table with Miss Turner driving the conversation to find out a bit about us.

Ginnie was indeed from the west country, outside Exeter, where her family ran a dairy farm near Woodbury, bordering the Clyst before it ran into the Exe estuary. One of the farm labourers was an ex-German prisoner of war who had stayed on after the war and brought his fiancée over to join him. Growing up on a busy farm, Ginnie had spent considerable time with his wife and this explained her command of German.

Miss Turner turned to me. "I understand you have a close German friend, William."

I tried not to tense up – my mother's blabbing about this to Mr. Sturr was coming home to roost. "That's right." I could see Miss Turner about to ask for more information.

Fortunately, Mr. Stock tapped his glass to get our attention.

"Fellow travellers, from now on we will speak only German amongst ourselves." He continued in German, "We will meet again in the Mallard Room in thirty minutes, where Miss Turner and I will provide you with some background on the German Democratic Republic and we will discuss our itinerary in more detail. There will then be some free time before dinner here at half-past six."

The afternoon session had us reading some articles from *Neues Deutschland* and discussing what they told us about how East German society was organised. My impression that the newspaper was only telling part of the story was unchanged. Peter was subdued, almost sulking it seemed, and he would not engage with me, even when I was speaking.

At dinner, we were told breakfast was at seven o'clock and to be packed and waiting in the reception area by eight o'clock for the bus to Heathrow.

By the time the bus picked us up in the morning to take us to the airport, I was starting to feel some excitement, despite my underlying concerns about the trip: I was about to take my first flight in an aeroplane in this life, and my young brain was excited. As we filed on to the small bus, I found myself next to Ginnie, who was sitting quietly, staring out of the window.

As we threaded our way through inner London and out on to the M4 motorway, I noticed she was twisting a handkerchief in her lap. "Is everything OK, Ginnie?"

Her hands stopped their twisting and she turned towards me. "I've not been in an aeroplane before." Now her hands had stopped moving, I could see them trembling.

"Neither have I." I smiled at her. "It's going to be exciting."

Her eyes flared with surprise. "What?" Her voice showed her total incredulity.

I tried to contain my enthusiasm. "I've wanted to fly, to be a pilot, for as long as I can remember."

Ginnie's face was questioning my sanity. "But why would you want to spend your life doing something that's so dangerous?"

It was my turn to be incredulous. "Why do you think that?"

"Because it is – you're always hearing of aircraft crashing."

"But cars crash every day," I countered.

"That's different." Ginnie's voice had an edge to it.

I remembered it was nearly impossible to counter an emotional argument with a logical one. "You're right, it is different." I saw some of Ginnie's hackles subsiding. "What can I do to help you?"

Ginnie leaned back against the window, half-turned towards me, some colour returning to her cheeks as she contemplated me. "You're unusual for your age, Will."

I managed to stifle the laugh that bubbled up inside me: *if she only knew.*

After appraising me for a few seconds, she turned away, staring at the back of the seat in front. "Could you sit beside me on the aeroplane, Will?"

She must have seen something in me to trust. "I think we are allocated seats, it's not like on a bus."

"Oh...I'm sure we could arrange it if we asked."

I wondered what Miss Turner would think of Ginnie wanting to sit next to me. "Would Miss Turner allow that?"

"She didn't say anything about us sitting together now." She paused and gave me a quirky smile. "It's not like we're alone in your room."

"Virginia Dawson," I joked. "What are you suggesting?"

Her face flared with an instant blush. "Nothing." And she quickly turned her back on me to stare out of the window.

Oops. I was used to joking like that with Col but Ginnie was unprepared for such a riposte.

"I'm sorry, Ginnie. I was joking, as I do with my girlfriend."

I saw her shoulders rise and fall with several breaths before she turned back to me. "You have a girlfriend?"

Now what was I going to do? My unthinking young brain...

"Yes, she's called Liliana."

"That's an unusual name."

"It's Polish, I think. Her family have been here since before the war. It's shortened to Lili." And I spelled it out for her.

"Please tell me about her."

We spent the rest of the journey to Heathrow in conversation, initially about Lili and me, but I was able to draw her out as well. Ginnie was an only child and her parents had both worked hard to make their dairy farm a success. Ginnie had gravitated towards Frau Klingmann, the farmhand's wife who helped around the house. She claimed to not remember learning German as Frau Klingmann had taken care of her almost from birth.

When we arrived at Heathrow for the BEA flight to Tempelhof, Ginnie spoke with Miss Turner at some length and came back to tell me that Miss Turner would see what she could do about us sitting together. We all went through passport control together and sat as a group waiting for our flight

211

to be called. I could see Ginnie getting more nervous again. To distract her, I asked her about her school.

"Oh, I will finish at Maynard's School for Girls after my A-levels in June."

"Is that a grammar school?"

Ginnie turned to me, with a frown. "No, my mother insisted that I go there even though it's far too expensive, at least for a dairy farmer." Ginnie sighed. "She wanted the best for me as she had not had any opportunity because of the depression and war."

"Do you like it there?"

"Well, it has a great academic record and that will help me get a place at university." She pursed her lips. "But, no, I don't like it. Most of the girls there are such snobs they won't have anything to do with a dirty farmer's daughter." Her voice took on the slow drawl evocative of the west country, mocking her classmates' view of her.

I nodded in understanding. "What do you want to study at University? Languages?"

"Oh no, not languages. I don't want to be a translator or a teacher, which seem to be the only possibilities if I do that." She seemed almost embarrassed to share her ambition. She turned back and almost whispered. "I want to study medicine."

"That's great, Ginnie. My mother's a doctor."

I saw the surprise in her eyes. "Really?"

"Yes, really. She was the only woman in her year at Guys Hospital in 1940."

"Oh, that must have been difficult." Ginnie shook her head, almost in wonder.

"I don't know. Perhaps." I half shrugged. "I've never heard her talk about it, but she has a pretty fierce reputation as a GP. She doesn't like people not following her advice and lets them know it."

Ginnie dropped her eyes. "I don't know that I could do that."

"Of course you could. You'd be the doctor who knew what she was doing – but I bet you'd be gentler about it than my mother."

Just then our flight was called, and we headed down to the bus that took us out to the aircraft. As the bus traversed the airfield, I was in my element, pointing out the aircraft types and their airlines to Ginnie. There was even a Tupolev Tu-104 in Aeroflot livery.

"Do you know every aircraft type?" I heard the amazement in Ginnie's voice.

"Of course not." I chuckled and then added, rather immodestly, "just most."

Ginnie smiled and raised her eyebrows. I gave her a playful grin with raised eyebrows in return.

The bus pulled up at our BEA Viscount and we clambered up the steps. The seats were in pairs on either side of the aisle.

"Do you want the window seat, Ginnie?"

She scrutinised her boarding card. "It says I'm in the aisle."

"That's all right – sit by the window if you want to, I don't mind."

We settled in and explored the seat pocket on the back of the seat in front.

"What's this?" Ginnie asked, holding up an airsick bag.

"That's in case you feel sick. You might not have time to get to the toilet – and even if you do, it might be occupied."

"Eww." Ginnie screwed up her nose and returned the bag to the seat pocket.

We were sitting within view of the port engine and watched as the propeller began to spin. Ginnie gulped and grasped the armrests tightly as the engine noise built and the plane began a gentle vibration.

"It's okay, Ginnie." I gave her what I hoped was a reassuring smile. "I'll tell you if something goes wrong."

Ginnie tensed and gazed out of the window. "What do you mean? What's going wrong?"

My attempts at humour were not helping. "Ginnie?" She didn't move; I gently put my left hand on top of hers where it gripped the armrest, giving it a gentle squeeze. She swivelled towards me with a small gasp.

"I'm sorry. Nothing's wrong." I lifted my hand off hers only for Ginnie to grab it and hold it in hers against the armrest. We stayed that way as the aircraft taxied out, with Ginnie squeezing my hand at every bump and change in noise. Eventually, it was our turn to take off and the engines wound up as we entered the runway. Ginnie closed her eyes and squeezed my hand. I heard her squeak when the brakes flicked off and we started accelerating down the runway.

Oh my. This was fantastic.

The reactions of two passengers could not have been more different: my old brain was exhilarated by what was for my young brain an almost spiritual experience. I watched out of the window whilst Ginnie sat as stiff as a board, eyes squeezed shut, holding my hand in a death grip. She squeaked and squeezed again at the sound of the undercarriage retracting.

"It's all right, Ginnie. We're airborne now. Look out of the window – it's fantastic."

Her eyes opened and she glanced sideways. "Oh goodness." Her eyes squeezed shut again. Just then we hit a bit of turbulence and the aircraft bounced slightly. She stiffened even more.

213

"Ginnie, please could you squeeze a bit more gently?"

After a moment, her eyes opened, and she stared down at our hands.

"Sorry." Her grip relaxed a bit and she gave me a tremulous smile.

"Thank you."

Once we flew out of the top of the stratus cloud and into the sunshine, Ginnie relaxed a little.

"It's quite smooth, isn't it?" she remarked once we levelled off.

"Once we're above the weather it's as smooth as milk most of the time unless you are very high, when there's some clear air turbulence, occasionally."

"How do you know about all this, Will, if it's your first flight too?"

I smiled. "Books, Ginnie. I have shelves of books about aircraft and flying." That was true, though most of those books were in some lost future – along with my glass of Shiraz and smartphone.

A stewardess pulled a cart past us to the front of the plane, wafting smells of lunch as she went. I saw Ginnie swallow. "Are you okay?"

She nodded and turned towards the window. I lowered her tray table, causing Ginnie to glance at me before she returned to the endless, brilliant white cloud tops.

Eventually, the lunch cart arrived at our row. The stewardess smiled at us and passed a lunch tray over to Ginnie and put one on my tray table. I started to explore my tray, pulling the cover off the main course as Ginnie watched. Roast chicken smells rose enticingly.

"Go on, Ginnie. Have something to eat."

She opened her main meal and started poking at it rather half-heartedly. After a few minutes, she stopped and returned to staring out of the window.

I munched my way through my tray. "Aren't you going to eat yours, Ginnie?"

She turned towards me and I could see she was pale, with sweat on her top lip.

"I don't feel well," she moaned.

Oh, dear. I quickly reached under my tray into the seat pocket and scrabbled out the airsick bag. "Here, use this if you're going to be sick." I opened the bag and pushed it across to her, then reached up to press the call button.

I heard a moan and then the unmistakable sound of someone vomiting. Ginnie had done well – it all went into the bag. I moistened a serviette with water and gave it to her. She gave me the sick bag in exchange, which I hastily closed, swallowing as the acrid smell got to me.

A stewardess appeared, quickly assessed the situation and removed our trays allowing me to stand up and let Ginnie out.

The stewardess took the sick bag from me and gave Ginnie an understanding smile. "The toilet's free, come with me and let's sort you out."

Miss Turner turned and saw me in the aisle. I walked up the two rows to her seat.

"Is Ginnie all right?"

I shook my head. "I'm afraid all the excitement must have got to her and she was sick."

"Oh…Does she need any help?"

"It's all right, I think. The stewardess is caring for her."

"Hm. Here, take this." Miss Turner handed me her lunch tray and stood up. "I'll go and find out what's happening." She had a strong sense of responsibility for her charges.

Leaving me standing with her lunch tray, she set off towards the toilets at the rear of the aircraft. I stood there wondering what to do for a moment, then put Miss Turner's tray back on her tray table. As there wasn't anything else I could do, I returned to my seat and sat, listening to the thrum of the turboprop engines, wishing for my noise-cancelling headset, lost with everything else in some weird time warp.

After a while, Ginnie returned, rather pale and wan, accompanied by Miss Turner, who said, "I think it would be best if Virginia sat in the aisle seat, Will."

"Of course." I moved to the window seat and a few minutes later we started our descent into Tempelhof airfield. The engines throttling down for the descent changed the noise in the cabin and Ginnie reached for my hand again. We stayed that way through the noises of flaps deploying, undercarriage going down and the varying engine sounds of our approach. The landing produced a gentle bump which caused Ginnie's grasp to tighten painfully.

"It's all right Ginnie, we've landed safely."

She relaxed a little and gave me an apologetic and grateful smile. "Thank you, Will."

I nodded in acknowledgement and we started sorting out our belongings now that we were in different seats.

Eventually, we exited the plane, went through passport control, retrieved our luggage and assembled in a group to wait for the bus to take us to the hotel. Once we were in the bus on our way out of the airport, the driver pointed out the *Hunger Kralle* – the memorial to the Berlin airlift that had kept West Berlin from starving and freezing to death during the winter of 1948/9 after the Russians closed road and rail access to West Berlin.

We wound through the western sector, reaching our hotel off *Bismarkstraße*. Ginnie's colour was much better now that we had spent some time back on the ground.

Before we went upstairs to our rooms, she turned to me, "Once you've put your luggage in your room, would you like to meet me here? We can go for a walk in the *Tiergarten*. I need some fresh air."

"Okay, see you back here in about ten minutes?"

Ginnie nodded and we headed upstairs.

When we met, Ginnie produced a map of Berlin and we walked through the *Tiergarten*, past the *Siegessäule* with its fabulous golden Winged Victory. We walked right up to the *Brandenburger Tor*, where we could see an East German police post on top of the gate.

The reality of what I was doing and what it could mean to Col and Mutti Frida if I was not careful struck home. I had an almost irresistible urge to turn and see if we were being followed, as if I had wandered into a le Carré novel. I think some of the unspoken threat of that guard post must also have pushed its way into Ginnie's mind, as we walked back to the hotel mostly in silence.

I acquired two postcards and stamps for England from reception and wrote to my mother and Lili – knowing that hers would be shared with Col and Mutti Frida.

After *Abendbrot (supper)* – I deposited these back at reception for posting and retired to my room, in a rather sombre mood.

Early – mid April 1964

I was woken during the night by the windows in my room rattling. My old brain knew this was caused by Russian Migs breaking the sound barrier over West Berlin – just part of the continuous intimidation against this western enclave in the Soviet empire. I drifted off to sleep, wondering what it must have been like to live every day with the fear of Soviet forces appearing in your city.

That unease must have weaved its way into my brain as I woke up in a fright. *What had I been thinking, bringing Oberstleutnant Schmidt's photo with me?* I feverishly grabbed my duffel bag and pulled out my Maths textbook. The newspaper cutting fluttered to the floor and I picked it up, staring at the face to fix it into my brain. After a couple of minutes, I tore it into shreds and put the pieces in my jacket pocket, dumping them down the toilet after I dressed.

At breakfast, we were told to meet back in the foyer with our luggage at half-past eight. I was about five minutes early but found Ginnie already there. "How are you feeling?"

"I'm fine, thanks, Will. The walk yesterday afternoon helped me calm down." She blushed slightly. "You must think I'm awfully silly, being sick on the plane like that."

I smiled, reassuringly. "New things usually cause some anxiety. What about the flight home?"

She swallowed. "I'll be fine…but please, sit with me?" I could see the uncertainty in her eyes.

"Okay."

Once everyone was there, Mr. Stock collected our passports, explaining that they had to be handed over to the East German authorities at Checkpoint Charlie. They would be returned when we cleared the border. We then put our bags in the back of the minivan and found seats. Once again, Ginnie saved me a seat next to her.

When we passed through Checkpoint Charlie into East Berlin, our minivan was waved into a bay. Mr. Stock got out with all our documents and was directed to a window in a building alongside. After about five minutes, an upright *Grenztruppen (Border guard)* officer walked up to him. After a few words, they approached the minivan and the officer followed Mr. Stock inside, stooping to avoid knocking his high-peaked cap on the roof. He scanned the bus, moving his head to pick up all our faces.

"You are the lucky winners of an essay competition, hmm? Welcome to the German Democratic Republic, we have been told to expect you this morning. I am *Major* Koch. We will need to wait a few minutes for the

217

person who will be your guide throughout your visit. Her name is Fräulein Elsa Hartmann." His English was accented, but excellent. As he knew about the competition, he must have known that we all spoke German; he must be taking the opportunity to practice his English, I thought, or perhaps he was showing off to the *Grenztruppen* guard watching us. He paused until he saw a young woman half running, half walking towards us. "Ah, here she comes." His voice gave away both annoyance and condescension.

A moment later a young woman in civilian clothes hurried up to the minivan. *"Herr Major."* She nodded in deference.

"Besser spät als nie, Fräulein Hartmann?" I heard the disapproval in his voice – and, from her worried frown and pursed lips, so could Fräulein Hartmann.

Despite her civilian clothes, was she a junior *Grenztruppen* officer or perhaps *Stasi*? Someone to make sure we are not spies or agents provocateurs?

"Travellers from England. Allow me to introduce your guide, Fräulein Elsa Hartmann. She will be accompanying you throughout your visit here." There was an almost sardonic emphasis on *Fräulein. Is she military in some way?*

Fräulein Hartmann nodded towards us and Major Koch waved Fräulein Hartmann into the front passenger seat beside our driver and turned back to us.

"Ich wünsche Ihnen einen schönen Besuch in unserem großartigen Land," (I trust you will have a pleasant stay in our great country,) he said, rather pompously, stepping out of the minivan.

Fräulein Hartmann leaned across to the driver and said something inaudible. The driver nodded and the minivan set off, presumably to our hotel, where we arrived about fifteen minutes later. Once we were off the minivan, Fräulein Hartmann waved us into a building. The FDJ logo announced it as student accommodation run by and for the FDJ – the *Freie Deutsche Jugend* that Col had mentioned. The FDJ was the official youth organisation of the *Sozialistische Einheitspartei Deutschlands* (Socialist Unity Party of Germany).

Mr. Stock and Miss Turner sorted out room allocations with Fräulein Hartmann and we were told to leave our bags in our rooms and come straight back to the entry. Peter Farquar strolled in about five minutes later than everyone else, causing Fräulein Hartmann to give him a short but sharp lecture on punctuality and its place in a community. There was something quite military about the way she dealt with Peter – as if she were giving a junior rank a dressing down.

She then turned to the rest of us. "This afternoon, we will have a tour of the city ending at six o'clock at *Karl Liebknecht Haus*, the FDJ headquarters, where you will be welcomed by and meet some of the youth leaders of the DDR and enjoy *Abendbrot*."

We took up our previous seats and spent a couple of hours touring East Berlin with appropriate socialist commentary by Fräulein Hartmann. Much was made of the rebuilding effort since the war, from blocky concrete apartment buildings in the suburbs for the workers to reconstructed historical buildings. Indeed, *Karl Liebknecht Haus* itself was an example of this reconstruction, as was the nearby *Volksbühne* theatre.

Touring around, the cityscape was different in a way that I could not quite put my finger on. I was still trying to work this out when Ginnie remarked that there was no advertising but lots of propaganda, which answered my unvoiced question.

We rolled up outside *Karl Liebknecht Haus* just before six o'clock and were ushered inside to a reception room where about a dozen young people came forward to greet us. In the background were four middle-aged people and I recalled what Mutti Frida had told me about never meeting ordinary people or having free conversations.

After a young woman gave a welcoming speech, there was an awkward pause as they were expecting one of us to respond, something none of us had expected.

I sidled up to Ginnie. "You'll have to say something, Ginnie. You're the only girl."

She shook her head, terrified at the idea.

"Just thank them for the welcome and tell them how much we are anticipating exploring their society and culture."

She hesitated, but I gently pushed her forward. Eyes swivelled towards her and she, with an increasing blush, repeated what I had suggested almost word for word. I saw expressions of relief on the faces of the rest of our party and, interestingly, on the faces of the young FDJ representatives. I also noticed several hard glances from the older East Germans directed towards Fräulein Hartmann. *Had she made another mistake by not briefing us properly?*

"That was truly terrifying, Will. Why did you do that?" Ginnie turned and hissed at me.

I smiled. "It might have been terrifying, but you did it beautifully."

Ginnie's frown softened slightly.

"Don't sell yourself short, Ginnie. You're very capable."

Ginnie took a deep breath and gave me a tentative smile. "All right, Will."

Waiters appeared, setting out several tables of finger food and circulating with glasses of wine and beer. Fortunately, there was also some water and glasses on the table as well.

I was hungry. "Come on Ginnie, let's get something to eat."

We filled our plates with the cold meats, cheeses and salads and perched ourselves on the chairs round the edge of the room. One of the FDJ young people walked across and pulled a chair out to sit opposite us, balancing a plate of food on his knees.

"Good evening. I am Friedrich Meyer." He smiled at Ginnie. "Thank you for your response."

Ginnie nodded in acknowledgement and we introduced ourselves.

"You both speak German well."

At that moment, a waiter appeared with what appeared to be glasses of Champagne.

Friedrich queried the waiter. "Is it *Rotkäppchen*?"

The waiter nodded.

"Ah." I heard the pride brimming in his voice. "You must try this – it is not available in the West. This trip will be your only opportunity."

After its reaction to the Schnapps, what would my young body make of wine?

Friedrich pressed a glass into our hands and raised his. "*Prost.*" *(Cheers.)*

Ginnie cast a sideways glance at me and I just shrugged. "*Prost.*" I raised the glass to my lips and took a sip.

Ginnie followed my example.

I was expecting something quite sweet, but this was a delicious dry sparkling wine. My old brain savoured the flavours that blossomed on my young tongue – *Pinot Chardonnay perhaps?*

I smiled at Friedrich. "This is good."

"You like this?" Ginnie asked. "I don't think I do."

"You prefer something a bit sweeter, perhaps?" Friedrich retrieved the glass from Ginnie's hand and accosted a different waiter, returning with a white wine. "Try this Riesling instead."

Ginnie took a tentative sip and smiled. "Thank you."

Miss Turner appeared behind Friedrich. "Will, you should not be drinking wine."

Friedrich stood and turned smoothly. "I'm sorry, but I insisted they try some of our great wines."

Miss Turner eyed him. "Will is only fourteen. Do children drink wine in East Germany?"

Friedrich gave Miss Turner an ingenuous smile. "Surely one glass is not dangerous?"

Miss Turner frowned at me. "All right, but just the one glass, Will." She turned to Ginnie. "And you be careful – keep an eye on Will."

Ginnie nodded and Miss Turner walked away. I watched her pick up a glass of *Rotkäppchen* and sip it appreciatively.

Friedrich talked to us about the FDJ and its important place in the DDR society. During this monologue, he acquired more wine for Ginnie and himself from a passing waiter. Eventually, he asked us about the youth organisations we were part of in England.

I shrugged. "I'm not a member of anything. I used to sing in a church choir, but not anymore."

Friedrich appeared surprised and turned to Ginnie. "And you?"

Ginnie seemed a little flushed. "I'm too busy with school and working on the farm."

"But that is good, Ginnie. Farm work is honest labour for your society." He gave me a thin smile. "You need to find a way to contribute too, Willi. But it is good you are no longer in the hands of the reactionary church."

Mr. Stock extracted himself from the group of older people and walked across to where we were sitting. "We will be leaving in a few minutes. Ginnie, when I gather everyone together, I would like you to say a few words of thanks for the FDJ's hospitality."

"Why me?" Ginnie blurted.

"Because you stepped up so well when we arrived, and they will expect it." He smiled reassuringly at her.

Perhaps the two glasses of wine had given Ginnie some Dutch courage, but her short speech graciously thanked the FDJ for the welcome and introduction to East Germany and earned her some polite applause.

Back in the minivan, Ginnie turned to me. "You're right, Will. I can do more than I think."

I wondered how much of this nascent self-confidence was the wine talking.

It turned out that perhaps some was due to the wine, but not all: the following day Ginnie spoke well, thanking the FDJ members who conducted us round the *Bode-Museum* and *Pergamonmuseum*. Both were fascinating – but the tractor factory on the following day not so much. We spent half a day there as earnest managers proudly showed us around their rather outdated factory making pre-war style tractors. Afterwards, on the way back to the hotel, Ginnie, who knew her tractors from working on the farm, was a bit caustic about the old-fashioned machinery, which visibly annoyed Fräulein Hartmann.

That evening we were guests at the *Staatsoper* for a performance of *Der fliegende Holländer*. My compatriots found the performance boring, unfortunately, but managed to be polite about it. Mr. Stock sensed my enthusiasm and asked me to make the speech of thanks to our FDJ hosts.

After breakfast the following morning, we left for Dresden, a trip of some two hundred kilometres, that would take nearly five hours. My old brain knew that this city was carpet-bombed by the British and Americans in February 1945, creating a firestorm that killed over twenty thousand people and largely destroyed the historic city centre. It would be interesting to see what reconstruction had occurred – and how a group of English people would be received.

As in Berlin, we were staying in student accommodation, this time at the *Technische Universität Dresden*, outside the city centre. We had a late lunch and then were joined by a pair of FDJ members who guided us around the city, rather usurping Fräulein Hartmann's role in the process. There were a few old buildings that showed no sign of any restoration. I was not surprised that the cathedral – the *Frauenkirche* – was still a ruin, given the regime's antipathy towards religion. Despite its still showing a great deal of damage, the work occurring on the baroque *Semperoper* was proudly pointed out to us as were the many new buildings in the centre of the old city. Our tour ended at the *Zwinger* – the baroque palace and gardens of the kings of Saxony. Our guides pointed out that this complex had been severely damaged by the bombing in 1945, but that work on restoration was started by the Soviet occupying forces almost immediately and had been continued and finished by the DDR. FDJ volunteers had helped in this work we were proudly advised.

I saw Ginnie staring around at the gorgeously restored interiors with some confusion. "Why is a communist state restoring a king's palace?"

One of our guides turned to her and said, "This is now owned by the people. Why would we not restore our own property? Besides, it is also important to learn the lessons of history, how the people of Saxony were oppressed allowing an elite to live in luxury."

I saw that Ginnie was about to ask another question, but she stopped and nodded. Then, as we continued following our guides, Ginnie whispered to me, "That interest in restoring history doesn't extend to a baroque church, though."

I raised an eyebrow and we walked on as our guide pointed out architectural and artistic highlights of the building and contents with socialist pride.

That evening we were again hosted by the FDJ, on this occasion at the *Hochschule für Musik*. We were treated to a movement from a piano quartet, which I did not recognise. I was told it was by Carl Maria von Weber, who spent a large part of his career as conductor of the *Semperoper*. After, the conversation accompanying the buffet was one-sided, with much exposition of the benefits of being a young person in the DDR. Mutti Frida was correct: I would not meet ordinary people and all I would hear was the party line. But I was sensing in the few questions the young people asked of us privately that there was interest in something different – and, thinking back, I had sensed this also at the tractor factory: a feeling that they could do better if they were allowed.

After breakfast the following day, we were driven out of the city to the industrial area. We visited a factory making radios – using valves. There were even 'portable' versions, weighing several kilograms with their heavy transformers and lead-acid rechargeable batteries. Back in England, Japanese transistor radios had appeared a year or so earlier – tiny radios that would fit in a trouser pocket. After my Premium Bond win, I had contemplated buying one but decided the lack of FM capability (or VHF as it was then being called) was a huge drawback in terms of listening quality. I wasn't interested in listening, again, to the pop music of the sixties: I wanted to tune in to the Third Program on FM, with its broadcasts of classical music and, increasingly, live concerts.

We had lunch in the factory canteen, joined by some of the workers and the manager who had been our guide. I asked if they had seen the tiny Japanese transistor radios available in the west. An embarrassed silence descended on the table until the manager leaned forward and said, "Yes, I have seen such things, but they are difficult and expensive to make. The factory would have to be completely changed." His voice took on an earnest tone. "We feel it is more important to provide all our people with a usable radio before we spend our resources trying to produce such things." There were murmurs of agreement around the table, but they did not sound heartfelt.

We spent two more days in Dresden, at a forest camp used by the FDJ in summer. It turned out we were part of a working party bringing the camp out of its winter hibernation ready for its summer visitors. On the first day, each of us was paired with an FDJ member, removing shutters from windows, piling them on to carts and depositing them at a storeroom where they were stacked to wait for autumn; then we cleaned the winter rubbish from outside the dormitories and the paths through the forest. Perhaps it was the shared work, but some of the reticence on both sides wore off and, after supper in the evenings, the talk round a glowing fire pit was more relaxed, with some veiled criticism of the way things were done in the DDR. On the second day, we spent a morning putting up posters promoting the FDJ and its activities. I thought one of these would make a great memento of the trip and asked if I could take one back to England. There was a modicum of surprise at this – the posters were definitely

223

propaganda and I had caught some sardonic remarks about their content from a few of the FDJ youth with us.

"What would you do with such a poster?"

I smiled. "I'd display it in my bedroom to remind me of the friends I made on this trip."

After some consultation, I was given the nod and chose a poster. I carefully rolled it up to fit in my suitcase and hopefully not get crushed.

After two days at the forest camp, we drove to Leipzig, where we were once again hosted by members of the FDJ at the University of Leipzig in *Augustusplatz* – near the *Gewandhaus* and the almost brand-new Opera House, on whose steps Col's father had been photographed.

This time, our hosts spent much more time with us, and I gained the impression that they were a bit dismissive of the central organisation as being a bit stuck in the past – *altmodisch* – as one of them said. I sensed that things might be about to loosen up in the Warsaw pact, or at least in the DDR. However, I caused a bit of a stir when I asked about a visit to *Thomaskirche*, where Bach was *Kantor*. The church in all its forms was officially regarded as a reactionary organisation and not something a proper FDJ member would be associated with and I didn't receive an answer.

Much to my delight, we were going to be treated to both a concert in the *Gewandhaus* and an opera – Mozart's *Die Zauberflöte*. There were rolled eyes by a few of my companions and Ginnie asked me what I saw in classical music. I was a bit stumped how to answer that without revealing too much, but then I thought of the essay I had written.

"I don't know – I suppose in part it's the music in my life, the music that speaks to me most deeply. I'll lend you the essay I wrote – that might help explain it."

I dug the copy of my essay out of my duffel bag and gave it to Ginnie at *Abendbrot*. She smiled and put it in her handbag, promising to return it in the morning.

The concert that evening featured Václav Neumann conducting Shostakovich's seventh Symphony – The Leningrad Symphony. The program notes talked at length about the great suffering during the siege and the symphony's first performance in the besieged city of Leningrad. I found this interesting, given the German audience, some of whom probably served in the *Wehrmacht* or had friends or relatives who had been involved on the Eastern Front during the war.

The following morning was a Sunday, and I was up early and walked out of the dormitory, heading for *Thomaskirche*. There were a few people in *Augustusplatz* and so I asked for directions.

An old woman eyed me with some suspicion. Perhaps my youth helped reassure her. "Go north to *Grimmaischer Straße* and then west. You can't miss it."

"Vielen Dank."

"Bitte sehr."

I set off towards *Grimmaischer Straße*, only to be pulled up by a voice calling my name in English, "William Johnstone. William Johnstone. Stop."

I turned round to see Fräulein Hartmann almost running to catch up with me.

I waited for her and she arrived, slightly dishevelled as if she had dressed hurriedly. When she reached me, she took several deep breaths and raked a hand through her hair.

"What are you doing, William?" I heard the annoyance in her voice.

"I want to visit Johan Sebastian Bach's church."

"But you were told that we would go everywhere as a group. You shouldn't be out by yourself." There was something in her voice behind the anger I was hearing.

"Why not? Is it dangerous here in Leipzig?" I knew I was twisting her tail, but I couldn't resist.

"Of course not. The whole of the DDR is peaceful and safe."

"Then why cannot I go out by myself?"

Fräulein Hartmann was a bit stumped for a response. After a moment, she summoned up, "Because you might get lost."

"I'm only going to *Thomaskirche* – it's just the other side of the university along *Grimmaischer Straße*. How could I possibly get lost?"

"How do you know that?" she snapped.

I shrugged. "I asked for directions from someone walking in the square."

Fräulein Hartmann swallowed and her eyes darted around.

"Come. We are going back to the FDJ *Wohnheim*." There it was again – but this time it was definitely fear that underlay her anger.

"But I don't want to go back to the dormitory. I want to visit *Thomaskirche*."

Fräulein Hartmann's head snapped back towards me. "*Wilhelm Johnstone. Du mußt mit mir zurückkommen.*" (*William Johnstone, you must come back with me.*) She commanded and without waiting, turned smartly on her heel and started walking back towards the university.

I was tempted to ignore her and carry on to *Thomaskirche*, but I remembered my mother's plea that I not cause any trouble. Suppressing a frustrated sigh, I turned and followed her. She must have heard my footfalls as I saw her shoulders relax slightly.

Back at the dormitory, breakfast was underway with a strong aroma of coffee in the room. Still upset at my aborted excursion, decades of habit kicked in and I acquired a cup of coffee without thinking and found a seat with Ginnie.

"You caused quite a stir, Will."

I shrugged. "I just wanted to visit Bach's church."

"I must have just missed you leaving, but I was sitting in the foyer waiting for breakfast to start when Fräulein Hartmann raced out of the building still adjusting her clothes." Ginnie smiled. "It was quite a sight."

I shrugged. "She found me in *Augustusplatz*. I had to ask directions to the church."

Mr. Stock came over and sat down with us.

"William, you were at the briefing in London when we made it clear that we must stay together, there was to be no going off alone."

I stared at him.

He shook his head. "Will, if we go off alone, the government might see us as *agents provocateurs* or even spies. It's not safe. Also, you are causing trouble for Fräulein Hartmann, who is responsible for us."

I said nothing – but I heard Mutti Frida's warning in my ears about the dangers to ordinary people if I spoke to them.

Mr. Stock sighed, softly. "I know it's quite different from how we live, but we are guests here and should abide by our host's rules." He leaned further across the table. "You must promise me that you will not go off on your own again. If you want to go somewhere, please speak to me and I will see what I can do."

I met his eye. "Okay," I said, grudgingly. "But, please, can you see if I can visit *Thomaskirche*? I was hoping to sit and listen to some of Bach's music in his church."

Mr. Stock's eyes opened in understanding. "That's right – you used to sing in a church choir, didn't you? You know much of Bach's music?"

My old brain knew quite a bit from singing in my local Bach Society Choir, to the annoyance of the choirmaster as I made no secret of my atheism. But I could not tell Mr. Stock that. "Well, I know a bit from listening on the radio, but not from singing it." I leaned forward. "I want to hear what it's like in Bach's church. It's like the difference between listening to an orchestra on the radio and being there in person in the Albert Hall."

Mr. Stock leaned back. "I'll see what I can do."

I picked up my coffee and tasted it for the first time. "Ugh." I spluttered. The coffee was like bitter mud, completely different from the sharp, aromatic *espresso* my old brain was accustomed to.

Ginnie laughed. "I've not seen you drink coffee before, Will."

"And I'm not going to drink this. It's awful."

"I don't like coffee either. I always drink tea at home but that's been hard to come by here."

Mr. Stock stood up and asked for our attention. "This morning, there is a tour of the University; please gather back in the foyer in fifteen minutes."

As I left, I saw him speaking with Fräulein Hartmann, who glanced across at me as they spoke. After this morning, I didn't expect my request would fall on fertile ground. Ginnie knocked on my door to return my essay as I was getting organised.

"Thanks for the read, Will. It was interesting to see how someone else tackled the essay, but I'm not sure it helped me understand your love of classical music."

I shrugged and stashed it back at the bottom of my duffel bag as I didn't think I'd need it again and we headed downstairs to meet up with everyone else.

The university tour proved more interesting than I expected. Not only did we tour the *Institut für Theoretische Physik*, but it turned out that one of the FDJ student guides was studying there and we ended up deep in conversation for most of the rest of the tour. This had its moments as we didn't share a technical vocabulary: there was shared laughter and a bit of hand waving.

At lunch, Ginnie asked me. "What were you talking about with that student?"

I didn't think before replying. "We were discussing theoretical Physics – principally quantum theory and the standard model."

"I thought you were doing languages at A level?"

I thought for a moment before answering as I didn't want to lie to Ginnie, but I was wary of being different. "I am."

"How do you know about this quantum thingy then?"

"I'm studying Physics too."

Ginnie stopped eating and stared at me.

After a moment, she put down her knife and fork. "Just what are you studying?"

I took a deep breath. "Does it matter?" I didn't want her – or anyone else – to start treating me as some kind of freak.

She leaned towards me. "Yes it does, Willi. I find you interesting and want to try to understand you."

I put down my knife and fork in turn, realising that perhaps being honest was the best way to deal with this. I did not want to prevaricate with Ginnie, but I kept my voice low. "All right. I'm studying double Maths, Physics, English, French and German. I dropped Latin as I couldn't find a way to fit it into my timetable."

Ginnie stiffened in surprise and she squeaked rather loudly, "And these are all at A level? All six of them?"

I was conscious of the silence that had descended on the table, everyone's face turned towards us. Damn – *this was not what I wanted.*

Ginnie was still waiting for an answer.

I sighed; I so did not want to be this different. "Yes, but I'm only first year A level," I added, trying to diminish the way it sounded.

From the other end of the table, Peter Farquar's voice sounded, "What a load of rubbish." His voice dripped derision. "He's just trying to big-note himself. No-one does six A levels, and certainly not at his age."

Miss Turner raised an eyebrow at me and leaned forward, staring down the table at Peter. "Well, I'm afraid you are wrong there, Mr. Farquar. I spoke with Will's school and he is indeed studying those subjects – and excelling." She glanced around the table. "It seems our William is a remarkable young man."

I wanted to sink into the floor – being different just caused problems.

Slowly, the conversations round the table picked up again and I noticed Fräulein Hartmann regarding me with great interest.

Ginnie was peering over at me. "Are you all right, Will?"

I shook my head. "No. I hate the way this drives wedges between me and everyone else."

"What do you mean?"

"I'm no different to you or ... or Peter Farquar. Just because I'm academically advanced doesn't make me a better or a worse person. But as soon as people find out, they treat me differently." I heard the frustration growing in my voice. "I have no friends at school – people in my classes see me as a threat and my age group see me as a freak." I glanced down at my plate, no longer hungry, my stomach roiling.

I turned to Ms. Turner. "Please excuse me, I've had enough to eat."

As I stood up, Ginnie grabbed my hand. "Will ..."

I gently removed her hand and went to my room. Not having Col, Lili and Mutti Frida – or even my mother – to turn to had left aching holes that I had only just realised were there. Col accepted me for who I was – and she knew me more deeply than anyone, but I felt that same acceptance from Lili and Mutti Frida. My relationship with my mother was more clouded, but there was acceptance, even though she did not understand who I was. There was nearly another week before we returned home, and I wasn't sure how I was going to make it through.

After a while, there was a soft voice at the door. "Will...Will. Are you all right?"

I closed my eyes. I didn't want company, but my old brain knew that pushing sincere people away when they wanted to help was not a great idea. I opened the door. "Hi, Ginnie."

"I'm sorry, Will. I didn't understand…" Her voice trailed away.

"Don't worry. It's not your fault, you couldn't have known."

Ginnie shook her head, walking into my room with her head down, deep in thought. "No, I should have realised back in London there was something special about you when you told me you were doing German A level."

"Um, Ginnie, I don't think you should be in my room."

Ginnie's face blushed almost to match her hair and she darted out of the room with an embarrassed squeak, nearly tripping herself on the carpet. She recovered her balance in a flurry of arms and legs and ended up leaning against the far wall. "Sorry, sorry. I wasn't thinking."

I smiled reassuringly. "You don't have to apologise, Ginnie. Thank you for coming to see if I was alright."

Her blush was fading, but her stance betrayed her feelings of awkwardness.

"Um. Perhaps we could find somewhere to sit and talk downstairs?" She fidgeted with her skirt. "We are going to a reception at the Opera House at five o'clock and we've free time until then." She glanced across at me. "But we have to stay here."

I gave a mirthless chuckle. "Right." I thought for a moment. "I'll bring a book down too. I've been neglecting my Maths during this trip."

"Okay, I'll see you in the foyer."

We spent the afternoon sitting in occasional conversation as our heads lifted out of our books. It was not the same as sharing a book with Col, but the quiet companionship proved a soothing balm. At about four o'clock we went back to our rooms to change for the reception and the opera,

Under the watchful eye of Fräulein Hartmann, we walked across *Augustusplatz* to the Opera, where we met several FDJ representatives. Waiters circulated with finger food and glasses of wine and Ms. Turner caught my eye, holding up a single finger to indicate I could have a single glass of wine. I nodded in acknowledgement and acquired a champagne flute, in the hope that it contained *Rotkäppchen*.

After a few minutes, one of the FDJ young men called for attention.

"We are pleased to welcome to Leipzig new friends from England and Poland. Our English friends are winners of an essay competition about the power of art and culture to spread peace and understanding. Our Polish friends are here to broaden the technical education links between our great socialist nations. Please enjoy the refreshments and, of course, the opera."

This was greeted with polite applause. A young man from the Polish delegation answered in Polish, noting, regretfully, his poor German. One of the FDJ translated for him. At a nod from Mr. Stock, Ginnie gave a short speech thanking the FDJ for their friendship and hospitality.

With the formalities over, people began to circulate, and I congratulated Ginnie on her excellent job of acting as our spokesperson. Inevitably, she blushed slightly and redirected the conversation.

"Do you know anything about the Opera we are seeing tonight?"

"It's by Mozart – *Die Zauberflötte* – the Magic Flute. It's an interesting choice for a communist country as it's all about the Masons."

"Oh."

"Mind you, it has comedy and some beautiful music including one of the most amazing but difficult soprano arias sung by the evil Queen of the Night."

People continued circulating whilst we nibbled and chatted. Suddenly I heard Fräulein Hartmann's voice from behind me, "*Herr Oberstleutnant*, I would like to introduce you to a remarkable young Englishman." I felt a hand on my shoulder. "William?"

A frisson ran up my spine and I turned to see Col's father standing in front of me. My stomach flipped and I swallowed hard. *Stay calm, stay calm.* My old brain clamped down on the surge of fear coursing through me.

Fräulein Hartmann's voice sounded almost proprietorial as she sang my praises. "Young William speaks several languages but is also studying Maths and Physics at *erweiterte Oberschule* – University entry-level. He wrote an interesting essay on how the shared cultural language of Europe should unite us." *How did she know that?*

"Hmm." *Oberstleutnant* Schmidt was in civilian clothes, but his eyes ran over me as if he were inspecting a recruit. "How old are you, young man?"

"I'm fourteen, sir." The honorific slipped from me without thinking and I saw Fräulein Hartmann's relieved smile. Tension was rising in my body and I hoped it was not obvious.

"And you think Europe will unify because of its shared culture?"

There was no way I wished to involve myself in a political discussion with Col's father. "It seems possible, sir."

"Of course, such unification will only be possible in a socialist Europe." He smiled, condescendingly, at Fräulein Hartmann.

I kept my face neutral.

Oberstleutnant Schmidt offered me a thin smile. "Well, young man, if you are interested in Physics, you should consider coming to study here. We have an excellent technical university in Leipzig, as I think you know.

Fräulein Hartmann, see that you send some information from the university to this young man."

Fräulein Hartmann nodded at me as they moved on. I took several deep breaths and turned back to Ginnie, to find her talking with the young Pole who had acknowledged the welcome earlier. It was clear that his poor German was a problem.

Summoning my less than perfect Polish, I slid into the conversation as the young man searched for a word. "*Dobry wieczór. Mówię trochę po polsku.*" (*Good evening. I speak a little Polish*).

The young man turned to me, smiling broadly. "Marvellous that you speak Polish. I am struggling here."

I smiled in return. "Yes, but not well. Please speak slowly."

Ginnie gasped. "You speak Polish as well?"

I shrugged diffidently and Ginnie and I introduced ourselves.

The young Pole leaned forward to shake our hands. "I am Lech Wałęsa, a trainee electrical technician from Gdansk."

Fortunately, neither Ginnie nor Lech noticed my eyes flaring in surprised recognition at the name and we started a three-way conversation in German and Polish, which I found quite wearing. It occurred to me that translators did not usually participate in the conversation and that probably made what I was doing more difficult, notwithstanding my less than perfect Polish. From what Lech was saying, the young people in Poland, like the young people we had met in Dresden and here in Leipzig were also seeking for a more relaxed society.

After about an hour, our host called us together for another short round of speech-making, with Ginnie again responding for our group. One of Lech's group who spoke quite good German responded for them.

From there, we were led into the opera house into excellent seats in the stalls. The opera was presented in modern dress and it was clear that the membership of the Masons was being used as a metaphor for party membership, which stretched things a bit in places, but the singing was excellent.

After the opera, there was a further reception where we were served *Kaffee und Kuchen*. Fortunately, Col's father was not there but Lech introduced me to the rest of his party, and I had to explain how I came to be learning Polish, but I was careful not to reveal Lili's name.

The following morning, we returned to Berlin for a day, touring factories (clothing and heavy machinery this time). On our last day before returning to West Berlin we were at a large reception at the *Palast der Republik* – the parliament house of East Germany. There were many young people there and Ginnie was relieved that she was not required to speak.

231

Leaving for home left me a bit deflated. I found that learning about the young people in the DDR (and a bit from Poland) was fascinating. Although being confronted by *Oberstleutnant* Schmidt had been unexpected and a shock, the trip had given me insights into eastern Europe: I would have quite a bit to talk about at home. It seemed that the young people behind the iron curtain – at least in Poland and the DDR – wanted to change their society to make it less regimented, more open, more modern. From hints talking with workers in the factories, that desire existed beyond the youth also. I suspected that this was probably true in the other Warsaw Pact countries but wondered about the USSR. *Would the young people there also feel this way?* In my old world, the first inkling that there was a mood for change behind the Iron Curtain was the abortive Prague Spring under Alexander Dubček's leadership in 1968, but that had ended swiftly when the Soviets rolled their tanks into Prague. *Would that happen in this world?*

The return to West Berlin was surprisingly simple once we had speedily cleared through the East German control point and farewelled Fräulein Hartmann at Checkpoint Charlie. From there, we drove straight to *Tempelhof* airport for our return flight, arriving at Heathrow just after lunch.

Ginnie was still nervous on the plane, but the experiences of the trip seemed to have strengthened her confidence. It turned out that she had been keeping a journal in an exercise book which she produced.

"Will, please could you give me your address and phone number?" she asked, with a smile and a slight blush. "I'd like to stay in touch."

I returned her smile and wrote this at the back of her journal. She then tore a sheet from the back, writing her contact details on it and gave it to me.

The bus from Heathrow did the rounds of the stations dropping Ginnie at Paddington to catch a train back to Exeter and finally deposited me at Victoria Station. I checked the trains and then rang home, leaving a message with my sister that I would arrive in Herne Bay at five past six. I waited on the platform for my train to pull in and then found a seat in an open carriage.

As it was a Sunday, the train was mostly empty, so I was surprised when a man sat down opposite me and practically stared at me. Something about him seemed familiar and then I recognised him: the man in the trilby hat I had seen at my departure nearly two weeks ago. He must have seen a flicker of recognition in my face, for he smiled slightly, raising his eyebrows.

He leaned forward, keeping his voice low. "I see you recognise me, William. But you don't know who I am, do you?"

How did he know my name? I glanced around, wondering if he was dangerous.

"It's all right, William." His smile was unsettling in some way I couldn't quite fathom. "I am Mr. Watling – I know you've heard of me."

I blinked: Mutti Frida's MI6 contact.

He leaned back in his seat. "Good." That smile again – and now I recognised its aura of superiority, of unassailable power and control. "Now, I think you have something for me."

I frowned. "Something for you?"

Mr. Watling just raised his eyebrows a millimetre as if bored by my obtuseness and nodded towards my duffel bag on the seat beside me. "Search your bag."

I felt for my bag, without moving my attention from Mr. Watling, not sure I could trust him. With it on my lap, I pulled out my books, my spare jumper and the copy of my essay.

"There's nothing there for you – that's all mine."

He shook his head. "Feel the bottom of the bag."

I stared into the bag but couldn't see anything.

"You need to feel around the bottom." He sounded almost bored.

I put in my hand and felt it – something was different, stiffer. I felt the edge, where the bottom met the sides – and lifted. I pulled it out and saw papers fixed to its underside.

"There you go," he said, like he was talking to a small child. "Pass it across to me." He carefully peeled the package of papers away from the false bottom, opened it and quickly rifled through them. From the brief glimpse I had, they appeared to be written in German, partly in the old-fashioned Gothic script.

Putting the papers back in their envelope, he stowed that securely inside his coat.

"Thank you, William. You did a wonderful job." He paused, smiling at me from under his eyebrows. "Although you caused a few heart-stopping moments in Leipzig with the attempted trip to Bach's church and your conversation with *Oberstleutnant* Schmidt."

I gasped. "You were watching me?"

"All the time, my boy…all the time." He smiled proprietorially. "The whole point was to get you to Leipzig to bring back that package." He was sounding ever more self-satisfied.

A few things clicked together in my mind. "Mutti Frida's evidence. That's what this is all about, isn't it?"

His eyes flicked up to my face and then he waved a hand at me. "What was in the package is of no concern to you." He was dismissive – I was just the courier, but I caught a hint of surprise in his manner.

233

The train was slowing, and Mr. Watling moved to his feet. "You do realise that you can't talk about this with anyone, don't you?" His voice had a hard and threatening edge to it. Then his voice softened, surprisingly. "Enjoy the rest of your journey."

The train pulled to a stop in Bromley South and Mr. Watling got off, walking to the exit with another man. As the train moved off, he turned and waved his trilby hat at me.

I sat there, thinking for a while. I had just been used as a secret service courier, which was quite an idea to get my head around and one that made me feel uncomfortable, although I could not put my finger on why. *What had happened to open up a place on the East German trip and how had I been selected to fill the gap?* It all felt decidedly suspicious now and I wondered if Mrs. Wiśniewski had been nudged into her actions.

As the train sped along the north Kent coast, I sat back and tried to make sense of everything that had happened – without getting anywhere.

We arrived at Herne Bay and my mother was waiting for me on the platform. She hugged me tightly. "I'm glad you're back, Will. Did you have a good time?"

"Yes, thank you," I responded a bit distractedly as my head was still trying to get round the encounter with Mr. Watling. I carried my bags out to the car and we drove home, with me answering my mother's questions about the trip as best I could.

Mid-April 1964 – September 1964

My mother closed the door behind us. "Go and unpack your bags, Will. Bring your dirty washing down and we'll get it done tomorrow."

"Okay. Can I ring Col to let him know I'm home safely?"

"Of course."

I talked with Col for a few minutes and arranged to go round in the morning. She told me that my postcard from West Berlin had arrived safely and she'd been seeing Lili most days while I was away.

Once in my room, I unpacked my case. The blue and yellow FDJ poster was slightly wrinkled and I hoped it would flatten satisfactorily as I thought its bold yellow and blue colours would make rather a fetching addition to my room. I gathered my dirty washing and carried it back downstairs. When I mentioned the wrinkled poster to my mother, she suggested I try ironing the poster with a cool iron; I retrieved it from my bedroom and spent half an hour carefully smoothing the wrinkles, removing almost all trace of them. I'd have to investigate getting it properly framed – perhaps Lili would know somewhere.

My father had stayed in London for the weekend, but my sister was at home. Over supper, I saw she was interested in my trip as I answered more of my mother's questions, but I think she was a bit jealous as she had yet to leave England. Once we had cleared up, I excused myself as I was feeling tired.

Lying in bed, I tried to work out what – if any – were the implications of Mr. Watling using me as a courier. I puzzled over this for a while, coming up with all sorts of strange theories but I had no data. I then began to wonder what it would mean for Mutti Frida now that the evidence she had gathered was with British Intelligence. *Would they leave her alone or would they come up with some further plan to involve her? Either way, what would this mean for Col?*

With my mind still gnawing at all this, I eventually tossed and turned myself to sleep.

***

After breakfast, I eagerly walked round to see Col. As soon as the front door closed behind me, she flung herself into my arms. We hugged and I felt a few tears on my neck. After a minute, she pulled back. "Oh, Willi. You're home safely." She wiped her cheek and sniffed, laughing at herself. "Come in and tell me all about it."

She pulled me into the kitchen where Mutti Frida was making coffee. "Milk and cake, Willi?" she asked.

The aroma of coffee tantalised me. "Could I try some coffee, please?"

"Coffee?" Mutti Frida's surprise was evident in her voice.

I explained how I had inadvertently picked up a cup of coffee in Leipzig and its aroma was enticing but it had tasted awful. The aroma of Mutti Frida's coffee was even better.

"OK, Willi." She poured me a small cup from the coffee machine on the stove: strong, dark and slightly bitter – pretty good, although not quite up to Melbourne *espresso* standards.

Col saw my appreciative smile and picked up my cup, taking a sip. "Ugh. That's awful." She shuddered with disgust.

I smiled at Mutti Frida. "You'll have to show me how to make this for myself, Mutti Frida. I like it."

Mutti Frida smiled and put slices of Mr. Searle's fruit cake on the table. "Tell us all about your trip, Willi." She settled on her chair, sipping her coffee.

I peered at them both, knowing what I had to say first would be difficult for them. I breathed in. "In Leipzig, I met *Oberstleutnant* Schmidt." Both of them paled slightly and I saw the sudden tension in their hands. "There was a reception at the Leipzig Opera, and I didn't realise he was there until I was being introduced to him."

I gazed into their eyes. There was fear there but something else – suspicion? Of me?

"We only talked for about a minute about my essay and the University – nothing else." Their eyes were still drilling into mine. "And then he moved on."

There was silence for a few more seconds and then Mutti Frida took a deep breath, shaking her head. "It's all right, Willi. You just surprised me," she said, and caught Col's eye. "Us."

Col reached for my hand and smiled. "It's all right, Willi, I know you would not betray us."

This was going to surprise them, too. "I also met Mr. Watling."

Mutti Frida was puzzled. "In Germany?"

I shook my head. "No – on the train, yesterday."

"Why would he want to meet you?"

I explained that I had seen him at the station when I left, although I didn't know who he was. Then he'd sat down opposite me on the train down from London. "I think my whole trip was 'arranged' by Mr. Watling and British security."

"What makes you think that?" Her voice held some disbelief.

"He told me he had me watched in the DDR and it turns out that, unbeknownst to me, I was bringing back a package of papers that, I think, was the evidence against your husband. It was hidden in a false bottom of my duffel bag."

"It's here? You have it?" I heard the relief in Mutti Frida's voice.

My voice was apologetic. "I'm afraid not. I didn't know I had it until Mr. Watling told me about it and then he took it."

Mutti Frida's gaze was intense. "Are you sure it was *my* evidence?"

"Well, Mr. Watling wouldn't tell me what the package was, but when I suggested that's what it was, he was quite uncomfortable and got rather huffy."

"You think British Intelligence set all this up so you could act as a courier?" I heard the disbelief in Col's voice more strongly. "They somehow arranged for a prize winner to withdraw and for you to be offered the prize instead?"

"I don't know that's what happened, but it certainly fits the facts."

Mutti Frida's face was quite hard. "They were playing a dangerous game if that's the case. What if you'd slipped up and revealed that you knew us?" She paused, her mouth working. "I'll have some hard words with Mr. Watling the next time I see him."

"No, you can't." I jumped in. "He told me not to tell anyone, but I had to share this with you."

Mutti Frida shook her head. "I'll have to see what he tells me the next time we talk." She let out a sigh of frustration and then turned to me. "Now, Willi, tell us all about your trip."

Col smiled. "How was your first flight in an aeroplane?"

"Fantastic – apart from Ginnie getting sick."

Col inclined her head slightly and her eyes showed a dangerous glint. "Who's Ginnie?"

I kept a straight face. "She's an attractive red-headed girl I sat with for most of the trip."

I saw Col tense and then I smiled. "It's all right, Col. She's much older than me, in her final year of high school and lives in Devon."

I saw that Mutti Frida's eyes were full of humour and she chuckled at Col's reaction.

"I think you'd like her, Col. She wants to be a doctor." I took a sip of my coffee. "She learned German from the wife of a German POW that stayed in England after the war, working on her parents' dairy farm."

I saw Col relax. She leaned across and punched me gently on the arm, realising she had been had.

"Ouch." I rubbed my arm, pretending she'd hit me much harder – and then smiled. "Ginnie was quite nervous on the plane and even though I tried to help her, the nerves got to her when she tried to eat lunch."

"Oh, the poor girl," Col empathised.

"She was fine once we landed – and we went for a walk in the *Tiergarten* for some fresh air once we got to our hotel."

"Was she all right on the flight home?"

"Oh yes. In fact, I think the trip has helped her self-confidence a heap. She had to make several speeches as she was the only girl on the trip."

"How many of you were there?" Mutti Frida asked.

"There were two chaperones – a man and a woman – and five of us prize winners. I was the youngest – all the others were about eighteen, in their final year of school. We were hosted everywhere by the FDJ – and I got to meet a young Polish delegation in Leipzig, too."

Mutti Frida stood up. "Well, I must get lunch together – Lili's going to join us. Why don't you two go and sit in the lounge room and talk so you're not under my feet?"

Col and I snuggled together on the couch, revelling in the closeness after two weeks apart. There were few words, but lots of kisses.

After a while, Col whispered, "When are we having that conversation with Mutti about our promise?"

I was conscious of the beautiful young woman I was snuggled up with. "Perhaps we need to talk about this when we're alone. Then when we are sure about what we want to do, we can talk to her."

"I'm already sure." Col found a way to snuggle closer and leaned in to give me a kiss, her tongue sliding over my lips.

"Well, perhaps first we need to talk about the things we can do that won't break our promise to her."

Col's eyes rested thoughtfully on mine and I knew she was about to speak when Lili knocked on the door. Col's face expressed her frustration, promising more discussion soon, and got up to let Lili in.

The three of us chatted about my trip until lunchtime. Unsurprisingly, Lili was interested in what the young Pole had told me about the views of young people in Poland and that of course led to my meeting with Col's father.

Eventually, Mutti Frida called us in for lunch and I realised that this was a Monday, and Mutti Frida should have been at work.

"I arranged to take the day off, Willi." She smiled. "I wanted to welcome you home and hear about your trip."

Lili grabbed my hand. "Oh, Willi, I nearly forgot. My mother wants to invite you to dinner at our house on Wednesday evening – you too, Col and Frau Schmidt. She wants to hear all about your trip, Willi."

Col caught my frown and elbowed me gently. "You're not surprised, surely? Not after all the effort she put in to get you to go?"

I huffed, remembering the worry Mrs. Wiśniewski had caused with the photographer and articles in the paper. "I suppose not, but I'll have to ask my mother if that's okay."

"It's early closing on Wednesdays," Mutti Frida reminded us. "We can walk down together from here. Do you want to spend Wednesday night here, Willi?"

"I'll speak to my mother and let you know tomorrow, Mutti Frida. Is that okay, Lili?"

She nodded.

We spent the afternoon chatting some more and then playing cards before Lili had to leave to get home for tea.

At home that evening, I asked my mother about having dinner at Lili's on Wednesday night and staying over with Col afterwards.

"You've been away for two weeks, Will. It would be nice for you to spend some time at home."

"I'm home now – and you'll have surgery on Wednesday, anyway."

My mother gave her head a dismissive shake. "All right, Will."

The following morning, I walked round to Col's house. Mutti Frida would not be there and we could have that talk. Col had been waiting for me as the door opened before I could knock. She led me into the lounge room, and we sat on the couch. She leaned in and we kissed for a while before she leaned back, a slight blush on her face. "Are you going to tell me about these other things we can do … things that won't get me pregnant?" The blush had deepened but her eyes were shining with desire. In spite of the boys' clothes she was wearing, she was gorgeous.

"I'm not sure that talking is the right way to go about this."

I slid my hand up her arm and caressed her neck. She leaned into my hand, rubbing her cheek against it like a cat enjoying the sensuous touch, her lips smiling invitingly. After a while of mutual exploration, she pulled back.

"Oh, goodness." Her eyes were languorous beneath those long eyelashes and she stretched, sinuously. "I think we'd better stop for now. I want more, but let's explore slowly."

I kissed her nose. "You're in charge, *liebling*."

We spent most of the day close together on the couch, reading and later in another gentle exploration that left us both breathing heavily. The following morning was filled with the same wondrous explorations – and we had yet to remove any clothing. Now the dark threat posed by my trip to the DDR was past, we both felt there was plenty of time for us, plenty of time for a slow exploration.

After we sat in companionable silence for a while, Col shifted in my arms. "Do you think it will take twenty-five years this time?"

I stared at her in confusion. "What will take twenty-five years?"

"For the Wall to come down. For the Soviet empire to collapse."

"I don't know."

Col swivelled on my lap, her eyes boring into mine. "Why not? Isn't it different this time? Can't you tell?"

I took a deep breath and slowly released it. "I don't know, Col. I'm sorry – I have no detailed knowledge of what it was like in the DDR in my previous life. I didn't visit it, meet and talk with young people last time. I have no way to make a comparison."

Col shook her head in frustration. "I don't want to spend the next twenty-five years in hiding, pretending to be a boy."

"Things are certainly different between now and the last time – you know that as we've talked about them. But I don't know what effect they'll have." I let out an exasperated sigh. "Perhaps the collapse will happen sooner, perhaps later. I just don't know."

Col closed her eyes and slumped back, leaning against me. "We have to find a way to end the hiding, then."

"I have no idea how to do that, Col ... perhaps Mutti Frida can talk to Herr Watling about it?"

We sat for a while; our mood darkened by the situation Col was in.

"Come on, Col." I pulled her to her feet. "Let's go for a walk, we need some fresh air."

Mutti Frida arrived home soon after we got back from a wander along the cliff tops and we sat down for lunch together.

Col glanced across at her mother. "Mutti, we need to ask Herr Watling how much longer we need to hide."

"Why's that so important, Col?"

"I want to stop being a boy. I want to become a girl again." I could hear the frustration and longing in her voice.

Mutti Frida nodded in understanding. "I know, Col, but we need to be safe. That comes first, sure ..."

"No, Mutti." Col leapt on to her mother's commitment to safety. "I want you to ask him. I'm fed up wearing boys clothes and I'm fed up with pretending to be a boy, which is getting more and more difficult." Her voice was sharp. "I want to be a girl with other girls."

Mutti Frida sighed. "All right Col, I'll ask him – and I'll point out the increasing difficulties we are going to have if we keep you as a boy."

Col seemed somewhat mollified and we carried on with lunch. Later, I changed into the smarter clothes I had brought with me while Mutti Frida and Col readied themselves. Then the three of us walked into town as a gentle dusk settled over the sea at the foot of the Downs.

Lili ushered us into Mrs. Wiśniewski's elegant drawing-room.

"So, Willi," Mrs. Wiśniewski said, after we had settled into our chairs. "How was the DDR?"

She had caused us such heartache that I thought I might play with her a bit. "I enjoyed it." I saw Mrs. Wiśniewski stiffen. "The people we were with were just like us and friendly."

Mrs. Wiśniewski frowned. "Friendly?"

"Yes. Young people from the FDJ escorted us around Berlin, Dresden and Leipzig, showing us the sights and talking to us about their country. They are like us in many ways."

I saw that Mrs. Wiśniewski was blinking. This was not what she was expecting – or wanting – to hear. Then she gathered herself. "But Willi, I told you to read between the lines and behind their words. Didn't you do that?"

I heard the irritation in her voice. *Time to let her know what I had heard and surmised.* "Oh, yes. I did indeed do that." I told them about Fräulein Hartmann's late arrival and *Major* Koch's irritation and then about the incident in the *Augustusplatz* when I had attempted to visit Bach's church.

I saw that Mrs. Wiśniewski was nodding as this agreed with her expectations.

"They kept you under quite a close watch, then?" Mutti Frida asked.

"Yes ... but I only truly noticed it when I tried to visit *Thomaskirche* in Leipzig – and there I had the impression that Fräulein Hartmann was mostly concerned about how her bosses would view her if I went off unsupervised." I peered across at Mrs. Wiśniewski. "We went everywhere as a group – except when we were at the FDJ camp, helping to bring that out of winter hibernation where we worked in pairs, one of us with one FDJ member."

"How long did you spend at the camp?" Lili asked.

"We were there for two nights. During the day we were working hard, opening the camp for the summer, but in the evening, we sat around a fire outside in the forest, just talking and singing songs." I smiled at the memory.

Mrs. Wiśniewski was still on her hobby horse. "And they told you how wonderful their society was, I suppose."

I thought about it for a moment. "That's not the impression I came away with."

Mrs. Wiśniewski blinked and shifted in her chair, but I did not give her a chance to interject.

"Outside of Berlin, all the FDJ people I talked with were viewing their society in a slightly critical way. They knew something about the west beyond the Soviet propaganda and did not want a society like ours, but

241

they felt that their society needed to change, to become more open and modern."

Mutti Frida and Col were both leaning in, fascinated by what I was telling them.

"You think that the young people are going to be able to change things?" Col asked.

"Perhaps." I shook my head. "I don't know. Berlin's control seems pretty strong, as I saw with the FDJ there. Outside Berlin, they certainly want to change – and it is wider than just the DDR. In Leipzig I met some Polish young people, well one young man, and he felt the same way."

An awful thought suddenly occurred to me, and I found myself blurting it,

"Please, you must not talk about this. If word got back to the DDR, I'm sure the *Stasi* would be able to track down the people we met and cause them problems. It would be the same in Poland, I expect."

Mrs. Wiśniewski nodded. "The Polish government has the *Urząd Bezpieczeństwa*, the Security Service. They are like the Stasi and KGB." She gave me a friendly smile. "All that was interesting, Willi. Thank you." She stood up, smiling. "Now, let us eat."

We had a pleasant meal chatting about school and our plans for the summer. It seemed the Wiśniewski family was going to spend two weeks in the south of France at the end of July. Col and I had no plans, it seemed, except a shared glance held promise of those not-plans including each other.

Once we were back in Col's house, drinking hot chocolate at the kitchen table, Mutti Frida quizzed me. "You saw a difference between the youth in Berlin and out in Dresden and Leipzig?"

I thought about it for a moment. "Well, the FDJ in Berlin were, I think, part of the central organisation – I don't know, but they came across like leaders. I don't think that gave them much leeway to say anything except the party line." I gave her a wry smile. "There were adults around all the time in Berlin."

"But outside Berlin it was different?"

"It was not something you could point to – it was just that there was not this strict adherence to whatever the party line might be. They were prepared to question and think for themselves about the answers." I stopped for a moment, trying to put my feelings into words. "I think that the Berlin FDJ would be like that too, if they felt safe."

"And the young Poles you met were questioning things too?"

I shrugged. "I only talked with one – a trainee electrical technician from Gdansk – but he certainly felt that the society in Poland needed to change in the same way." As I thought about this, everything I had seen and heard fell quietly into place, the jigsaw pieces assembling themselves in my head.

"None of them wanted revolution, to throw over the current socialist order, but they all want to make it softer, more open...more...able to grow." The jigsaw pieces were adopting a clearer pattern. "The society they want is definitely socialist – they did not like what they knew of the West with its privileged class exploiting everyone else."

"That's not the way England is." Col interjected.

I raised my eyebrows at her. "No, you're right, that is an exaggeration – but it is an exaggeration of a truth. There is a privileged class here in England and the ordinary English worker is exploited to a lesser or greater extent, that's why people join trade unions, why there is a Labour Party."

"But there's a privileged class in the DDR, too," Mutti Frida said, softly. "I know, as should you, Col, for we were part of it."

Col blinked.

"I think that is part of what the young people see is wrong with the society in the DDR, one of the things they want to change," I added.

Mutti Frida nodded, then glanced up at the clock. "Plenty to think about, but we need to get your bed organised as it's getting late."

That weekend marked the end of the Easter Holidays and on Monday we resumed our now usual school day activities. Monday was a Polish day and we walked back from Lili's house telling Mutti Frida about our respective first day back in that language. For nearly two weeks, Col had spent most days with Lili and her Polish had certainly accelerated past mine. I had some catching up to do.

Tuesday started out as usual, chatting with Col and Lili as we headed to Canterbury, but when I boarded the bus that afternoon, there was no sign of Col, just a worried Lili.

"Where's Col?" I asked, my eyes skipping round the bus as if she might be hiding somewhere.

"I don't know." Lili shook her head in confusion. "She was called out of class before lunch and I haven't seen her since. I asked at the office, but they wouldn't tell me anything."

"Was she ill or something?"

"No Willi. I told you. She was called to the office."

I had a sudden thought. "What about her bag?"

"Someone collected it to take to the office." Lili frowned. "It was like she was in trouble, but that can't be right. We're together all the time and she's not done anything wrong."

I sat, wondering what had happened. *Was Mutti Frida sick?*

"Oh, God." A terrible thought occurred to me. "Has her father found them?"

Lili's face was anguished. "Oh, Willi. Surely not?" Her eyes flared. "What are we going to do?"

I heard the distress in Lili's voice and I grabbed her hand; mine was sweaty with fear, but the contact helped steady us both. I thought frantically for a moment.

"There's a number seven bus that should come in about ten minutes. We'll get off at the next stop and get on the number seven. That way we'll be at Col's house as soon as possible. Let's hope she and Mutti Frida are there."

"Okay, Willi."

At the next stop we got off and got on to the number seven about five minutes later. We sat in silence, lost in our own swirling thoughts until we approached the stop at the end of my road.

"This is it, Lili." And we went to wait at the front of the bus.

Once off, we walked quickly past my house, round the corner into Sea View Avenue and along to Col's house. We knocked on the door – nothing. I led Lili round the back to the kitchen door, searching in vain for an open window. Like the front, the back door was locked. There was no movement and no response to our knocking.

Lili held her hand against the glass, peering inside. "I wonder where they are?"

I closed my eyes, trying to blot out all the wild, awful thoughts: trying to think of what to do. "Let's go down to the shop where Mutti Frida works."

"Okay – but let's leave a note here in case we miss them, that way, they'll know what we are doing."

"Good idea."

I tore a page from the back of an exercise book, divided it two and wrote a quick note on each half, telling Col and Mutti Frida what was happening and where to find us and slid one under the back door and the other through the letter box in the front door. Then we walked quickly down into the High Street.

At the shop, we explained who we were. They told us Mutti Frida had gone to do some shopping at lunchtime, but not returned. I saw that the owner was annoyed at what she saw as Mutti Frida's unusual irresponsible behaviour. Lili sensed I was teetering on the edge of panic.

"We'd better go to my house," Lili suggested, taking my hand and leading me out.

We walked on to the seafront and along to her house, with the pavement feeling increasingly insubstantial beneath my feet. Once inside I sat down and took some deep breaths, trying to still the spiral of fear and guilt twisting inside me.

Then a thought occurred to me. "Can I use your phone, please Lili?"

"You're going to phone Col's house?"

I nodded. Out in the hall, I dialled Col's number. It didn't ring but came back with a strange sound I hadn't heard before.

"I think there's something wrong with their phone."

Lili dialled Col's number herself. "You're right. Perhaps if we phone the exchange, they can check the line."

The exchange advised that the number had been disconnected.

I felt a numbness creeping over me as the dark spiral tightened round my chest. Something terrible had happened to Col and Mutti Frida – and I had caused it by going to the DDR. Overwhelmed by the tightening braid of guilt and fear around my heart, my world greyed out to black.

***

Vaguely, I heard my mother's voice calling me softly. "Will, Will?" I felt a hand gently stroking my hair.

My eyes opened slowly – I was lying on a couch in Lili's lounge room, my mother leaning over me.

My mother tried to hide her concern. "Can you sit up?"

I thought about that and it seemed possible, so I did.

My mother quietly checked me over and seemed satisfied there was nothing obviously wrong. "Come on, Will. Let's get you home."

With Lili giving me support on one side and my mother's arm around me, they got me out into my mother's car with Mrs. Wiśniewski watching worriedly.

During the drive home, I realised we should have called the police straight away. *Idiot!* It might be too late now.

"Mum, we need to ring the police and report Mutti Frida and Col as missing."

"It's all right Will, we've already done that."

At home, she sat me down at the kitchen table. "Here, drink some water." She watched me closely whilst I drank. "How about some soup? Hmm?"

I wasn't hungry, but perhaps I should eat something. I nodded and my mother turned on the stove and found a tin of soup and some bread. I sat there, crushed by the knowledge that things in this world were repeating themselves – I had lost contact with my closest friend, again. But this time it was different. This time, somehow, I had betrayed Col.

"What do you think has happened?" My mother asked, drawing me out of the gyre of my guilt and shame.

I could not voice my fears, constrained by Col's secret. "I don't know, but it's ... strange that their phone has been disconnected."

My mother's eyes lingered on me at that morsel of information.

I sat in silence with my black guilt lapping greasily at my mind. After a while, my mother placed a bowl of cream of mushroom soup in front of me and a plate with two slices of buttered bread. Then she sat down opposite me with hers. For a while, I sipped disconsolately at the soup and then gave up.

"Thanks, Mummy, but I'm going to bed."

"Are you okay?" I heard the worry in my mother's voice. Twice, now, I'd collapsed in shock in the last six months, I realised.

I tried to reassure her. "I'm sure I'll be fine. I just need to sleep."

I felt my mother's eyes on me as I headed off to bed.

I lay there, wondering if I'd ever be okay again. Somehow, I had brought down *Oberstleutnant* Schmidt's wrath on Col and Mutti Frida's heads. I almost wished that I would wake up, back in my old world, that all this had just been a weird dream.

Sleep wouldn't come for hours. When I woke still in my childhood bedroom, the sun was streaming through the window. I lay there confused in my depression, but eventually I had to go to the loo.

My mother must have heard me moving, for she was waiting when I came out.

I blinked, my fogged brain struggling to work out why she was not at work. "It's not Sunday, is it?"

"No, Will." Her eyes swept over me, a doctor's quick assessment. "I let you sleep. Dr Jones is covering my morning surgery." She searched my face again. "Breakfast?"

I nodded, despite feeling drained, I realised I had to try to eat.

"Get dressed and I'll make you some scrambled eggs and Marmite toast."

Ten minutes later I dragged myself downstairs and my mother set a plate in front of me. "I phoned the school and told them you were sick."

I nodded. "Did Lili ring? Is there any news?"

My mother shook her head and clattered around in the kitchen, keeping half an eye on me. When she saw I had left half of my food on the plate, she sat down. "What's going on, Will? How come Col and his mother have both disappeared?"

I just stared at her face, unable to answer.

My mother pursed her lips. "Will, something strange is going on and I suspect you know quite a bit about it." Her eyes were full of compassion, but I saw her incisive intelligence there, too.

I didn't move.

Eventually. "Your silence is quite eloquent, Will." She reached across to take my hand. "If they are not found soon, the police will want to talk with you and Lili. If you stay silent with them, I don't know what will happen."

"Mummy, it's not my secret to tell – and if I do tell it, both Col and Mutti Frida would be in danger. I – we – can't risk that."

She leaned back with a small sigh. "You're close to Col, aren't you? So is Lili."

I took a deep breath, trying to hold down my guilt and fear, and nodded. "She's my closest friend."

"Lili?" My mother's face showed her confusion and then she stiffened in realisation. "She?" Her eyes bored into me. "Are you telling me Col's a girl?"

My heart was suddenly pounding, my eyes locked on to my mother's. "You must not tell anyone that."

My mother gazed off into the distance, lips pursed, and then murmured, "Why would Frau Schmidt want to pass her daughter off as her son? Is Frau Schmidt in trouble?" Her face softened. "Running from her husband, perhaps?"

I closed my eyes. She was close to at least a part of the truth. When I opened my eyes, my mother's eyes were pensive. After a few seconds, she half-smiled. "Col being a girl is actually a relief – in a way. I have been worrying for some time about the two of you and your close relationship." Her voice tightened. "Society is, unfortunately, intolerant of homosexuality."

I knew it would take half a century for that to change and even then, the acceptance was far from complete. I shook myself, trying to concentrate. "Please, Mummy, you have to keep Col's secret. Just letting out that she's a girl might be enough to put them in real danger."

"Will, if they might be in danger you must tell the police about it."

I leaned towards her, my voice intense. "I can't. Neither can you and nor can Lili."

"Lili knows Col's a girl?"

My big mouth. "Yes." I sighed, recalling the near disaster at Mrs. Wiśniewski 's Christmas party. "She saw Col and I kissing at her Christmas party and we had to tell her. But she's Polish and…" I managed to stop myself.

"What has her being Polish got to do with anything?" She paused again. "This makes no sense." Eventually, she shook her head and, as she got up, she turned to me. "I've got a surgery this afternoon and evening. Will you be okay by yourself?"

"I'll be fine." I hoped this continued to make no sense to her. After she left, I spent an hour or so moping about, unable to focus on anything, trying not to slip into that deep black hole from which there might be no return. After a while I rang Col's phone, only to hear that same noise, telling me it was disconnected. I couldn't stand it any longer and went through our secret garden to Col's house. I peered through all the windows: the house was still and empty, robbed of all the comfort and warmth of Col's and Mutti Frida's presence. In the lounge room I noticed that the bookcase we kept our books in had been cleared. Eventually, I went back over the fence and across to our secret garden.

I stopped under the tree. The cedar was redolent with memories both good and bad – her face staring down at me that first Sunday, sitting there knife poised and her saving my life beneath its branches, our times shared with Lili in its arms, reading aloud as Lili sketched us in the needle-dimmed sunlight. I sat down at the foot of the tree, head resting back against its solidity, and tried to calm myself whilst tears of guilt scorched my face. After a while I managed to rouse myself and head home, but I could feel my reserves were nearly depleted.

That afternoon after school, Lili knocked on our door. I took her out into the garden, sitting side by side on the rockery, so we could talk privately if my sister came home.

"You weren't on the bus this morning. I caught a number seven and came straight here. Have you heard anything?" Lili asked.

I shook my head. "I went over to their house earlier. There was no-one there and all their stuff has been taken away."

Lili had a puzzled frown on her face. "I tried asking again at school today, but the office told me nothing. Col's locker was unlocked and empty. She must have taken everything with her."

I felt my world closing in around me. *Col wasn't coming back.*

I started to sink into myself. "I must have made a mistake and betrayed them. I don't know what I did, but I must have done something." My voice cracked. "I did something and now they've been taken."

I felt Lili take my hand. "Willi…Willi…" She shook my hand. "Willi. Look at me."

Lili was searching my face.

"Willi, Col told me that if you ever got…um…down, I was to let her know at once." Her eyes narrowed. "She told me it was terribly important that I tell her – at once." I saw that Col had impressed this deeply on her.

I breathed in, closing my eyes as I tried to hold myself together. Col cared so much she had set Lili to help watch my moods.

"Willi, I know you are distraught at what has happened – but ... I can't tell her. She's not here." The anguish in her voice dragged my eyelids up.

248

I felt tears gathering in the corners of my eyes and collapsed onto Lili's shoulder. After a while, I pulled myself back. "What are we going to do?" I searched Lili's eyes for help.

She gave a shuddering breath and shook her head. "I don't know, Willi." Her voice echoed my hurt, but then her hands grabbed my shoulders and her voice firmed. "But I can tell you what we're not going to do – and that's collapse in a quivering heap." She held my eyes, her hands giving me a shake when I tried to shift my eyes away.

"I'll try." My voice was as thin as water.

"Not good enough, Willi. We have to be here for each other, for Col, however long it takes." This was a part of Lili I had not seen before: such hidden strength. I felt I had none; I hoped she had enough for both of us.

From somewhere, I summoned a nod.

"We'll still see each other every day on the bus and after school." It was a statement and not a question. "We'll carry on doing our homework together and we'll try and find her."

I swallowed. "Okay."

And that's what we did as the days of the summer term rolled into weeks, a month, with no news. It soon became clear that the police weren't interested in what had happened: a mother and her daughter had disappeared together without any sign of foul play: nothing to see here. They never properly interviewed us, despite our pestering at the police station. Eventually, they told us to go away. They would contact us if they heard anything.

Lili's strength seemed indomitable, keeping me afloat, insisting on our homework club and daily language lessons in French, German and Polish as a thread of normality to which I could cling.

One afternoon at Lili's house I remembered that Mrs. Wiśniewski had contacts that might be useful. "Lili, do you think your mother might be able to help? Do you think her contacts could find Mr. Watling, Mutti Frida's MI6 contact?"

"Perhaps – it's worth a try," Lili agreed.

When Mrs. Wiśniewski returned home, I asked if she could help us.

"What do you need help with, Willi?"

"We were wondering if any of your contacts could help us find out what had happened to Col and Mutti Frida."

Mrs. Wiśniewski remained motionless.

"You see, the police don't seem interested, but we thought maybe…" My voice petered out in the face of Mrs. Wiśniewski 's cold expression.

"Please Mama," Lili's voice was pleading. "We don't know what else to do. You have friends that might be able to help us, don't you?"

Mrs. Wiśniewski's lips were pursed. After a few seconds she stood up. "All right, I doubt if they can help, but I'll ask."

Each day, Lili and I caught the bus back and forward to school in Canterbury, Col's absence a hole that was impossible to fill. We pushed ourselves hard in our studies. For me it helped hold back the ever-threatening darkness; I think Lili pushed herself to keep me engaged. As a result, her French improved greatly and she topped her class at the end of term. Her German and my Polish also improved.

In the middle of the summer term a fat envelope arrived from Leipzig. My heart blazed with hope and fear, but then I saw the sender: *Institut für Theoretische Physik* at Leipzig University. That evening at the opera snapped back into scalpel-sharp focus: *Oberstleutnant* Schmidt inspecting me, instructing Fräulein Hartmann to see that I was sent information about the University. I took the envelope up to my room, unopened and slid it between two books on my bookshelf: I couldn't open it for what it symbolised. *Had his interest in me led him here?*

What had I done in Leipzig that had betrayed Mutti Frida and Col?

The summer holidays arrived, leaving vast deserts of time, empty of life, empty of Col. All I had to ward off the dark sea that lapped at the edges of my consciousness was study and I found solace in Maths and Physics: the timeless beauty of Maths and the endless searching of Physics. There was escape, too, in the literature I was studying.

During the holidays, Lili and I did not see one another as much as during term time. Unsurprisingly, there was a boy – well a young man – in her life and they wanted some alone time. One summer morning just before Lili left for the south of France, she knocked on our door. After I invited her in and we sat down, she pulled a tubular package wrapped in brown paper from her voluminous artist's satchel. Somewhat diffidently, she handed it to me. "This is for you."

Without opening it, I knew what it was.

Lili saw me struggle; her voice was gentle with compassion. "If you can't bear to have it, I think I understand." Then her voice firmed. "But this belongs with you. Open it, Willi."

After a few seconds of warring emotions, I pulled off the wrapping, carefully unrolling the thick drawing paper: there she was. It was better than a photograph for Lili had captured Col – her curiosity and humour, her strength and deep empathy. For some uncounted time, I could hardly breathe, let alone speak, Col's eyes holding mine.

I finally took a deep breath and dragged my eyes away from hers and up to Lili's. "Thank you."

"It's been sprayed with fixative, but you should have it mounted under glass, so it doesn't fade." Lili smiled diffidently, packing up her satchel. At the door she drew me into a hug. "I'll see you in a couple of weeks, Willi." Her eyes searched mine. "Take care of you." There was a murmur of uncertainty in her voice.

All I could do was nod, silenced by my emotions.

Lili's voice firmed. "Remember your promise to Col." She gave my hand a squeeze.

I glanced up, startled. How much had Col told her?

Lili just smiled enigmatically and walked off.

September 1964 – August 1970

I spent some of my Premium Bond money on proper framing. Lili's pencil and crayon portrait of Col then adorned my bedroom wall, along with the FDJ poster. I often found myself sitting on my bed, sharing her gaze. The feeling that it had been something I had done that had resulted in their betrayal to *Oberstleutnant* Schmidt grew in me. I sat there, sifting my memories of our time in East Germany trying to identify my mistake. At times, Col's eyes seemed to be filled with subtle accusation.

When we restarted our homework meetings in September, I found Lili had a smaller version of the portrait which she had kept for herself – apparently the final essay before the larger version she had given me.

Our relationship had changed with the loss of Col. She was much of the glue that held us together and we had to search for a different way of relating. Lili was an artist of growing confidence and ability, but she had none of Col's curiosity for science. We still shared our languages and the literature they allowed us to access, but Lili was striking out on her own path, where I was stumbling into growing darkness. Early in the autumn term, she called off our homework club on a few occasions, perhaps to be with her boyfriend. There was a growing distance between us, probably caused in part by my need for her support while I had little to give her but darkness and my academic ability.

Every day, my old brain fought with the roiling sea that threatened to engulf my young brain. My mother knew I was having a hard time and watched, unsure how to help. Bound up in my misery, I did not notice her suffering.

One October afternoon, for some reason my feet took me the long way round from Lili's house – up the Downs and along Sea View Road past Col's house. During the summer I had checked the house with decreasing frequency as it became evermore clear that they were not returning. Today it remained still and empty, the garden unkempt. I pulled myself away and my feet traced over the path back to my house. They had grown to know each crack in the pavement, each uneven surface intimately in the eighteen months that Col and Mutti Frida had lived there.

I was surprised to find my mother in the kitchen.

"No evening surgery?" I asked.

"Come and sit down, Will. We need to have a talk."

I saw that my mother was troubled. I hung up my coat and sat down opposite her.

"Will…" She petered out, then took a deep breath and started again. "Will, your father and I are separating."

I nodded, my eyes searching her face. Given what I knew, this was not a surprise and I was glad to have him out of my life completely, but it must still have been hard for her.

"I have decided that I...we...all need a clean break." She paused, her eyes in turn searching mine for...something, almost afraid of what she might find. "We are selling the house. I am leaving the surgery here and have taken up a position in Leicester. Your father is moving into a flat in London ..."

"And...?"

"We – that's you, me and Hilary – are moving in two weeks."

My stomach flipped – another break with my past. This had been my childhood home until I finally broke free at age seventeen. My parents had continued to live here even after they retired in the 1980s, sharing an uneasy peace.

"What about school?"

"I've arranged for you to stay with a friend of mine in Canterbury for the rest of the academic year."

I just sat there, thinking about how my life was being completely turned upside down.

My mother reached across the table, taking my hand. "I'm sorry, Will, I know this comes at a bad time for you." She gave my hand a squeeze. "Please try not to let it disrupt your studies."

It was only in bed that night that I realised that once we moved it would be more difficult for Col to find me – if, despite my betrayal, she was going to do so. I was sure she'd try to contact Lili though; I would make sure Lili knew where I was.

Our homework club and my Herne Bay life ended precipitously. My mother and Hilary moved to Leicester one weekend, dropping me at Dr Cassidy's house beyond the Westgate in Canterbury. When Lili and I parted, she gave me a fierce hug and we promised to stay in touch, which we did by letters every week or two; Lili's usually included a sketch of Rupert, her cat, or a view around Herne Bay. Underneath everything she wrote and drew, I felt her still sharing her strength in spite of the distance that had opened in our relationship.

Leafing through the local newspaper a week before Christmas, there was a picture of a completely wrecked car on page three. I would not normally read such depressing material, but a name leapt off the page at me. The accompanying article told me the Ford Prefect was flattened by a truck that lost control on the Thanet Way, killing the entire Wiśniewski family – mother, father and two children. I found my fingers didn't have the strength to turn the page but soon I could not see the awful photograph through the tears. Beautiful, talented Lili with sparkling blue eyes and an indomitable strength was gone.

It felt as if every part of my life was being shredded – and every link with Col erased, piece by piece.

Somehow, I found the will to keep on keeping on. Perhaps it was so that a part of Col's life remained in my memories of her and perhaps I was keeping my promise to her. I had no-one I could talk with about the darkness that swirled at the shores of my mind; I would lie on my bed and converse silently with Col's portrait, which sometimes helped but at other times the accusation in her eyes became too hard and I turned her face to the wall.

Nothing had come from our attempts to involve Mrs. Wiśniewski and that option was now forever closed. After Christmas, rather naively, I tried writing to MI6 in the hope I could find out what had happened to Col and Mutti Frida, perhaps speak to Mr. Watling, but after two unanswered attempts I gave up.

My established habit of reading the newspaper continued – but now in the school library where I went through *The Times* before morning assembly. In the background, the race to the moon was heating up and I followed the press coverage, ticking off events as they coincided with my memories from my previous life. One morning shortly before the Easter term ended, I read that Ladbrokes were offering odds on who would get to the moon first – Russia or America – and when. I realised that this was an opportunity to make some money using my foreknowledge – provided the Apollo program was as successful in this world as it had been in mine and the Russian N1 rocket the same unmitigated disaster. Laying a bet was also a statement that I was trying to make a future for myself: it felt a bit like nailing my colours to the mast.

I knew well enough that this world was different from that of my old life, but the space program did seem to be following the track I recalled. The more I thought about it, the more the reward seemed worth the risk, with its commitment to my future strengthening the case. I took one hundred pounds out of my Post Office account and went to the Ladbrokes shop in Canterbury High Street, having disguised my school uniform as best I could. They could see I was underage, but I explained I was placing the bet for my dad. The size of the bet probably helped convince them of this and I walked away with the betting slip made out to Mr. William Johnstone at odds of 950:1 for an American moon landing and safe return to earth before the end of 1969. This was a bit less than the odds quoted in the newspaper, but I suppose I wasn't the only one having a flutter and the odds had shortened. I carefully put the ticket in the frame behind Col's portrait.

The habit of burying myself in my studies carried me though the rest of my 'A' level year and I won a scholarship to study Physics at Cambridge. Col's portrait accompanied me there, along with the FDJ poster, both of which elicited nosy questions, which I ignored, from the infrequent visitors I allowed into my room.

As my first term at Cambridge drew to a close, I managed to screw up my courage and head to London to see if I could get anywhere with MI6 in person where my letters had failed. I was expecting the sort of security arrangements seen in 2000 era Bond films, but in 1965 MI6 seemed almost comically relaxed when I walked up the steps and into the foyer. There was a reception desk and beyond that a guarded security gate. Summoning my courage, I walked up to the reception desk, that was shielded behind what I suspected was bullet proof glass.

The young man behind the desk had a friendly smile. "Yes?"

I spoke through the grill. "I'd like to speak to Mr. Watling, please."

"And you are?"

"I'm William Johnstone."

I didn't suppose many teenagers came into MI6; he gazed at me for a few seconds, deciding what to do.

"Okay." It was drawn out as he continued to decide what to do with me. "Let me check." He turned to a table behind him and rifled through what I took to be a directory.

"I'm sorry, but I can't find such a person."

I had been prepared for this as Watling was probably a false name. "Well then, I need to speak to someone about a defector from the DDR – East Germany."

The young man smiled indulgently at me. "And what would you know about a defector from East Germany?"

"I know where she lived in Kent until recently, and I also know she had evidence that a senior *Stasi* officer was guilty of war crimes."

The young man scrutinised me for a few seconds and then reached for a phone. His other hand came up and flicked the grill closed, excluding me from his conversation. After a minute, he put down the phone and opened the grill. "Just wait there a minute, please." He gestured at a hard bench to one side of the reception counter. I sat down and watched what little traffic there was in the foyer, trying to prevent hope that I was getting somewhere from burgeoning.

"William Johnstone, would you come with me please?"

I glanced up. He was a rather non-descript man in a grey suit. "You're not Mr. Watling," I said, accusingly.

"You're right there," he said, smiling down at me. "But perhaps we can talk about this somewhere more private than the foyer?" He raised an eyebrow, gesturing towards the security gate. "Please come with me."

Perhaps I was getting somewhere. I stood up and followed him. At the gate, he pulled out an ID card and gestured towards me. The guard nodded and we entered the interior of the building. Following a ride in a lift and a short walk down a corridor, we arrived in a small room that reminded me of an old-fashioned interview room from a 60s TV police show.

"Please sit down, William. I am Mr. Pritchard."

As I took my seat, the door opened and a woman, her grey hair pulled back into a tight bun, walked in. I stood up again, as I had been trained to by my mother.

The lady paused, her hand on the doorknob staring past me at Mr. Pritchard with a wry smile on her face. "Well, Geoffrey, at least someone has some manners."

Mr. Pritchard stared back at her stonily but remained seated. The lady pushed the door closed, walking with a slight limp to sit down opposite me. She placed a slim folder on the table and surveyed me for a few long seconds. The scrutiny was intense and left me feeling I was lacking...something.

Finally she sniffed, almost dismissively. "Well, William Johnstone, you're young to be up at Cambridge." She paused, continuing to watch me. "But it's clear from your file that you are quite a *special* young man." There was more than a hint of derision in her tone.

Mr. Pritchard pulled the file closer and flipped it open, leafing through the few pages.

"You have a file on me? Why?"

The lady gave me a smile that was almost condescending and responded in perfectly accented German. "How many fourteen-year-olds visit East Germany, do you think? In particular, young men that speak multiple languages and who go on to win scholarships to read Physics at Cambridge?"

The lady wanted to try out my German? Fair enough.

Mr. Pritchard glanced sideways at the lady. Before he closed the file, I caught a glimpse of one of the letters I had written: they had *chosen* not to answer me; I felt a surge of anger but contained it.

"Now, what's this about a defector from East Germany?" he asked in English.

I stared him in the eye and replied in German. "If you have a file on me, that file would tell you the information you need to know – or MI6 must be even more inefficient than the CIA believes."

Mr. Pritchard leaned back in his chair, his face hardening. "Now..."

The lady put a hand on his arm. "Thank you, Geoffrey." Her tone was commanding, and she was back in English. She acknowledged the barb and language competition as a draw with a slight nod. "If you know what's in your file, why are you here?"

"Because I want to know where they are. I want to know what happened to them." I heard an edge of panic in my voice, so I took a deep breath. I needed to hold things together.

"What happened to whom?"

Was she being deliberately evasive? I closed my eyes, took another deep breath. "To Colette Schmidt and her mother Frida Schmidt, who until early May last year lived in Sea View Avenue, Herne Bay, Kent. Frau Schmidt, whose husband is *Oberstleutnant* Schmidt, second in command of the Leipzig *Staatssicherheitsdienst* office." I paused, seeking a reaction that I did not get. "Returning from the DDR in April last year, I unwittingly couriered back Mutti Frida's assembled evidence that *Oberstleutnant* Schmidt was a Nazi war criminal."

There was a stony silence from the other side of the table.

I waited a few seconds and then continued, "On the train home from London I gave that evidence to Mr. Watling, Mutti Frida's MI6 contact." I laughed, slightly cynically. "Perhaps a more accurate description was that Mr. Watling took it from me."

There was no motion from the other side of the table, and we sat staring at one another. The lady was quite imposing, and it was only my need to find out what had happened that prevented me from wilting under her harsh gaze. After several seconds, she gave me a slightly crooked smile and spoke to me again in German.

"You knew Frau Schmidt well enough to call her Mutti Frida – you were close to her?"

"Yes." I stared her hard in the eye. "And to her daughter."

"I see." She paused, raising an eyebrow. "You knew Colette was not a boy, then."

It was a statement not a question, so I remained silent.

The lady studied me across the table. Long seconds dragged past. Finally, she leant back in her chair, distancing herself from me and returned to speaking in English. "We don't know what happened to them." Her voice was as hard and flat as a steel plate.

"I ..." My voice choked. I started again, almost croaking my throat was so tight. "I betrayed them." The black tide of guilt and shame roared in and I collapsed slowly forward, my forehead coming to rest on the table.

"William?" A hand grabbed my hair, jerking me up so the lady could see my face. "What makes you think you betrayed them?" Now her eyes held something dangerous.

"I don't know," I almost wailed. "I must have let something slip. Why else would they disappear so soon after my return?" My voice seemed to come from a distance, my chest heaving.

She released my hair, but when my head dropped back on to the table, she grabbed it again, forcing my head back up. "William, we only have the barest information." I saw that she was deciding how much – or how little – to tell me. "Colette – or rather her alter-ego the boy Col – was collected from her school by a perfectly normal taxi that took her to meet her mother just outside Canterbury. There were two men with Frau Schmidt and the taxi driver left as they were all getting into a large black car – a Humber, he thinks. There was no sign of force being used, according to the taxi driver." She stopped, letting the implications of that sink in for a few seconds. "After that we have no trace of them, or the car." Her face was flat and hard, devoid of sympathy. "We have to assume that they were smuggled out of the country – willingly or unwillingly – and are now back behind the iron curtain."

I closed my eyes for a moment, trying to control my emotions, sensing she had more to say.

The lady's voice was matter of fact as her eyes scanned me like some strange radar, searching for truth. "It is, I suppose, possible that you said or did something whilst in the DDR that led to their discovery. But we know that *Oberstleutnant* Schmidt was searching for them and …" her eyes flicked towards Mr. Pritchard, "we think there might have been a leak."

Using my hair, she tossed me backwards into my chair. Standing up, she gave me a cold stare. "Whatever happened, they're gone." Her eyes were full of ice: no empathy, no compassion. "Best you get on with your life and forget about them." She picked up my file and walked out of the room, her gait displaying a slight hitch.

Mr. Pritchard's face declared his distaste for her demeanour. He watched the door close behind her and then took a deep breath. "She's extremely good at her job, but her…experiences…in the war cauterised her humanity." I caught a sort of apologetic tone in his voice.

I sat there, trying to take on board what had been said, but all I could think of was that Col and Mutti Frida had disappeared behind the Iron Curtain.

And I would never see them again.

Mr. Pritchard stood up. "Right, let's get you out of here."

A few minutes later, I was standing on the Embankment, dazed by the emotions running through me. I walked up on to Vauxhall Bridge and stood there, leaning against the balustrade, staring down at the river as it flowed away towards its end in the sea. The temptation was there, skittering across my thoughts, whispered in my ears by the breeze, flicked into my eyes by the water's coruscations; but I managed to just … stand.

Slowly, I dragged myself away and returned to Cambridge, where Col's eyes were accusing, yet full of compassion. The MI6 woman had intimated that perhaps Col and Mutti Frida had returned to the DDR willingly – and that implied they had lied to me – and to Lili.

That thought haunted me for a few days. *Could they have so misled me?* The longer I thought about this, the more ridiculous it was. Whoever that woman was, she was a masterful player, and her seed of doubt came close to germinating. But now, however, it lay sterile. I was certain that Col and Mutti Frida were who they said they were, not agents from the Eastern Bloc.

Eventually I realised that life goes on – and my promise to Col remained, wherever she was.

At Cambridge, I was much younger than everyone else in first year Physics and that made me different, which I hated as it always led to problems. I should have been used to this by now, but I wasn't. In an attempt to appear a bit older, I tried to grow a beard, but every attempt was a laughable straggle of patchy hairs and I ended up shaving it off, only to try again a few months later.

My tutor, Dr Finlay, kept trying to involve me in things beyond my studies, trying to help me fit into university society. There were departmental staff-student do's, but these centred mostly around a keg of beer which, because I was under eighteen, I was not allowed to drink. I did join the German and French clubs, which allowed me to practice some of my languages. With my fellow students, I gained a reputation as a hard worker, someone to have in your lab group, someone who had the answers to the difficult questions on the tutorial worksheets, but the age gap, my intolerance of stupidity and my morose nature kept me from forming any real relationships.

I ended my first year with A's across the board – and I started to feel the eyes of some of my lecturers on me.

The summer vacation was another expanse of time to fill. I knew no-one in Leicester except my mother and sister – and she, as usual, would have nothing to do with me. It seemed I was to blame for the family break up which had removed her from her circle of friends.

I scouted around and found a part-time job washing cars at a local garage. I had picked up my textbooks for second year before I left, another use for the Premium Bond winnings, and I worked my way through these with my mother's FM radio at my side, giving me access to classical music on the BBC. By early September I had finished the textbooks and my part time work had replenished my finances. Sitting around left far too much time to think and I was scared where that might lead. I realised I knew the centres of Dresden and Leipzig better than my country's capital and, after a bit of to and fro with my mother, I booked myself into the central London Youth Hostel for a week.

For a couple of days I did the usual tourist things – Tower of London, Buckingham Palace and down to Kew Gardens, but then the weather turned cold and wet and I resorted to the Museum strip in South Kensington. My first port of call was the Science Museum: the old steam engines were fascinating, gleaming in polished brass and bright red and green paint, as was the top floor which was the aviation section: I lingered beneath a hanging Spitfire, amazed at how much bigger it was than my young brain expected.

I was standing waiting for the Foucault's pendulum to be re-swung when I noticed a head of red hair joining the crowd: something about the way the head moved seemed familiar, so I carefully sidled through the gathered people until I could see the face. Once the pendulum was set in motion (by burning a restraining thread with a match) and the explanation of the pendulum's motion was complete, people started to move away, and I could get close enough to speak.

"Hello, Ginnie."

Her head turned towards me and after a moment her puzzled face broke into a smile. "Will, long time, no see."

I smiled in return. "Likewise. How are things going? Are you studying medicine?"

"Yes. I'm well, thank you. I made it into St Thomas Hospital. I'm about to start my third year. It's terrifying in a way but quite amazing. What are you doing?"

"I'm studying Physics."

Ginnie nodded. "Of course you are." She glanced around. "Hmm, I think there's a cafe here, shall we get a pot of tea and catch up?"

"Okay ... but it'll be coffee for me."

She laughed. "You got over that terrible cup in Leipzig, then?"

I smiled at the shared memory. "Yes."

We found our way to the cafe and ordered a pot of Earl Grey tea for one. When I realised the coffee would be instant, I settled on an orange juice and we found a table.

"You never replied to my letter." Ginnie accused me.

I blinked. "What letter?"

"I wrote to you once I had settled into St Thomas, that October after the DDR trip. I meant to write sooner, but I was so busy after we got back, what with exams, the farm and organising myself up to London."

"My parents separated, and we moved to Leicester in mid-October. Your letter should have been forwarded, but I never got it. I'm sorry, Ginnie."

"Oh, Willi, I'm sorry to hear that." She gave me a wry smile. "Are you keeping your languages up?" She asked, pouring her tea and changing the subject to something safer.

"There's French and German clubs at Cambridge, but Polish is more of a problem. What about your German?"

"I'm afraid I don't get to use it enough, only when I go home." Her head was cocked slightly to one side. "You're studying ... Physics ... at Cambridge?"

"I'm about to start my second year."

"Well done, Willi. You've kept ahead of the pack then ... is that still causing problems?"

"Well, I haven't had a Peter Farquar recently." I pulled a face at the memory. "But I still don't fit in."

Ginnie appeared a little flustered, remembering the attention she had inadvertently drawn on me that lunchtime in Leipzig. She changed the subject again. "Do you still have that German girlfriend ... umm ... Lili was it?" She picked up her teacup, sipping the hot tea carefully.

I couldn't control the tension that stiffened my body and I saw Ginnie's eyes widen. "Willi, what is it?" The teacup paused, suspended in its return to the saucer.

"It's...complicated, Ginnie." I closed my eyes, taking a few breaths, clinging to the cliff face of control.

The teacup clinked on the saucer and I felt a hand on mine, then a soft, intimate voice in my ear. "If you want to talk about it, I'm here."

Ginnie had been my companion and became a supportive friend during our trip and I felt she was owed the truth.

"Lili wasn't my girlfriend, and she wasn't German."

"What? ... Wasn't?"

"I'm sorry, but I had to lie." I stared at her face, seeking forgiveness. "Lili was my – our – friend. She was Polish and it was her that was teaching Col and I Polish." I took a deep breath. "She was killed in a car crash with the rest of her family just before Christmas a couple of years ago."

"Oh, Willi. That's terrible." I saw the questions behind her eyes.

"Col was my German girlfriend. She was from Leipzig – she and her mother had defected when she discovered her husband was a Nazi war criminal."

"Was...not her too?" I saw the horror on Ginnie's face."

261

"No – at least I don't think so." I breathed deeply for a moment. "Ten days after we got back from Germany, both she and her mother disappeared. MI6 think they were kidnapped back to the DDR. Col's father is a senior officer in the *Stasi* – the east German secret police."

Ginnie sat there, her tea forgotten.

I felt my old brain struggling for control. "And I think I somehow betrayed her when I was in the DDR." My voice cracked with the anguish I was feeling.

"Betrayed her? How?" I heard the disbelief in her voice.

I shook my head. "I don't know – I've been over everything we did, everything I talked about and I can't think of anything...except..." I dribbled to a halt, my throat constricting.

Ginnie stroked my hand. "Except?"

"At the opera reception, do you remember a tall, greying man talking to me?"

"Um – vaguely."

"That was Col's father – *Oberstleutnant* Schmidt, second in command of the Leipzig *Stasi* office." I fought for a breath against the constriction in my chest. "Fräulein Hartmann introduced me to him, I think because of my interest in the Physics department of the University. He must have had me investigated and found Col and Mutti Frida."

I watched Ginnie's face change from concern to horror as realisation struck her. "Oh, no. Fräulein Hartmann was there at that lunch, when I drew all that attention to you." She slumped back in her chair. "It's my fault she introduced you to him."

"I don't think so." I shook my head, trying to convince her she had no blame in this. "I think it was me showing off my knowledge of Physics at the university that was the reason. After...after they disappeared, I received a package of information about the *Institut für Theoretische Physik*."

Ginnie peered across at me for a moment and then dropped her eyes, fiddling with her teacup. "And ... you were in love with her, weren't you?"

I nodded. I felt tears pooling in the corners of my eyes. "I still am."

Ginnie gazed at me for a few seconds before saying, "Come on, Will. We'll go for a walk in Hyde Park...like we did in the *Tiergarten*."

The rain had stopped but it seemed like it could start again at any time. Ginnie retrieved a folding umbrella from her bag and we smiled at the similarity with our walk in West Berlin. As we walked along the wet paths, Ginnie told me about her desire to qualify and then specialise in obstetrics and I invited her to come and visit us in Leicester and meet my mother. We exchanged student addresses before we parted.

"Are you all right, Will?" Perhaps she was remembering me nearly losing it at that lunch in Leipzig.

I gave her a grim smile. "Mostly. When it gets difficult, I just concentrate harder on my studies."

"Stay in touch, please Will." She gave me a gentle hug.

I nodded, finding no words. As I walked back down to South Kensington tube station, I realised I had spread my guilt about Col and Mutti Frida onto Ginnie. *What sort of a friend was I?*

For the rest of my time in London I drifted, memories of our trip to the DDR assailing my dreams and waking thoughts, so I spent those days in a sort of fog, not experiencing the capital at all. After a couple of days back in Leicester, I returned to Cambridge for my second year of studies to find a chatty letter from Ginnie which helped me settle back into the life I was living.

Everyone had said that the second year of the degree program was heavy going – and that proved quite correct. I was glad I'd been through the textbooks during the vacation as that kept the workload reasonable, for me at least. That was certainly not true for everyone and I was able to provide help to some of my peers, which by Christmas had earned me grudging respect and envy in about equal proportions.

I found Christmas itself difficult – my best Christmas memories were the two celebrations I had enjoyed at Col's house. But their soft glow also cast long shadows of pain and guilt as the faces of Col, Mutti Frida and Lili peopled my dreams and waking thoughts; there were so many 'if only' thoughts. I escaped back to Cambridge as quickly as possible and buried myself in study, the only thing that seemed worthwhile in my life.

The catastrophic capsule fire of Apollo 1 in January 1967 occurred as I remembered, so I decided to risk another hundred pounds that things would turn out in this world as they had in my old one. The odds had shortened to five hundred to one though, despite the recent tragedy. But that restatement of a belief in my future helped provide some continued direction to my life beyond study. I didn't know what I would do, but I was making a commitment to be there and to do ... something.

Ginnie and I had exchanged a few letters and she invited me to stay at their farm for a week over Easter. We both had a heavy load of work, revising for the end of year exams, so our forays amongst the cows were punctuations in the time we spent sitting at her parents dining room table studying, frequently talking in German. I found the memories this evoked quite challenging and Ginnie sensed this. During a longer walk around the farm, she gently encouraged me to talk, extracting the story of the homework club I had shared with Col and Lili. By the time we wound our way back to the farmhouse, I was feeling less tense.

I complemented her on her bedside manner, and she blushed. The green shoots of confidence I had first seen during our trip to the DDR had burgeoned and blossomed. At the end of the week, we travelled up to London together on the train, talking only German for practice, which caused a few sideways glances from people around us. We parted at Paddington, Ginnie heading for her shared house and me across London for a Cambridge train.

I ended my second undergraduate year with excellent results and left for Leicester with the books I would need for my final year's study. These kept me occupied along with picking up a part time job cleaning four days a week in the canteen of a shoe factory. I hated that job, but it was all I could find. I had to be there at eight o'clock in the morning to clean up after breakfast, then help set up for lunch and clean after that; then get set up for tea if the factory was working overtime on a rush job or for breakfast if not. The canteen was redolent with the aroma of boiled cabbage and no matter how hard I scrubbed; every surface seemed to retain a patina of grease that made my skin crawl with revulsion. I felt the need for a bath every day when I returned home. My old brain would have preferred a shower, but they were uncommon in English houses back then. Still, the work replenished my finances for my final undergraduate year, a most important consideration which allowed me to preserve my Premium Bond winnings.

In late October 1967, early in my final undergraduate year, my tutor inquired what I intended to do next. He intimated that there might be a place for me as a graduate student at the Cavendish Laboratory, should I maintain my current high undergraduate standing, which I had every intention of doing.

I went home for Christmas pondering this offer, trying to decide what I wanted for the rest of my life from this, my second time around. I had left my world in 2020, a year that had seen Australia savaged by the effects of climate change: widespread coral bleaching, a deepening drought, horrific bushfires and finally floods. Perhaps I could use my growing expertise in Physics to work on ways to reduce emissions: I would take up the Cavendish post if it were offered and otherwise find somewhere else to commence postgraduate studies.

With the award of a First in June 1968, the hint from the Cavendish Laboratory became a firm offer and in October I would join the Cavendish as a junior member of a team chasing the ever-receding dream of fusion power, which in my world had still not born fruit by 2020. I had the advantage of knowing what was showing promise in 2020 and could introduce the idea of braided magnetic field confinement and renew the flagging interest in Stellarators: perhaps that would be enough to tip the balance. For my supervising professor, I had expressed an interest in working on the plasma instability problem in Tokamaks and would work to refine this to a thesis once I started there in late September.

The implosion of the Soviet empire in the late summer of 1968 as I transitioned into my postgraduate studies was almost unbelievable, but I recalled those discussions with the FDJ, so perhaps not so incredible – even if twenty years earlier than I expected.

It started with a black day in mid-August: the Soviets rolled their tanks into Prague to suppress Alexander Dubcek's Prague Spring – an event I recalled from my old world but had forgotten about until it occurred. But differences soon became apparent.

The invasion sparked demonstrations in Poland that grew as unions joined the students on the street, fearing that the loosening bonds happening in Poland would lead to a similar suppression. Within days, the demonstrations spread to the Baltic states, DDR, Hungary and Rumania. Only the USSR and Tito's Yugoslavia remained, at least outwardly, calm. The Soviets and the various Warsaw Pact governments were immobilised by indecision in the face of massive and spreading dissent – and that emboldened the Czechs, who surged onto the streets one sunny Sunday morning five days after the invasion.

Western media carried TV footage of Czech students holding hands and dancing round the Russian tanks, inviting the soldiers to join them, which increasingly some did. In the DDR, protesters marched to the Wall in Berlin and overnight demolished large sections, helped by some of the guards whilst others watched, bemused by events. Demonstrations started on the streets of Moscow, Kiev and several other Soviet cities, with banners demanding freedom. Within days, one by one, the governments of the Warsaw pact countries resigned, collapsing like dominos led by the DDR. In Russia, the authorities called out the army to clear the streets but almost *en masse* the army joined with the demonstrators and the Soviet era was over. Those young people I had met in Dresden and Leipzig had achieved their open society – they now needed to sort out what that meant.

Slowly, order returned to eastern Europe and information leaked out that the Soviets had tried to make the other Warsaw pact countries participate in the invasion of Czechoslovakia, but they had all refused. In Germany, east and west stared at one another over what was now a meaningless border – and started moves to reunify their divided country, awakening historical fears in England and France.

I had no idea what had happened to Col and Mutti Frida, but I suspected that I might be able to pick up something that would help me find them in Leipzig. As things settled during the autumn, I thought about a holiday in Leipzig over Christmas. But it didn't happen, in part because graduate

265

students are the slave labourers for their professor's research and that made it difficult to get away, but mostly because I was afraid that if I went, I would not find Col and if I did, that she would reject me because of my betrayal. This guilt and fear pinned me down in England, furious with myself for my cowardice but too ashamed and afraid to try to find her.

All of this boiled over on New Year's Eve, when our neighbours, also students in a shared house, had a party. They invited our house not because we were friends but because that way we wouldn't complain about the noise. My young body was not used to alcohol and I got very drunk before my old brain realised there was a problem. I have a vague recollection of being taken home and tossed onto my bed. The hangover when I finally stumbled out to the toilet did not help the darkness rising in my mind, but it did physically incapacitate me so I could not put into action the ending I was contemplating.

I spent New Year's Day mostly in bed and the sleeping continued into the night. I was dragged out of bed about ten o'clock the following morning when Jim, one of my housemates, banged on my door, yelling that I had a visitor and I'd better get downstairs quickly. I scrambled into some clothes, wondering who could possibly be coming to visit me, and stumbled downstairs to find Ginnie sitting coolly at the kitchen table, being chatted up by Jim.

"Goodness gracious, Will. You're a bit under the weather."

I blinked, finding it hard to summon any sort of enthusiasm. "Um ... I overdid New Year a bit." I stared blankly at her. "What are you doing here?"

"Visiting you. Didn't you get my letter – again?"

I shook my head, careful to be gentle with my lingering headache. "'Fraid not ... it must be held up in all the Christmas post or something."

At that point, Jim sat up with an embarrassed start. "Um ... wait a moment." He darted out of the kitchen and we heard him rush upstairs and, after a minute or so, back down again, whereupon he handed me an envelope. "Sorry, Will. I picked it up with a bunch of my post and forgot to give it to you."

Ginnie rolled her eyes. "Well, I'm here interviewing for a houseman position at Addenbrooke's Hospital later today and I thought I'd come up early and catch up with you."

"What time's the interview?"

"Not until three o'clock." She surveyed the untidy kitchen. "Do you want to go and find somewhere to have lunch?"

Ginnie's unexpected presence was pushing back the darkness. "Can you give me half an hour to have a shower? I was asleep when you arrived."

"If you can make me a pot of tea," she said, smiling.

266

I glanced at Jim. "Your penance for failing to give me my mail is to make tea for a beautiful red-head."

He smiled and nodded as I headed back upstairs. One of the reasons I had selected this house was because it had a shower, which I stood under for ten minutes, feeling it wash some of the darkness from my mind. I was back downstairs well before thirty minutes and we headed off to a nearby pub that offered reasonably priced hot lunches.

Ginnie claimed us a table near the open fire and I picked up a menu, a gin and tonic for Ginnie and an orange juice for me: I'd had quite enough alcohol for a while.

We both picked Shepherd's pie with chips and peas. I went to get up and Ginnie reached over. "No Will, I'll get the food."

"Thank you."

After placing the order, she settled herself back into her chair and sat gazing thoughtfully at me for a couple of seconds. "Out with it, Will. I can see there's something eating away at you."

I closed my eyes, breathing deeply to try and hold the cocktail of guilt and shame at bay.

I heard Ginnie's chair scrape on the floor and she took my hand.

"I'm here, Will. Perhaps I can help." A gentle statement, without any pressure.

I opened my eyes to find she'd moved round the table to be closer to me. I drank some of my orange juice, carefully replacing my glass on the table. "It's Col."

Ginnie blinked. "You've found her?"

I stared at the table, unable to speak until I felt Ginnie's hand give mine an encouraging squeeze.

"No ... it's ..." I stuttered to a stop, berated my cowardice and found the strength to go on. "I can't go and search for her."

"What do you mean?"

I closed my eyes, trying to shut out the terrible visions of Col and Mutti Frida languishing in a prison ... or worse. But as always, they remained. "I should have gone to Leipzig to see if I could trace her, but I didn't ... I couldn't ..."

Motion caught the corner of my eye – the bar girl was standing there with our meals, unwilling to break into the tension at the table. Ginnie blushed faintly and gestured for her to put the plates and cutlery on the table, which she did, warily glancing back at the intense aura of emotion she had felt. Ginnie busied herself for a moment, sorting out the table. "Will, shall we eat and then go for a walk? You can tell me what's going on then, like you did at the farm." Her voice was soft, full of concern.

I took a breath and nodded. During lunch, Ginnie regaled me with her experiences as a medical student. After we finished our meal, she produced a map from her handbag, and we walked towards Addenbrooke's Hospital. I told her about starting to plan a visit to Leipzig but giving up in the face of my guilt and shame.

"But there's more, isn't there, Willi?" she asked, gently.

I walked several paces before I turned towards her, tears blurring my vision. "If I do find her, she might not want to have anything to do with me … or she might have found someone else."

Ginnie pulled me to a stop. "Oh, Willi." Compassion shone through her words and she pulled me into a hug as tears ran down my face.

After a minute, I pulled away. "Sorry. Sorry." I wiped my face and felt in my pockets for a hanky I knew wasn't there.

"Oh Will, don't apologise." Ginnie pulled some tissues from her bag and handed them to me. "I can see you're hurting." We stood there for a while as I blew my nose and sorted myself out a bit.

She smiled comfortingly and then glanced at her watch. "I need you to do something for me."

"What do you mean?"

"I want you to go back to your house and wait there for me. I'll be there as soon as my interview is over, and we can talk some more." She gave my hand a squeeze. "Can you do that for me?"

I didn't have the energy to argue, so I just nodded.

"Okay – off you go," she encouraged me with a smile.

I gazed around to get my bearings and set off towards my house. I turned back as I crossed the road to see Ginnie standing there, watching. She gave me a wave and then started walking towards the hospital. I made my way home, went up to my bedroom and collapsed on the bed. I must have fallen asleep and was woken by Ginnie covering me with a blanket.

"Oh, you're awake. I'm sorry, I was just trying to cover you as it is getting cold."

"It's okay, Ginnie." I pulled myself up and leant against the wall, rubbing the sleep from my eyes. "How did the interview go?"

Ginnie shrugged. "Okay, I suppose. It's hard to tell what they want."

I nodded.

Ginnie sat sideways on the bed, her eyes searching my face. "I'm worried about you, Willi."

"I'm okay."

"No, Willi, be honest, with yourself – and with me." She took my hands in hers, stroking the backs with her thumbs. "I don't know much about psychiatry as we've only had an introductory course, but I can see there's something wrong." Her eyes stared, questing, into mine. "And it scares me."

I stared at her. *Did I want to unload on her…and would that help either of us?* I'd already made her feel guilty by telling her about *Oberstleutnant* Schmidt…and what about my suicidal thoughts?

Ginnie rotated my hands and inspected my wrists. I tried to pull them away, but she held me. I could see fear and pain in her eyes.

"You've thought about killing yourself, haven't you?" The question lacked judgement but was full of compassion.

I closed my eyes and tried to hold myself together, but the darkness rushed in and I collapsed into Ginnie's arms. Quite some time passed before I was aware of my surroundings again – under a blanket, cradled in Ginnie's arms.

Slowly, she got me talking about everything that had happened during that amazing period of my life I spent with Col, first as a boy and then gloriously as herself. We must have lain there talking for well over an hour and by the end I was drained.

When I ran down, we lay there for a while, before Ginnie turned her head. "Col extracted a promise from you that you would talk to her if you ever felt suicidal… and you've been keeping that promise, even though it's been hard?"

I nodded – the memory of that time under the cedar tree was a beacon in my memories.

"And she set Lili to watching you as well?"

Again, I nodded.

She held my eyes for a while. After a minute or so she reached up and stroked my cheek. "I know Lili's gone – but Col isn't. She's out there, waiting for you to find her."

I tried to turn away. "You can't know that."

The hand on my cheek held me, her eyes peering into mine. "And you can't know that she isn't." She was smiling, then her face became more serious. "You need to do something about that. Perhaps you're not ready yet, but you have to try ... sometime." Her eyes bored into mine. "And in the meantime, you have to keep your promise to her."

We lay there for a while longer with Ginnie lending me her strength, before she roused herself. "I have to go, Will. I have to be back in London tonight as I go on shift at half past six in the morning."

When we appeared downstairs, there were knowing smiles and some muttered comments from my housemates, which caused Ginnie to blush and me to give them a furious glare. I rang for a taxi to take her to the station and walked out with her when it arrived.

"Keep your promise to Col, Will." Her soft voice belied its steel as she leaned in and kissed my cheek.

I drew her into a hug.

"Take care of you, Ginnie." I stood and watched the taxi drive away, pondering on the good fortune that had given me such amazing women in my life. Ginnie was right, I would have to try and find Col, but I knew I wasn't ready. I needed more strength so I could face the rejection that I felt was owing to me. And I had no idea how long accruing that strength would take.

Ginnie wrote to me a few weeks later that she had not got the job in Cambridge, but was at the Royal Devon and Exeter hospital, which must have pleased her parents as she was so much closer to them. I struggled on with life from day to day, with my research the only light in my life.

The Apollo program was building to a crescendo. Christmas 1968 saw *Apollo 8* orbiting the moon, gifting us that incredible earthrise photograph. *Apollo 9* confirmed the operation of all the mission elements in earth orbit and *Apollo 10* did all that again in lunar orbit – even if they did briefly lose control of the LEM at one point.

Work at the labs came to a practical halt with the launch of *Apollo 11* in mid-July as everyone was glued to the BBC TV coverage of this epic voyage. I sat with my housemates as we listened to Armstrong and Aldrin make the descent, remembering what had happened in my old life and mentally ticking off the computer errors and fuel warnings as they happened.

"Houston. Tranquility base here. The Eagle has landed."

We all started breathing again, along with Charlie Duke and the entire mission control room in Houston: they had landed with just fifteen seconds of fuel remaining.

Hours later, I went to bed having watched the first moon walk and listened again to Neil Armstrong's famous words. This was the first time that I felt a real emotional connection with my old life. Somehow, because that connection was to a world event rather than a personal one it brought a strange feeling of peace and I drifted off to sleep with unaccustomed ease.

A few days later after the successful splashdown I walked into the local Ladbrokes office and presented my two betting slips. They caused a bit of a stir and the manager went off to make a phone call. After a while he came out and presented me with a cheque for a large amount of money. He then spent some time trying to get me to agree to some publicity, which I politely but firmly refused. I walked round to the bank and deposited the cheque, the size of the deposit raising the eyebrows of the cashier. I now had the financial resources to search for Col, but I still lacked the mental ones.

Ginnie and I exchanged letters irregularly and so I knew she was moving closer to her desire to become a specialist in obstetrics a few years hence. In return, I told her about the ups and downs of my research. Whilst I could find analytical solutions to simple plasma control situations using braided magnetic fields, I needed numerical solutions as I moved towards more complex arrangements – and these required more computing power than I had access to. My professor seemed unable – or unwilling – to push harder to give me increased computer access. In the meantime, I was working on a small test rig that would – at a tiny fraction of the plasma energies needed for fusion – allow me to explore braided fields in what was essentially a model stellarator. The design of this took most of the second half of the year. I became reasonably expert, after quite a few abject failures, at hand winding coils using coated wire only slightly thicker than a human hair as I moved into the construction phase during the winter.

I was so engrossed in my research rig and its inevitable feedback into the theory behind my design that I was conscious of little else. It came as a complete surprise when my professor advised me I was to accompany him to the European fusion conference in August. Rather brusquely I was told to get my passport organised. I didn't say I already had one as I wasn't sure if one with a picture of me age fourteen would be adequate. The following morning, I diverted to the post office with my passport and was told that they could update the photo. I found a photographer and a few days later returned to the post office with the photos and the form they had given me, both signed by my professor as a witness that I was who I said I was.

I was not going to speak at the conference, but my magnetic containment research was deemed sufficiently worthy by the conference organisers to warrant a poster exhibition. The conference was in August – two months away – so I did have time to pull things together. This included having the lab's photographer spend a day with me getting photos of the research rig that was nearly finished. I spent most of the time trying to make sure he didn't touch anything, or drape lighting cables close to magnetically sensitive parts of the rig.

About a week before we were to leave for the conference, I attended a meeting of our team at which our itinerary was handed out. We were going to the *Institut für Theoretische Physik* in Leipzig.

The room faded out for a few seconds and only came back into focus when I swallowed what felt like my entire stomach. Fortunately, it seemed no-one had noticed. I tuned back in to discover that I was the only grad student in the team, and I was there to cover the sessions of lesser interest to the professors and post-docs, taking notes so I could brief them. I was also given instructions to make sure I took a suit with me for my poster day and other official events. My fellow grad students who weren't going on an

271

all-expenses paid holiday to Leipzig insisted I buy a round of beers to compensate them.

That evening, back from the pub, I sat on my bed, communing with Lili's portrait of Col, awash with both excitement and fear. I knew I would be so busy during the conference I would have no time to go searching – but I could, perhaps, stay on for a few days afterwards. I had not reached a decision to stay on the following morning but decided to enquire if that was possible. After explaining to my professor that I had visited Leipzig six years earlier and wanted to see how much it had changed by staying a few extra days, he grunted and said he would see if it were possible.

I left his office convinced he would soon forget, and nothing would come of it – which meant I didn't need to decide, which in its own way was a relief. We had a final meeting on the Friday morning before we were due to leave early on Saturday, travelling by train, ferry and train, arriving in Leipzig late on Saturday evening.

The lab manager was there at the end and handed out our travel documents. "Here's yours Will. You'll need to find somewhere to stay for the extra days – but I think you should be able to stay on in the university dormitory if you ask on arrival."

I glanced at him, surprise showing on my face. He raised his eyebrows at me. "You did ask to stay on for a few days, didn't you?"

I nodded. It seemed the decision had been made for me – ready or not, I would have time in Leipzig to seek out traces of Col and Mutti Frida. I spent the rest of Friday putting the posters and photos into a large travelling tube I had borrowed from the lab manager before heading back to the share house to pack, including the ready to wear grey suit I had altered to fit me.

We arrived in Leipzig late on the Saturday, staying once again in student dormitories. As on that previous occasion, I was up early on Sunday morning and finally visited *Thomaskirche* – hearing the distant echo of Fräulein Hartmann's voice as I walked across *Augustusplatz*. I stood at the back of the church, enthralled by a *cantata* before I had to leave to help finalise our participation in the conference. My contribution to the meeting was to sit and listen to everyone else and have jobs 'delegated' to me: as I said, slave labour. By evening I was exhausted from racing around but did have time to investigate the Leipzig telephone directory: unsurprisingly, there were hundreds of Schmidts listed – that was not going to help. I had heard the *Stasi* files had been opened to the public, but I had no idea how to gain access to them. I would have to find out about that after the conference finished. I could feel my anxiety rising at the thought of possibly meeting Col and Mutti Frida. *Would I have the strength to start the search? To continue it?*

The conference started on Monday, with the usual plenary session before breaking up into smaller groups. I spent the day taking notes for my professor in the breakout sessions I had been told to attend. That evening I set up my poster show in the foyer, which I would stand beside to answer questions at morning and afternoon tea on Tuesday. That made me late for the reception, but I managed to scrounge one glass of *Rotkäppchen.*

In bed, I wondered how I could go about trying to find Col and Mutti Frida. I hadn't thought this through at all, but now I was here I had to try to find them, in spite of my misgivings on how I might be received. I didn't think I was likely to have much immediate success given that MI6 hadn't been able to trace them. I ended up tossing and turning for some time as my stomach was quite unsettled by my emotions.

On Tuesday, there were four of us 'poster boys' – well, poster people, as one of us was a nerdy French woman who refused to engage with the rest of us – displaying our research in the foyer outside the main conference hall. Fortunately, given my emotional state, the morning tea session was a bit slow for me with only a couple of desultory enquiries. The afternoon tea session was quite different – both in terms of my attention to the task and the number of people wanting to speak to me.

Apparently, a question was asked in one session about the problems of stabilising plasma and someone had mentioned my research as 'promising': at afternoon tea I found myself with a small crowd around me as I answered questions mostly in English, but with some German and French as well. I noticed the French lady cocking an eyebrow at me when she heard me discussing, in French, my use of Laplace transforms to solve one of the equations. As the crowd thinned out, a grey-haired professor, from Moscow according to his name tag, was trying to query me, but his English was almost non-existent, and I spoke no Russian. I tried him in German, French and Polish with no success.

He raised a finger and in a frustrated and peremptory voice, instructed, "Wait." It was clearly a command.

I nodded – I was not going to risk annoying some probably influential Russian professor who could then stir up my supervisor and cause me problems.

After a few minutes he returned and walked up to me. "Soon. Translate." Then he turned his back on me to examine my poster board, muttering to himself and occasionally nodding. I got involved with a post doc from Imperial College in a deep discussion about the second order effects of the braided magnetic fields I was using.

"Ah." The Russian professor grabbed my shoulder and spun me round. "Translate."

I blinked, taking a half-step backwards in surprise. "Mutti Frida!"

273

She peered at me, perhaps my current scraggly attempt at a beard was confusing her. "Willi?" Her voice was tentative, as if not quite convinced or ...

Had she forgotten me ... or was she deciding what to say to the person who had betrayed her? Time slowed, but my heart raced. The room irised down until all I saw was Mutti Frida's face; all I heard was the wild thudding of my heart; all I felt was the roiling of my stomach: I could never be ready for this rejection ...

"Oh, Willi!" Her smile blazed and I was enveloped in a crushing embrace, its intensity left us gasping deep lungsful of joy.

After some uncounted time, we were interrupted by a rather impatient cough. *"Извините меня."* (Excuse me.)

Mutti Frida turned, clasping my hand tightly as if afraid I would try to escape, and spouted rapid fire Russian at the professor. His frown evaporated and he looked at me with an amused smile. There was a brief exchange and then he reached across, shaking my hand and giving me his card. My face must have shown my total confusion.

He nodded, smiling across at Mutti Frida.

I stared between the two of them. "What's going on, Mutti Frida?" My mind was racing in tiny circles but there was still the potentially career-limiting issue of not annoying an eminent Russian professor.

He just smiled some more, pointed at Mutti Frida and walked off, chuckling quietly and shaking his head.

Mutti Frida turned back to me, taking me by both hands and running her eyes gently over me from head to foot, her inspection finally travelling back to my face. "You never added Russian to your other languages," Mutti Frida said. "I'm so glad you didn't, or we might not have met." She lifted a hand and ran her fingers softly over my cheek through my straggly beard. "It is so good to see you." Her eyes radiated happiness and then one eyebrow cocked. "but perhaps you might rethink the beard?"

My mind was in turmoil, but I needed to sort this out first. "The professor, Mutti Frida – what did he say?" I glanced uneasily across the foyer, but he had disappeared.

Mutti Frida's face glowed. "Tomorrow, you must meet him here, thirty minutes before the conference starts – I will be here to translate." She turned, pulling my hand. "But now, come with me."

I was so disorientated by what was going on, I let her drag me down a corridor to a side room marked *Nur Übersetzer* (*Translators only*) overlooking the main conference floor. Mutti Frida opened the door, gently pushing me inside.

A dark-haired head turned, a glint of a thin gold chain at her neck, and we arrived home in our shared gaze.

Afterword

There is a free prequel short story, *Mrs. Henderson's Limp*, giving the back story to the woman Will meets at MI6 HQ. You can get a FREE copy of *Mrs Henderson's Limp* and stay in touch with Robert's work by subscribing to his newsletter at *https://dl.bookfunnel.com/muop564zlq*

Do you want to know what happened to Col and Mutti Frida? If so, the sequel Through different Eyes is underway and will be released soon. Here's an excerpt from the first chapter...

***

I woke in confusion as I hit the back of the seat in front of me and ended on the floor with Mutti on top of me. As we struggled to sort ourselves out, there were several loud pairs of bangs – gunshots? – and Mutti stopped struggling to get up, pressing me down as low as possible. *"Unten bleiben, Col." (Stay down, Col.)*. We lay there for what felt like several minutes but was probably much less. I could hear moaning from the front seat and muffled voices and then the rear doors both opened. In the glare from headlights of a vehicle behind us I saw a man pointing a pistol at us.

About The Author

Robert was born in Nigeria but grew up mostly in the UK and was educated there. Upon completion of a degree in Aerospace Engineering, he migrated to Australia, where he lives with his wife, three ginger cats and a black labradoodle.

He reads widely and loves classical music and opera, regularly attending live performances. He has been a glider pilot since he was fifteen and still enjoys soaring with the eagles.

As mentioned, you can stay in touch with Robert by subscribing to his newsletter at *https://dl.bookfunnel.com/muop564zlq* which will also allow you to download a free copy of *Mrs Henderson's Limp*.

Brisbane, Australia
December 2021